'Many authors can write compelling[y] ~~about~~ [falling] in love . . . but it takes a deft hand (or two, in this case) to write compellingly about staying in love. Luckily, we have Wibbroka, who have crafted a novel about marriage that is honest to the bone, refreshing and – like a long-term relationship – deliciously surprising'

Jodi Picoult, *New York Times* bestselling author
of *Wish You Were Here*

'*Do I Know You?* shows the pure magic of that pivotal moment when two people make the choice to fight for each other. This book is more than a story of a marriage in trouble. It's the story of a spark rekindled, and the new flames deliver all the warmth you could want in a novel. Full of humour and heart, *Do I Know You?* had me in my feelings!'

Denise Williams, author of
The Fastest Way to Fall

'*Do I Know You?* offers the fresh twist on a marriage in crisis that I didn't know I needed! Wibbroka does it again with a magnetically raw and intimate portrayal of where love begins, fades and begins again. Flirty, sweeping and hopeful, readers will clutch their chests and root for Eliza and Graham until the very last page'

Amy Lea, international bestselling
author of *Set on You*

'Reading Wibberley and Siegemund-Broka's prose is like sliding into the crisp sheets of a luxury hotel bed. *Do I Know You?* is such an inventive take on a "marriage in trouble" story, showing the fragility that can sometimes hide behind familiarity. By the end, I cared about the fate of Eliza and Graham's relationship like I knew them personally'

Alicia Thompson, bestselling
author of *Love in the Time of Serial Killers*

'Readers won't be able to turn the pages fast enough'

Publishers Weekly

'I love, love, LOVED this book. It sucks you into a slow, sexy burn from page one and keeps you hooked with its layered, heart-wrenching honesty. This is contemporary romance at its best!'

Lyssa Kay Adams, author of *A Very Merry Bromance*

'Together, Emily Wibberley and Austin Siegemund-Broka produce a seamless voice that is compulsively readable. Their characters spark to life immediately on the page and are so real and relatable that I'm still thinking about them days later'

Jen DeLuca, *USA Today* bestselling author of *Well Traveled*

'There isn't a single page of *The Roughest Draft*, not one, that doesn't contain a sentence I had to reread twice just to savor. I'm going to be thinking about this heartbreakingly lovely, vividly emotional book for a long time. These authors are masters of their craft and their writing is such a treat to read'

Sarah Hogle, author of *Twice Shy*

'Searingly insightful and achingly romantic, *The Roughest Draft* is a sweep-you-off-your-feet celebration of love and creativity in all its mess. Emily Wibberley and Austin Siegemund-Broka plunge readers into the world of co-writing with a depth and vulnerability that is sure to delight and fascinate'

Sarah Grunder Ruiz, author of *Luck and Last Resorts*

'*The Roughest Draft* offers the most tantalizing romantic tension with a giant helping of swoon'

Trish Doller, author of *The Suite Spot*

'*The Roughest Draft* turns the act of co-writing a novel into one of the most soulful expressions of love I've ever read. Smart, tender and deeply romantic, this book is an unforgettable, page-turning knockout'

Bridget Morrissey, author of *A Thousand Miles*

'Utterly engrossing and beautifully wrought, *The Roughest Draft* is an intimate and authentic portrayal of human connection and the creative process. An exquisite love story that will leave you spellbound and longing for more'

Libby Hubscher, author of *If You Ask Me*

Titles by Emily Wibberley & Austin Siegemund-Broka

The Roughest Draft
Do I Know You?
The Breakup Tour

The Breakup Tour

EMILY WIBBERLEY

AUSTIN SIEGEMUND-BROKA

PAN BOOKS

First published 2024 by Berkley,
an imprint of Penguin Random House LLC, New York

First published in the UK 2024 by Pan Books
an imprint of Pan Macmillan
The Smithson, 6 Briset Street, London EC1M 5NR
EU representative: Macmillan Publishers Ireland Ltd, 1st Floor,
The Liffey Trust Centre, 117–126 Sheriff Street Upper,
Dublin 1, D01 YC43
Associated companies throughout the world
www.panmacmillan.com

ISBN 978-1-0350-2012-6

1 3 5 7 9 8 6 4 2

A CIP catalogue record for this book is available from the British Library.

Printed and bound by CPI Group (UK) Ltd, Croydon, CR0 4YY

Visit **www.panmacmillan.com** to read more about all our books
and to buy them. You will also find features, author interviews and
news of any author events, and you can sign up for e-newsletters
so that you're always first to hear about our new releases.

To the Swifties,

and Miss Swift,

for inspiration evermore

PROLOGUE

Riley

THERE'S NOTHING LIKE the sound of heartbreak.

I lower my lips from the microphone, exhaustion deep in my chest, head humming with restless melody. I've immersed myself for weeks in the hardest memories of my life, the deepest hurt, searching them for inspiration. It's where I'll find what I need, I know it is. I just need to keep listening.

I'm frustrated, honestly. When I've spent fifteen hours in the studio, I expect to have polished whatever I'm working on to perfection.

Instead, nothing is working. The chorus is cheaply grand, synthetically sorrowful. The verses have no culmination, no urgency. The instrumentals have come out well enough—it's my singing I can't get right. I sound like I'm performing, not like I'm *myself*. It's left me here, rerecording vocals. The more I wrestle with the song, the farther I get from the music in my heart, refrains insisting I let them free.

I wish I could. It physically pains me how much I wish I

could. This song was supposed to be my masterpiece. It needs to be my masterpiece. It deserves to be my masterpiece.

He deserves to be my masterpiece.

Sighing in exasperation, I roll my shoulders under the shining studio lights. In the expansive soundproofed space, it's easy to forget it's one in the morning. Nothing changes in the windowless, sterile room of microphones and minimal furniture. Usually I welcome the emptiness, the lack of distraction, the freedom to pursue whatever musical inspiration I'm hearing.

In this moment, however, it just reminds me of the progress I'm *not* making on the song I can't finish.

Part of me wants to resign for the night. I'm half-desperate to surrender to the impersonal comfort of my suite, my home for the past few months. The Victory Hotel off San Vicente near Sunset, one of Los Angeles's highest-powered entertainment industry neighborhoods, has hosted me in discretion while I procrastinated on house-hunting, instead hurling myself headlong into my music.

I couldn't help it. After my divorce, what else could I do?

The end of my marriage was a summons. I knew I could write us unforgettably. The whole perfect, painful ruin. Everything I hoped with him, everything I imagined. I chased the promise of the *song of us* until finally, "One Minute" was finished.

Moving out of our house, packing my possessions into suitcases, I listened to the demo on repeat. Over and over, the reminder of the music I found in the hurt kept me from sobbing. My ex wasn't home—he let me relocate in peace, one of his few recent kindnesses. I packed rhythmically until, in one unassuming moment, it happened.

Inspiration.

I was proud of how I'd rendered our whole relationship in one song. It gave me the idea for my entire next album. I pitched my label the premise, which they loved. I started writing, and once I started, I couldn't stop. It consumed me. Writing shifted into recording, and many days I did some of each.

I've practically lived here in Stereosonic's huge recording studio, spending wild hours of productivity playing and polishing, often sleeping on the couch. When I'm chasing inspiration, sacking out on the cushions is just easier. Honestly, I'm probably the Victory Hotel's favorite guest.

The songs emerged, each memorializing a relationship. I worked and worked until they were exactly the way I wanted. The process was like no inspiration I've ever experienced. I could hear *everything* I wanted. I worked relentlessly until I executed them flawlessly. Eleven of them.

Everything was magic. *The sound of heartbreak*. It was going startlingly well.

Until now.

At first, I didn't even know whether I wanted to write the song I'm struggling with. Our relationship was long ago, in the privacy of the past. It holds no public recognizability unlike my infamous flings and marriage. It's not even a footnote in the many, *many* stories of the musicians and movie stars I've loved and lost.

Yet I decided I had to include him, for one undeniable reason.

I know, quite simply, I loved him most. I heard every harmony. I could feel the wonder of every coming reprise. I was unforgettably in love with him.

The song I wrote for him has eluded me for days. Once I finish the recording, the album is done. In the weeks since I wrote the lyrics, I've recorded plenty of passes—none of them satisfying. Whenever I fell short, I would procrastinate, redirecting my efforts to one of the album's other songs.

Now I'm out of unfinished songs.

Fuck, I feel wrecked. My voice is sore. My back hurts from the stool where I've sat for hours in front of the studio microphone.

The Victory is nine minutes from here on the empty streets of midnight in West Hollywood. I imagine the cool comfort of the marble floor under my feet, the windows' gauzy curtains letting the light of the low skyline into the room, contouring the furnishings in gentle gray-white. The pillowed comforter of my California king, solitude I reassure myself is independence.

Instead, I wander over to the studio couch. I won't permit myself the comforts of "home," I decide. Not when I've failed so profoundly. Spending the night in the studio is my reminder to myself of the work yet undone.

In the dark of my mind, a dangerous possibility lurks. *What if I only have eleven songs of heartbreak in me?* This song is desperately important to me. What if importance isn't enough? What if I've exhausted myself in months of divorce and relentless heartsick songwriting?

It's unimaginably depressing. I force the idea away.

However, I do need sleep. What I'm feeling now is no way to record. I'm miserable. Defeated, frustrated, hopeless. I feel like—

I sit up straight.

What if it's the perfect way to record?

With every urge in me demanding I rest, I return instead to the microphone. My heart is racing. This album is about the deepest hurts of my life, the struggles. The wounds of love. It's dedicated to devotion and defeat.

It's supposed to sound this way, I realize. It's *supposed to hurt*.

I start the recording, having put in enough hours here recently to know how everything works without the help of my engineer or producer, who have gone home given the hour. The piano fills my ears.

When the verse comes, I sing. I sing like it's the last chance I'll give myself. I sing like I'm giving up. I sing like I'm saying goodbye.

I put everything into the music like I know my everything isn't enough. Like I know I can't be what the song needs.

It hurts. It hurts so much.

With the emotion I'm devoting to every note, it never fails to surprise me how fast three verses, three choruses, and one bridge pass. The music ends, and the rest is silence. Withdrawing from the microphone, I wipe my eyes with shaking hands. I didn't even know I was crying. Of course I was, I guess.

In the hushed studio, I hesitate. I'm out of inspiration, out of fight, out of everything except one fragile hope. I don't know how I'll cope if this song breaks my heart like the man who inspired it.

I play the recording. The song I've worked on for days, weeks, months fills the room. I listen closely.

It's ... perfect. Fucking perfect.

It was worth it, I remind myself while I walk with heavy steps over to the couch, knowing I'll nod off in the Uber if I head for the hotel. The pain I gave it was worth everything I'm certain this song will give me.

The recording feels ... life-changing. Undeniable. It feels like my hit. It sounds like my legacy.

It was worth it, I repeat to myself, my only lullaby in this windowless room. *You made it worth it*.

FOUR
MONTHS
LATER

ONE

Max

I REMEMBER EXACTLY what song was playing when I started my car on the night I got my heart broken.

I cranked the key in the ignition. The radio came on—Joni Mitchell's "The Same Situation" filled the interior of the used Camry I'd gotten for two thousand dollars when I graduated from high school. Feeling foolish, pretending I was fine, I let the song play, even while I knew it would entwine itself with the day's sad memories. I drove home on Los Angeles's silent freeways, recognizing in the pit of my stomach how Joni's voice would haunt me from then on.

Which is why a decade later I find myself hovering my finger over my laptop's space bar, unable to press play.

Open on Spotify is Riley Wynn's new album, framed on my screen in the small office I share with my sister in Harcourt Homes, the senior assisted-living facility I run with her help. It's just me in here right now, waiting for myself, ignoring the spreadsheets printed out on my desk. January is the coldest the San

Fernando Valley gets. The California chill surrounds me, invading my fingertips, expectant, urging. *Listen, Max. Just listen.*

I know what will happen when I start the first song. *If* I start the first song. The voice of the country's new favorite pop prophetess will steal into my soul the way only she can.

I should listen, I know I should. Hit play. Let Riley's music— her magic—ensnare me. Especially "Until You," the undisputed song of the year. I've had to work to escape hearing it because it hides around every corner in the labyrinth of the same songs every radio station plays.

I haven't entirely succeeded, instead hearing snatches in the supermarket or when I'm changing stations. Then there are the billboards, Riley looming over my commute on Sunset. She stands in the wedding dress she's wearing on the album cover, looking caught off guard while fire licks the edges of her veil. The *Rolling Stone* email with her featured interview hit my inbox a week ago.

Yet, I've resisted Riley's new music until today, when I suddenly knew I could hold out no longer—gravity was pulling me. Of what heavenly body, I don't know. Stars have gravity, but so do black holes. Like one inside the other, Riley's eyes stare out from my laptop screen.

My hesitation is sort of pathetic, I know. In fairness, however, not many people in the world face the question I do when it comes to Riley Wynn's new album.

How do you listen to *The Breakup Record* when one of the songs is about you?

Maybe we should form a support group—me and the eleven other people Riley's immortalized on her chart-smashing second LP. It's the gripping, genius conceit of her new collection of songs—each one centers on a romantic split of Riley's life.

Which means our nine months together in college is presumably included in the company of Hollywood-headline relationships, of short-lived flings, of her notorious divorce. Nine months when I dated the woman who would become one of the most famous musicians in the world. Nine months in which I felt like I'd found the chorus to my verse in Riley Wynn—whose lips made me ignite, whose smile looked like stage lights, whose laughter played secret chords on my heartstrings.

There's a chance I'm not included, some hopeful part of me whispers. What if our relationship didn't register enough to make the cut?

On second thought, that might be worse.

Riley is known for her breakup songs. Renowned or infamous, depending on the source of the judgment. On her first album and EPs—when she was popular, just not yet the most loved figure in the contemporary music industry—the songs of heartbreak were the hits.

It was easy to understand why. When I listened to them once or twice, out of nostalgia or masochistic indulgence or some combination, Riley's preoccupation with the pain or pleasure of romantic endings was evident in the power of her voice, the sharpness of her structures, and the keenness of her lyrics.

Her reputation was made. "The Breakup Queen," the music press calls her.

The Breakup Record is her meta-manifestation of her own reputation, self-commentary and self-realization in one. It's ingeniously Riley, making masterpieces out of misadventures, conferring ironic honor on romantic failures memorable enough to spawn songs. While I'm pretty much the opposite of fame-hungry, even I would prefer Riley Wynn's songwriting scalpel over the ignominy of being the forgotten ex.

I know there's only one way to find out whether she wrote us into song. It's just—how do I prepare myself for what feels like walking into the fire on the album's cover?

Melodies hold memories. Like nothing else on earth, they re-call feelings, places, moments—the needle dropping into the groove of the soul's record player. I remember what song was playing when I had my first kiss, what I put on while having din-ner alone the night I moved into my first apartment, what was on the radio while my father stiffly said I would need to run Har-court Homes if I wanted it to stay open because my parents could no longer manage the property.

Whenever I listen to them, I'm there.

The same will happen here. When I play whatever Riley's written for us, I'll find myself reliving a part of my life I'm not sure I'm over, even ten years later.

"Did you listen yet?"

The sound of Jess's voice has me snapping my laptop shut. In-stantly, my furtiveness embarrasses me. It's not like I was watch-ing porn or something.

Sure enough, my sister smiles. She's opened the door just a little to poke her head into the office. The loose curls of her chestnut hair hang past her collarbone. The sparkle in her green eyes says she knows exactly what hell I'm presently in. We're obviously siblings, matched in every significant physical characteristic—the perfect pair for, say, the "About Us" page on retirement home websites.

"I've heard it," I say neutrally.

"Liar," Jess replies. She slouches in mock desperation. "Come *on*. I need you to listen and tell me which one is about you."

"You don't know if any of them are about me." Hearing my own lack of conviction, I wince.

Jess rolls her eyes. "Um, you and Riley were obsessed with each other. I'm one gazillion percent certain there's a song about you." She shrugs, pretending she's indulging in casual speculation, which I know she is not. "My guess is 'Until You,'" she says.

I frown. Surely Jess is messing with me now. I probably have *a* song—not *the* song. The lead single. No fucking way. I'm surely relegated to the second to last track or something. The filler. The one that barely made it onto the album.

"I'm sure 'Until You' is about that guy," I say.

Jess looks incredulous. "Her ex-husband, Wesley Jameson? He's an Emmy-nominated actor, collective crush of the internet. He's not '*that guy*,'" my sister informs me witheringly.

"Whatever. Him," I say, feeling my face heat. I definitely know exactly who Riley's ex-husband is. I don't know why I in- sinuated otherwise. "The song is about him. Isn't that what everyone is saying?"

It's not like I seek out gossip headlines. When it comes to Ri- ley, however, they're hard to miss. Riley has shot to the kind of stardom that makes speculation about her love life a national pastime. Everyone online is saying the biggest hit on the album is about Wesley, Riley's husband of three months.

Had it surprised me when Riley married one of prime time's hottest stars? No, absolutely not. Riley is . . . everything. She's gorgeous, smart, quick-witted, uncompromising. She'd want someone who could complement her. Who could keep pace with her own relentless incandescence.

Jameson made sense. He's machine-pressed handsome, with sharp, planar features, his eyes squinted ruggedly in every one of his numerous photoshoots. Like Jess remarked, he's undeniably internet-crushable, with his wavy dark hair, his sinister somberness. He's captivating onscreen, launching himself from a conflicted criminal on HBO to the leading man of fans' fantasies.

His relationship with Riley captured the public's obsession instantly. Photos of them close, of him whispering in her ear, found their way online from one charity event or magazine party or other. They weren't world news, not yet. Riley wasn't famous like she is now. In fact, *he* was the famous one then. Rumors followed his potent combination of popular and prestige, of roles in consideration, of other women.

The photos of them together were what caught fans' imaginations—the dazzle of Riley's delight, the glint in Jameson's eye. The dark prince who snared the sharp-tongued starlet. Each garnered more and more retweets and comments until Riley Wynn and Wesley Jameson were iconic "main characters" on the public stage.

Two months later, they were married. Three months later, they were divorced.

It was the perfect reflection of the differences in the lives we'd led. Obviously I wasn't just home on the couch swiping through photos of Riley with Wesley Jameson—I've had relationships of my own, some of them serious.

They're passages of memory unnerving in their finitude, disappearing from my life so completely it's hard to remember how much of it they once occupied. Kendra, who had her MFA in design and worked on the new progressive mayor's campaign, and loved herbal tea and her sister. Elizabeth, one of our residents' granddaughters, who worked in employment law, never liked Los Angeles, and dreamed of living in France.

In the year I spent with each woman, I meant it when I said I loved her. It just . . . never worked out. It wasn't right.

Or, *I* wasn't right. I can claim fault for the end of each relationship. The same thing happened—when the idea of moving in arose, I withdrew. Not immediately, yet unmistakably. Dinners got quieter. Futures faded into uncertainty. I could feel something missing, or I convinced myself I could. Either way, it scared me, and I ran.

In the meantime, I've enjoyed myself well enough with the one-night stands the right combination of tousled hair and glasses will earn.

Jess is watching me with skeptical wonderment. "You really haven't listened to it, have you?" she asks.

I stand, knowing it's confirmation enough. "I'm late," I say instead, struggling to keep annoyance out of my voice. The problem with working with your family is that you can't hide from them, even when you want to. "I'm due in the dining room." I pass Jess in the doorway, hoping she'll let the subject drop.

Of course, she doesn't.

"One of those songs *is* about you, Max," she says.

I don't reply, heading into the hallway on the second floor. My sister's inquisitiveness is expected, honestly. Everyone who knows me personally—which, okay, isn't very many people outside of Harcourt Homes, where the residents don't exactly listen to the SiriusXM hits station—has asked me eagerly which song is about me.

I've found refuge in saying I don't know. I don't *want* to know. Ten years isn't enough time to get over Riley Wynn. Maybe twenty years will be. What is it Springsteen sings? *In twenty years, I'm sure it'll just seem funny.*

I head down the wide staircase into the lobby, ignoring patches of peeling paint near the carpet curling up from the floor. Details our residents don't notice, or I hope they don't. They stand out sneeringly to me, though. Guilty indications of places where I couldn't keep up with the demands of the property.

Once our parents' business, now our own, Harcourt Homes is the legacy I carry proudly despite its heavy weight. In the Valley's flatlands, only minutes outside of, yet unmistakable for, Los Angeles, we keep residents' lives from changing. It's the point of what we do, conserving health, comfort, consistency. It's the business of waiting, of holding on.

Holding on despite what I found in the spreadsheets on my desk, the monthly financials I've printed out, no different from last month's.

I've pored over them, searching for costs to cut or secret efficiencies to exploit, struggling to do right by this place. There's nothing—except for the outright cruelty of raising prices on our residents, which we would never do. Planning for retirement is nearly impossible. When someone doesn't correctly calculate how many years they need to save for, we work out new rates with their family based on what they can pay. Unfortunately, it's left Harcourt Homes on the edge of bankruptcy.

I wanted to help. It's why I changed my major from music to business. I even *did* help, for the first few years, keeping the home running. Only when I faced the ongoing downward spiral did I realize I couldn't find the fixes we needed, which left me in this precarious position, learning habits for cost-cutting wherever I could.

I know the *real* conversation is coming. The one where we face the music, so to speak. Where I gather everyone and admit Harcourt Homes cannot continue. I just can't dwell on it right now.

Not with the piano waiting for me.

In minutes, I'll play for everyone, our residents and their families. I don't want my stress over the home's finances to bleed into my performance this evening, but of course it would if I let the harsh realities preoccupy me. Everything I feel finds its way into my music.

Music is the life in the lungs of Harcourt Homes, the sustaining spark in these walls. Whether it's old standards I let echo from the record player into the halls, or me playing for residents during dinner, music helps us forget life's peeling paint. Since high school, I've hardly ever missed my Sunday piano revue.

The dining room is full of familiar faces when I enter off the main hallway. The four octogenarians who always wear Navy hats occupy one corner. Keri eats with Grant, the pair having become inseparable since they realized their names combined into one old Hollywood star. Imelda regales her indulgent daughter with resident gossip—of which, make no mistake, there is plenty. I cross the room, nodding to the residents.

When I sit down at the ancient upright piano, I feel like I'm home.

"*Finally*, Maxwell."

I smile, hardly surprised. The voice is Linda's. Of course, my favorite Harcourt Homes resident is seated right next to the piano.

"My potatoes are already cold," she remarks, playful petulance in her eyes.

"I'm sorry," I say earnestly. "How about Sinatra to make up for it?"

Linda smiles magnanimously, satisfied, and I start playing.

The home's upright is the piano I learned to play on. It's *not* the nicest piano I've ever played, not by far, but it's my favorite. The rich sound, the worn feel of the keys—it's perfect. Part of the reason I never went on to pursue music despite initially majoring in piano performance is this wonderful instrument's unwieldy logistics. I can't just pack the piano up and haul it to gigs with me.

I place my fingers on the keys, feeling the warmth of their welcome. This piano is part of me. When my foot finds the pedal, I feel like I'm stretching my hamstrings to sprint. When I inch forward on the bench, it's like inhaling deeply.

I play, and it's like coming to life.

The song spills from me, rolling like the wind over the hills of Mulholland Drive ten minutes from here. "Come Fly with Me" is one of the residents' favorites, ebulliently quick on the keys and sprightly syncopated. It plays like its title, the rush of landing gear lifting off the runway.

Half the dining room hushes to listen. The other half continues conversing. I don't mind. Music doesn't have to demand everyone's attention. It's there for those who need it. Not every song preaches from the pulpit—some hold your hand from the passenger seat.

I run down my repertoire of the residents' favorites, from

Sinatra to Elvis, Bobby Darin to Etta James. When I play, I forget the minutes drifting past on weightless currents of melody. I'm perfectly content. Everything else vanishes—the financial pressures of Harcourt Homes, the idea of returning to my empty apartment, the pattern of watching my friends from music school either make it or give up their dreams for steady jobs and families they find equally fulfilling.

I forget about the hit song I've possibly inspired. I forget *The Breakup Record.* I forget—

Well, no. I never quite forget Riley.

Dessert signals the end of my dinner revue. While staff serve key lime pie, my father's recipe—one of the ways in which my parents' presence lingers here, despite them having retired to Palm Springs—I finish my final song and stand, bowing my head to scattered applause. Not every table is occupied, I note with discomfort clenching in my chest, reminding me we're not at full capacity. I can't move in anyone new, though, not without the money for more staff.

It's remarkable how quickly stress wraps me again in its clenching wires. How quickly the respite of music's exhilarating ease has disappeared into the past. Looking out over the residents enjoying meals in this home, the idea of everyone we might fail is overwhelming.

"Encore!"

The single word rings out over the applause. The voice is young, female, and flickering with confident humor.

Saying it distracts me is the understatement of the century. It stops my heart.

Glancing into the back corner, I blink, certain I'm hallucinating. The figment of my overwrought imagination, the result of the billboards I saw on my drive in this morning. Of staring at the album art on Spotify.

Of remembering the sound of her small intake of breath before she would strum the first chord of her songs in college.

The figure seated inconspicuously near the entrance to the kitchen is miragelike. I feel my heart pick up its pace, emotions I can't name crescendoing into one forbidden harmony.

While her hair is dyed sun-spun gold, her roots remain dark. She's dressed in jet-black jeans, with the black fabric of the top she's tucked in clinging to her frame, covering her chest and carelessly and recklessly revealing the skin of her sides. No bra. She never wore one when I knew her. If she turned to the left, I could see the first word of the line of poetry tattooed under her breast. It's Mary Oliver, her favorite.

Who ever made music of a mild day?

She's heart-stoppingly gorgeous and looking right at me. With her head slanted coyly to the side, her smile says she knows she's walked out of my daydreams.

In honesty, *daydream* isn't half description enough for her sense-warping effect on me. She's a symphony when you're expecting a solo. She's heartbreak. She's my first favorite song.

In the corner of the room, Riley Wynn raises her hand *hello*.

TWO

Riley

THE RETIREMENT HOME hasn't changed. I remember the décor, the floorplan, the smell. Every detail of the drive, the dry, winding hills giving way to the comforting flat sprawl of the San Fernando Valley, is familiar. I even recognize some of the residents from the last time I was here nearly a decade ago. Harcourt Homes is just the same.

Max Harcourt, not so much.

With how attuned I was to every facet of his person while we were together, of course the changes over the years leap out to me now. His shoulders have broadened, his jaw sharpened. Stubble shadows his chin where he was clean-shaven in college. The russet hair I remember being unruly is now lightly tousled.

Hands lined with veins like highways on a map to my favorite places. Granite-cut smile made for offering small graces.

I'm writing him into lyrics before I've even spoken to him. No surprise there, I suppose.

His sense of style has changed, too. When I knew him, he lived in T-shirts and jeans. Now, his dark olive pants compliment his gray tee with nice understatement. His glasses are round, the metal frames delicate.

He's more handsome, no doubt. Yet every change reminds me how, when we last spoke, we were just kids, sophomores in college. The decade I've lived since has changed me, inspired me, scared me—and every day of it was without Max. I've spent years feeling like I was playing sold-out shows on lonely stages. I've lived love songs he's never heard.

I won't pretend the years weren't solitary—this shiny life of striving for new heights while losing the people I wanted to share them with. I let the days fly past while I outran hurt or doubt. The small clubs and radio interviews where I started changed into the life I live now—of office visits to *Billboard* or YouTube, of photographers getting coverage of me outside the house where I lived when I signed my first major-label deal, of my name in the now-ubiquitous font of my logo.

I've never chased the relationships I committed into song out of some vain effort to fight the loneliness. I wasn't with Hawk, or Kai, or Wesley Jameson because I missed Max, or because I needed companionship.

I was with them because I really, really thought I'd found love. It's my gift, sometimes my curse. My fierce conviction that every dream is within reach. Waiting to be seized. Stardom. Musicality. Love. Everything in my reach, for one inviolable reason.

I'm Riley *fucking* Wynn.

Riley Wynn, who loves loud. Riley Wynn, who hurts loud.

Riley Wynn, who's maybe a little scared she needs to shine to be seen, or to suffer to be heard.

Everyone's convinced it's why my love life looks like it does. In the commentary surrounding *The Breakup Record*, I've heard the smirking suspicion I *cause* my breakups to keep writing great songs. People saying I'm "crazy" to drive partners off on purpose, or I dump them unceremoniously only to weep over them into the mic.

It's fucking ridiculous, obviously. There's nothing contrived in my fraught romantic history, nothing except genuine passion followed by genuine pain. While I voice them in song, the hurt is very real.

Even with Max. *Especially* with Max.

He's studying me now, dissonance in his eyes. I keep clapping, my calls of "encore" earning me glances from my table. Thankfully, a woman up front has joined my refrain, and it's picking up momentum.

Finally, with effort, Max pulls his eyes off me. He holds his hands up in surrender to the crowd, then sits back down at the piano.

When he starts playing, I feel my knees weaken with quiet delight. The song he's chosen is "It's Been a Long, Long Time." While it's possible the song is Eustace's or Ethel's favorite, or just one more in Max's impressive repertoire of old standards, I doubt it. I'm pretty certain he's replying to my entrance in the language we used to speak to each other.

Watching him play, joy steals over me. He's like no one I've heard in years of playing with some of the country's finest session musicians. When Max immerses himself in the keys, it's like he *is* the music. Like Max Harcourt is a memory, leaving in his place this shimmering shape of resonant sound. He doesn't play the songs—he embodies them.

It's why I fell in love with him, on the night we met. It was one in the morning, and he'd brought his keyboard out into the lounge of our dorm. He explained later his roommate couldn't fall sleep to the quiet clicking of Max's keys while Max played with his headphones on. So whenever he was compelled to some nocturnal practicing, Max would haul his keyboard out into the vacant lounge.

Except, one night in September, I was sleeping on the lounge's couch because I'd found my roommate hooking up with someone in *my* bed. I woke up to—of course—the clicking of Max's keys, finding this contemplative boy playing with his headphones on, enraptured by a melody only he could hear. His bashful smile when he noticed me watching had me canceling the date I was supposed to go on the following night right then and there.

I guess one thing about Max Harcourt hasn't changed, then.

He finishes the song and is met with renewed applause. I join in. The man next to me does not, instead sticking his fork into his pie. Smiling, I lean over. "Enjoying the dessert?" I ask him.

He glances up like he didn't expect to be spoken to. When he looks me over, surprise enters his eyes. Recognition, however, does not. I know I stand out just about everywhere I go— especially in a retirement home. Still, I'd be willing to bet no one here recognizes me.

"It's delicious," my dinner companion replies. The impressive mustache under his large glasses moves expressively with every word he says. "Hank's key lime pie is half the reason I chose this home."

I coat my voice in charm. "Can I have a bite?"

"It's not every day I get to share my pie with a beautiful woman." He slides his plate over.

I'm of the opinion that nothing holds memories the way songs do. However, home-baked key lime pie offers stiff competition.

With one taste of the custard filling from my dinner date's plate, everything rushes over me—warm waves of reminiscence, of dinners in this very room, of the sweetness of finding what felt like my second home.

"Come on, I'm sure you shared plenty of pies in your day," I reply, pushing past the comforting curtains of nostalgia. I love having conversations with strangers. While I might be known for my breakup songs, one of my favorite truths I've discovered in my line of work is how inspiration hides everywhere. It's intuitive, once you realize it. Songwriting is storytelling. Everyone is in the midst of the story of their lives. Which means everyone has songs to share, in some form.

You just have to listen.

He sits up a little straighter, pride unmissable in how he squares his shoulders. "You could say that," he begins, looking like he's going to elaborate.

Instead, Max's voice interrupts us.

"Riley."

The low sound of my name from his lips is shockingly familiar. He's shrouded the short word in layers of reserve. It's a half-guarded, half-ordinary hello.

Of the pair of us, I know I'm the one *less* surprised by the flashback whiplash. Max didn't even know I was coming. While, granted, it's easier for him to hear my voice these days than it is for me to hear his, I doubt Max has listened to mine much, either.

I turn, finding his eyes right on me. There's no hint of what's going on underneath their perfect green.

"Max, you know this young lady?" my dinner companion asks.

"I used to," Max says. His reply isn't devoid of emotion, not exactly. It sounds more like he's restraining every emotion in the world. "Why are you here?"

Smiling, I shrug one shoulder while I lounge in my seat. The man sitting next to me looks like he's riveted by our every word. Lucky for him, I'm physically unable to avoid making a spectacle out of everything I can.

"I came for the pie," I say sweetly, taking another bite.

Max stares at me for a moment, then seems to accept my answer. "Let me know if there's anything else I can get for you." He starts to leave.

I frown. I should've known Max wouldn't play my game. "Excuse me," I say to the gentleman next to me.

I get up hurriedly and follow Max out of the dining room. While his stride is clipped, I chase off the idea he's fleeing from me deliberately. He's just done with his dinnertime show. Just has other stuff to do.

"Max," I say, stopping him. I feel foolish for the urgency in my voice, not far from pleading. "Is there somewhere we could have a word?" I ask more softly.

His gaze settles on me. "So you're not here for the pie," he replies. It isn't a question. I listen for playfulness in his quiet validation.

"No," I confirm. "I'm not."

He studies me for a long moment. I recognize the look from how his eyes would rove over the staves, the rests, the notes of new pieces of music. He's . . . sight-reading me.

I wonder what song he hears. If I'm winsome, sweet, like our fondest memories, or if I'm something sad—or if I'm nothing but the nostalgic melody he remembers from when he was younger. I don't dare hope I'm the song he can't get out of his head.

"Come with me," he finally says. I was worried he would be cold when he saw me, but he isn't. He doesn't look happy, but if he ever held a grudge, he's released it into the past.

I never resented him, either. I knew I could. His choices were most responsible for ending our relationship. I just . . . didn't. I don't. Of the notebooks I could fill on Max Harcourt, words I've condensed into one heart-split piece of poetry, not one would be written out of resentment. He's not my *enemy*, or even just my ex.

He is my enigma.

The question of how he left us has lingered in the periphery of my mind for the last decade. I understood perfectly the choice he made while understanding nothing of why he was making it. I can ignore the riddle or write its verses into song, but even now, I can't answer it.

Following him into the entryway, I notice the front desk, where his mom, Ruth, would welcome visitors, is empty.

The sight saddens me. Not everything stayed the same here in the years I haven't visited, I guess. I hope she's well.

We continue up the stairs. While Harcourt Homes looks much like I remember, I can't help wrestling with how the context of this place has changed for me.

The home is, of course, what Max left me for. It isn't just where he works. It's the person he's become. Noticing new wear on the washed-out paint, I feel like I'm entering the embodiment of Max himself, walking the hallways of his heart.

He offers no glancing smiles or efforts to make conversation on our way up the stairs. I'm fighting not to let his indifference wound my ego. Of course I've looked him up over the years, but he's not really one for social media. Maybe he's married and uncomfortable to see me again. Maybe what we had was just one in a long string of his romances.

Maybe it didn't mean to him what it did to me.

We walk down the second floor's long main hallway. I know where we're heading. Sure enough, when we reach the end, Max opens the door to the small office I remember used to be his dad's.

Inside, his sister Jess squeals when she sees me.

"*Oh my fucking god*," she says.

Shaken out of my rumination, I can't help smiling. I hold my arms out for a hug. "It's so nice to see you," I say honestly. "You grew up."

When I last saw Jess, she was in high school and unsure of herself. Now, she's her own person, with an understated classic style. Curls of her hair frame her face like they have a vibrant life of their own. She looks, simply, cool. Like when I saw Max, it makes me feel mixed up. I'm happy she's doing well. I'm sad I missed years of this life while I was out living my own.

Her grin goes wide. In my fifteen years of exes, I've found sisters either warily judgmental or conspiratorially friendly. Jess Harcourt was very much the latter. Within minutes of meeting me, she was showing me videos of five-year-old Max from his piano recitals.

"You're, like, famous now," Jess says when she pulls out of my hug.

Self-consciousness never fails to steal into me when I'm reminded of my public image. Still, I've had enough practice playing it off casually. "It's weird, right?" I ask.

Max's sister scrunches her face up in dramatic denial. "No. What would be weird is if you hadn't become famous."

I'm touched by her ready endorsement. Max, however, doesn't let the moment linger. "Jess," he says gently, "can we have the room?"

"Right. Yes." Jess passes me, heading for the door. "But Riley, I'm going to need a selfie and an autograph before you leave. *Oh my god*," she exclaims like she's just remembered. When she grips my elbow, I have to smile. "The album. It's so good."

My eyes flit to Max, who I find watching me. His silence is like a record spinning without the needle. He doesn't echo his sister's praise—I wonder if he's listened to *The Breakup Record*.

"I'll find you before I leave. Promise," I tell Jess.

Jess shoots me playful *you better* eyes, then walks out and closes the door behind her. When Max leans on the wall, I'm instantly aware of the small space we're in. We made out in here once. It had been hot, the way many nights in the Valley are. Max's deft hands had found my hair, the curve of my neck, my hips while I perched on this very desk. He played every inch of my skin like a scale. His lips were sweet like key lime pie.

Remembering how I felt wrapped in him makes me feel passionate. It wakes me up. While Max may have the perfect music-nerd image, the look suggests none of his natural finesse and heartrending passion in . . . other respects. He kissed with fervent devotion. His hands explored me like I was his favorite obsession. His fingers possessed skills not even the piano knows.

I remember it now, the recollection rushing over me. Despite how out of context the feeling is, how incoherent with his stiff manner, I don't chastise myself for the warm flash. I've learned to fend off embarrassment or regret—they're no use to me when I'm searching my life for songs.

Remember fearlessly, I remind myself. *Feel fearlessly.*

"It's good to see you again," he says.

I raise an eyebrow. "Is it?"

"It's always good to see you, Riley." His features soften just slightly. "That's never changed."

His earnest words warm me like no rave review or Pitchfork profile ever could. "It's good to see you, too," I say with no swagger. "You look good. You play beautifully."

Sitting down in his desk chair, he motions for me to take Jess's vacated seat. It's striking how naturally he fills the space. He's grown up, too. "The piano is a little out of tune," he demurs.

I shrug. "Some songs sound better a little out of tune."

"That's *not* true." He sounds scandalized.

"In the era of synthesized instruments, it is," I press. "It's like a live show. Sometimes you want the artist to mess up the lyrics just so you know they're really singing."

"You never mess up your lyrics," Max says.

I wonder if he knows how much the offhand observation means to me. It's just, lyrics are the whole point of songs for me. I would never want to mess them up. I choose every word carefully, much like I'm doing right now. As if this conversation, this reunion, is a song I'm writing for just one listener.

Crossing my legs, I eye him with curiosity I hope comes off casual. "Been to one of my shows?"

"No, I just know you," he replies. When he realizes what he's just confirmed, his color drains. "I mean, it's not like I'm not interested in going—" he continues hastily.

"Hey, no worries," I reassure him. I mean it 99 percent. Only the smallest, most guarded part of me is wounded. I've played for hundreds of thousands of people over the years, way more if you count the viewership of *Saturday Night Live* last weekend. Was

Max *never* one of them? "I didn't expect you to come to my shows."

Max swallows like he doesn't know what to say. I wish I could sight-read him the way he did me.

I change the subject instead. "How's your family?"

Relieved, Max nods. "Good. Everyone's good," he says with enthusiasm for this surer conversational footing. "Jess is probably moving to New York for the girlfriend's job soon. My parents retired to Palm Springs, but they visit every month, usually more. They're excited for Jess, but I can see they're sort of sad she's leaving."

"The girlfriend," I repeat. "Wow. Serious?"

"Very."

"You?" I ask.

"I'm happy for Jess, yeah."

"No, I mean—is—" I stumble over my words the way I never would in front of the microphone. "Is there anyone serious for you?" Hearing how clumsily I've led into the question, I cringe.

Max looks away. In his pause, I decide I hate silence. Hate it. This feeling isn't just the war I wage on silence every night I fill a stage with sound. It's deep, heart-sickening resentment of the quiet I'm desperate for Max to dispel.

"Not right now," he says.

Instantly, follow-up questions explode into my heart. Only with incredible effort do I restrain myself. Prying into every detail of Max Harcourt's love life isn't why I'm here.

"This is weird," Max says. "I could ask about you, but, um . . ."

There's no mirth in the smile I flash him now. "But you've seen the headlines."

"Hard not to," he replies. While the comment could be

flippant, it isn't. Not the way he says it. "I'm sorry about the divorce. How are you?" He speaks like he doesn't know how to have this conversation, which is understandable.

I shrug. "We were only together for five months." The observation is my go-to when discussing Wesley, instinctual now. It's not untrue, yet it reveals nothing. It leaves the listener free to infer whatever they'd like, which satisfies them enough to keep the conversation from continuing. "You and I—" I start to say, then stop myself.

"—were together longer than that," he finishes my sentence. While what he's said is simple, it sounds riddled with footnotes I can't quite read. He's capable like no one I've ever known of converting statements into questions. I just wish I knew what they were.

I settle for smiling again. "Right. I'm fine."

Max starts to smile back until something new crosses his expression, shifting the room into a minor key.

"Why are you here, Riley?" he asks.

Of course he understands I didn't just drop in to catch up. I take a breath, feeling like I'm onstage, readying myself to sing my first notes. I'm honestly not sure where the stakes feel higher. Starting every show, knowing the smallest failure or shortfall could hurt my career, or here, in this fragile flashback with the man I used to love.

"I have a favor to ask you," I say.

THREE

Max

I LEAN FORWARD in my chair. *Riley Wynn has a favor to ask* me? She's up out of her seat now, pacing the small space like staying still was starting to prickle under her skin. I watch her nervousness with mounting confusion. It's out of character with the renegade firework of confidence I've known Riley to be since the night I met her.

I can't believe she's actually here.

When she walks to the window, I see her top has no back, just skin all the way to the waistband of her jeans. The sight is jarring in ways hearing her voice or having her in front of me isn't, this reminder of the places I've had my hands when she was mine to hold.

I sit on my fingers to restrain myself from reaching out for her. I know how she would feel, sweetly soft—or sweat-slicked if she was fresh from the stage, or fresh from our first round and daring me for the next. Her scent would kiss me even when her lips wouldn't, the intoxicating promise of how I would feel wrapped in her.

Riley.

She's ruthless magic. I lower my eyes, struggling.

I honestly never imagined I would see Riley again except in carefully orchestrated camera angles and photo shoots. Instead, I feel like we're living the cover song of our lives. Every lyric, every move of the melody, is the same—yet the tempo is changed, the instrumentation stripped to the lonely notes, the charge coursing under them something I've never heard. They flicker in my fingertips the way only unforgettable songs do.

The ones I want to play over and over.

"You've heard the album, right?" she asks, facing her half reflection in the window.

"I haven't had the chance," I admit.

She spins, incredulity replacing her nervousness entirely. It's momentarily stunning how emotion lights her up, like staring into a camera flash. "You don't go to my shows and you haven't heard my music. You're really not a fan, are you?" She nods to herself, processing. "This is good. I needed this. Fame really messes with your head. It's good to be humbled by your college boyfriend."

"Hey," I reply defensively. "You try having your ex go on to be—*you*."

Riley laughs. I nearly short-circuit from the sheer joy of the sound. *Hundreds of flashbulbs.* "Max, I've dated, like, three musicians with relatively popular music."

"Do you listen to their stuff?"

"Hell yeah I do," she exclaims. "One of them wrote this song about me that is so mean. I love it."

Now I laugh. "No you don't," I say. Except, part of me knows I'm wrong. Riley works to find inspiration for songs, but she lives like she wants to inspire them.

"I do," she insists. "It's my workout jam."

My merciless mind provides me with the image of Riley in workout wear, perfectly stretched fabric covering the body I know like the keys of my piano. I scold the idea instantly. "So if I were to play it right now . . ." I reach for my computer.

"I'd sing along. It's called 'Nightmare Girl.'"

I falter. "Wait, really?" Riley wasn't wrong. The radio-friendly cut of resentment she's just named *is* incredibly mean, which is unsurprising given its perpetually leather-clad creator's reputation for narcissistic scorn. "You dated Hawk Henderson?"

"Unfortunately, yes," Riley says, unfazed. "You're honestly the last nice guy I was ever with."

Not knowing what to say, I open my laptop. Of course, the moment I do, Riley's face pops up onscreen on the Spotify page of her album.

Riley rounds on me, the gleam of victory dancing electric in her eyes. "Well, well, well," she chides. "What's this?"

When I start to close the computer, she stops me. Her hand on my arm halts my movement, not to mention my heartbeat. Even the momentary contact is shocking, the white-hot remembered charge of every single other moment her skin met mine, sitting next to me at the piano, or—

"So you *do* listen," she says.

"I was . . . thinking about it," I reply, flustered. "I haven't yet."

She drags her chair closer, perilously close, and sits down again. Her scent is devastatingly familiar. Sweet, smoky, like flowers on fire. Her eyes sparkle in that way that always made me itch to caress her.

When she speaks, it's like hearing the devil on my shoulder whispering in my ear.

"Don't you at least want to hear your song?"

Your song.

"I wondered if I'd made the cut," I confess. "It was so long ago, and we were so young."

She doesn't shift her gaze. "You made the cut. In fact, yours is sort of the star of the album."

My stomach drops. I'd sincerely meant my denial when Jess suggested *I* was the inspiration for the song of the summer, the chart-topping masterpiece described in hundreds of headlines— of streaming records smashed, TikTok trends, Grammy predictions.

It's . . . about me. About us.

"'Until You,'" I say.

Riley smiles. The faintest hint of shyness flickers in the reckless joy lighting up her features.

"You're sure you don't want to hear it?" she asks.

"I'd sooner if it *weren't* about me." I keep my voice even only with effort. In fact, I'm very much wrestling with the entire idea. Nothing prepares you for learning your intense, ill-fated first love is the subject of the song millions of people have memorized, sung in the shower, driven home to, and played for their friends.

Riley studies me. "I don't get you," she finally says.

"No, you don't."

The reply slips quickly from me. The way Riley goes quiet says she knows why. I don't often permit myself to pass into the purgatory of remembering the reasons for our breakup, the doldrums of *what if.* In weaker moments, I've wondered if Riley does. I guess if I listened to the country's new favorite song, I could find out.

When Riley sighs in exasperation, it's like she's shaking off the memories. "Well, it is about you. The problem is," she contin-ues, "no one *knows* it's about you." Despite the decade since our last conversation, I'm caught up short when I recognize the shadow darkening her eyes. She's hurt. "Instead," she goes on sharply, "my ex-husband has started saying *he's* the inspiration for 'Until You' in interviews lately. And I just fucking hate how he's using me like this. I mean, the guy divorced me because of the song I wrote for *Only Once.*"

I nod, remembering. *The Breakup Record* wasn't yet announced when Riley, off the recognition for her second album, got asked to write the end-credits song for a major movie adaptation of a prizewinning novel. While she wasn't nominated in the end, I remember there was a moment last October when Riley was in the Oscars conversation.

I can only imagine how Jameson reacted.

Riley shakes her head in soft fury. "He'll never admit it, but he hated the idea I might be more famous than him."

Once more, she stands up. Except now, when she starts pac-ing, it isn't like she's strutting up to the microphone. It's like she's in a cage.

"I started the album the day I moved out. He knew my label wanted something new from me. He was dreading it," Riley ex-plains, her voice sparking like stripped wire. "When I was alone in my empty hotel room, I wrote 'Until You,' and I just . . . knew. It was *the* song. I spent weeks recording it, redoing it over and over while I worked on other songs on the album, knowing I could get it perfect. When I sent in my final version, they replied in like . . . minutes."

Even in the midst of her frustrated explanation, Riley smiles fondly. It's fleeting, gone when she shakes her head.

"If you'd listen to the lyrics you'd *know* it's about you. Just like he knows it's not about him." She scowls. "Yet he's publicly pretending it is, just so my success can still be in his shadow."

Saying it drains her in ways I've honestly never seen. She stops pacing. Her shoulders sag.

Her words hit me, knifelike, right in the chest. While Riley and I don't understand each other, not entirely, it's not hard to imagine how wrenching it would feel to have the heart of your proudest creation ripped out of your control.

"I'm sorry," I say earnestly. "That's horrible."

Riley's laugh is sandpaper rubbed together. "That's Wesley for you." Her distant eyes return to me, the focus in them renewed. "So that's why I'm here. I want to announce the song is about my college boyfriend, not Wesley."

I nod. "Me," I say.

"Yes," Riley confirms. "You."

I think it over. "I don't see anything wrong with that. It's not like you'd use my name."

The smile she gives me is playfully pitying. "The fans will figure it out in, like, two seconds."

"Oh," I say. "In that case, no."

"No," Riley repeats like she doesn't know the word.

"Yeah, I'd rather not. Thanks for asking, though."

I recognize the stunned incomprehension in Riley's eyes from our relationship's few fatal fractures. "Max, *why*?"

"Do people not say no to you very often?" I inquire politely.

Riley's eyebrows rise. "Not often," she grumbles.

"It's good for you. Like you said, everyone needs to be humbled," I offer teasingly.

"Yeah, well." Riley puts her hand on her hip impertinently,

like she's practiced the posture in music videos. She lifts her chin, the picture of self-possession. "I've decided I don't like it."

I laugh, even though I'm really starting to understand *why* people don't say no to her very often. Her very presence is persuasive. I don't know how she does it—while Riley is on the shorter side, she makes five-foot-two feel imposing over my six feet. *Does* is the wrong verb, really. It's something in the way Riley *is*.

"Just make someone up," I tell her. "Just say the song is about whoever."

I'm surprised when Riley's eyes flash. "That would be a lie. My songs aren't lies. Come on," she implores me, her voice like hardened honey, "what can I do to convince you?"

I shift in my seat. Patiently, I formulate my next words. "The only thing worse than having your ex-girlfriend become the singer-songwriter of your generation and write a hit song about you is having your ex-girlfriend become the singer-songwriter of your generation and write a hit song *everyone knows* is about you."

Finally, Riley is quiet.

I get the impression she's reckoning with what I've spent years coming to recognize. Riley is everything I'm not. Which is surreal, since we were once so similar. In the decade since we dated, we haven't just separated—we've gone in opposite directions, her into a high-flying, headline-wrapped world of sound and flash, me into obligation, into order, the pleasant confines of home wrapped up in necessity. Riley married her famous ex while I retreated from unsuccessful relationships. Ten years is plenty of time for us to change into completely different people who only look like the partners we used to love.

It's several long seconds until she replies. When she does, her veneer of celebrity is gone. She's just the unguarded girl I used to know. "You really won't budge," she says.

"You know I won't."

She smiles sadly. "Yeah. I do."

While the office is silent, it's like something has crashed through the door, carrying the past into the room with us. The pressure of regretful recollections, of love left unfinished. Riley glances down, looking uncomfortable.

"I have to say," she starts.

It startles me anew how instantly I recognize the light edge in her voice. How well I remember exactly the way Riley's intonation would set the stage when she wanted to pick fights. While we didn't fight often, we didn't fight *never*. We were everything to each other, which raises the stakes and heightens the friction.

It's funny how something like eagerness wakes up in me. I'm not stuck in the past, my past with Riley—honestly, I'm not. It's some rogue, guilty part of me I feel yearning for the chance to relive us in the form of harsh words.

"It's sort of a relief to see you still here," Riley goes on. "You're doing exactly what you left me for."

I wait for the punch line. Or, the resolution. When dissonant notes reprise into harmony.

"Like, at least you stayed with what you chose over me," she says.

There it is. I have lost count of the nights I've passed wondering if we would ever have this conversation. If Riley Wynn, new superstar, would ever have it out with her outstandingly ordinary ex over how we fell apart. "You left me, too," I remind her stiffly. "I was always here. You didn't come back."

The summer we broke up, I wondered every day if Riley

would invite me to return to her life. I watched my phone like it held my whole world, which it sort of did. It held my only hope of hearing from the girl who made stages feel intimate and made ordinary days feel like standing in the spotlight.

Weeks passed. Months.

Maybe ebbed into *no*, like it does.

"There was nothing to come back to," she replies. "Not really."

I hear her meaning with cutting clarity. Her gift, just like in her lyrics. *Nothing she wanted.* Not the life she needed. Nothing except the man who'd let her down.

"Tell me you're happy, though," she says. "That you *chose right.* That you don't think about the road we didn't take together."

I know she's not looking for comfort, for me to say *everything worked out in the end.* She's goading me. While I'm not quick to frustration, I'm not the one who showed up to *her* place of work with no care for how I would upend her life. "I don't regret staying at Harcourt Homes," I reply shortly. "Do you regret not coming back?"

"No."

"Good. I'm glad to hear it, Riley." The forced pleasantry is making my heart pound hard. "I really am."

"I'm happy to hear you're happy, Max." Riley's fast reply says everything. The pink in her cheeks says even more. "Well," she continues, "I guess I don't have a reason to be here, then. I'd give you tickets to the LA show on my tour, but you already made it clear you're not a fan."

The idea makes my resentment falter. Riley interrogating me on my life choices, rubbing in the reason for our split, is unpleasant. Her feeling like I don't care for her music is intolerable.

"Riley, that's not it at all," I say, schooling the spite out of my voice. I need her to know I care for her music even if I no longer have the privilege of caring for her. In fact, how much I care is why I *can't* listen. While I wish she understood, I can't face saying out loud, *The memories in your songs would run me ragged.*

"It's fine." With her hand on the door, she smiles. "It's funny. Millions of listeners, and the one person I wrote the song for hasn't heard it. Take care, Max."

Like a melody lost on the wind, she walks out.

FOUR

Riley

I PARK IN front of the vegan Mexican place where I'm meeting my mom for dinner. The restaurant, on the fancy stretch of mid-Melrose, is one of my favorites. While I'm not vegan, I strictly follow whatever diet involves consuming this place's soyrizo burritos in high quantities. In more practical terms, I've learned the restaurant's cozy relationship with celebrities means they understand important points like discreet seat placement.

I power off my car's electric engine. Usually, this is when my music system would fade out. Tonight, however, there's only continued silence. I drove here from Harcourt Homes without music, which I only do when I'm really rattled.

I'm going to need some exquisite vegan horchata to wash from my mouth the taste of my conversation with Max. What frustrates me isn't just his refusal. It's the revelation that he *doesn't even listen to my music.* If Max were releasing music, I'd be following him on Spotify, streaming on every release day.

But Max gave up music in college.

I figured he was watching my career with even the slightest

interest. Finding out he's not, I don't know how I feel. My pride hurts. Maybe my heart, too.

I'm not still *in love* with Max Harcourt. He's just . . . still important to me, in some way my soul refuses to forget. It's like knowing which way the compass points even when my life's journey is leading me in other directions. I guess I just wanted some sign I was important to him, too.

Whatever. This is the best year of my career. I'm determined to enjoy it, no matter whether Max Harcourt listens to my music or not.

In the restaurant's entryway, the heavy heels of my boots thud on the intricate tile under the conical overhead lights. The design here coheres in unexpected ways, this perfect mélange of old-school character and modern California cool. Conversation carries in from the patio over the clinking of glasses with elaborate garnishes.

I follow the sound onto the expansive flagstone space. In the corner, I find my mom seated at our table. She's left me the chair facing away from the street.

I used to get recognized occasionally before *The Breakup Record*, more often when I was out with Wesley. Now, if I'm not careful, it's unnervingly easy for crowds to form, crushing in with cameras and prying questions. Going out in public feels like feeding wolves. Of *course* they're excited to see you. It's just very easy for the excitement to darken into something more ravenous.

The fame I've found with *The Breakup Record* intimidates even while it exhilarates me, honestly. The "M" for millions on the follower count under the checkmark next to my name on Instagram, the heyday surrounding my label's SUV leaving *The Tonight Show* when I debuted "The Final Word," one of my favorite new songs. Sharing my music with countless listeners on the country's largest stages is the stuff of my lifelong dreams.

Yet—fame like this is irreversible in ways I'm still grappling with. I remember when, inside the last nine months, I could grab sushi in Santa Monica, smile in some fans' selfies, then head home to my pre-Wesley house off the curb on Crescent Heights, where I never worried whether the hedges were high enough to keep paparazzi out.

Melrose fortunately has the benefit of being peppered with celebrities and having a culture of *be cool* around them. Half the people on this patio are probably in either the film or music industry.

I sit. Despite my dark mood, I have to smile when I notice how much my mom stands out here. In this expanse of high fashion, Carrie Wynn, with her short blond hair looking exactly like it does on every other occasion, is wearing her favorite purple sweater, which eschews style for comfort. My mom is Midwestern to the max. It's from her I get my genuineness, never mind how different our genuine selves look.

She glances up from the menu, pleasantly surprised. "You're on time," she observes. "You said you would be late."

"My errand wrapped up faster than I thought," I say lightly.

"Everything okay?" Mom's eyes laser in on me. I pretend to read the menu, hoping I can evade her intuition.

"Everything is great," I lie. "Should we get the nachos?"

This underhanded ploy works exactly like I expected. The mention of the nachos distracts my mother. "I can make those at home," she says disapprovingly.

I purse my lips to suppress my laugh. My mother has long held the philosophy of never ordering from a restaurant something she already has a tried-and-true recipe for. Which, for me, includes the entire menu. My mom, however, former housewife and personal chef to my dad and me my whole life, has developed a formidable culinary repertoire. While I'm not certain she could recreate *these* nachos—which infuse dragon fruit with mole-drizzled cashew cheese covering effervescently crunchy chips—I don't point this out.

"Okay, you pick," I reply.

"Why don't we get the gorditas," she declares. While what she's said is grammatically a question, she's not asking.

I wave down our waiter. When he swings by our table, I notice his jolt of recognition, then he recovers his composure. "What can I get started for you?" His voice is friendly, casual. He's pretty good, this one.

I match his noncommittal warmth, following one of my publicist's pointers. *If you're overfriendly, people will think you're obsessed with being recognized. If you're disaffected, they'll think you're a bitch.* "The gorditas to start, please," I say, smiling. "And horchata for both of us."

When he leaves, my mom wastes no time. "So the furniture is fully moved. I've unpacked your bathrooms, your kitchen. You're a thirty-year-old woman, and you can unpack your clothes. Besides, you have so many of them, I wouldn't know where to start. It's time I book my ticket home."

My smile slips. "You don't have to leave so fast."

"Yes. I do." In my mom's immediate reply, I'm pretty sure I hear something other than impatience. "You don't need me, and you certainly don't want to be living with your mother. I have to go home. Sort through my own house."

I fall silent, wishing I had my horchata just for something to do with my hands. Like our matching brown eyes, my mom and I now have matching divorces, just months apart. Of course, my parents' ended thirty-five years of marriage; mine, three months. When I asked her to fly to LA to help me move out of the Malibu house I'd just bought with Wesley and into my new place in the Hills, I knew my mom would welcome the distraction. We both would.

"Dealing with . . . home could wait, Mom," I say. In the humming glow of the patio heaters, I wonder if it's visible how my cheeks color from my ineloquence. When you center your entire career on evoking emotion with the perfect lyrics, it's funny how the right words sometimes desert you when you need them. I press on. "How about you come on tour with me instead?"

Mom lets out a baffled laugh.

"Tour is . . . your dad's thing," she explains when she realizes I'm not joking. "You know I'm so proud of you, but I'd just get in the way. I need to live my own life, hon."

I nod patiently, having known she would say this. It's true my dad taught me guitar. On my first tour, he came to half my shows. Would he be delighted to come on my next tour? Of course he would. In fact, I know he would.

"I actually talked to Dad about this," I say delicately.

Immediately, my mom's forced sunniness clouds over.

"It was his idea," I continue.

I went on a long drive days ago in between tour rehearsals so I could catch up with him, his gravelly voice from my car's speakers filling the quiet interior while I followed the Pacific Coast Highway without destination. The conversation was nice, if a little painful. Although the divorce was mutual, neither of my parents is *happy* with the development.

However, my dad has his career, land surveying in St. Louis. My mom gave up hers when she had me. I have no siblings, and neither does she. Even the saddest songs I've ever heard don't capture the hurt of imagining my mom alone in her house—our house, once—with no one. My dad felt the same way.

Mom fusses petulantly in her seat. "I thought one of the effects of divorce was *not* having to listen to what my ex-husband thinks I should do."

"He still cares about you. He worries," I say gently. "And he's not the only one."

Knowing every line on my mom's face means I can pick out exactly when her resistance softens, despite her expression hardly changing. Unspeaking, she gazes past me to where the string lights illuminating the intricately gardened patio glow over the diners. "I'm *fine*," she says, scoffing unconvincingly.

I shift my head to find her eyes. My penetrating stare is the one I learned from her.

It works. "Okay, I'm not *fine*-fine," she amends. "I'm getting there, though. I'm fine enough on my own, hon," she says, her voice settling into the self-sacrificial conviction I know she's spent decades learning. "You don't have to take your sad divorced mom on tour with you. I don't need a babysitter."

"What if *I* do?" I improvise. I pride myself on my capacity for winging it, inventing magic from nothing. No matter how prepared everything I do is nowadays, nobody gets where I have without knowing how to improvise. "This tour is going to be huge," I go on. "Everyone on my team acts like they're on my side, but really they're in it for themselves. I could use someone who is there just for me. The person, not, you know—*Riley*

Wynn." I say my name like it's written in lights. "I need *you*," I finish.

The moment I do, I know I've found my angle. It feels like hearing the perfect riff unfold from my fingertips. Playing on my mom's instinct to do whatever I need is how I'll convince her to do what *she* needs.

"You butt," Mom says, evidently feeling my rhetorical hand.

I laugh—noticing she's not arguing. Like when I feel the audience is with me, I ride my momentum. "It'll be fun!" I promise her. "Single ladies on tour! Hey, you can stay on the bus with me! We'll watch bad movies and eat crap!"

While my mom frowns, the disapproval doesn't reach her eyes. She's warming up to the idea.

I'm preparing to extol the virtues of Tour Bus Movie Nights when my phone vibrates. My publicist's name on the notification gets me to reluctantly swipe the conversation open.

My ex-husband's face greets me in the iMessage conversation. His unchanging grin stares out from the still of the TikTok my publicist sent me. Feeling less hungry now, I click the link.

When I hear the music, I'm grateful I keep my phone's volume low. The piano rhythm under the first verse of "Until You" is one song I do not need noticed coming out of *my* speakers in the middle of dinner on Melrose.

In the video, Wesley brushes his teeth shirtless, obviously proud of the shower-glistening pecs he's developed for the medieval period drama he just signed on to. While he's not the hunky sort, he's conscious enough of his ebony-haired, chiseled gravitas to understand "unlikely" sex symbol status is one more opportunity to exploit for his own gain.

In front of the mirror in the modern bathroom I called ours for, like, six weeks, he grooves to the most recognizable lyrics in the country right now. My lyrics. *Woke up with my heart under your fingers*, I sing near the end of the opening verse.

When I reach *under your fingers*, he winks into the camera.

Indignation pounding in my heart, I check out the video's specifics. Millions of views since he posted this morning. *Of course*. Of course he's reaping only rewards for this shit. He knows what he's doing on social media, feeding #WesleyTok with fancast responses, winking references to rumors, everything to boost his internet-loved persona.

The video is far from his first featuring my music. When we were married, he would humorously caption clips of him frowning with idiosyncratic stuff I'd "gotten mad at him for," with some of my more vengeful songs for musical accompaniment.

His viewers lapped up the self-deprecating clowning—and certain male-pattern fanboys loved how *relatable* the complaints of his *nasty* wife made him. *Ignore the comments*, Wesley would say.

Of course, my label fucking loves it. While I've refrained from requesting my publicist chasten his for content like he's just posted, I'm honestly not sure the label would cooperate if I did. They wish I would hype my music on social media more, which I won't. Frankly, my label flacks have no idea how it feels reading the shit I expose myself to whenever I post.

The fact that Wesley is doing the new-media promo for them, even if it shifts the glory to him, makes him their hero. One of the flashiest rising stars in the world promoting my music online? Well, who cares how much it hurts the musician.

Fury unfurls in my cheeks, searing my face unpleasantly under the restaurant's patio heaters.

It's nothing compared to how I feel when I open the caption, though.

Divorced life = not so bad when you inspired Riley's best bop.

I feel my fingers clench on the custom iPhone case I commissioned from one of my favorite social media–famous designers. What pisses me off isn't just Wesley racking up more internet credit for my work. Not this time.

It's his fucking word choice. *Bop?* I love songs I would consider bops, including songs of mine. "Until You" isn't one of them. While Wesley knows nothing of the songwriting of "Until You," the whole point is the ripped-open longing I put into every note. Fucking "bop" changes not the song's value but its *purpose.* Its meaning, to listeners, to me.

Which he knows. He went to Yale Drama. He's done Shakespeare. He knows what words mean, how words feel. He knows *me* well enough to understand how it would crawl under my skin for him to misconstrue the work I'm proudest of in this way.

"What's wrong?" My mom's question is part instantaneous protectiveness, part relief that she's no longer the subject of inquisition.

"Just the same. Fucking Wesley," I say honestly. "I can't believe I actually married that asshole." Grunting in frustration, I flip my phone face down on the table. Mom needs no more explanation—when we weren't unpacking silverware or framed photographs, we spent nights unpacking my ill-fated marriage. There were tears. There were hugs like I haven't needed since I was sixteen.

She's silent for a moment. I start figuring out my response to my publicist. While I don't want them to feel like I endorse or welcome Wesley's ill-intentioned humor, if I resist overenthusiastically, they'll pressure me to do my own social media instead. I'll have to say something noncommittally sarcastic—

"Maybe I can come on *part* of the tour," my mom says.

I look up, hope leaping into my heart. Of course the moment I wasn't plying her to join me on tour is what persuaded her. Nothing reaches people like real emotion. Just like songwriting. "Oh my god, *yes*," I reply instantly. "It's going to be so much fun. I promise."

Mom rolls her eyes, looking pleased. "You're going to be sick of me in three cities," she comments as the waiter returns with our gorditas. "I guarantee it."

When the horchata is set down, I pounce on mine. It's perfect. Milky, sweet comfort over ice. "We'll see," I say playfully, not meaning it. My plan may have been to ease my mom's transition to divorce, but I can feel the truth even now. I might need my mom more than my mom needs this tour.

FIVE

Max

WELL, WHY THE hell did you let her *get away, Maxwell?*

While I wash dishes, Linda's self-satisfied reprimand repeats endlessly in my head. In the day since Riley's unexpected visit, inquisitive residents have pestered me nonstop about my "girl-friend." I've lost count of how often I've explained the super-famous, striking—okay, unbelievably sexy—woman who dropped into our lives yesterday is *not* my girlfriend.

Linda, of course, pressed me with endless follow-up questions. I felt like I'd covered up Watergate from the way she cornered me during dinner service. *You sure she's not your lady friend? Never? Well, I'm not surprised. When? How long? Nine months? Only nine?*

Well, why the hell did you let her *get away, Maxwell?*

None of my explanations satisfied her.

I scrub the final pan of the night, letting Stevie Wonder wash over me. The keyboardist extraordinaire is my cleaning music of choice—soothing, lively, joyous. His catalogue is endless, sort of like doing the dishes.

While "Love's in Need of Love Today" winds down on the speakers I've linked to my iPhone, I feel good. Sure, Riley's visit yesterday shook things up. Still, nothing changes how workdays here always leave me. Satisfied. Like the day meant something.

When my parents got here this morning for one of their usual visits, I caught myself enjoying showing them what was *working*, what was going *right*. Sure, some of the paint might be fading. What isn't is the way this place feels like home. Not just for our residents—for me, too. For my family.

"Max, can we talk?"

My upbeat mood disappears like the last of the pan's char swirling down the drain. There's no mishearing the stiff sadness in my mother's voice.

Hastily I shut off Stevie Wonder, not wanting to risk the Joni Mitchell effect of whatever's coming imprinting in my mind onto this lovely song. I face my mom, finding her stretched expression looking nothing like how upbeat she seemed today.

"Of course," I say, shutting off the faucet. "Um. Why?"

"It's . . . the business," Mom manages. "We should sit down. The four of us."

I'm struck with strange foreboding, noticing how *familiar* every detail of Harcourt Homes' restaurant-style kitchen is— the placement of every pan, the layout of ingredients in the small fridge near the stoves, the patterns on the hand towels.

The business? I follow my mom out of the room, my chest clenching. In the now-empty, half-lit dining room, she sits down next to Dad and Jess. No one meets my eyes.

I take the table's open seat. Instead of waiting, I start in. I want everyone to understand the facts—no hasty decisions. "I know income isn't good," I say. "We're going to need to make cuts. Layoffs, new suppliers. I've reached out—"

"Max," my mom says.

The strangled pinch in her voice stops me short. It's Carole King in my ears now, not Joni Mitchell. I look up, starting to feel the very ground moving under my feet while I'm standing still.

"We know how the business is doing. We've known how the business is doing," my mom continues. "It's not—we're not—"

"We'd like to sell," my dad elaborates.

Shock swipes my next reassurance from my lips. Of the difficult conversations I've imagined concerning the home's finances, this was not one of them.

When my parents left the business in my charge, they made me and Jess part owners while keeping their own share. The idea was we'd eventually buy them out, supplementing their retirement savings—more than fair recognition of this business they've built for us to carry on—or inherit it. What's never entered consideration, even in the worst downturns my parents ever faced running this place, was selling out of the family.

"What's—" I falter. "Is everything okay with your retirement savings?"

My dad shrugs. "We're fine. With cost of living, especially in California, we could be better, but we're fine. This decision isn't because we need cash."

"Then what is it?"

My dad won't meet my eyes. "It . . . This place is declining, Max. The offer we've received is from developers who don't just want the land. They want to try to keep the home running." I notice something flit into his expression, some hungry hope, when he continues. "It might be the last offer like this we ever get, to purchase the operating business, until the home goes under. Maybe things would be different if the business could recover, but it won't, not the way we've been doing things. It's been this way for years. Things won't get better. Which means it's . . . well, it's now or never."

He pauses.

"Of course, the developers will only purchase the entire property. So we'd like you to sell with us," he finishes. "Let this place go."

Silence falls devastatingly in the space his words leave. My dad, who could barely get them out, looks down. In the half light, every line on his face is shadowed into a canyon. In many ways I resemble him, his sweep of hair graying where mine isn't, his glasses frames square instead of round. It isn't just painful to see him felled this way—it's harrowing.

I know I can't fathom what this feels like for him, for them. My parents built this business up from nothing thirty years ago. Still, what he's said sticks in my throat like tears I can't swallow down.

"Sell?" I manage. "The new owners will raise the rates. Half of our residents won't be able to pay."

"Which is why we're going out of business," my mom replies, her voice stretched, imploring me to understand.

I know deep down I *do* understand. I just don't want to. "It's not fair to our residents," I protest.

"It's not fair to your staff if Harcourt Homes"—my dad starts in sternly, then loses his momentum when he reaches the home's name—"or whatever they call it, goes out of business," he continues. "They have families, too. Look, we're profoundly grateful for what you've done here, both of you. Especially you, Max. The way you've stepped up, you've given us—our residents, our staff, everyone—years this place would never have had with us in charge. None of us want this." He sighs heavily, then shrugs without much life. "But maybe it's not the worst thing."

I stare, feeling like I've just heard him say he prefers *Magical Mystery Tour* to *Sgt. Pepper's*.

"Not the worst thing?" I repeat.

Half-confrontational, like he's convincing me of something he doesn't believe himself, my dad looks up. "Well, Jess is moving to New York. Your mom and I have retired. We only visit for the memories. You don't need to keep this place up on your own, Max."

I force myself to reply patiently. "I know I don't. Jess"—I face my sister, who looks uncomfortable like I've rarely ever seen her—"you're going to love New York," I say. "Mom, Dad, you deserve to visit this incredible place *you* founded. I can do this," I insist. "I'll—I'll figure this out. If the developers think they can run this business instead of knocking the place down, I can, too."

My explanation is not met with gratitude or surprise. While I see the look my parents exchange, it's not one I know how to decode. Being married business partners for decades, my parents practically have their own silent language.

"What?" I ask.

It's neither of them who speaks up.

"What do you *want* to do?" Jess's voice searches delicately. "Like, with your life. What's your dream?"

I meet her gaze, feeling suddenly defensive. "I'm doing it," I reply.

"It's just," my mom starts right where my sister left off, "maybe this could be good for you, Max. It's been wonderful having you both here, but we never wanted our dream to become your burden."

"It's not," I insist, feeling frustration spring from new sources. I expected the somber summaries of our financials, not this existential inquest. I'm not sure where it's coming from, frankly— this suspicion I'm secretly resenting my purpose here. I was *just* feeling satisfied with the day's work, contently scrubbing pans to Stevie Wonder, wasn't I? Ever since I can remember, I've spent my life here willingly. No one ever made me help out. When I graduated from college, I didn't even apply to other jobs—I knew what I wanted.

"God knows we needed you," my dad remarks. He removes his glasses to wipe the lenses on his sleeve, the way I do when I need to read music. "Changing your major, studying business. You gave us ten more years." He returns his glasses to their perch on his nose like he's putting the world into focus. "I just can't help worrying about what it cost you."

I open my mouth to protest.

"Look at Riley," my sister says.

Her rhetorical pivot strikes something in me. I round on her slowly, realizing this whole conversation, its focus on me, is starting to feel . . . coordinated. Uncomfortably intervention-like. When I reply, I only just manage to match her equanimity. "What does Riley have to do with anything?"

Jess shrugs stiffly. Distantly I recognize this sort of direct soul-searching isn't exactly my freewheeling sister's default— which means whatever she's going for here is genuinely important to her. "When you and Riley were together you were . . .

writing music and gigging," Jess explains. "You were so good, and now . . . Look at her. She's . . ."

When Jess pauses, I get the sense it's out of reluctance, not uncertainty.

"She's living your dream," my sister finishes.

I simmer, not wanting to snap when I know the subject of Harcourt Homes' future isn't easy for any of us. Still, the way my family is spinning the issue only heightens my indignation. Do they really imagine I've *never* considered this? Do they think they're shedding new light on the situation?

Yes, my ex-girlfriend, with whom I once joyously made music, is now one of the most famous musicians in the world. Don't they know this fact *would've* devoured me if I weren't content with how I've lived my life instead?

"I'm happy for Riley," I grind out. While I'm pissed Jess dragged her into the conversation, I want them to hear conviction in my voice, not frustration. "Really. She has her dream. I gave music up for what *I* wanted."

Did I want the same dream once? Knowing my music was loved by people worldwide? Of course I did. Was the dream part of why Riley and I fell in love so fast? Sharing the same grand hope for our futures, like harmonies on the same melody?

Of course it was.

Our relationship only unraveled when I did something my family can't comprehend. *I changed my mind.* My relationship with Riley didn't end when I fell out of love with her. We ended when I fell out of love with the dream, with fanning the shared flame Riley kept raging.

"Honey." My mom's voice smothers gently. "You always wanted

to be a musician. I know you like it here. It's just, you never even got a chance to pursue it. I know you still love music. When you perform here, you're magnificent. You deserve to play for more people than"—she gestures to the piano in the darkness—"this old dining room."

Moving on impulse, I stand up. I note my mom's startled expression, which I understand—like interrogation doesn't come easily to Jess, harshness doesn't come easily to me. I can't contain myself now, however. I'm *done*. It's one thing for my family to fold our beloved business, but to spin it like it's some favor to me? I just can't stand it.

"You think"—I shove my chair in—"I'm just the noble, dutiful son, long-suffering, lashed to the old family shop. I don't know how to convince you I'm not. *This* is what I want." Shaking my head, I start to leave.

"Max."

The sharpness in my sister's voice catches me. I pause, facing her, finding no sting in her eyes. It's not the final word she wants. It's one more chance to convince me.

"Look at me and tell me you're happy," Jess implores. I hear Riley's refrain in her words. *Tell me you're happy.* "All you do is work in the tiny office upstairs, play the same songs every week, and then go home to your empty apartment where you never even hung up drapes."

I don't understand the significance my sister is placing on my window dressings. While I love working here, I'm not exactly rolling in dough. Spending fifty dollars on cheap screw-in rods for green fabric from HomeGoods isn't my highest-priority expenditure.

I don't have the chance to explain. Jess charges on. "When

Kendra wanted to move in with you, you broke up," she says. "Same with Elizabeth."

Now I have no explanation to offer. I wonder if Jess knows the sore spot she's struck—while I'm deeply, earnestly happy for her upcoming move and the companionship she's found with April, I can't ignore the contrast with my own relationship status. Yes, I'm sometimes surprised to notice I've replaced the guy who listened to cracked earphones during calculus class with a diligent manager in charge of property, employees, salaries, and the future of his family enterprise. Nevertheless, while my sister is moving out, flourishing in love, I've found myself unable to move past my empty apartment and my failed relationships.

Jess softens in my silence. "You never push for what you want. You say the home is your passion, but you've been avoiding this conversation for months. Just . . . waiting until someone forces you to have it. You're living in limbo," she says. "I know you can't see it, but you need more than this."

I darken, only resisting anger because I love Jess, who I know wants to do the right thing. Still, I'm thirty years old—I've done okay so far without my precocious younger sister prescribing my life to me, insisting I *need more*, like I'm a houseplant kept out of the sun.

Even so, I honestly don't want to make this conversation worse, not when I know everyone is struggling in their own way.

So, with my family's invocation of Riley stuck in my head, I do what I did when I wrote songs. I stick with the truth.

"You're wrong," I say. "All of you."

I don't hesitate now. I leave the dining room, ignoring my father's defeated sigh, my mom's plaintive intonations of my name.

"See? You're doing it right now," I hear Jess call out. "Walking out instead of fighting."

In the lobby, I grit my teeth. *Now* she wants the final word. Refusing to give in, I continue out the front door without slowing my step.

Nights in the Valley look like streetlights. It's the one constant, everywhere you go, past trees, powerlines, laundromats, or the marquees of restaurants—streetlights, running in neat yellow rows, latticing every avenue like fireflies in formation. Under a lone sallow ring, I find my car. It isn't Joni Mitchell or Stevie Wonder playing when I crank the key, fortunately. For the past few years, I've sated my musical curiosity by flipping radio stations, immersing myself in whatever the hits or the oldies channels serve up.

I drive, letting songs I know well rub elbows with songs I don't, fighting to forget the conversation with my family. While I search the stations, I exit the hills, where chaparral changes to concrete, where the city streets welcome drivers out of Laurel Canyon. I follow my usual route, onto Sunset, heading for West Hollywood.

Sunset Boulevard is the crass shell of the sinful, star-studded street rock documentaries depict, where Janis Joplin partied, where Petty cruised with Springsteen, where the Doors sprung from the Whisky a Go Go. Nowadays, while landmarks like the Whisky remain, they're wedged in among generic restaurants under the skyscrapers of media conglomerates. Financiers who wear sneakers with suits flock into Soho House while furniture stores display drab minimalist pieces. The old Tower Records plays host to Instagrammable pop-up experiences.

Out of this landscape rises Riley's huge billboard.

Of course it's in front of one of the street's longest stoplights, where I wait. Instead of pretending the billboard isn't there the way I sometimes do, I stare up at her—on fire and indignant and beautiful.

When one of her songs comes on the radio, I reach on instinct to change it, then stop myself.

It's not "Until You." I recognize the title on the radio display from the Spotify page I spent yesterday fretting over. "Home-made Rollercoaster" is quick, yet quiet, with charged urgency in the country-tinged up-and-down of Riley's voice. Involuntarily I meet her eyes on the billboard when the chorus comes in, leaving me with the feeling she's singing to me. The siren of the Sunset Strip.

Knowing it's not about me, I let myself enjoy the song. It isn't difficult. Riley has always had unnatural songwriting skill. Her ear for melody is unparalleled, and at Chapman she didn't study music, choosing English instead to focus on poetry classes. In the decade since, her poetry has sharpened, and her voice is stronger.

I'm . . . hooked. Captivated, in my car filled with her voice. *Damn it, Riley.*

When I reach the next red light, I switch from the radio to my phone's audio. "Homemade Rollercoaster" is the first song on the album—not letting myself lose my nerve, I open Spotify, where I start the second. *The Breakup Record* unravels for me pop portraits of Riley out of love. One is for Wesley—I don't let myself speculate which. Each is full of Riley, her pounding, restless heart seeping into every flourish, every chord, every verse.

Who ever made music of a mild day?

I remember when the words on her skin first ensnared my

eye, when we first had sex. We were neither of each other's firsts—yet, somehow, we felt like each other's first *something*. When Riley cast off her shirt, revealing the ink inscribed on her chest, I paused in the midst of what we were doing, intrigued. With wry Riley humor, she nonchalantly inquired whether instead of where the night was heading I'd prefer to read some poetry.

Every inch of you is poetry, I replied.

Riley holds me in her spell the whole way home, where I switch Spotify to my wireless headphones. I'm walking into my—okay, yes, empty, dull, drape-less—apartment when "Until You" starts.

I recognize the near-murmur of the opening piano rhythm, often my cue to change the song. Pulled into the album now, however, I let Riley's playing draw me in. It's one more of her uncanny skills, her power for starting songs with instantaneous never-letting-go imperative.

Standing in the middle of my dark living room—while I've closed the front door, I haven't even hit the lights—I listen.

First, my musician's mind makes one instant evaluation. "Until You" is not just a hit. It's not just iconic, not just the "song of the summer." It is a masterpiece. Riley's structured it cleverly, writing the first verse in past tense, the second in present, and the third in future. It's the sort of poetic flourish she'd engage in simply out of impulsive inspiration. She cements the concept in verb shifts in the chorus.

I didn't know what love is
I don't know what love is
I won't know what love is
Until you

Of course, once my head has heard the song, my heart kicks in.

What fixes me in place is the idea Riley felt this way about me. *Ever.* While of course I was head over heels for her, either she's found a compelling story in our long-over romance, or . . . she once loved me as much as I loved her.

I wish I could revel in the feeling. Or even just enjoy the song—just feel glad my ex-girlfriend's music career is flourishing. I wish my heart rested easily enough with the end of our love for this song to ring in my ears like nothing except enchanting music.

Instead, I . . . hate it.

Not Riley's musicianship, of course, nor her success. I hate the way she's diminished the heartsick riddle of my life into one short single. It wrecked me for years—it isn't three minutes of *verse-chorus-verse-chorus* followed by the repeat button.

In many ways, Riley is the unforgettable marking point in my life. I've spent countless irreplaceable nights studying the wounds our relationship left on me while they slowly closed. *They* were supposed to be our love's legacy. Instead, Riley's photographed my heart's secrets, then displayed them fifty feet high on Sunset fucking Boulevard, pretending they're the real thing.

When the song ends, I don't let the next one start. I hit repeat. It's masochistic pleasure, pressing my resentment deeper. *Is this what you wanted, Riley? Is this what we were?* I say to myself in the dark. *You've written us in chords and colors even I never imagined, only to pretend it's what our love was. You win.*

Make me your song, Riley.

On my next play, details stand out in the first verse.

Late nights, new homes
Your hands on the piano
Woke up with my heart under your fingers
Played me slowly so the notes would linger

Riley's describing the night we met, I realize. She explained to me once with no hint of shyness why she fell for me, the guy who unintentionally woke her up with his midnight piano playing.

I sink onto my couch—noticing how ugly the gray fabric seems right now, how Jess's characterization of my uninspiring present living situation is painting everything here in shades of pathetic. I remind myself of what else my family said. Songwriting superstardom was Riley's dream, one she was willing to chase no matter the cost. She's reached it in *The Breakup Record* by converting the people of her romantic past into characters in her songs.

People including me. "Until You" is a song. It's the idea of Riley she's casting to draw her listeners in, like she drew me in. It's not how she feels *now*, not really—just one of the many characters Riley plays for her audiences. It shares nothing with the intricately devastating ways I've wrestled with the end of our relationship.

Still...

In my songwriting days, the idea of "sticking to the truth" didn't come from me. It came from Riley. It was her guiding principle, inspiration she passed on to me.

I doubt it's faded now. Which means somewhere in her is . . . the girl who means what she's singing in "Until You."

I play the song over five times. I find myself loving how much I hate it, which maybe just means I love it. It's like how the hurt of heartbreak doesn't negate love—it reflects it.

With each repetition, I surrender to wondering if my family was right. *Do I give up? Am I afraid of pushing for what I want?* With Riley's voice ringing in my ears, my family's words hold more power.

After all, they aren't the first to say them. Riley did, when she dumped me.

We were supposed to spend the summer in Nashville, the city where one-day superstars rise from the small stages of crowded rooms. Riley planned everything. Our "tour," she would say half-reverently. Venues with open mics, the occasional booked gig, cheap places to stay. Everything we needed to sustain weeks of playing our music together, far from home.

Until I dropped out. The day we were set to leave, I told her Harcourt Homes needed me. I watched the Nashville skyline crumble in Riley's eyes when I explained I couldn't come with her.

"Until You" chastises me in my headphones.

The day of, I want you
High roads, see us through
You look like you're hoping I'll be fine
I know I'm helpless even when I try

We know it isn't true
when you say you'll see me soon
Cut me cleanly with your gemstone eyes
which is when I realize . . .

I drove home, knowing she was going on the tour without me. While she broke my heart, I knew I'd broken hers first, differently. So when she walked away, I let her.

What if I should have fought harder?

For Riley. For music. For the dreams we shared.

In the dark, the nothingness of my home looms forth. I have one picture on the kitchen pass-through, of my family when we went to the Grand Canyon. My furniture is cheap, functional. While I don't need to direct my joy into drapes, the fact is, there's *nothing* here in which I've invested pride, permanence, or love. When my exes would spend nights or weekends here, they would leave behind jackets or hairbrushes or other casual items—little claims staked. Gone now, into memory.

Reckoning with my family's characterization of my life, I decide they were wrong in only one way. I love Harcourt Homes. Which makes this worse. We're going to lose the one—

I sit up straight. I shut off Riley's song.

What if I could give my old dreams one last shot *while* saving Harcourt Homes?

The one thing Harcourt Homes' prospective buyer has that I don't is funding to invest in it. What if I could come into enough money to make the improvements I need?

Fingers racing with inspiration, I text Jess.

> Did you happen to get Riley's number today?

Jess replies immediately with no mention of our fight or lingering hostility. It's how it is with us. Our family is too close to let fights drive wedges between us.

She never changed it

I exhale. Nothing stands in my way now, no logistics holding me from the hugest leap of my life. If there's one thing scarier than taking chances, it might be taking *second* chances.

Scrolling my contacts, I find the one I could never force myself to delete—one I haven't used in a decade.

SIX

Riley

WHEN THE DOORBELL rings, I've just spilled detergent on myself. Half the bottle, from the looks of the stain spreading over my jeans.

The frustration puts tears into my eyes. It's not just because of the detergent, obviously, despite the volume of liquid dousing my denim. It's everything. It's how empty the echoing hallways of this house feel. It's my mom leaving last night, headed home to pack for the tour. It's how much I already wish she hadn't left.

I've never lived alone in my whole life. In college, I had roommates. When I dropped out of college, I found other roommates. I had no money—playing sporadic shows while scooping fancy ice cream in Los Feliz wasn't exactly filling the coffers.

Even while my career was picking up, I didn't move out. I didn't have free time to tour houses while I was in the midst of studio time, label meetings, and playing shows, and I've never craved space.

Only marrying Wesley compelled me to buy a house. Our Malibu place, with windows like massive microscope slides. I didn't object to him keeping the house, leaving me recognizing the views in his TikToks like fragments of forgotten dreams.

I wish my new house felt like home. In recent weeks, I've walked its hallways, waiting for it to feel, I don't know, right. It mocks me with how perfect every detail is, reminding me I have no excuse not to love the refurbished four-bedroom.

Nestled in the Hollywood Hills, the house is infuriatingly lovely, with exposed ceiling beams, warm hardwood floors perfect for the rugs I've laid down, and views of the canyon from the roomy kitchen overlooking the sagebrush. I imagined I would feel happy here, right up until the door closed with only me inside.

I'm not sure I'm made for living alone. I woke up five times last night convinced I heard ghosts in my picturesque kitchen, rattling the gorgeous copper pots I have no idea how to use. I'd get a dog, except my touring schedule feels unfair to a pet. I'd find new roommates, except I think I'm too famous for that now. I'd ask my mom to move in permanently, except it would ruin my whole carefree rock star vibe.

Instead, it's just me and my ghosts.

God, I can't wait for my tour. I don't care if it's grueling. It'll surround me with *people*.

The doorbell rings again, the sound warbling cheerfully into the laundry room.

I strip off my jeans. When I've chucked them into the washing machine, I press start and step quickly into my house's unfamiliar hallway. In the living room, sunlight slants on the floor in playful geometries. I fling open the front door.

Max stands on my doorstep. His cream-colored button-down polo looks like fifties vacation-wear, cool for how un-trendy it is. He's combed his hair, which is half-dry out of the shower.

He opens his mouth to speak, then his gaze travels to my bare legs and the underwear beneath my too-short T-shirt. He swallows his greeting.

"Sorry," I say, flustered with myself. "I can put on pants if you want."

His eyes—the eyes I immortalized in the second verse of "Until You"—return to mine. They're uncommonly difficult to read, which is one reason I find I can't look away. The other reason is they're his.

"If I . . . want?" he repeats.

"Definitely pants," I answer for him. Swinging the door wider, I let him into my still sparsely decorated living room. "I've sort of just gotten used to being naked around random people," I offer as explanation. "Not that you're random. Shit, no, wait—that sounded worse, like I intended to be naked around you. My current nudity was not premeditated."

"It's fine, Riley." While his expression says nothing, his voice is smiling.

I reach for one of the cardboard boxes labeled "Closet" sitting on the stairs. Opening the flaps, I pray there's something I can wear in here instead of shoes or, god forbid, more underwear. I couldn't handle the irony. Luckily, right under the flaps is a pair of sweat shorts I haven't worn since college. I pull them on.

When I return to Max, he's standing in the middle of the living room, his eyes roaming the space, lingering on every detail.

Cut me cleanly with your gemstone eyes.

Out of his sight, I shake my head. It's habitual, the incessant self-editing of everything I've ever written, whether lyrics or melody. *Gemstone eyes* isn't right. I recorded it into the most popular song in the country, but it isn't right. Max's eyes don't glitter, they don't cut. They pull inward.

Dark magnets.

Ugh—there's no changing it now.

While I figured it would be weird reconnecting with the man who inspired lyrics I lovingly crafted, what I feel now is different. I should have expected it. The Max of "Until You" is the Max of my memories fused with the Max of my imagination. The Max in front of me is someone else, something else. He *hasn't* stepped out of my lyrics. He's the living revision of my songwriting, standing in my home.

The dusty front room, specifically, with cardboard boxes just outside.

Self-consciousness streaks into me. When I invited him over in response to his text last night saying he wanted to discuss something with me, I should have probably cleaned up.

"I like your place," he says. "Did you just move in?" He faces me, his gaze snagging on my shorts. I know he remembers them. Remembers nights spent curled up in his too-small bed, sneaking into the dorm showers together, eating Chinese food on the floor while we wrote music.

"If this counts as having successfully moved. My mom just left, figuring I could finish unpacking on my own," I reply. "Clearly, I cannot."

"Carrie?" He recalls my mom's name with ease. "How is she?"

"She's great," I say, then catch myself on the impulse to provide fake pleasantries. "I mean, she's not great. She's also recently divorced. So we're just . . . a couple of divorced gals."

His shoulders slump just slightly. I snatch up the detail,

realizing how hungrily I'm starting to hoard my observations of the new Max.

"I'm sorry. I didn't know your parents split up," he says genuinely. He's always genuine. It's what's so disarming about him. Most musicians have to practice putting emotion into their performances. Not Max. He feels so easily.

"Thanks. It's—whatever," I say, not liking my own evasiveness. "I'm a thirty-year-old woman."

Max puts his hands in his pockets. The shift in his stance repositions him just right, letting one of the sunbeams touch his lips. "I don't think you grow out of caring about your parents being together."

I soften or maybe sag with relief. With all my dreams exploding to life this year, my sadness over my parents' split has felt childish, even selfish. I've stuffed the messy knot of feelings out of sight, pretending the Riley Wynn who shined under stage lights wasn't the Riley who mourned the idea of visiting her parents under one roof. It's nice to have Max validate my feelings.

I sit down on the ottoman, curling one leg under me. The furniture in this room is the set the house was staged with. Lightly funky, California cool, pretending it's not expensive. It reminds me of rooms where I've posed for magazine photos, idealized spaces imagined for someone like me.

Someone like you. It's who one producer said I should write for. Though they're my lyrics, my life, I'm not writing them just for me. I've known other musicians who find the idea depersonalizing, even violating. Not me. I find the challenge invigorating, the results inspiring. I'm not cutting off pieces of myself for others. I'm sharing them. Daring to stretch the limits of where *I* becomes *we*.

"So you wanted to meet about the song. Does that mean you listened to it?" I ask.

Max sits nearby on the soft caramel leather couch. "I did," he says. I find myself leaning in. "It's good."

I laugh, feeling stung. *It's good.* His sparse reaction says everything. I remember how he would praise my work when we were together. His eyes would light up like he could see new colors. He'd elaborate on what my every chord progression meant to him. I know exactly how it would sound if he loved "Until You," if it reached him the way I intended—I've even imagined it sometimes, in weak little fantasies.

Now I know how it sounds for him not to.

"No, really. It's . . . ," he starts to elaborate. "You're . . . an incredible storyteller. It's easy to be swept away by it."

I frown. "It wasn't just a story," I say. "It's my life. I wrote it from the heart." Is *this* why he's disdainful? He's presuming I'm overdramatizing my feelings, my experiences, in the name of radio-friendly pity-partying? I expected such scorn from music reviewers, from faux-intellectual social commentators who deem my writing the overwrought clichés of a dramatic girl. I never expected it from Max.

He looks away. "If it were entirely true," he replies, "the rest of the album wouldn't exist."

Like it has nowhere else to go, his gaze finds refuge in a corner of my rug. Something in his expression says he knows I didn't choose the furniture myself.

"That's not what I came here to talk about, though. You asked if you could reveal that the song is about me," he says, his eyes meeting mine once more.

"And you said no," I remind him.

"I have something to offer you instead."

Memory strikes me like lighting. My guitar in my lap. I'm strumming while Max plays his keyboard. We're in his bedroom. "One more run-through before your roommate gets back?" I say.

"Or . . ." Max plucks my guitar from my hands while leaning down to kiss me slowly. "I have something to offer you instead."

I focus on the Max in front of me, hiding how breathless the memory of him has left me. He hasn't heard the same echo of his words. He looks composed.

"Let me play 'Until You' on tour with you," he says. "You can reveal who the song is about, but I'll get something out of it, too."

My breath leaves me for a different reason. The suggestion startles me so completely I can't reply for several seconds. The first coherent thought to come to my mind makes it out of me in a squeak. "Why? You quit music."

He nods like he expected the point. "I didn't quit music. You saw me playing at the home. I just quit performing for money," he explains. He steeples his hands in his lap. "I'm not here to unload all my emotional baggage on you, but Harcourt Homes is struggling . . . and I want to give music one last try. In case I made the wrong decision ten years ago."

The words feel double-edged. What he's saying reverses the riddle I've spent these years pondering, the constant companion he wasn't. We were perfect for each other in every way except him giving up music while I would do anything and everything in pursuit of it.

If it isn't our one inescapable divergence, I don't know where we're left. He's no longer just my revision. He's ripped up the entire page.

"You want me to pay you to go on tour," I clarify. The logistics are what I can focus on right now.

"Just whatever you would ordinarily pay a touring band member."

I stand, needing to pace while I consider. The habit centers me in part for how it reminds me of strutting onstage. The imaginary weight of my guitar strap rests on my shoulders.

Instantly, I'm distrustful of Max's idea. The whole reason I want to reveal Max is because my ex is trying to take credit for my success, to step into my spotlight. Max joining me on tour feels no different, putting him on the same stage, literally.

Then I start to wonder if I'm only thinking this way because of Wesley. He made me doubt myself in ways I'm not used to. Whether in the way he positioned himself next to me on the red carpet for his indie film, or how he would casually-not-casually drop my name in interviews, he used me constantly in subtle ways, like he knew how nicely I underlined his fame.

Max, however, isn't Wesley. When I was with him, I never assumed his motives were anything except what he said.

Still . . . the Breakup Tour is *my* tour. It's my career.

I pause in my pacing. Max meets my eyes, the sun lighting him with photo-ready clarity. "If we do this—" I start. "If you come on tour, it's on my terms. This is my album, my story to tell."

"Of course," he replies.

I walk into the center of the room, starting to feel less nervous, more in control. My mind works fast through every angle of how to spin this. The industry press, the ever-shifting internet conversation surrounding me, everything.

"You come on tour," I say. "You come out to play 'Until You.' I say you're an old friend from college. The narrative writes itself. The speculation will be louder than Wesley, louder than just announcing you as the subject, too. Let them debate and analyze every one of our glances."

I'm not surprised when he stiffens. He was never willing to see fame for what it is—a battle to be won every minute of every day. He studies me from my pre-selected couch, and I don't shrink, unafraid of his judgment. I've shot photos in sets designed to feel like homes—now I'm sitting in my home that feels like a set, the home of *someone like me*, with Max Harcourt. His eyes look like gemstones now.

"I understand," he says.

Standing up, he holds his hand out to me. I laugh.

"Max, you still have to audition," I explain. "I can't just hire you for the biggest music tour of the year without hearing you play the song."

He straightens. Confidence sparks in his eyes. "I'd love to play for you."

Our gazes meet. I hear harmony ringing in my ears.

"Do you have a piano here, or—" he starts.

"Follow me." I lead him past the kitchen into the sitting room I've converted into my music room. It's the only space in the house showing convincing signs of life. One of my guitars rests on the velvet couch, my bass on the floor next to my unfinished LaCroix from last night. Capos and picks scatter the coffee table.

Under the window overlooking the orange tree outside sits my upright piano.

Max's eyes fix on the instrument first. They wander from there, fixing on every detail, every little piece of my process.

I wonder if I looked like this entering his office. With the room under his roaming gaze, I feel barer than when I answered the door in my underwear. In this room—possibly only in this room—I'm my most vulnerable self.

He walks to the piano bench. "May I?" He gestures to the seat.

"Please," I reply, reaching down to collect one of the pages on the rug, lyrics strewn with my hectic handwriting. Where did I leave my pen, though? "Let me just find something to write you the chords—" I start.

Max sits. "No need," he says.

He places his hands on the keys. Into the room resonates the opening notes of "Until You," played perfectly from memory.

It strikes me silent. In the past couple days, he's not only listened to the song, he's immersed himself in it fully enough to memorize every note. The way he's playing stills me except for my insistent heartbeat. The way he caresses the melody, welcoming it like the song is returning home to him.

Which, in some sense, I guess it is. He's playing it exactly right. No, better than exactly. Piano isn't my strongest instrument. I only chose it for "Until You" because it's Max's instrument. I never expected him to play it, of course. I just—Max *is* the piano for me. If I was writing about him, I wanted it to be in his instrument.

I don't have the skill to fill out every chord the way he's doing. Even his embellishments, the new harmonic lines he weaves in, are beyond me and yet exactly right. He plays it the way I heard it in my head while I was writing it.

Watching him, I realize I was wrong. This song is no longer just my story to tell. Not when Max will be playing it with me.

Having him onstage with me will shape it in ways I can already see shifting, like the melody under his fingers.

The idea doesn't make me nervous or defensive—it's exhilarating. The changes, the conjoined inspiration, feel like what "Until You" was meant for. It's why I love live music. It reverts recordings to *songs*, incandescent spirits reborn nightly under the lights.

The same magic surrounds us, Max's playing holding me under the notes' perfect sway. With sound seeming to vibrate in the room's white corners, I'm struck by the sudden impression— for once, my house feels like home.

He finishes the song with no ceremony. The piano falls silent.

When he stands, he faces me with what looks charmingly like cockiness. "Well?" he asks. "Did I book the gig?"

Starting to smile, I hold out my hand.

"You're hired, Max Harcourt," I say.

SEVEN

Max

I'M NOT SURE I'm cut out for New York City.

Stepping off the subway onto the clamor of the platform, I'm conscious of how even the passage of time feels different here. Impatient, like some unseen conductor is constantly waving the city's tempo faster.

I spent the morning checking out apartments with Jess, who flew out with me, and April, who is already living here. Jess will follow in the next couple months. Of course, my sister loved every single one we saw, and April, who started work last week with the New York Foundation for the Arts, loves Jess, so I suspect the decision-making process will not go swiftly. I couldn't help smiling, watching how comfortable my sister was while imagined futures unfurled in her eyes. Standing in the small rooms, however, I only felt how different they were from home.

I'm happy for Jess. Not so much for myself. One day into this four-month tour, and I'm already missing home.

It's why I'm here, I remind myself while walking up the steps coated in exhaust residue, past the metal signs surrounding the subway entrance, up to the street where the February snow is solidifying into ice. I need this. Not just the money, but the chance to find out if I made a mistake a decade ago. So I know just how hard to fight for the future of Harcourt Homes.

The neighborhood into which I've emerged isn't much like Williamsburg, where I've spent the day with Jess, except for the overall New York-iness of everything. Instead of the eclectic collection of walkable shops, skyscrapers littered with light-up signs stand high over streets clogged with pedestrians.

Following the map on my phone, I find my way to the staff entrance, where metal barricades prevent onlookers from getting too close. I inch up to one of the security guys, who I show my ID to.

In recent weeks, I've immersed myself in my Harcourt Homes duties, distracting myself from the charged, conflicted excitement of this day. Of course, I've practiced "Until You," ensuring every chord stays inscribed in my memory. It wasn't difficult. Riley's songwriting comes maddeningly, wonderfully naturally to me.

This, though, is not just *practice*. This is the first stadium rehearsal of the Breakup Tour.

Into the daylight rises the colossal cylinder of the venue. *Madison Square Garden*. The most intimidating place for Max Harcourt to kick off his first-ever music tour.

When I pass the fences, I take in the tour buses. Three of them, each bigger than the apartments I toured with Jess. They wait, formidable, impressive sentinels of the stadium. People haul luggage and guitar cases in and out. Watching the logistics, something like stage fright settles onto me.

What distracts me is the unexpected swell of pride I feel

seeing Riley's name in huge letters on each bus. While I don't know if I deserve to be proud of Riley Wynn, I don't know how not to be.

Hiking the strap of my duffel higher on my shoulder, I march forward.

I see her immediately. It's hard not to. She's leaning over the barricade, posing for selfies with fans who've recognized her.

Her smile is incandescent. Her hair is perfect, spun gold shining in the February sun. Her wool coat is instantly iconic, ready for fashion headlines. The fans look rapturous.

It hits me the way the tour buses did—Riley's *really* famous. I knew she was, of course. I've seen her on TV, in photos from red carpets. But watching her in person works on me differently, combining the fame I knew of with the woman I used to know in new ways. She looks larger than life. Out of reach.

Which she is. She's so forceful, so quicksilver stunning, the idea of touching her is like reaching out to hold on to lightning. I'm not sure it's even physically possible. If it is, it would undoubtedly electrify you within an inch of your life.

I'm not imagining touching Riley Wynn, though. I've long since chased such ideas from my dreams so fiercely they've stopped returning.

Or mostly stopped. I could never fully vanquish my desire for Riley.

"Keys?"

I turn, not recognizing the voice. The tall woman I find standing behind me waits expectantly.

"You're the keyboard player, right?" she clarifies.

"Yeah, sorry," I say, recovering. "I was—"

She grins. "Starstruck, by the looks of it."

I don't object. This woman is right, though she doesn't know I was starstruck by Riley long before she released her first single.

"You're new here," she comments. "Do you usually tour on the West Coast? I'm Vanessa." She holds out her hand.

"Max," I say. We shake. "And no. This is my first tour, actually."

If her eyes widen, the change is imperceptible. "Interesting. Well, I'm drums," she says.

I'm picking up her personality quickly. She projects control, stability. Not surprising for the musician who will provide the rhythmic scaffold of our songs.

"Hamid"—she continues, gesturing to the lanky guy in an Eagles shirt nearby—"is on guitar. Kev is bass, and Savannah is backup vocals," she says, indicating the red-headed guy loading up his luggage and the short-haired woman on her phone, respectively. In the midst of everything, one middle-aged woman watches, carefully controlled stress hiding in her expression. "That's Eileen Yeh, Riley's manager," Vanessa says, following my gaze. "There's a page running around here, too, but I haven't met him yet."

I nod, grateful. While the stage fright lingers, the disorientation is lessening. "Thanks. Do you, like, all know each other already?" I ask.

Vanessa smiles. "I've toured with Kev a couple times. We go way back. But everyone's met once or twice. Sometimes a band member is sick and can't go on for a night, so you want to keep contacts in every city of people you like to work with. Who put you up for this gig?"

"I did," I say.

The drummer's surprise is impossible to miss this time. Her eyebrows rise.

I shuffle my feet, self-conscious. While I know I need to explain, I'm not sure how much. "I auditioned for Riley," I settle for saying. The memory still feels like the snatches of dreams you can recollect the moment you wake up—playing "Until You" in Riley's music room, the only lived-in space in her new home.

It was exactly the house you would imagine for Riley if you didn't know her. No matter how homey, how nicely decorated, how reminiscent of the Laurel Canyon icons she loves, it didn't fit with the woman who ended our relationship over our tour in Nashville, one I knew meant everything to her. Without momentum, without crowds, the house could never be *home* for Riley Wynn. I remember how she stood in the middle of the rooms, looking like she was posing, not living.

Nothing like she looks now.

"No shit," Vanessa says. She calls out over her shoulder. "Hey Kev, come here. Our keyboardist knows Riley."

"I wouldn't say I *know* her," I start while the redhead hustles over, giving me the same evaluative glance Vanessa did.

"What's her vibe?" Kev asks. "What kind of tour are we in for? Wynn doesn't have a reputation in the industry yet."

I realize I don't really know how to respond, which saddens me unexpectedly. The fact is, if we were in college, without the stretch of life separating now from then, I know *exactly* what I would say. Right down to every pre-performance ritual and preference. For us, they were details more intimate than knowing what side of the bed someone sleeps on or how they smell without perfume. Now . . . I have no idea what superstar Riley Wynn's "vibe" is.

Shrugging, I try not to look stiff or insecure. "I really don't know her well enough to speculate."

They look disappointed by my answer. Past Kev, out of the

corner of my eye, I watch Riley finish her fan photos. When her eyes move to us, I see the moment she notices I'm here. While she's out of earshot, she's close enough to come over to us. Which she does—promptly wrapping me in a hug.

The familiarity so startles me, I barely catch her in time. *Holding lightning*, the idea flashes in my head. I'm not sure if I'm more struck by the fact I'm hugging one of the most famous women in the country or by how it feels just like the last time I hugged her.

"You made it," she says enthusiastically.

I'm conscious of how the crowd of fans who were just taking photos with Riley have started taking photos of me with Riley. But I'm only half-aware, because the rest of me is consumed with the place where Riley's chest touches mine.

"I made it," I confirm. It's just like Riley to have me echoing her words in the first sentence I've spoken to her in New York. The rest of the band has been rehearsing together for the past week. Because I'm only joining for "Until You," which is just with Riley, I wasn't needed until now.

When Riley withdraws from the hug, she looks up, right into my eyes. She's smiling. While her vibrance is stunning, I can't help feeling like she's drawing out every moment on purpose.

"Get settled in," she says. "I have to run—we'll chat soon."

I don't have the chance to reply before she's off, slipping into one of the buses out of view of the onlookers.

"Looks like you know her," Vanessa says dryly.

I watch the bus doors slide shut, noticing how strangely empty the sidewalk feels now. "We're old friends from college. We haven't spoken in years," I say, my voice cooling while I urge my skin to forget how Riley felt pressed to me.

With exacting rationality, I work through what just happened. Riley didn't hug *me*. She didn't hug me in Harcourt Homes or when I visited her house in the hills. Because there was no one around to see.

Riley is a show-woman. She doesn't need a stage to perform whatever narrative she knows will entice or enthrall. I won't let myself forget it.

I face the other musicians, who I find watching me skeptically, clearly coming to the conclusions Riley designed. Ones I don't want to discuss further. I need to redirect. "Do you know which bus I should put my stuff on?" I ask.

I'm grateful when, despite the flicker of understanding in her eyes, Vanessa doesn't call me on my evasion. "The lists are posted on the doors," she replies.

"Thanks," I say. "It was nice meeting you."

I head for the bus Savannah just entered and find the list on the doors. It doesn't include my name. Resolutely, I continue to the second-closest bus. On its doors I find Vanessa's name under Kevin's, but not mine. It leaves only one bus left.

I inhale through my nose. Then, knowing what I'll find, I walk to the final set of doors.

I'm conscious of everyone's eyes on me. On Max Harcourt, whose name Riley's crowds don't know yet, but they will soon. Max Harcourt, who walked out of his ordinary life into the love song on everyone's lips, lips now exchanging whispers while curious cell phone cameras follow me.

Max Harcourt. My name is, of course, on this bus's doors, right under the first name on the list.

Riley Wynn.

EIGHT

Riley

I HOLD UP the dress bag my mom flew out with, feeling the electricity I get in my movements whenever I have shows coming up. It's not just excitement—it's more like the feeling of coming home to myself. Like the real Riley Wynn is the one who steps out under the stage lights. I feel her close now.

I'm reaching for the zipper when the bus doors open.

On the steps is Max. He does not, I cannot help noticing, look happy. His eyes remind me now of dark skies, not gemstones.

It's . . . interesting. I raise an eyebrow, waiting for him to speak.

I don't need him to, of course. I would be lying if I said hugging him in front of everyone was innocent, and I knew Max would understand it wasn't. It was intended to spark rumors, which I know my fans well enough to feel certain it has. I wanted to see how Max would respond.

Not well, it seems.

His gaze fixed on me, he mounts the first few steps. "I didn't agree to pretending we're togeth—" he starts, stopping short when he notices the other person on the bus. My mother watches him from over my shoulder with undisguised curiosity. Max's manner changes instantly, his anger evaporating. "Carrie," he says with surprise mirroring hers. "It's nice to see you again. How are you?"

Like she's remembered herself, my mom moves past me, reaching to wrap Max in a hug. "I'm good," she says, then withdraws with her hands remaining on his shoulders. "But look at you. You're so grown-up!"

Max smiles. "Am I? Sometimes I'm not so sure," he replies with gentle warmth.

It is sucker-punch endearing, right to my heart. *Yes*, I want to say, *and no*.

In fact, every moment I spend with him, every moment he even crossed my mind since my visit to Harcourt Homes, has left me contending with the dual man he is. I know, realistically, he's the Max who's lived the past decade without me. Whose jaw is stronger, frame sturdier.

Yet sometimes, when I see him in the right light or when I hear the way he speaks to my mom, I see the shimmering mirage flash of the Max I used to know. The Max who meant everything to me.

The memory slips over me of bringing him home for our relationship's only Christmas. He met my whole extended family. We had sex in my car when I excused myself on a supply run, fighting off the cold in the sedan's interior on the vacant street we found. I remember flattening his wrinkled shirt on our way in to dinner, smiling smiles only we could read, the strung-up lights painting us in the warm glow that looked like how I felt around him. I didn't know if I could ever capture in lyrics the love in my heart then.

If I couldn't write our love song, however, I knew what I could write. I decided right then that I would give Max my heart, and if he broke it, I would write the moment into our breakup song. Knowing I wouldn't walk away empty-handed even if he hurt me had given me the courage to love him fully.

> *Little lights, close hearts*
> *I felt the end in the start*

I wasn't left empty-handed.

"Are you seeing Riley off?" Max asks my mom. His perfectly pleasant demeanor says I'm the only one surfacing from the reverie of memory. I feel sheepish until I remind myself not to. *Feel fearlessly.* My dearest songwriting principle, inscribed into my heart with years of practice.

I drape the garment bag over the nearest chair. "My mom is coming on tour with us," I say. "I was just showing her around."

"I hear we're all going to be roommates," my mom chimes in with enthusiasm. I know she isn't oblivious to the tension in the room. She's not hiding from it, either. She's smiling in its face, saying *You don't scare Carrie Wynn.*

"That's cool with you, right?" I fix Max with my cheeriest smile, mustering my own imitation of my mom's indefatigable Midwestern nonchalance. "There just isn't enough room on the other buses. I could ask someone to switch, but they might wonder why." I let my meaningful look linger, watching him weigh my words, realize how it would only increase gossip in the crew.

Max pauses. His gaze remains on mine, the hollow moment widening. He's a very good pauser, I have to concede. Like rests in music, he speaks with silence.

Until finally, he lowers his duffel bag from his shoulder.

"It's your name on the bus window," he says. "I'll go wherever you want me."

I wanted you to go where I go, something raw screams in me. *I wanted you to* want *to go where I go*. Does he not realize what different lives we could have lived if he'd only *gone where I wanted him*—where I wanted *us*—when we were younger?

I suppose it's definitive proof of which Max stands here in this cramped corridor. It certainly isn't the Max I still feel could have been my everything, the Max of my memories. This is the Max who wouldn't follow me when I desperately wanted him to.

Because, like he's just reminded me, no matter what we were to each other, he's only with me now because of my fucking name on the window.

I let none of this onto my face, of course. Instead, I grin, hiding my little maelstrom from him. "Perfect. Well, with you both here, I can give you the tour." *Distraction*, I reassure myself. "This is the kitchen and living space. The pantry will be stocked with whatever you tell the page to grab."

I gesture to the cupboards over the counter, the lacquered wood reflecting the overhead lights. Next to me is a built-in booth of soft white leather. Everything is upscale-RV standard, pleasantly personality-less.

Still, I'm relieved to feel my restless heartache changing into something else. I can't fight my excitement. Never mind the close quarters, the hotel-on-wheels furnishings. *This* feels like home.

I lead them backward through the bus, pausing by a door on one side of the corridor. "Bathroom is in here." We pass the narrow rows of bunks to reach the bedroom. "Mom, this is where you'll sleep."

When I slide open the door, my mom walks past me into the room, evaluating its unexpected spaciousness. Wide windows let the winter sunlight in on three sides. The large bed is done up with a surprisingly luxurious duvet, leaving just enough room for a small vanity in the corner.

"Riley, this looks like it's supposed to be your room," she says skeptically, like she's wary of putting me out. "Where's your bed?"

Stepping back, I pat the closest bunk. "Right here."

Mom frowns in righteous indignation, her usual reaction to receiving generosity from others. "No. This is *your* tour. You're going to be working hard. You need your rest. I'm just . . . here."

"I invited you," I point out, playing to her sense of etiquette. "Just accept the VIP treatment." *Just let someone take care of you for once*, I want to say, but I don't.

Mom opens her mouth, objections ready.

"I want to sleep in the bunk anyway," I continue hastily. "It's part of the tour magic."

While she looks only half-convinced, she doesn't get the chance to object. I hear the bus doors open, and in steps an older man with an impressive gray-black beard and a shiny bald head.

"Frank!" I squeal, delighted to see him. He was the driver on my first smaller tour, and I specifically requested him for this one. He's worked in the industry for forty years, yet never once talked down to me. During our nights on the road, I started to see him as my "tour dad." When I was wired from performing, he would exchange favorite pieces of music lore with me until sunrise. When I wasn't, he drove smoothly enough I could actually sleep.

His smile matches mine, his eyes crinkling exactly like I remember. "Hey, Ri," he says. "Congrats on the record. Pretty sure I recognized a couple of those licks from late-night writing on the road. Well done, kiddo."

My heart warms to hear he remembers. In fact, he's not wrong. I wrote parts of what would become *The Breakup Record* tracks on our bus years ago. I know some songwriters don't like writing on the road, despite how modern release schedules often necessitate the practice. I'm the opposite. I love when songs reach me somewhere inconvenient. Like they're reminding me they're their own masters.

"This is Max," I say when he steps up next to me. "Our pianist. And this is Carrie, my mom."

Frank extends his hand eagerly to each of them. His quick cheer is entirely free of posturing or hesitation. It's my favorite of his qualities. Not swapping music stories or even pleasant driving. It's his openness. His every gesture is like the crinkles next to his eyes—they show what he's feeling right on the surface.

"So you're where Riley gets it," he says to my mom.

When my mom laughs, visibly perplexed, Frank looks twice at her. "Certainly not," she demurs. "I can't carry a tune or speak in front of a crowd."

"I meant her eyes," he says.

I have to purse my lips to suck in my surprise. My mom goes the pinkest shade of pink I've ever seen in her cheeks. "Oh," she manages. In seconds, she recovers. "Yes, those I take credit for."

"You could practically get a cut of the royalties," Frank replies easily, then looks to me before I take offense. "I said *practically*. Your talent speaks for itself, Riley Wynn."

Pleased, I nod.

"How long have you been a driver?" my mom asks.

Knowing where the story starts—with every grunge band I'd ever heard of, with whom Frank crossed the country on countless occasions—I let him regale my mom while I glance back. Max has retreated to the bunk corridor and is stowing clothes from his duffel in the slim closet space. I drift over to join him.

"So," I start. Hitting questions head-on is my style, and no delicate eloquence could ease the coming conversation. "Are you more pissed about sharing a bus with me or that I hugged you in front of the band?"

He doesn't turn, doesn't falter in his unpacking. I watch his jacket join his shirts in the closet.

I press him. Silence isn't for flinching. It's for filling. "Remember how I told you this was my tour and I was going to spin a narrative around you?"

Now he looks right into my eyes.

"Did I not do *exactly* what I warned you I would?" I ask.

The storm in his eyes roils. I ride it out, meeting his gaze, perversely glad. Max retreated from me once. I lost him then. I'm entitled to none of him now. Which is why I'm deeply, desperately hopeful he won't retreat from what he wants to say in this moment.

I nearly go weak when he finally lets out a breath.

"I guess I didn't expect you to insinuate we're currently together," he explains, his voice measured, his syllables metronomic. "I don't want to be part of some pretend showmance offstage."

"Fair," I say, straightening up. I'm glad he's not cloaking this conversation in inscrutable glances or long pauses. "I'll dial it back in front of the crew. Look, the bus thing really was because someone has to share with my mom and me. You seemed like the best option. Besides"—I smile winningly, my encore smile—"it's a bus with my *mother*. When the band meets her, they'll realize there's nothing at all sexy about our sleeping arrangements."

Max laughs. The sound is low and strikingly sincere. It's my favorite sort of flashback. I feel tension I didn't notice I was holding on to slip soothingly through my fingers.

"Just—when it's only us," he says, "I want the truth. In here, I don't want to feel like I'm in front of an audience."

I stare at him, reality and song lyrics overwriting each other in front of me. *The truth.*

What I wrote *is* the truth. "Until You" was written from deep within me, dark sparks struck in corners of my soul. The feelings I put into song never fade, not fully. The love never fades, like how the half-remembered man I once loved never quite stops flickering over the one in front of me now. I'm not sure if the songs preserve them or if I preserve them for the songs, but they're never really gone.

"I'm always in front of an audience, Max," I say, softer.

His smile slips.

"I suppose you are," he says.

I don't need an experienced ear to discern the disappointment in his voice. It isn't just the sting of judgment I feel, either.

He doesn't understand me, or this part of me. He assumes the performance is the lie, like everyone does, like the critics who chasten my heartsick songs. On his own, he's concluded the me who stands onstage or in front of paparazzi cameras isn't real.

I didn't force him to come on this tour, I remind myself. I didn't even ask him. It was his idea. I don't owe it to him to live the lie he decided was the truth. Pretending I'm not the same woman, in the same spotlight, living the same endless song, even when I'm offstage.

Still, the idea of him walking out now has fear stretching the strings of my heart. I've heard our duet ringing in my head, in my dreams. It would rip something out of me to never live it out loud.

He doesn't leave.

With solemn resolve, he turns back to his bunk. "I can move my stuff if this is the bed you wanted," he says.

"Oh." The relief is instantaneous. Relearning Max's indirect way of speaking, I recognize his logistical comment for what it is. His peace offering. "No," I reply. "I'm good. I'll take this one." I tap the bunk not three feet from his.

Without reply, he resumes unpacking his clothes. While I'm grateful he's still here, our conversation clearly isn't finished. I don't know where we'll stand tomorrow.

I linger in the hallway, feeling like Max somehow makes our mutual silence sound like its own duet. Maybe, I rationalize, it's because we're realizing the same thing. We'll be sleeping side by side, close enough to hold hands.

I hear my own refrain, repeating hollowly in my head.

Nothing at all sexy about our sleeping arrangements.

NINE

Max

I START TO panic during the second verse of "One Minute."

The band is incredible. They're startlingly synchronous, reading each other's moves with uncanny intuition. It's clear they've not only been rehearsing together for weeks—they're professionals who've been performing for years, even decades. Riley slots into the group effortlessly.

I'm the odd one out. Way, *way* out. I'm Max Harcourt, who last week was playing Sinatra for thirty octogenarians under failing halogen lights. It's nowhere near prepared me for this. What was I thinking when I suggested joining Riley on tour? I can't do this. I couldn't do it when I was twenty. I *definitely* can't do it now.

I'm standing in the front metal-gated section of the pit, sweating profusely. The heated interior of Madison Square Garden isn't charitable to the nervous. Nor is the fact that I have some time before I'm needed onstage, with "Until You" later in the set list. "One Minute," which the band is launching into now, is the opener.

Behind me, the stadium is empty except for security and

other staff. In the center sits the platform stage on which Riley will perform. The lighting scaffolds extend their latticed ribs overhead, while past the stage is the small encampment of tents constructed for backstage logistics.

Standing in the midst of this space, I feel row upon row of seats holding their breath. Even in its unpolished, pre-performance state, it's impossible to overlook the place's striking presence, not unlike the time I've spent with Riley herself lately.

Onstage, she charges forth, unifying the band like she commands sound itself. She's everything. Rock star, seraphim, girl next door.

Watching her, I start to understand what she meant on the bus. The woman in front of me is the real Riley, while the one without a microphone is only half of her.

When they finish the third song, they break so Riley can do a wardrobe fitting. Overwhelmed, I head into one of the concrete corridors from which players emerge onto the court when the Garden hosts sports. I know it's nonsensical, retreating like my stage fright is some horror-movie monster I can escape in the shadows. I just need some distance.

In the tents, I can see the other musicians chatting, practicing riffs, testing mics. They look comfortable, even excited.

It makes me want to shrink deeper into the passageway. I'm desperate to escape the feeling I don't belong here. Which I don't. I'm no expert touring musician. When I suggested this, I had only a vague idea of the scale. Now, with the seemingly endless rows of seats waiting for an audience, I'm worried I'm going to sit down at the piano and forget how to play. I'll embarrass myself and ruin Riley's moment.

I pull out my phone.

I'm dropping out. I can't do this.

Jess replies instantaneously.

> Yes you can. The seniors of Harcourt
> Homes are a way rougher crowd than
> Riley's adoring fans. You're not even
> going to have to break the news we're
> out of chocolate pudding.

I laugh despite my nerves. Leave it to Jess to make me smile while I'm weighing the decision of whether to disappoint the woman I used to love or wind up on YouTube for forgetting how to play the most popular song in the country.

Though her reminder of the chocolate pudding fiasco is welcome, it doesn't exactly ease my misgivings. I'm writing my next message when Jess sends another. I scroll up to find a video.

Intrigued, I open it.

In the handheld footage framed in the iPhone's rectangular dimensions, I sit at the piano in Harcourt Homes. Riley is next to me on the bench, her head on my shoulder while I play the elegant opening of "Bridge Over Troubled Water." It's from early in our relationship. The younger versions of ourselves strike something hidden in me, some chord I'd forgotten how to play.

When she straightens up to sing, the me in the video smiles fondly down at the keys. Our eyes lock, and it's like we're only performing for us.

Which we sort of are. No one in the dining room is listening.

I remember how it felt. Not in the moment in the video, exactly. Just . . . playing with Riley. I wanted—*needed*—everyone to hear the sound we were finding, the push-pull meshing of our styles, the perfect joining of her music with mine. Yet, with every note she sang directly to the center of me, I was more convinced no one could *ever* hear what we heard, could ever experience how it sounded when the songs of separate hearts entwined into one. The contradiction lingered with me in every performance.

Even then, she was rending my soul down the middle.

I listen for the same strains of feeling now, watching the video, reaching out with parts of myself I've left quiet for years. While faint, hiding under the shrill of nervousness, they're there.

I never knew this video existed. Jess understandably never had a reason to send it to me after Riley and I broke up. I don't even remember this specific performance—in those days it never much mattered to me what song we were playing, not when every song instantly felt like ours. I understand why Jess sent it, though. It's not just how confident I look. It's how I look with Riley. Like we were meant to play together.

One more message from Jess scrolls onto my screen.

You've got this.

I save the video into my camera roll.

I can't believe you've had this the whole time.

Well, if you completely choke onstage, I think I could probably sell it to the tabloids and make enough to keep HH running for a couple months.

I laugh to myself until I hear the opening of "Novembers," the fourth track on *The Breakup Record*. I've familiarized myself intently with Riley's work in the past weeks, preparing for tour. I love this song. I wish I could enjoy it.

Instead, it just reminds me of how my number is next.

I slide my phone into my pocket, feeling marginally more confident. The video Jess sent helps me frame how I'm going to think of this. Just me and Riley.

I head to the tent on one of the wings of the stage, mentally running through my song. Even preoccupied, I'm impressed by the intricacy of the highly functional labyrinth of operations surrounding the stage. Crew members hustle in every direction with rhythmic efficiency. One hands me an earpiece, explaining they'll count me off and can provide a metronome if I want. I decline, pretty sure it'll just distract me.

When "Novembers" ends, I walk discreetly onstage, eyes downcast to avoid seeing the empty stadium. I need no extra reminders of how many people will be here tomorrow night. At the front of the stage, I hear Riley, the sun of the solar system in which I'm one small moon. She's talking to someone in the pit about the lighting. I focus on familiarizing myself with the piano.

It's a baby grand. I haven't played on one in years. I fixate on the keys, reminding myself they're the same eighty-eight strips of ebony and ivory no matter where you play. Madison Square Garden or Harcourt Homes, where I can almost convince myself I'm seated right now.

Until Riley walks up to me, and I see what she's wearing.

It's a wedding dress.

No, it's *the* wedding dress. Perfectly Riley in every way. Simple satin hugs her body close, clinging to every curve and dipping dangerously low down her back. The hem brushes the black snakeskin boots she's wearing.

Everything exits my mind for a moment. It isn't the fact that Riley looks like she's stepped right out of the record itself I'm struck by. This entire tour is designed to disintegrate the separation of Riley the person from Riley the icon of her music.

No, it's how she's walked right out of my own forgotten dreams.

There were a couple months while we were dating when I started to entertain the fondest of guilty pleasures. I knew I was jumping the gun, hoping prematurely. I just couldn't help imagining I might marry Riley one day.

I knew I wanted to, deeply, fundamentally, the way I read music with only a glance. Like how I heard melodies instantly from the intricate notation, I heard wedding bells in the memories I started to see when I was with Riley. Songwriting sessions, fifteen-dollar local concerts, great sex. *Late nights, new homes.* I heard our whole future in the chords we played on each other.

In white satin, she's literally the Riley of my dreams.

Now those dreams will be onstage.

My stomach knots. I wish my performance was still the only stress on my mind. Instead, I'm reckoning with having my heart's secret desires on the video screens in Madison Square Garden.

"Hey, we'll start in a sec," Riley says, unimaginably casually. "There was a mix-up with the lights I wanted to sort out."

I can hardly process her words. "What are you wearing?" I ask, halfway to desperate.

Riley looks down like she's forgotten. She frowns. "*Not* the right outfit. This is for 'One Minute,' but I should be changed out of it long before 'Until You.' Nothing is ready yet. Opening night is going to be . . . fun."

"Quite the costume," I remark. I know I'm fussing with this detail I can't ignore.

She laughs. "It's better than a costume. It's the real thing. I figured the marriage didn't work out, but the money I spent on this dress didn't need to be wasted," she explains, shadows of victory dancing in her eyes.

Uncomprehending, I say nothing. In my earpiece, a woman's voice says the crew is ready now. Riley grins with magnetic delight and moves up to the front of the stage, where she starts her introduction.

While I know I should focus on the keys, preparing myself for our song, I can't. I'm lost. Stuck in the distorted reality Riley is summoning where fun house mirrors make the floor seem to slant under me. She's using her own wedding dress as a *prop*.

Like she's using me.

If Riley wants to change pieces of her past into gimmicks for public consumption, she's entitled to. I'm just not sure I want to be one of them. Is this what I am to her now? Months of happiness, of love, she's now ensuring weren't wasted?

When I hear my cue, my hands play the opening melody of "Until You." My heart isn't with them. I push in vain to lose myself in the song. But when Riley starts singing, I can't look at her.

Her voice is heartrending. I play perfectly. I just can't meet her eyes the way I did in the video. When it was real between us.

This is the opposite. I've never felt more like strangers than hearing her perform in the dress of my wildest dreams.

TEN

Riley

IT'S MIDNIGHT BEFORE the biggest day of my life. The first show of the Breakup Tour. I'm fucking wired, of course. Keeping everything in my head, from cues to costume changes, lighting to lyrics, feels like holding on to music itself. On the very verge of impossible.

I'm sitting on the floor of my hotel suite to try to stay grounded. *Grounded.* My distractable, lyrical mind unfolds the word's metaphorical options on instinct. Planes? No. Conduction. I want to be grounded because I feel like lightning.

Eileen sits on the couch nearby while I read out the items on my iPhone's to-do list. "The mic—" I begin.

Eileen interrupts me. "—is being touched up now. No more missing rhinestones. It'll be finished before sound check."

I nod. "And they're moving the guitar stand to where I taped, right?"

Eileen smiles patiently. "Riley, everything is in motion. Let me handle it." She rises from the couch, yawning. My stomach swoops with dread. "The only thing you need to worry about is getting some sleep. You're about to be in for a lot of late nights."

I don't reply, wrestling with my selfish desire for her to stay. I won't make her, of course. But I'm stuck, unforgiving hopes holding me hostage. There's everything to get right tomorrow. I might never have a moment like this again. Honestly, I probably won't. There's a unique pressure to achieving your dreams, to wringing out every ounce of joy you can from them. Within my excitement, I'm counting every second.

Nothing feels as ready as I want yet. Especially "Until You." It's not Max's fault exactly. He's playing wonderfully. We just haven't locked in yet. I haven't wanted to over-rehearse us, though—the issue isn't one practice will fix.

Our connection needs to feel earnest. Natural. If it doesn't, I'll need to use the acting lessons I never asked for but nonetheless received when I would run lines with my ex-husband.

When Eileen walks to the door, I manage to look up. "Good night," I say, feeling like I'm shutting myself in my own prison of doubt. "You get some sleep, too."

"I will if you will," she says, giving me a knowing glance before leaving.

I pull myself off the floor, eyeing the room's massive bed. Everyone in the tour has hotel rooms until after the show, when we'll load onto the buses with most of our things waiting for us. But I'd rather be on the bus now. This room is suffocatingly quiet, imposingly luxurious. I wish I didn't feel its uncomfortable ironies, how uneasy the gentle lighting on the white marble makes me, how confined I am in its spacious dimensions. I'm devoid of inspiration in here, suffocating in its glass walls.

More pertinently, I'm pretty sure I'll struggle to sleep. I'm way past exhaustion, on into perpetual motion. Combined with the well-meaning discomfort of my hotel, I do not foresee sleep in my near future. I need to get up, do something.

Even my muscles feel like there's somewhere they'd rather be. I cross the room to grab my shoes, seizing on the first idea I get. In the hallway—fancily sterile, the idea of luxury with none of the feeling—I stop outside my mom's door. I was serious when I proposed tour-bus movie night in my first pitch for her to come on tour with me. Now feels like the perfect opportunity.

I knock gently, not wanting to wake her if she's gone to sleep.

Which . . . she has, I deduce disappointedly when there's no response. I could knock harder. Just wake her up.

It feels childish, though. I don't need *my mom* to entertain me.

It's funny—while I'm not loving the confusing cliché of the pop star who doesn't know how to be on her own, unprogrammed, unsupervised, for one second, I simultaneously feel entitled to it. So what if I don't know how to be on my own? Some people don't. Do I not get to be this way?

I've found myself caught in this existential shift more than usual lately, of remembering I'm *me*, the human being, who needs, who wants, who gets bored or nervous or needy. I love becoming the RILEY WYNN on the billboards, I do. It's just new—the feeling of being the person inside the icon. Surprising, in moments like now, when thirty feels too young to be *here*, putting *this much* heartbreak into this much fame, yet too old to be standing outside my mom's door.

I push myself to focus. Pondering imponderables is for songwriting, not for dealing with my sleepless night. I just need to *do something*. This tour has required hundreds, even thousands of decisions of me—set list, costuming, lighting, everything. What's one more?

With renewed decisiveness, I head for the elevator block. Strictly speaking, I probably shouldn't go out on my own. But the hotel's rooftop bar is contained, without high traffic since the elevator requires a room key. Besides, without makeup and wearing a simple black cotton dress that hugs my hips, I don't think I'm giving off celebrity.

I ride the elevator up in forgettable seconds of silence. When the stainless-steel door slides open, welcoming me onto the mood-lit rooftop, I step out.

It's nice here—the hotel is equipped for the lacerating cold of New York winter. The radiance of overhead heaters warms the patio, where gentle night winds ruffle cocktail napkins past the glass surrounding the space.

Approaching the bar, I avoid making eye contact with the guests whose gazes I feel lingering on me. I've learned if I don't engage, people generally feel too uncomfortable to come up to me. I'll give myself to my fans for the next few months. Tonight is my last night that's just for me.

I reach the stools, finding my eyes drawn to the one man seated on his own at the end of the long bar. When he looks up, his gaze flits past me. *Perfect.*

He's about my age, his dress shirt's collar unbuttoned, his sleeves rolled up under the heaters. He's giving off work-trip vibes. Just here killing time, like me. He looks good. More importantly, he looks interesting. Spending the night with him would be fun. Leaving him in the morning would be the stuff of songs yet unwritten.

I sit down next to him.

When he glances over, I give him a friendly smile, stretching old, stiff muscles I haven't used since Wesley and I decided to become exclusive. I was nowhere near this famous then, leaving me feeling unsure how to do this now. I've never flirted with someone while knowing my face is on billboards in Times Square.

Of course, I've never let uncertainty keep me from chasing what I want, either.

Want is probably the wrong word here, in fact. I'm single, I'm fresh off a divorce, and I'm about to spend months on a small bus with my ex. I *need* this. "Can I buy you a drink?" I ask.

He raises his eyebrows. "I think that's my line," my stranger says. His voice is steady, sure. It fits him, his straight brown hair, his clean-shaven chin. He's quietly confident in being what's expected. I'm going to enjoy giving him the unexpected.

"Didn't hear you say it, though," I reply.

His embarrassed laugh shakes the facade. I smile, intrigued. *Rooftop laughter, no happy-ever-after.* Yes. I grab on to the gossamer strand of inspiration. I'll spin it into something later.

He puts his hand into his pocket. I expect he'll pull out cash or his card. The scene writes itself in my head. He'll buy my drink. We'll exchange nothing sentences, vague summaries of what we're doing in the city, wasting time in this modern mating dance.

One of us will say *It's getting late.* The other will say *My room's on the fifteenth floor.* It'll be the oldest story, one I can sing new in fresh ink.

I'll call it, "It's Getting Late."

Instead, he pulls out a black ring box.

My eyes widen. "You move fast," I remark.

"I'm proposing to the love of my life tomorrow morning," he says.

I'm not embarrassed or disappointed. While he's certainly ripped up my first lyrical draft, he's now snared my curiosity completely. I lean forward, thrilled with this twist. "Congratulations," I say. "Let me buy you a drink anyway, as a friend. Tell me about her."

He eyes me, bemusement playing gently over his features. "You don't have to," he finally says.

"I insist," I reply. "I love love stories."

When he shifts in his seat, the bar's strung lights reflect in his eyes like stars. "Well, we have a good one."

"What's her name?"

"Nina," he says, caressing the syllables. I order two glasses of wine from the bartender and slide one to my non-hook up. "You really want to know our story? It's kind of long," he cautions me.

"Hell yeah, I do," I say. "No offense, but this is way better than picking you up." The one-night stand I'd planned for us, however passionate, was unoriginal. I'm not leading this story, though. I'm following it.

He laughs. The same laugh, sweetly embarrassed. I imagine how he must make Nina's cheeks go pink. "She dated my college roommate for four years. I hated the guy. Only lived with him freshman year, but they got together early on, so she basically lived in our dorm with us. It was . . . torture."

I wince, enjoying the commiseration. "You were into her right away?" I ask.

He smiles softly. "She would bring me cupcakes whenever she spent the night. I overheard their conversations about what movies she liked, what research she was doing, how her day was. It was obvious how smart and passionate she is. Of course I was in love with her right away." He drinks deeply from his glass, familiar ghosts in his eyes. What is "Until You" except my own exercise in how some yearning never fades? "But we were just friends, even when her boyfriend and I stopped living together."

When he pauses, lingering in the reminiscence, I widen my eyes playfully. "Well, man, did you break them up?" I demand.

He frowns. In the same moment, the cold wind gusts over the rooftop, jostling the lights. It's perfect, the imagery I would have written if I needed to. "I wish I did," he says. "I thought she was out of my league, so I did nothing. Until she broke up with him. The next day, I showed up to her door with cupcakes."

I toast him, impressed. "Nice."

He nods, permitting himself the slightest smugness.

"Let me guess," I continue. "The waiting was worth it?"

"God, no," he says flatly, then catches himself. "No, I mean, if I'd needed to wait, I would have. Forever. *But I didn't need to.*" When his eyes flit to mine with sudden intensity, I realize the vein I've hit is important. "The years I waited weren't some bridge to the future," he says. "They were only time I wasted not being with her."

I say nothing, letting his words ring. I'd wondered if we would get here, to this truth. Everyone is a songwriter if you listen.

Reaching forward, I tap his ring box with one finger. "Hence the no more waiting."

When he grins, it's marvelously human. His clean-pressed features crack open with victorious joy. "Exactly."

Downing the rest of my drink, I stand up. "Not that you need it, but good luck tomorrow."

"Thanks. Honestly, after talking to you, I feel less nervous." He holds out his hand. "I'm Jason, by the way."

I shake it. "Riley."

He pauses, the skin of his palm pressed to mine. I feel the heavy familiarity of watching what I said register with him. "No," he says.

"No what?" I reply dutifully.

"You're not Riley Wynn, are you?" He sounds like he's losing the fight with his own skepticism.

I chew my lip. It's confession enough, I know. *I should've known*, I scold myself. Should've known I would wind up in some iteration of this interaction. While Jason seems reasonable, many people do until they don't. I prepare myself for the instant cloying hunger I've seen painfully often lately.

Instead, he releases my hand from his, which flies to his forehead.

"I feel awful," he moans. "Nina is a *huge* fan. I thought I recognized you, but, you know, nervousness about tomorrow sort of distracted me. If she finds out I met you and didn't call her to come get a photo, she's going to kill me, but if I call her, my proposal surprise will be ruined. She thinks I'm traveling for work right now."

I smile, remembering how it's exactly what I predicted he was doing. He's very much captured the spirit of his excuse.

Relief starting to slow my heart rate, I reach for the pen behind the bar. "Email this woman," I say, jotting Eileen's address onto my napkin. "I'm playing a concert tomorrow. We'll get you in for a meet and greet if you want."

His eyes light up. "Really? Now she's going to say yes for sure."

I laugh, feeling strangely, vicariously happy for him. I'm spending the next few months of my professional life commemorating my romantic collapses. I guess it's nice to cheer a love story for once. "See you and your *fiancée*," I emphasize meaningfully, "tomorrow."

Jason grins hugely, overjoyed. It's very endearing.

Yet, leaving the bar, I feel suddenly sad. The vicarious hope drains right out of me. I remember painfully well when I was in Nina's position. The day Wesley proposed. He flew me out to the location where he'd been filming in Croatia. He'd sent me pictures of the stunning castle, promising we'd visit, then surprised me with the flight. I remember shrieking *yes* with the wind in my hair. I remember how happy I was. I remember feeling like it was very *us*.

Now I realize it was just very him.

I step in to the elevator's open doors. The mirrored walls show me by myself. For the thirteenth time, I'm alone again. I'm part of no love story except ones I happen to peer into or ones with heartbroken endings. While it hurts, I feel guilty for the clenching in my chest. Heartbreak is what led to this moment, to my dreams coming true. I should be grateful.

I ride the elevator down. In the long hallway to my room, I refocus, examining the yield of my wounding hunt.

Waiting was the worst thing I ever knew
Until I felt having and then losing you . . .

When I return to my room, it no longer feels quiet.

ELEVEN

Max

I woke up the morning of the show feeling good. Everything was within reach, like fifths on the piano. I know "Until You" by heart. Yesterday's rehearsals went perfectly fine. I don't have to look at Riley when I play. As long as I'm not messing up the song, it's fine. I could handle this.

I, Max Harcourt, could play for thousands in Madison Square Garden. Sure, I was somewhat nervous. On the whole, however, I felt good.

Until my mom's name lit up my phone screen.

I vaguely recognized the link in her message. It was one of those Instagram accounts where people submit photos of spotted celebrities. I honestly didn't know why my mom knew what it was. It didn't matter. The photo was unmistakable.

Riley looked stunning. She leaps out of photographs in this way I've never understood, like she warps light itself. The laws of physics ceding to her unstoppable presence. Of course, this unique effect wasn't the reason these photos were on Instagram. I recognized the location—our hotel's sleek rooftop bar. The face of the man Riley was sitting next to wasn't visible, but Riley's was, her smile incandescent while she slid him a drink.

My mom's message wasn't idle. Her question after the link was cheerfully straightforward. *Why haven't you asked Riley out if she's already moved on from her divorce?*

I stood, hair mussed from sleep, in my sterile-seeming hotel room for four full minutes, wrestling with how to reply. The rooftop bar hung over me like storm clouds. The sunlight shooting in from the crack in the curtains, which I had found encouraging in its promise of the fresh day when I had woken up, suddenly reminded me of the harsh stage lights I had performed under yesterday.

Finally, I settled for shrugging my mom off with noncommittal nonchalance. I wasn't lying, either. *I'm not here for romantic reasons. I'm here to play music.*

Definitely *not* to get back together with Riley Wynn.

Except the photos gave me no peace for the rest of the morning.

Riley's smile stuck in my heart while I showered in the modern white stall in my bathroom—lingered with me while I grabbed coffee and breakfast from the crowded bagel shop down the block—followed me the whole trip to the stadium. It turned out the way to take my mind off playing for twenty thousand people was four blurry iPhone photos of Riley sitting with a stranger.

I feel guilty for my exhaustive perusal of the images. Riley has said in interviews that she wishes her love life was under less scrutiny. She finds the pressure exhausting, the feeling of never making private decisions privately, and when she wants her artistry to make her famous, she resents the impression that people value her for relationship gossip instead. It's part of why she wrote *The Breakup Record*, she explained—wanting to rub in listeners' faces their feeling of entitlement to her private life and the hunger of their focus.

These pictures invade her privacy, I know they do. I don't want to provide them the clicks they're seeking. I want to resist the compulsion to see every one, to know where she was, who she left with, how she smiled.

I *want* to. I just . . . can't. I'm powerless.

Frustrated, I consider finding myself the same kind of diversion. I'm not useless in the flirting department. I play music professionally—for the moment—on the stages of the hottest music tour of the year. I could lose myself in someone else's arms, someone else's sheets, while forgetting how Riley makes me feel.

Except I wouldn't, my discouraging mind points out.

No matter who I went home with, I would know I was running from *this*.

Now, while I sit in the Garden's greenroom, the photos stick with me like unwanted guests in my uneasy mind. With the TV on the wall counting down to showtime, I find I'm not nervous— I'm frustrated.

Frustrated because I'm *jealous*. There's no denying what this feeling is, however juvenile, however unjustified. If my confident comfort this morning felt like easy chords, this feels like the notes one misses sight-reading something for the first time—the quick wince of unintended discord.

What I know won't help is seeing Riley. She's elsewhere for much of the day, handling publicity or other obligations. I wait, my mood souring itself further.

The greenroom is not what I expected. It's part hotel

ballroom, part living room for the tour's impromptu family. Crewmembers' jackets rest on the couches. Water bottles litter the tables. Marigold carpet runs from wall to wall, on which framed photos commemorate iconic performances, while one long window overlooks Manhattan.

When Riley finally enters, everything starts for real. Her voice is vibrant when she talks to her dad on the phone and congratulates the band and crew, her movements quick with exuberant impatience when she updates her fans on social media with pre-show photos.

I want to look away. Concentrate on the music, on the performance.

Of course I can't.

In a short silk robe over the white sequined bodysuit she wears under her costumes, the sculpted cut showing an endless stretch of her leg, she sparkles beneath the lights of the room. I can't stop staring, every detail of her inscribed with diamond precision on my helpless heart.

She's stunning. Yet how she looks isn't even what hits me hardest.

It's the way she luminesces with pride, with the excitement of dreams captured. If she's gorgeous no matter what, joy makes her radiant.

Which I have no right to notice, I remind myself. *Just like I have no right to jealousy.* The vinegar filling my heart is entirely unreasonable. Riley's been dating for ten years without it sending me into this spiral. *I've* been dating without caring who she was with. Now is no different.

Except . . . it *is* different, sort of. I'm going to be sharing a tour bus with her. Will she bring flirtations back to those close-pressed bunks with her? Would it be worse if she didn't? Every night she's not on the bus, I'll know it's because she could be with someone else instead. Riley might be the songwriter, but I'll have no trouble writing wounded vignettes for my petty heart whenever she is.

It's the final nudge I needed for my mood to collapse from precarious into miserable. Grabbing a drink from the green-room's fridge, I head into the corner of the room for what passes here for solitude.

I just need to keep it together for long enough to play my ex's devastatingly perfect breakup song about me in front of her countless clamoring fans. *Easy.*

"Max, may I sit with you?"

Surprised to recognize the voice, I look up from my ruminations. Riley's mom, Carrie, joins me on the couch, her no-nonsense features softened with sympathy. I nod, of course, not sure what's prompting this. When I dated Riley, I stayed with her parents for one short visit over Christmas. I didn't really get to know her family since I was so wrapped up in Riley. I remember sneaking away every chance we got for some privacy.

I realize now Carrie certainly knew what we were doing. Regardless, I've had few conversations with Riley's mother.

"I don't really know what to do with myself here," she confesses. She doesn't sound sad—just honest, which, it occurs to me, might be why Riley's songwriting shares the same quality. "Riley doesn't need me, and any time I offer to help, I get the sense I'm just getting in the way of a well-oiled machine."

Managing to pull my gaze from Riley, I look at her mother. "Does Riley need any of us? She could go onstage with nothing but herself and bring the house down."

Carrie laughs. The sound is quick, real.

"Still," I continue, "I think she's glad you're here." I remember Riley in her lovely, lonely house. She's uncomfortable in solitude. When we were in college, we had only been dating a week before she began making excuses for why she needed to sleep over. It took five days for me to tell her she didn't need an excuse.

I know why she's restless by herself. She strives to fill the vacuum with sound, with light, with presence. The effort wears on her. Riley finds being on her own like playing for empty stadiums.

"I didn't know you were still close with my daughter," Carrie remarks inquisitively.

I shift in my seat, flushing with embarrassment. "Oh," I fumble to say. "I'm not, really. Just, you know, when I *did* know her . . ." Carrie is right. It's presumptuous of me to pretend to know Riley's feelings. Like it's presumptuous to be jealous.

"I'm teasing you," Carrie replies. When her smile catches the glint of having completely gotten me, I'm relieved. "Riley told me how she dropped in on you at the home and how easy it still is to talk to you. I think it's very mature you two are doing this together as friends. You've grown up so much since you were sneaking out of our house to go hook up in Riley's car," she says, lightly sarcastic.

I would succumb to embarrassment once more if I weren't intensely curious instead. Riley mentioned her visit to Harcourt Homes? She said I was easy to talk to? What else did she say? What were her exact words? Could this conversation possibly be transcribed for my review?

I don't get the chance to ask. I hear Vanessa say Riley's name, drawing my attention.

"Hey, Riley, is the hottie from last night coming to the show?"

Out of the corner of my eye, I see Vanessa holding up her phone. I know perfectly well what's on the screen. The first in a series of Instagram stories.

Riley shushes her. "A little louder," she says. "I'm not sure my mother heard you."

They laugh together. I'd be impressed how swiftly Riley makes her band her friends and equals if I weren't utterly engrossed in the subject of their conversation.

"He's coming," Riley says, her voice lower. "But we didn't hook up."

"Mmm." Vanessa hums like she's not convinced.

"Really," Riley insists. "It wasn't like that. He's bringing his fiancée to the show. Eileen set them up with tickets."

The relief I feel crushes me. While I know the reaction should make me guilty, I'm no longer sure I care. Riley has me celebrating victories in wars with myself I shouldn't wage. I find myself smiling down at my shoes until I feel Carrie's stare on me. She doesn't say anything. Even so, I know she saw me eavesdropping, and worse, saw my reaction to learning Riley didn't hook up with anyone last night.

I wrestle with the silence. I don't know if I should say something or if it would just be more incriminating to downplay what I was caught in.

Ultimately, it isn't me who ends the silence. Instead, a moment later, Riley approaches. Carrie gives me a conspiratorial smile before looking up at her daughter. "Mom, it's probably time for you to get to your seat," Riley says with unhidden eagerness.

Carrie stands. She hugs Riley, then faces us. "Break a leg," she says. "You two are going to be great." With the pointed glance she shoots me, I hear her double meaning.

When she follows a crew member out, I'm left with Riley in the crowded green room. Alone-ish, separate yet surrounded.

"Thanks for hanging out with my mom," Riley says.

"Oh, no need to thank me," I reply honestly. "It was . . . enlightening."

"Uh-oh." Riley's voice is playful, her expression unperturbed. "What did she say about me?"

"You? Not so much," I say, stretching the moment, daring to match her joking flair. "How much have you said about me, however?"

Riley's grin widens, which I didn't expect. I should have, I realize. "Oh, lots," she says cheerfully. "That can't surprise you, Max. You were my first love. I wrote a whole song about you. Of course you've come up in conversation with my mom."

"Right," I say. "But, like, recently?"

She pauses. Or falters. It's striking, the combination of her incredible poise colliding with her caught-off-guard stillness. Her hair is dyed freshly blond, her makeup dramatic. Still, I notice pink stealing into her cheeks. "Is Riley Wynn blushing?" I ask.

Riley laughs like she's amused by her own emotion. The setting sun sinks into the window's view, letting vermilion rays into the room. The effect is stunning, like the skyline is laughing with her.

"Wow, I am," she says.

I find her eyes. "Now," I pry, "what could you have said to make you blush? Did you tell her I'm easy to talk to?"

"Sounds right," she replies.

The little half shrug she gives emboldens me. I'm enjoying this conversation, this off-the-cuff exchange with the girl I remember playing piano for in my dorm room. For once on this tour, I feel like I'm in the right place. Riley might be made for stages—I might be made for greenrooms.

"What about that it was good to see me again?" I ask, drawing out the question.

Riley lifts her chin just slightly. Confrontation meeting invitation. "Most likely," she says.

I lean a little closer, my quiet way of showing her this conversation is only for us despite the hectic room. I chase the little voice in me demanding I keep this up—prove to myself, to her, to every random guy she might meet, that I can still flirt with her, even if it's just for fun. I can still strike the chords we learned from each other when we first met.

"How about," I say leadingly, "that I'm even more handsome than I was ten years ago?"

"I'm pretty sure it came up, yes." Riley looks me right in the eye.

Even with the charge mounting in this exchange, I'm lightly surprised. I find I've entirely forgotten we're about to go onstage. "Did it really?" I ask.

Riley rolls her eyes. The sheepish flicker in her expression is desperately charming. "The years have been very kind to you, Max," she informs me. "You look good. I'm not embarrassed to say so. Admitting it isn't some huge declaration of love."

The lights flash, signaling the show is going to start. My bravado fades, our flirtation smothered by the promise of stage lights. "I know it isn't," I say, hearing how my voice sounds—like myself, my usual self. "But still, thanks. You look good, too."

Good? I chasten myself for my insipid word choice. Even if I'm echoing Riley, the understatement feels criminal. *You look like harmony in human form,* I could say. Instead, I settled for the confines she drew. *You look good.*

Around us, the room is swept up in sudden urgency. While Riley looks eagerly at everyone, like some primal force is drawing her to join them, she pauses. She pulls her eyes to me. "Max—" she starts.

I wait, wondering what she wants to add. The moment is over, the reminder of the expectant audience separating us.

"Have fun up there," she concludes stiffly. It's obviously not what she wanted to say.

I nod, disappointed. She walks into the center of the room to address the band.

I wrench my gaze from her while I still can, stuck with the feeling our duets only sound like harmony when no one else is listening.

TWELVE

Riley

I FINISH "NOVEMBERS" with sweat glistening on my arms, feeling like I've run marathons down memory lanes. I'm immersed in the song, emerging from the person I was in its lyrics, the girl saying goodbye to the singer-songwriter she dated for exactly one year.

She was twenty-seven, sitting in her car under Crescent Heights's streetlights, pulling up her iPhone notes so the lyrics wouldn't leave her. She'd just gotten dumped one year to the day since her first hookup with the guy she'd met before his Palladium show. Reflecting on the calendar quirk, she'd started to feel like every beginning was just the beginning of something ending. *What's November in love over November in pain? What's November mean when every one's the same?*

In the roar of the crowd, I pause, returning to the Riley who stands on this stage, no more or less me than the one in the song.

I live for shows. The kaleidoscope they let me become, how I shift through pieces of my past, memories summoned on guitar strings. The three-minute slivers of my soul I pull on like the costumes waiting for me in my wardrobe.

With every song I've played tonight, I've uncovered past versions of myself. Past Rileys who fell in love and had their heart broken. It doesn't matter how many people stand in front of me, screaming my lyrics. While my hands are on my guitar, my lips pressed to the mic, each song is a time capsule containing pieces of my heart.

When the reverberating echoes of the song fade, I feel connected. Not only to the people surrounding me, the glittering dark expanse of cell phones held high over the heads of the crowd. I feel connected to myself.

The lighting changes, and I place my guitar on the stand positioned exactly where I requested it. With a sip of water, I collect myself. I let go of the girl who wrote "Novembers." I close my eyes, immersing myself in the sounds of the stadium, ready to become the next Riley.

Every stage is its own field of play, with its own feel, in its own relationship with the surrounding space. Mine is curved, made of smooth gray paneling with metal lips. I step up to the mic stand, where I notch the microphone into the clip.

The audience waits. I smile. "Has your life ever changed in a moment?" I ask.

They cheer. The roar is exhilarating. It's what popular music is meant to do, what popular art is meant to do. The point isn't just pleasure. It's unity.

"This next song changed my life forever. Because of you." When they cheer louder, I look out over the endless lights.

It was worth it. Every hurt, every breakup—all of it was worth it to be standing here now.

"The subject of this song probably doesn't know he changed my life twice," I go on. "Once when he first kissed me on a piano bench, then again when I thought about that kiss years later and got my guitar out in the middle of the night to write a song."

I feel my heart pounding. It's not nerves—it's the new Riley. She's laying herself open, her soul naked.

I know Max is listening, and I'm not embarrassed. When you've written a breakup song about a guy who splintered your heart ten years ago, it's hard to be embarrassed about anything. The vulnerability in my voice is no stage persona, no rehearsed intro. It's real.

In the drum of Madison Square Garden, I know my introduction is working. The crowd is fervent. I hear cheers, screams, even crying. The anticipation rolls over the stage in electric heat-waves.

I let them. I welcome them.

Finally, I speak again.

"This one is called 'Until You,'" I say. Into the eruption of sound, I go on. "And I'd like to invite an old friend of mine up to play it with me."

I look back over my shoulder, expectant.

Max stumbles onto the stage. He appears immediately out of place. Not just because he's dressed *not* like a rock star in slacks and a button-down, but because he's a piece of my past, stepping into my present. He's a secret standing in plain sight. He's a name I used to whisper on my lips now surrounded by speakers.

"Max Harcourt and I used to play together when we were twenty," I explain, feeling like I'm walking out to the edge of everything. The fans know a piece of our story without knowing it's *our* story—yet. "He's still the best piano player I've worked with, and since this song has to be played on piano, I knew I had to have Max join me."

Max looks up into the lights while the audience welcomes him. The spotlight's powerful glare glints off the lenses of his glasses. It's like he'd rather reflect the light instead of stand in it.

The piano is on the side of the stage, dark finish shining, the polished white keys stark in hyper-saturated contrast. When Max steps forward, the audience hushes. Suddenly, I feel the first nudge of nerves of the night. What if this doesn't work? What if we perform so stiffly together everyone ignores Max completely?

Then Max sits down at the keys, and his eyes find mine.

When I nod, he begins the intro.

In a few notes, he transforms. He's a different person—or, he's the person I fell in love with years ago. The feelings overwhelm me. It's hard to recognize they're from the past when he's right in front of me. *I'm not in love*, I need to remind myself. I've just opened the time capsule.

He plays with methodical grace, his shoulders rolling while his hands cover the keys. His hair, swept up from his forehead, stays in place precariously, like it was combed quickly. His expression is intense, his eyes fixed on the instrument. Visible beneath his rolled-up cuffs, I watch familiar forearms ripple with elegant motion.

Remembering how I would notice those forearms while those fingers were on me, it occurs to me playing piano is one of the sexiest things men can do.

"*Late nights, new homes,*" I sing, my melody joining perfectly with his. I feel him in his playing, and I know he feels me, the language we used to speak to each other rushing back.

I'm reaching the first chorus when he finally looks up. Right at me.

His eyes light up with luminescence I'm pretty sure isn't from the spotlights. Instantly, it's like he can't look away. Singing the chorus, I'm struck by how it's the look he would give me when we used to perform while we were dating, the one I've noticed in old videos of our earliest performances. I feel like I'm in possession of something stolen, recognition circumstance meant to deny me. Like I wasn't supposed to know how familiar every movement of his hands on the keys is. Like I wasn't intended to feel my heart swell desperately when his gaze says mine is the voice he hears in his dreams.

It makes me pull my eyes from his.

In the final notes of the chorus, I'm hit with flashing fury. I'm not supposed to *remember* the expression on Max's face or the way his hands caress the keys. I'm supposed to have lived with them for the past decade. Circumstance didn't deny me them—he did.

In the slipstream of the stage, something happens. The Riley I change into is one I haven't entirely inhabited even in the many previous performances of this song. I felt the memory of her, the ghost. She walked with me down the sad pathways of "Until You" in studios and soundstages.

Now I feel her fully. Like she's drawn to the one new piece of tonight's performance.

Max.

I'm twenty, packing my car, my heart racing with happiness. Our amps, mine and Max's. My guitar. My luggage, clothing enough for fifteen days in Nashville. The June sun sweltered down on the driveway of my place, from which we were planning to leave because it was closer to the freeway. I didn't even care how much I was sweating. I felt like nothing could shake my excitement. *Nothing.*

The only missing piece was Max. He was driving over with his luggage and, of course, his keyboard. I remember how with every car I heard on my profoundly ordinary street, I got the same giddy rush of hope.

Music meant only joy to me then. It meant only harmony. It meant only companionship.

Only love.

Except finally Max's car did get there. I'd never seen the expression on his face when he stepped out into the glaring day.

He said nothing. It said everything.

With frantic disbelief I stared past him into his car. In the Camry's windows, it was unmistakable. His luggage was nowhere in sight. Nor his keyboard. My heart stuck in my throat.

"What's going on?" I mustered.

"I'm so sorry," Max started.

I was struck by the lack of *baby* or *love*, the pet names Max had started shyly using in recent months. They were very *him.* Nothing exaggerated, yet everything he meant.

"I'm not going to come with you," he went on.

"Why?" I gulped out.

Standing in Madison Square Garden's lights, I *still* feel embarrassed for how fast I searched for other explanations. *God, I hope nothing happened with his family.* Or . . . *Maybe he dropped his keyboard. Maybe it's smashed into plastic pieces.* Or . . .

I ran out of other possibilities quickly. *It was none of those things,* my mind's cruelest voice reminds me. *It was you, Riley. You weren't what he wanted.*

"I need to stay here. I need to start running Harcourt Homes," he explained.

The heaviness in his voice conveyed what his succinct explanations didn't. He wasn't saying the roof would fall in or the money would run out or the residents would riot if he, Max Harcourt, were not personally calling bingo that summer. He didn't mean the home needed him. He meant he needed the home.

"I shouldn't—" He struggled to explain himself. "I'm not . . . meant for doing music with you. It's not . . . me," he said.

I knew it was his choice. His right to live the life *he* wanted. He wasn't who he was on purpose, wasn't choosing what he chose out of spite. It's why I haven't spent the past decade hating him.

Yet—somewhat selfishly, I recognize—I was hurt. I didn't just feel like we'd realized we were incompatible. I felt rejected. I felt startled to learn the man I was head over heels in love with had suddenly come to the conclusion that the core of my hopes and dreams wasn't worth very much to him.

I did something I haven't done much since. I started to cry. "Please, Max," I whimpered. "We've planned this for months."

He shook his head.

"I can't," he said.

Not *I won't*. I could have found hope in *I won't*. *I won't* can change into *maybe*, even one day into *yes*.

I can't was impossible.

Except it wasn't, I guess. Here he is, coaxing wonder from the keys like I knew he would. *I can't*. For months, Max Harcourt filled my heart with three little words. With two, he shattered it in ways I'm not sure I ever mended. This, touring together, was our plan ten years ago. Instead, we're only here now.

It isn't even because he wants to resuscitate our dream, either. He just wants to try on my life before returning home.

I went on our Nashville tour. I stayed in the unspeakably shitty hotel room I'd dreamed of sharing with Max, instead using the exhausting vigor of the performing schedule to distract myself from the gutting loneliness.

In my unexpected spare time, I found myself writing new songs—my first breakup songs. I could write one complete song during the day, premiere the song for my small crowd of patrons, then repeat the process with something new the next day.

With each night, I started to notice the strange effect of this wretched routine. My breakup songs were the ones my listeners loved. While they nodded their heads passively to my up-tempo paeans of young freedom, I could watch their faces change when my wounded chords grabbed hold of them.

I immersed myself in it with wild, reckless zeal. I wrote more new lyrics, using Max for inspiration. I lived my feelings out loud, covering every sad song in my repertoire. It worked, every night.

It's worked for ten years since.

What I'd discovered was undeniable. Heartbreak was horrible, powerful magic.

It was Max's dark gift. In rending my heart, he reinvented my entire relationship with music, leaving me with what I'd suspected. What doesn't kill you makes you a great songwriter.

It's no longer only my proudest joy. It's my first instinct when I'm hurting—how I reach impulsively to stretch the strings of my guitar so they sing the pain in my chest. It's the lover I come to with my sadness as well as my passion.

Instincts hard-won from him. From the music we never got to make.

What a legacy.

This emotional hurricane has swept me up in the short moments separating chorus from verse. Madison Square Garden is resonating with Max's playing, the notes filling up the darkness. If I get madder, the rage in me will interfere with the performance. I turn my back on him. I won't finish the song with the memory of lost gazes looking me right in the face.

"Little lights, close hearts . . ." I sing to the crowd, feeling disappointed with myself. The point of bringing Max on tour is to heighten the song's mythos. I want them to see the music rendered in life in front of them, feel the lyrics written into reality. If I can't make eye contact while singing, then I might as well be onstage by myself.

Hitting the second chorus, I reach inside myself. I'm *Riley Wynn*. I'm in Madison Square Garden. I didn't get here because I flinch easily. When Max crushed my heart, I didn't collapse—instead, I remade myself onstage.

I won't ruin this night, the launch of my tour, because I can't control my heartsick resentment. I need to find my way forward.

When I returned from Nashville, I was single. I remember the shock of realizing my pride was starting to outweigh my pain. If I no longer had Max, I had myself. I had my musicianship. I had my voice. I had stories—sad ones, now, which I was learning to use to spellbinding effect.

I had started living the songs I wanted to make my name, and I had no intention of stopping.

As I sing, I remind myself Max Harcourt isn't the love of my life. He's just a great song.

THIRTEEN

Max

ON THE DRIVE to Ohio, I'm hiding in my bunk.

Hours after the concert ended, the rest of the band is celebrating here in Riley's bus. I hear them outside my flimsy curtains, exchanging tour stories over drinks. Even Carrie is part of the celebrations. Riley's voice—like always—stands out to my stage-weary ears, her laughter ebullient.

During our performance, she was incandescent. It's why I'm here, instead of out there. I couldn't drag my eyes from her, her lips shaping every lyric, her dress shimmering under the lights like they gave her life.

I couldn't stop watching, even when she wasn't singing to me. She sang our song to the fans, who echoed every lyric. It was weird enough knowing everyone was listening to our story. Watching it happen was entirely something else—watching our song become theirs.

I gaze out the strip of window in my bunk, restless. Outside is pitch dark, the road rushing smoothly under us, the vehicle's weight smothering the vibrations the terrain would offer. Interrupting my view is part of the decal on the side of the bus. Riley's name. I've got the long diagonal line on the left of the capital "W."

I shift on top of my blankets, not sure what to do with myself. I don't want to join the celebration.

Instead, I just think. It isn't only the communal experience of "Until You" on my mind. It's how I had to watch Riley sing every *other* song on the album, about every other guy who had feelings for her. I heard the real emotion in every song, saw the heartache vivid on her features. I realized—ours isn't special. It's just the one she gave the hit melody.

I hear the bathroom door rattle open nearby. Footsteps come closer, and my curtain slides open. It's Vanessa, who grins. She still has on her thick eyeliner, her loose hair wild from her night of drumming. "You know, it's hard to hide from a party on a bus," she notes. "Impressive."

I smile graciously, not willing to confess I can't stand to be near Riley right now. "I'm exhausted," I say instead. "I don't know how you all are still standing, and I only played one song."

"Oh, I'm dead," she replies. "But the buzz hasn't let me realize it yet."

She knocks on the bunk in farewell, leaving my curtain open when she returns to the party. I'm left with the festivities in partial view, every one of my fellow musicians celebrating like they feel unstoppable.

I look away. The darkness outside my window is comforting, free of invitation or expectation. I *don't* feel buzzed. I feel . . . I'm not sure. I know what I'll need to figure it out, though. Time, and space from Riley.

Riley, who sang like she still isn't over twelve breakups tonight, who made thousands of people love her. In mythology, sirens would lure sailors to rocky shores with intoxicating voices. I'm starting to feel like I've just heard one sing in Madison Square Garden, wearing her old wedding dress. It's impossible to watch Riley Wynn perform and not feel drawn in, impossible not to do everything I can to remain close.

Did I like performing tonight? Or did I like performing with *her*?

I don't know.

It's frustrating. Notwithstanding Harcourt Homes' finances, I wanted to use this tour to figure out whether I regretted giving up on playing music professionally. I'd hoped stage lights would cast out the shadows in the riddle's corners.

Instead, I'm worried I'll just end up proving how easily I can come under her spell, even ten years later.

I feel the bus slow gradually to a stop. Outside, the illuminated sign of the gas station we've pulled into glares in my window. The party breaks up, everyone filing into the bright store. When they come out, they're bearing plastic bags of Cheetos, Red Vines, AriZona iced tea, Hostess. Like they're not rock stars—like they're teenagers on a road trip.

They return to their buses, presumably to get some sleep. It's past three in the morning.

When we start moving again, it's quiet. Just Carrie, Riley, and me. The space somehow feels smaller without the rest of the musicians. Not intimate—claustrophobic. The cramped confines press in, the cabinets reflecting the overhead lights' glassy glare.

I'm conscious of Riley's every move. She starts picking up the party's refuse with her mom, tossing cups into trash bags.

I climb out of my bunk to help them, impressed but not surprised superstar Riley Wynn still picks up her own garbage. She glances up in surprise, her hair drying slick from onstage sweat, her eyes luminous. She looks exhausted and like she could stay up for days.

"I thought you were asleep," she says. "You don't have to clean up. None of this is your mess." Her voice is rough, exertion finally catching up with her. Involuntarily, I remember how sexy I found it when she would sound this way, when we would head home from our earliest performances.

"I don't mind," I say, not dishonestly. I wipe chips off the leather booth into the closest trash bag.

We work in silence, or near silence, the hum of the road under us reminding me of our constant movement, until Carrie yawns.

"I haven't stayed up this late since you broke your curfew when you were sixteen," she comments to her daughter.

Guilt flashes over Riley's features. Not, I assume, for the curfew violation. "Mom, go to sleep," she says like she's just remembered her mother isn't used to nights like these.

"This isn't done," Carrie protests, gesturing to the spilled liquor on the table.

Riley straightens up. She lifts her eyebrows sternly. "I'm not five. I can clean up my own messes." Carrie hesitates, and Riley pulls the Hefty bag out of her hands. "I'm sending you to bed." Riley points to the back of the bus.

Carrie laughs. "You can't send your own mother to bed."

"My name's on the bus, isn't it?" Riley returns. "Which reminds me, we need a system. The three of us."

In the midst of grabbing paper towels, I pause, not expecting to be brought into the conversation. "System for what?" I ask.

"If we ever want to bring someone back to the bus," she explains.

Embarrassing heat invades my cheeks. Her nonchalance hits me in the way the rest of her songs did. Peering into fragile places I'd prefer to leave unexamined. Immediately, I find the spill on the table very fascinating.

Carrie eyes her daughter, genuinely inquisitive. "What would we bring someone back for?"

"For fun!" Riley says. Her choice of euphemism is the smallest of graces. "It's a music tour!"

Mopping the spill, I contemplate how none of my expectations for this tour included discussing sexile systems with my celebrity ex-girlfriend and her mom. I wonder if Frank could pull over to let me off. I'll just walk to Ohio. It's not far.

In the exhausted recesses of my mind, it occurs to me I started the day simmering over photos of Riley having what could have been fun with the stranger she met last night. Now I'm feeling much the same, state lines later, with dawn drawing closer. Will these feelings never leave me?

"Riley Eleanora Wynn," Carrie gasps, half-serious. "I will not be bringing anyone back for *fun*. I'm going to bed."

"Duct tape on the door," Riley declares, ignoring her mother's retreat. "That'll be the signal. I'll leave it here by the stairs."

"Goodnight, Max!" Carrie calls out in reply.

I can't help chuckling as Carrie closes her door.

When the latch clicks, I'm left in the quiet of the nearly clean living space with my ex, who plans on leaving duct tape on the door. She's disarmingly cheerful, continuing to methodically pick up the room while the ghost of her smile lifts her cheeks.

We say nothing until she suddenly speaks. "Did you enjoy the show?"

The question's context gives me pause. It's one she's probably asked countless fans, friends, even exes, meaning something completely different. It's what she would've said to me if I'd come to one of her shows. The idea of it, this misplaced parallel-universe dialogue, reminds me how just last month, we weren't even in each other's lives.

"Our song, I mean," Riley clarifies, like she's reading my mind. It would not be the first time. "Did you enjoy performing?"

I reopen the riddle I was struggling with in my bunk. "Enjoy?" I repeat. "I don't know. But there was a moment when everyone was singing the lyrics back to us. I felt . . . connected."

Riley grins wide. "Incredible, right?" Her smile could outshine the moon, which is faintly visible outside the decaled window.

I nod, the motion making the feeling real. It *was* incredible, I hear some deep, urging voice in me say. Maybe it's how late it is, how adrenaline and exhaustion have pushed me past the edge of reason, or maybe it's just because Riley has always drawn my feelings from me. Whatever it is, it compels me to break our silence once more.

"The dress," I say. Venturing into the subject feels like stepping onstage did. "Does it really not hurt to wear?"

I wonder if she hears the question's hidden weight, if she knows I'm not only asking about her wedding dress. It's . . . every song. Every severed relationship sculpted into stadium-worthy lyrics. It's me. How does she excavate her heartbreak every night? How does she wear every cut like a crown?

Riley leans on the counter, rubbing her wrist the way I've noticed she habitually does. The little weight of weariness in her expression isn't easy to discern. "Of course it hurts," she says.

The admission is almost a relief. Proof it's not just pageantry—we're not just props. I'm left feeling half-guilty, realizing I'm glad to know Riley hurts. Because if the pain is real, the love was real. I want to know it was real for her. If she feels the loss I did, it's because she felt the love I did.

"I didn't want *this* to be the legacy of my wedding dress," she goes on. "I thought maybe he and I would make it."

Impulse makes me look away. I wish I had the liquor spill to preoccupy me. It's erased now, like it was never there.

"But I knew we weren't perfect for each other, Wesley and I," she says. "I *wanted* it to work. If it didn't, though, I knew it would make one hell of a song."

Her words yank my head up sharply. I hardly recognize how urgently my reply flies out of me. "So, what? That's reason enough to *marry* someone? To do . . . anything? For the song?"

Riley doesn't flinch. "Yes."

Her hand moves to her side, where Mary Oliver's words rest. I traced the lettering once, holding her close in my dorm room, wrapped in my sheets. *Who ever made music of a mild day?*

"I have to live—*really* live—to write music," she insists. Her voice holds the quiet intensity of decisions made after midnight in the confines of sleepless nights, of words repeated to herself when they were her only handholds.

"You're more than your music, Riley," I reply. It comes out the way I'm feeling, half-gentle, half-exasperated. "We're all more than music."

"I know," she says. She doesn't sound offended or defensive. She's patient, like she's had this debate with herself. "It's not just for the music, though. If I weren't looking for inspiration in my life, I don't know if I would *live*. The material for great songs makes for great living."

I don't know what to say. Or rather, I don't want to say what I know I would. While I'm used to silence, even sometimes comforted in its inexpectant constancy, I distrust the sort of stiff, waiting emptiness filling the tour bus now.

I don't want to tell Riley how to live or what her relationship with her music needs to be. I'm certainly no expert on living. In fact, I'm only here in hopes of dispelling doubts I could no longer ignore, of pulling cast-off dreams over my shoulders to find out if they fit.

Nor do I have the final word on songwriting. When I went my way, into the sweltering stasis of the Valley, Riley went hers— into her own journey of entwining her life with song.

Nevertheless, I hope she won't lose herself in service of her music. Her life inspiring her songs is one thing. Her life *becoming* her songs is something else.

"Do you ever wonder where we would be if you'd come with me that summer?" she asks. Onstage her voice is volatile, volcanic, everywhere. Right now, it's the exact opposite. Stripped down to unvarnished honesty.

She watches me closely. If she wanted the rhetorical sting of her question to silence me, I know I'll have to disappoint.

"Yes," I answer. "All the time."

What if I'd gone on the tour we'd planned together? If I'd spent the past ten years orbiting her sun? What kind of life would I have now? Even contemplating the possibility feels like gazing down curved highways. I can start to see where the road goes, until I can't. If I'd spent the journey as Riley's passenger I don't know if I'd care where our path wound.

Her expression shows me she understands what I'm saying.

Fragility steals into the slight waver of her lips, the defensive slant of her shoulders. With the kitchen cabinets framing her, it's easy to forget this is the girl who stands fifty feet high on Sunset Boulevard.

My admission doesn't make her happy. Of course it doesn't. It just reopens the heartbreak like not even a song can. We can't reverse time or rewrite our lives. This tour doesn't replace the tour we would have taken a decade ago.

I remember explaining myself, standing in her driveway on the morning we were supposed to leave for Nashville. Or, sort of explaining myself. I was racked with the guilty enormity of what I was doing. I knew how much it would hurt Riley, and yet I knew I had to. I wasn't scared of commitment or the stage. I just couldn't ignore how launching myself into the life Riley wanted had increasingly felt misaligned with myself.

She had pleaded with me to come. She'd cried. Riley's strength has never come from smothering her feelings. Rather, she felt everything, finding her way through every hurt or struggle.

I watched it happen, under the improperly cheerful sun. Riley repaired herself, pulling her shattered pieces into sharp new resolve.

"Well," she finally said. "I guess I'm going to Nashville without you, then."

While I'd earnestly wondered whether she would, her decision did not surprise me. Riley's fierce momentum is powerful enough to withstand disappointment.

"We can talk when you get back," I'd weakly replied.

Riley only nodded. I did not need her poetry classes to understand the subtext of the silent gesture. In honesty, this did not surprise me, either. I'd ground the summer she had dreamed of under my heel in my inelegant dance of existential uncertainty. I couldn't claim not to have expected she would want nothing to do with me when she returned home.

Yet still, I hoped.

I waited fifteen days, the duration of the tour we'd planned. I kept waiting. Masochistically, I checked her social media. I noticed when she posted photos from a show at the Palladium, a fifteen-minute drive from Harcourt Homes. She was home from Nashville and gone from my life.

I never reached out. I had no right. I knew I was the one who'd hurt her, even if she was the one continuing to make her disinterest in forgiveness clear. The way we left our final conversation in her driveway, what she wanted was unmistakable. Glaring like spotlights, screaming like speakers.

I knew without a doubt her choice was made. We weren't holding out hope for each other, like we'd split hastily, with only vexing variables like miscommunication and overthought separating us. When Riley returned home and didn't contact me, I knew she had made her choice without reservation or regret.

It was welcome, in a way. I was certain my pain was inevitable, which made it strangely more manageable.

Or so I lectured myself.

I'm here now wondering if what silenced me for the past decade was not only resolute respect for Riley's choices. What if it was complacency? What if it was fear?

Riley's reemergence in my life cracked the door of doubt. Which is horrible, because no matter what I would find if I pulled the door wide, I can't change the past. Neither of us can change what happened. I lost her. Riley became *Riley Wynn*. Tears were shed. Years were lived. In the end, we're left with nothing except regret and one immortal song.

I stand up slowly, knowing we've silently decided this conversation is over. When I pass her on my way into the hall, her scent strikes me. She smells like the stage, like the party, like *her*. I have to push myself forward, which I do, climbing into my bunk and closing the curtain.

Sometime later, I hear Riley climb into hers. We're so close we could be sleeping in the same bed.

But we're not.

FOURTEEN

Riley

I LOVE THE bus. I love the feeling of staying constantly in motion, like no one city can contain me. I love the way the scenery changes, landscapes like melodies played out over crescendos of mountains ceding to flatline rests. I love the contact high of new places full of new people, wells of inspiration in lives in the middle of being lived.

I don't, however, love *sleeping* on the bus.

When I emerge in the morning, drowsy from only a couple hours of interrupted sleep, stiff from the confines of my bunk, I find Max in the living space. He's sitting at the table, coffee from the pod machine steaming in front of him, looking like he didn't sleep at all.

Honestly, while I know I'm not the picture of well-rested readiness for the day, he looks like hell. His hair is dramatically mussed. The rings under his eyes could hold up the weight of years of conversations never had. His expression is emptily dour.

I don't know what to say to him after last night. Our exchange lingers in the room the way every song rings in my ears when I've finished the final chorus. *He wonders what our lives would be like.* The question of what he imagines clung on to me in every sleepless moment during the night.

We went on tour together. Did we find the fame I did?

Did it matter?

Were we happy?

I meant what I said in Harcourt Homes. I regret nothing. It isn't just my *Riley Wynn, Breakup Queen* gimmick. I don't regret loving Max fiercely. I don't regret going on tour without him. I don't regret discovering how I could change sadness into songs like forbidden alchemy.

It'll probably be the title of my fucking memoir one day. *Riley Wynn: I Regret Nothing.*

I don't even regret never contacting him, despite his well-intentioned, utterly meaningless *we can talk when you're home,* or whatever he'd said. My silence wasn't sprung from resentment, or even from the selfish urge to sustain the heartbreak I found uniquely inspiring. It honestly wasn't.

I just knew, deep down in my soul, there was no reason for me to reach out. I didn't *choose* the life I was chasing, music stardom, legendary songs, stage lights. It *was* me. It *is* me. It didn't matter if Max wanted to reconnect when I returned from Nashville—in our final conversation, he was clear that the life I wanted could never be his. I mean, he walked out on our first tour *the morning of.* I can't imagine more punishing proof of our misalignment.

Still, I wonder, too.

It's why every conversation we've had over the past weeks has felt impossibly fragile, fraught with uncertainty. Is he hesitantly considering upending the understanding of each other on which I've founded a decade of sad silence?

Or is he just getting ready to leave me and my dreams once again?

I'm scared to ask, so I don't. The reaction leaves me a little furious with myself. It's not me. This flight response is the *opposite* of me. *Feel fearlessly.* I don't just write every song with the imperative in mind. I live every day with it.

Except now, with Max. He's my weakness.

The rest of the morning, neither of us speaks. We drink our coffees in silence.

The tour continues over the next weeks. We play shows in Columbus, Foxborough, Philadelphia, D.C. Everything goes well—incredibly well, in fact—from the candidly impressed *Rolling Stone* coverage to the endless expanses of fans with my name on their shirts, from the exultation of choreographed lights in the huge dark of stadiums to the unimaginable connection of countless hearts united under one lyric.

It's the Breakup Tour. Everything is perfect.

Everything, of course, except for the one detail I can't get out of my head.

When I'm not rehearsing, I check the online chatter obsessively. Some fans have started to comment on the cute pianist I introduce before "Until You," but without real speculation. Meanwhile, gossipier outlets note how Wesley continues to connect himself with the song.

The publicists for my label even *congratulate* me on the media fascination "Until You" is earning due to his efforts. On the drive from Philadelphia into the nation's capital, I end up email warring with Larissa, my head publicist, who grabs on to the idea of my ex-husband.

While I read my iPad in irritation, she proposes viral

moments, meetups on the road. She wants me to "reply" to his highest-performing TikToks with clips from his filmography. She wants us submitted as co-presenters for one award show or other. The last pitch is comically unpleasant—yes, I'll just do a round of pre-Golden Globes humor with the man who in mere months relentlessly destroyed my every hope of loving him.

I put my foot down, rejecting every idea involving Wesley. Past my resentment of Larissa's persistence, I'm hurt, in a weird way. While *I* decide my performing persona, it's uncomfortable to feel like what I represent to my promoters is just the paper doll of Riley Wynn they'll pose however they want.

Part of me feels guilty for my uncooperativeness, which rattles me even more. Don't I have the right to decide how my public and private lives overlap without feeling *guilty* for my choices?

It leaves me even more frustrated with the failure of "Until You." I know why it's not working, why nobody's grabbing on to the story I'm spinning for them with Max onstage. It's because I don't know how to sing *to* him. Every show I tell myself I'll block out every conversation we've had in the past weeks, and I'll wrap myself in memories and sing to the man I used to love.

Every week, I fail.

It's not just me. Something is off in Max's playing. Not technically, of course—from a musicianship standpoint, he's improved with each show, developing his finesse for pauses, for emphases, for how to fill stadiums with his piano.

No, it's something else. I don't just *remember* how Max sounds when he puts everything into the song he's playing—I never forgot.

I don't hear his singular magic now. He's holding something

back. His renditions of "Until You" come from his hands, from his head. Not from his heart.

Each performance lets dismal fears into my relentless heart. *It must mean something*, my insecurities insist every day. My psyche's prevailing interpretation is disconnection with Max. I'd premised the plan of reshaping the public story of "Until You" on us getting onstage together, playing with even the ghost of the emotion our duets once shared. Instead, we're up there every show, disjointed, even wary of each other.

I know we're different people, getting to know each other musically after years of silence. The conclusion I'm dreading is deeper—it feels like not enough of our love survived.

The quandary sits on my shoulders in every spare moment, making me restless. The drive from D.C. to Nashville is the longest leg of our tour yet. We leave streets showing the first cherry blossoms of the season for hours of green highway winding over the state's famous rolling hills. It's depressingly lovely weather, the open skies incompatible with my sullen stress.

Near the state line, we stop somewhere called Gray so Frank and the other drivers can take a break. The second we park, everyone flies out of the bus doors, eager to stretch their legs in the direction of the diner on the main drag.

I don't follow them. I've spent the past hours feet away from Max, our unfinished conversations, stolen glances, and uncomfortable silences piling up on me. I need to figure out how to fix our performances, and the perfectionist in me won't let me enjoy the afternoon until I do.

I settle in at the table with my laptop, ready to watch every video people have posted of "Until You." It's punishing work, watching yourself over and over. Finding the phrases you hide your nerves behind onstage, the awkward gestures that don't at all look the way you imagined. I study everything. Every time Max skirts my gaze, every moment of disconnect. Every failure.

Until my laptop is snapped closed.

Frank stands over me, his mouth a straight line.

"Um, hello, Frank," I say uncertainly. "I was sort of in the middle of something." I reach for my computer.

He slides it out of my reach, shaking his head. "I'm kicking you off the bus."

I laugh, affronted. "It's my—"

"Your name is on the bus, but as long as I'm the driver, it's my bus," he corrects me, his eyes crinkled with hints of humor. "You need some air."

"I appreciate you're trying to help, but I don't need air."

"I'm *not* trying to help. I'm trying to kick you off the bus. And now, I'm officially working during my break." Despite his words, he sits down across from me. His rough-hewn features relax into real sympathy. "What's going on, kiddo?"

I almost cry just from his kindness. Well, and the poor sleep and peak levels of stress I'm living with daily. "'Until You' isn't right yet," I admit, guilty for taking his time.

He doesn't look like he's in a rush to get up, though. He shrugs. "No one starts a tour without a couple kinks. You have to give it time."

"People spent money on these tickets. They're supporting my career. I can't just *give it time*. It needs to be perfect."

Frank nods like he expected me to say that. "Riley, you put on a fucking great show. I'm sorry it's not what you want it to be yet. I understand, I really do. But is the fix really in this bus?"

"It might be!" I say petulantly enough that even I have to smile at my own childishness.

"Can I give you some advice?"

"Since when do you ask for permission?"

"Get some air. Find inspiration in the world. Music isn't a problem you can solve by looking at the mistakes. You need to look *past* the mistakes," he says softly. "Keep moving. Keep reaching."

I let out my breath, knowing he's right. Frank is always right when it comes to music. I stand up. "I'm sorry I took time off your break," I say, meaning it.

He waves his hand. I want to hug him, except I kind of feel like oversentimentality would mess up the gentle understatement of his care. Instead, I just smile. If I know Frank, he'll read the depth of gratitude in my expression.

Leaving my laptop, I head for the door on shaky legs. The day outside is refreshing, the perfect in-between of springtime sunlight with winter chill. I decide I'll go for a walk. Clear my head.

I know I'm not myself when solitude sounds nice. Still, I have to do something. I walk into Gray, head held high. *Keep reaching.*

Despite the name, the small city is verdant, nearly entirely green. Patchworked lawns only reluctantly leave space for paved roads. Shaggy trees hunch over shingled rooftops. I pass churches, car repair shops, houses with old pickups out front.

While the many nights onstage make my feet perpetually sore, I don't care. I love exploring. It's one of my favorite parts of touring, of travel. The world yields details I couldn't possibly invent on my own. I file them into memory for future lyricism, filling up my magpie hoard of rough gems.

The stress of the drive starts to leave me slowly. In all honesty, approaching Nashville has me out of sorts. Memories shadow me, unshakable, reminding me how Max and I were supposed to spend the summer here ten years ago. I've visited the city enough since then to find myself comfortable there under ordinary circumstances—label events, promotional TV features, other shows.

We're not driving in today under ordinary circumstances, though.

Instead, nearing Nashville, Max and I are immersing ourselves in the reprise of decade-old dreams. The memories have found me now, the opposite of nostalgia. Places, plans, possibilities I imagined when I was younger, except everything feels different with the context changed, like revisiting your hometown once you've grown up.

It's not culminative or reassuring. It just feels . . . late.

Under my feet, the cracks in the pavement look like the Mississippi River. My little outing undoubtedly looks surreal— superstar Riley Wynn wandering the empty streets of the city of Gray, reflecting on what could have been. *Stars, they punish themselves for old dreams just like us!*

I wonder if Max is ruminating this way, wrestling with the feeling of finally living out hopes we once deferred. He's probably not. For him, this is no lost dream. It's just a memory, like the phone number of his family's old landline.

When I return to the gas station, I hear music echoing from the doors of one of the band's buses. Intrigued, I follow the sound up the short set of stairs inside. It's wonderfully loud in the small kitchenette where everyone's set up. I'm surprised to find Max sitting in the booth with someone's portable keyboard in front of him on the table. Hamid sits on the couch, his guitar in his hands, while Savannah sings. They're in the middle of Howlin' Wolf's "Killing Floor," their rendition languidly emotional. They sound great.

I join Kev and Vanessa to watch them. When Max notices me enter, he looks up for a heartbeat but doesn't stop playing. I applaud with everyone else when the song finishes.

Hamid eyes Max. "You really don't play in a jam band? Nothing? Just the old folks' home?"

Over the past weeks, I've found our guitarist disciplined, perfectionistic, sometimes sarcastic. He is not overwhelmingly enthusiastic or encouraging. The excitement in his voice for Max's playing is genuine.

"Just the old folks' home," Max confirms somewhat sheepishly. He pauses like he's deciding if he wants to say more. "Riley and I used to play together, though," he ventures. "A long, long while ago."

I straighten up, surprised. Heads swivel in my direction.

It's unlike Max to invoke our past. He's skirted the subject in other conversations like this one, friendly questions I've overheard on why he joined the tour or how long he's been playing. I start to smile, wondering if he'll say more.

Instead, he meets my eyes. It reminds me, slightly shockingly, of when we used to play together, the moment right before I'd come in with vocals and he would glance at me to line up our timing.

I hear what his silence says. *You tell them.*

Needing no more encouragement, I nod. "The first time I performed for complete strangers was with Max," I say, enjoying the way the revelation makes everyone's eyes widen. "We used to gig anywhere that would let us, but usually we played at Harcourt Homes. The 'old folks' home,'" I clarify with Hamid's phrasing.

We'd found the Harcourt Homes dining room the ideal place to practice performing for other people. While the stakes weren't high, the audience was vocal and easy to lose. We learned showmanship. We considered the careful discipline of set list creation. We were often paid in key lime pie. It was perfect.

Hamid's keen eyes move from me to Max. "Why did you stop gigging together?"

Max says nothing. His hands return absentmindedly to the keys, like he's relying on the piano to say what he can't figure out how to. The chords he plays don't come from any discernable song. Just patterns, frills. Meditations in minor keys.

I'm reaching for one cliché or other—*creative differences, we just went separate ways eventually*, whatever—when suddenly Max speaks.

"We were going to tour together," he says. "I dropped out."

While the confession leaves me open-mouthed, the feeling is nothing compared to what hits me when Max repositions his hands on the keys.

The chords change into ones I recognize instantly. They pierce my heart all the way through, memories like nails pinning me in place.

He's playing "Unchained Melody," a song he used to play with me often. While I loved following its heart-aching contours in front of Harcourt Homes or whatever small venue we could find, I loved it most when it was just us. I would sing to Max. He would play for me. It was like few other moments of connection in my life.

The other musicians recognize the chords instantly. Sighs and smiles go up from the group. Vanessa closes her eyes. Hamid nods in sanction of the choice.

Max plays like they're not there. He plays like he's confessing every note to the keys. Or imploring them, wanting the piano to fill places in his heart he doesn't know how to on his own. He plays with whatever singular devotion is missing in every night's rendition of "Until You."

I join in, singing over his keys with everything in my heart.

Max doesn't seem surprised. He keeps playing like he knew I would step in, like the song could not have been played without me in the room. He redoubles the piano line's intensity, the music rising to meet me, joining us. When I hit the chorus's questions about long-ago love and whether it remains, he looks up, right at me.

I don't look away.

Max smiles with joy, his expression one I haven't seen in five weeks and a decade.

Everything changes in the length of the chord he's playing. His smile is boyish, the Max I knew in our closest moments. The happiness he reserved for songs played perfectly for the first time, for new music recommendations shared, for whenever I presented him with lyrics I'd just finished, my heart pounding with pride.

The rest of the room vanishes. I'm no longer lost in the fog of memories. I'm floating on them. It's easy, like music is the air we're breathing together.

When he releases the keys of the final chord, the room is hushed.

Only when Vanessa slowly claps do I even remember our

small, informal audience. The rest of the group joins in. Hamid whoops. Kev whistles. Quickly, the cheering gets loud, filling the windowed space.

His cheeks reddening, Max's gaze drops from mine. The self-conscious stain on his fine features says he's remembered parts of himself four minutes of melody permitted him to forget.

It knocks the wind out of me, how fast our synchrony snaps. It didn't feel fragile or fought-for in the moment. It felt sure. Soaring. Effortless. *Didn't it?*

I feel my own expression wobbling. Not like I'm crying, just—the surprise grip of hurt in my chest making my cheeks waver unexpectedly. What Max's reaction means is painfully obvious, harshly undeniable. Without the music, nothing connects us anymore.

While I'm working up to suggesting he play Fleetwood Mac's "Songbird," however, the drivers return, dashing my hopes. The slap of disappointment shakes me up. Shouldn't I feel like the star of this tour, not someone watching the school dance while hugging the wall?

The impromptu jam session ends without ceremony, everyone stowing their instruments in preparation for the final few hours into Nashville. With his usual reserved friendliness returning, Max thanks Kev for the use of the portable keyboard. When he passes me on his way out the door, his shoulder barely brushes mine. His gaze remains elusive.

I linger, knowing we need to get underway. Savannah hops up to sit on the counter, where Vanessa joins her, playing some vibey R&B from her iPhone speakers. Hamid returns to the couch, sipping the coffee he grabbed from the fridge. Everyone looks . . . comfortable.

What waits for me in my bus is the opposite. It's hours more with Max while this pressure mounts, pulling us like strings ready to snap.

I should make the effort, the nobler voice in me whispers. It's my tour. My songs. In the end, he's my musician. I should push myself to find the connection, or remake it, however we're going to.

I just . . . can't. I sing my heartbreaks every night onstage. There's only so much I can stand to stare them in the face in my hours off.

Instead, I stay here. I sit down on the couch next to Hamid, who looks lightly surprised. "Cold brew in the fridge if you want," he offers.

"Thanks, man," I say. "With the sleep I've gotten recently, I definitely do."

He chuckles. While it sounds like he knows I don't just mean the joys of curling up in our bunks every night, he doesn't inquire further.

We start to move, pulling out of Gray. I return from the fridge with the cold coffee to sit on the couch, where I stare out the window with my headphones in. While part of me wants to socialize with everyone, getting to know the musicians better, I find myself exhaustedly stuck in my mind. The riddle of Max consumes me.

"Unchained Melody" repeats in my head, a one-song playlist I can't shut off. I know if we'd performed what we just did onstage, we would have *captivated* the audience. Absolutely everyone would know one of my songs was about him.

Which means the problem isn't us, or the way we play together. It isn't even Max's reluctance to find our old connection, or mine. In one of our familiar favorite songs, each of us reached for shared passion we haven't felt since we first fell in love.

No, the issue is something else. My fraught process of elimination leaves only one possibility.

The problem is "Until You."

FIFTEEN

Max

I REALLY EXPECTED that space from Riley would help.

Help I sorely needed, what with how Nashville went. Playing "Unchained Melody" with Riley shook me in ways I couldn't entertain, not if I was going to perform "Until You" hours later. The very idea of Nashville with her was hard enough. Then I had to face the musical city with the new painful, wondrous reminder of how playing with Riley could feel like fucking magic.

Would have felt, if I'd visited this place with her when we first planned.

While the other musicians enjoyed our newest destination, I used none of our pre-rehearsal hours for exploring the streets or—no way—daring to imagine what I would have felt singing "Unchained Melody" on the stage of some folksy venue with the woman I loved. If I ventured into Nashville, I knew other questions of *would* and *should* would follow my every step.

I couldn't.

Instead, I slept. I curled up, hiding from the daylight. I passed the couple hours until rehearsal fighting to forget where I was, and when, and with whom.

Rehearsing led right into the show, where I dutifully performed "Until You" while now-routinized questions repeated in my head. Did I like the feeling of the spotlights illuminating my keyboard gleaming white? What did I feel when I heard the crowd cheer, their phones lighting up the venue like stars in the night sky?

In this city, onstage, with my guard forced down under the elegiac power of Riley's voice, the questions I'd fled finally confronted me. How would I feel if I were *returning* to Nashville with Riley instead of here with her only now? If I really regretted running from this, how could I live with the years of this dream I'd lost?

The years of *Riley* I'd lost?

I ignored the questions fiercely. If I listened any closer, their uproar would overwhelm me, like playing every song I've ever heard at once.

The result was self-inflicted disappointment. Nashville left me with nothing. The blacked-out blur of the Breakup Tour's half day in the music capital of the country was the worst sort of frustration—frustration with myself, frustration I struck into every keystroke onstage. I could have looked for reckoning in the city's music halls or clarity in the venues I'd decided not to play.

Instead, I hid.

From it all.

When the show was over, we returned to our bus, where we exchanged the perfunctory conversation the past days have reduced us to. I hate it. It was complicated enough feeling like pieces of each other's pasts. Now we feel like *exes*.

We drove on to New Orleans, where we're staying now. No

difficult dynamics with Riley could challenge the profound relief of checking in to the hotel where we'll be sleeping for the
next couple nights since we're playing two shows in the Superdome. We'll end our stay in the city with a day off for the crew
while Riley does press.

The hotel is in the city's French Quarter, which is half his-
toric neighborhood, half urban downtown. Colorful facades in
the city's iconic design sit next to warehouses and the occasional
skyscraper. Our hotel is luxuriously stylish, stone exteriors surrounding swanky rooms with old-school funk.

When we arrived half an hour ago, everyone separated for
some much-needed space. I was no exception. I went to my
room, savoring the openness, the fabricated silence hotels have,
the crispness of the carpet. Eager to wash off the feel of the bus, I
headed immediately into the shower.

Standing under the steam, I welcome the solitude.

Finally, distance from Riley. It *should* help, I reason with myself, hearing how desperate I'm starting to sound. For days I've
felt like if I could just get some space from her, I might be able to
reflect on how I've felt performing for crowds nearly every night.
I could maybe convert some of my insistent questions into answers.

Instead . . . the shower doesn't do what it's supposed to. My
muscles don't unwind. The steam feels like humidity. The warm
water feels scalding.

It's funny, if darkly.

Here I am, floors separating me from Riley, and I feel edgy.
Like I'm in withdrawal.

I scrub myself, then step out of the shower, demoralized.
Frustrated, even. Not wanting to explore New Orleans when

we've spent the past weeks constantly on the move, I decide to FaceTime my parents, who have stepped out of retirement to run Harcourt Homes while I'm on tour. I'm not surprised when seeing them in the dining room hits me with a rush of homesickness.

Still, while we talk, my favorite piano sitting in the background, I feel perfectly torn down the middle.

Yes, I'd be happy at home. Homesickness, however, isn't what's ripping my heart's edges ragged right now. If I *were* home, I would feel the same restlessness I feel right now magnified a millionfold, so far from Riley. I mean, I feel the way I do sitting in the middle of my hotel room *in the same hotel where she's staying*, having spent the past few weeks in nearly constant contact.

With more separating us—state lines, career paths—how could I imagine *not* feeling like I'd had deep, fundamental pieces pulled out of me?

It's the first occasion on which I find myself wondering how I'll walk out of her life for the *second* time. I spent years repairing myself the first time.

The Riley I know now is not the girl I fell in love with, either. The Riley I met when I was twenty was the girl of my dreams. This Riley is . . . everything. She's not *more*, exactly, with her stardom, her presence, her name in lights—rather, she's more *herself*. On stages the size of the ones she electrifies now, she looks like she's the Riley she's dreamed of being her whole life.

It makes her radiant.

I shake off the thought. If I do end up separating myself from her, from the life she lives now, in which she's provided me this strangest of second chances, indulging every such observation will only make leaving harder.

The problem is, when I'm with her, I'm not exactly happy,

either. I'm confused yet captivated, like I'm on the edge of something dangerous, high from the adrenaline.

It makes me suddenly want off the call with my parents. Getting some space in my hotel room was the last resort I'd longed for. Instead, it's managing only to intensify the questions. The need for clarity, for certainty, is overwhelming, leaving me wishing to lie in the dark and for *one hour* feel like I know what I want.

With rushed goodbyes, I end the FaceTime. Out my full-length window, the French Quarter exists oblivious to what I'm contending with. I collapse onto my bed, where I close my eyes.

My exhaustion isn't just emotional exhaustion wrought from the question of Riley. It's real physical exhaustion. I haven't had a good night's sleep since the tour started, and I have a feeling it has nothing to do with the struggles of sleeping on a moving vehicle. No, it has everything to do with sleeping just feet away from Riley.

Every night, the same intoxicating misery. I hear the rise and fall of her chest, the unconscious movements she makes. I know what the country's favorite singer sounds like when she dreams.

When I close my eyes in the hotel room, though, someone knocks on my door.

I consider ignoring it, but the possibility it's Riley has me pulling myself up from the comforter despite my weariness, equally hoping it's her and hoping it's not.

It's not. When I open the door, I find Eileen in the hall. I'm embarrassed how disappointed I am.

"You busy? Riley wants a word," Eileen says.

My heart leaps. Instantly, I chastise myself for its sudden movement. I can't live every moment like a roller coaster, unsure if Riley is the highs or the lows.

"I'm not busy," I say.

"Perfect." Eileen's delivery is fast, her intonation revealing nothing. It reminds me of how nurses inject shots while you're distracted.

I follow her down the hallway to the elevators. We ride up in silence, giving me the opportunity to hear my pulse pounding in my ears, quickening with every step closer to Riley. On the hotel's highest floor, we continue to one of the few doors off the elevator lobby. Eileen unlocks it, revealing the nicest hotel room I've ever seen.

Riley's suite is palatial. Marble floors, a spacious living room decorated with furniture halfway to modern sculpture, floor-to-ceiling windows overlooking the city in the mid-March sunlight.

And in the center of the space, a white baby grand piano.

Riley sits on the bench, her back to the keys, a computer on her lap. She's a shock of color in the sleekly white room, her green jumpsuit standing out ferociously. When we walk in, she looks up, her eyes disarmingly distracted for the quickest second until she focuses on us. "Thank you for coming," she says.

"Of course," I reply, finding myself echoing her neutral politeness. We're stilted again, not at all like we were when we were jamming on the bus, when we could fall back on the songs we used to play together. I look to Eileen, who remains standing by the door. "I feel like I'm being fired," I venture. While I'm going for joking, I end up just sounding uneven.

Eileen doesn't laugh. My stomach twists. Am *I being fired*?

Riley smiles weakly. One frantic impulse seizes me—*I can't go home, not yet.* The rushing of my heart rate changes to roaring in my ears. "Our performances haven't been what I'd hoped," Riley says gently. She presses the space bar and rotates the computer on her lap so I can see the screen.

It's us. The Nashville show, where I'm playing like I'm performing for one of my old professors, while Riley sings "Until
You" like someone else wrote it.

Desperation grips me. I don't want to be sent home. I don't
want to be exiled from Riley.

In the clutches of the feeling, I step forward impulsively, reaching out to stop the video with one stroke of the space bar. The still
frames Riley's face, staring past me with searching intensity.

"I'm trying," I say. It's half defense, half longing plea. Even so,
I won't resist whatever her decision is. I know she wants this to
work—in fact, it's one of Riley's defining traits. *She wants. She
believes.* But I know this tour is important to her, too. She won't
let me drag it down.

It would make miserable sense, I rationalize. Maybe after our
conversation on the bus, when I confessed I had regrets I couldn't
name, she decided she no longer wanted to face me, let alone sing
with me.

Riley sets the computer aside. "It's not all on you," she says
slowly, like she's only reluctantly admitting the problem's complexity. "We're in this performance together. I want to rehearse
more. Without the crowds. Find out what the issue is."

The relief douses me like ice water. Comfortable? Not exactly.
Exhilarating? Yes. I'm still part of the tour.

I don't say anything. I don't need to "find out what the issue is."

Instead, I only nod. I walk up to the piano, noticing how
perfectly the view of the city skyline past the instrument complements the experience. I feel like I'm walking up to the edge of
somewhere very high, peering over the top of one of Riley's
fifteen-story billboards.

Riley stands up. I sit down.

"I heard you jamming on the bus the other day," Eileen says. "You were perfect. Exactly what we envisioned when we put this duet together. We just need to translate that into 'Until You.'"

"I get it. I want to make it work," I reply, looking at Riley.

While her eyes don't say she's convinced, they don't skirt mine, either. She holds my gaze, her expression like the one she's wearing on the screen. Searching. "Let's just have fun with it," she finally suggests.

I put on a grin, privately struggling with the impossible weight she's handed me. I *can't* have fun with it. Not this song. Still, I start in, fighting to relax my shoulders. The piano fills the room, the marble scattering the sound everywhere. When Riley sings, I pretend this isn't a song she wrote about us. It's just a song, like the hundreds we've played together.

Like I'm posing myself, I look to Riley. I smile.

She smiles.

It's simple harmony. Precise. Maybe we're pulling this off. Maybe if I just don't think—

"Okay," Eileen interrupts. "Maybe don't smile. It's a sad song, right?"

Riley flushes. It's startling—on her face, embarrassment is like a home intruder. Frustration instantly smothering her self-consciousness, she paces the marble floor of the foyer, then returns to the edge of the piano.

"Max. Do you like the song?" she asks.

It takes everything in me not to drop her gaze. "I've told you. It's an incredible song."

Exasperation worries under Riley's patient expression. "Yes," she replies. "But do you *like* it? What does the song make you feel?"

I clench my jaw, half-scared my real answer will fly right out of me. *I feel like the hardest choice I've ever made has become everyone's favorite playlisted plaything.* The moment is horribly strained.

Riley looks to Eileen. "Maybe give us a couple minutes."

Eileen steps out, not hiding her skepticism. I understand where she's coming from. They can't have someone on tour who hates the centerpiece song. When the door closes behind Eileen with the grinding click of hotel locks, silence reigns.

Until Riley fixes me with undeniable eyes. "Play it with feeling, Max."

Frustration steals into my voice. "I *am*," I insist.

"No," she says. "Play it the way the song makes *you* feel. Not the way you know it should make you feel."

I look down. The keys stretch out in front of me like smiling jaws. Or perhaps they're prison bars, or ladder rungs leading up to harrowing views where even the one in front of us would look small. Every possibility is perilous.

"I don't think that's a good idea," I finally say.

"Humor me," she presses. Her voice says she knows what hell I'm in. It says she's interested in joining me.

I look up at her, warring with myself. I don't want to play what she wants to hear. I don't want my feelings out in the open, not when Riley watching me will feel like wind whistling over open wounds. But I also don't want to go home.

With a resigned breath, I start the intro again. This time, I play it the way *I* hear it—hauntingly. Like memory's music box echoing a melody down the hallways of somewhere I used to live. I let my unease out through my fingers, ratcheting the notes with percussive flicks that explode into the measure where Riley comes in. She joins me seamlessly, yet for once, I'm the one leading the song forward. While she sings, I let anger, hurt, resentment, regret flow out of me. I'm consumed. I'm a fucking symphony of spite.

Riley's eyes widen. She doesn't stop singing, though. Instead, she keeps eye contact with me and feeds on my emotions, returning them to me in the song.

We near the first chorus like we're charging for a head-on collision. Riley uses my interpretation, lighting up the mournful lyrics with prosecutorial fury. "*I felt the end in the start,*" she sings. "*Words I didn't know you didn't mean. 'I' and 'love' and 'you' would make me see.*"

Instead of emphasizing "'I' and 'love' and 'you'" the way she has in our shows, she doubles down on the line's slippery poetics, hitting "you would make me see" like a warning.

I match her in every note. I play like I'm pushing her away, like I did a decade ago. I prepare myself for Riley to shut the song down. For her to interrupt like Eileen did. *It's not working. You're doing everything wrong. We can't play this in front of the fans.* She'll fire me. She'll exile me.

Instead, she steps closer.

She joins her voice with my playing, fusing our sounds into one conjoined strand of pure emotion. Her eyes never leave me, even when mine stray to my keys. Not because I need reminders of where to position my hands next—I could easily play "Until You" with my eyes closed. No, the sheer force of Riley's focus is what diverts me.

The feeling is indescribable. It is—I can't help recognizing—impossibly intimate. I've known closeness to Riley in every way, her hair splayed out on her pillow, her uninterrupted skin waiting for me. It wasn't like this.

We reach the chorus, mounting its famous heights together.

I didn't know what love is
I don't know what love is
I won't know what love is
until you
Opened the door.

With the end of the chorus, Riley sits down next to me. We're side by side while the song's journey continues, one of us the passenger, one of us driving. Neither of us knows who is who.

Her voice remains nothing like the performances. It isn't wistful or yearning. She sounds vindictive, matching the vengeance of my playing. We're each pressing deliberately into old wounds, just to fascinate ourselves with the perverse pleasure of the pain.

In the second verse, the lyrics switch to present tense. Whatever my feelings on the song, its structure is fascinating, Riley's proof of poetry existing in pop. It is my least favorite verse—like she's writing crime journalism, she diagrams the final day of our relationship. The wording is vague enough for relatability, not to mention discretion, but I remember too well exactly the moments she means.

"*The day of, I want you,*" she sings. "*High roads, see us through.*"

She isn't speaking idiomatically. She means the tour we intended to take. The next step in our musical-romantic relationship, the one she hoped would see us through together.

I urge the melody forward. It's like we're arguing. Like I'm seizing the chance to say in chords everything I couldn't when we left each other's lives. *It was Nashville or nothing? I wasn't the man you loved if I wouldn't play music with you?*

No wonder you wrote me into song when you could've called me, even once, over the past decade.

Of course, you didn't.

The hurt is only worthwhile if it's a hit, right?

I get the strangest feeling Riley hears me. Sitting next to me, she presses on, opening her heart in the middle of the second verse. I feel her every movement, her slight sway with every word she sings, the rise and fall of her chest with her every inhalation. The impossible closeness of the skin of her arm right next to mine. Invitation and condemnation.

Her gorgeous mouth, shaping the lyrics I can't figure out how not to hate.

"*You look like you're hoping I'll be fine,*" she sings. "*I know I'm helpless even when I try.*"

I know what's coming. My heart pounds, the waver in my fingers finding its vibrating way into the melody. When I return to the verse-opening notes, Riley will hit the hardest lines for me to hear. *We know it isn't true when you say you'll see me soon.*

She does this pain-stretched note on "see me soon" I can hardly stand to hear onstage. I'm not sure I can manage it now. With my hands still on the piano, I face her, my eyes locking on hers.

She breathes in.

I kiss her.

Everything stops. The sound of the piano ends sharply. The lyric I knew was coming is swallowed under my lips meeting hers.

Every sense hurtles forward in me with head-rush intensity.

Her mouth under mine is still half forming its stolen syllables. Her scent, sweet like summer nights, is everywhere.

She kisses me back, and our music changes from melodies into the beating of our hearts, the blood whispering in our veins. Leaning forward, she presses us closer. Once more, we're urging each other forward, leading each other in voiceless harmony.

If I'd permitted myself to imagine this moment, I would have expected it would feel like a familiar reprise. Now, kissing Riley feels like we're writing something new.

I pull her closer to me, hungry to touch more of her. The movement surprises her. I hear it in the soft intake of her breath as she sits on my lap, her fingers gripping the collar of my shirt. Her hips press tantalizingly into me, and I hold her face, her back, clinging to her like I'm trying to capture sunlight in my hands. Impossible, but maybe, just maybe, I'll open my palm and find it's not empty.

When we break apart, it's only because the hotel door beeps. Riley slides off my lap, and Eileen enters, undoubtedly drawn in by the music's sudden stop. Reality returns in one harsh kick. The searing white stone of the floor, the glaring day outside. The swift impossibility of the situation. We did this once. It ended in heartbreak. Nothing has changed. Nothing will. Sunlight can't be held. My hands are empty.

Riley stares at me, her fingers pressed to her lips, shock in her eyes. She's quiet.

I stand sharply and walk out, feeling everything. Regret, desire, fear, longing.

I hear no melody in my head now—only noise.

SIXTEEN

Riley

I WALK OFFSTAGE after our first show in New Orleans close to crying. The Superdome crowd I just left cheering has no idea how I'm feeling, which I'm glad of. In the miniature galaxy of the stadium, the dark dome filled with collective emotion, I gave them enough. I gave them what I could.

Still, the performance of "Until You" was our worst yet. Creativity comes with plenty of volatile shifts from highs to lows. On lows like tonight my frustration feels like drowning, choking my exhausted lungs with fury.

When I pass Eileen, I hold up my hand, knowing what she's going to say. Our rehearsal in the hotel room set us back. *Of course* it did. Because Max kissed me, then clearly regretted it.

For the record, I don't regret it. Sure, it was probably a bad idea in the long run, but I don't believe in regrets. Even if I did, I could never regret kissing Max Harcourt. Kissing Max was like hearing a forgotten favorite song for the first time in years.

It obviously wasn't the same for him. I'm unable to shake the memory of the hurricane in his eyes when he stood up from the piano, the . . . resentment. Writing songs ripped from my own emotions, I've started to suspect people forget I *feel* the emotions first. When they find their way into my voice, it's only because I've walked through them, shouldered them myself, first.

It's what I do now with the lingering sting of where our kiss left us. The feeling follows me into the dark wings, down into the greenroom.

Under the uniform metallic lights of the stadium's inner workings, I smile in reply to every perfunctory congratulation from everyone I pass, wishing I could meet them with more enthusiasm, like I wish I could've given fans more in our performance of "Until You." When everyone, every crewperson, every fan, is there for *my* show, the guilt of every rough day or distracted moment is overwhelming.

It's how I felt struggling through "Until You" onstage. This mess with Max is making me disappoint everyone.

In my private dressing room, I take my time changing out of my costume, hiding in the solitude. I know I'm going to have to face Max. Talk this out. Figure out what happened, what we can do, how we save the song. I'm putting it off, though, because I suspect when we discuss it, Max will choose to leave rather than find a way to move forward. We've been down this road once, and while the breakup inspired the biggest hit of my career, I'm not eager to walk it again.

I meet my eyes in my dressing room mirror. I look nothing like the star who lit up the video screens in the stadium, my digital replicas moving in synchrony. I look miserable. Small. Overwrought.

I don't want to return to my room, the scene of our kiss, where the baby grand piano looks like a gravestone standing in the middle of the space. Nor do I want to regroup with Eileen to discuss what I already know I need to fix in the show. Instead, I straighten up. In the mirror, I shake off some of my disappointment. *No more moping.* I leave the dressing room, looking for my mom.

HOLDING WARM BEIGNETS, we walk through the French Quarter. It's late, but New Orleans isn't asleep. Its lively cheer is charming, music spilling from second-story windows over the friendly clamor of the nightlife.

I feel happier, stabler, more like myself. It's remarkable what wonders New Orleans donuts and hanging out with my mom can work.

People we pass ask me for photos or autographs, which I oblige until more start to congregate, drawn by the crowd. I keep my crowd face on, reminding myself how genuinely grateful I am for fans' support, despite the inescapable nervousness of moments like this.

It's fine until I hear one voice call out, "Give Wesley another chance!"

In fact, in the past couple months, I've noticed darker currents emerge in *The Breakup Record*'s public discourse. Plenty of Wesley's fans have eagerly pinned our divorce on me, with collections of misconstrued quotes combined with outlandish cheating conspiracies.

His worshippers don't make me fear for my safety in public, despite the distaste of the invocation of Wesley. However, they're not the only faction who worry me. Worse have been the dude-bro defenders of Jacob Prince, who I memorialized on one of *The*

Breakup Record's less flattering portraits. Jacob went on to star in some superhero movies. The macho ones, not the fun ones.

In some startled late-night internet sessions, I found out I'm exactly the sort of woman his fans hate. In the months since, I've generally learned which forums not to peruse and what sorts of profile pictures to scroll past. Still, the stuff some commenters wish would happen to me, or want to do to me—it's upsetting reading.

While everyone in the French Quarter right now looks welcoming, the mention of one of my famous exes has me on edge. I know people have unwanted opinions on my love life. I know I even invite them. Still, I don't need to hear them personally, and I definitely don't want to hear them—or worse, whatever insults or complaints the crowd might have for me—when I'm practically on my own in public past midnight.

I decide I need to make my escape. "Hey, everyone," I call out, projecting my voice with exhausted muscles. "Sorry I can't stay—I'm with my mom—but thank you so much for your support. It's sincerely so nice to see you!"

I start pushing my way through the crowd. Just when I'm wondering whether I should've brought security, Mom grabs hold of me and fearlessly strong-arms me away in a manner that screams *don't mess with the pop star's mother*.

We finally get free, rounding the corner. This street is no more vacant, the never-ending party spilling from the nightclubs. However, nobody in my immediate vicinity recognizes me—yet.

"Here." My mom pulls sunglasses from her purse.

I put them on gratefully despite the hour, then pull my hair out of my sweat-slick post-concert braid. "Thanks," I say. "Sorry.

I know dealing with crowds is . . . not normal mother-daughter stuff."

Mom laughs. "Honey, *no* part of this tour is normal for me. I mean, it's a Thursday night, and I'm walking around New Orleans after a rock concert. A year ago, I never would have imagined any of this."

The second the sentence is out of her mouth, her smile slips. I know what she's remembering, what she's realizing she just said. *Of course* she wouldn't have imagined this a year ago. A year ago, she was married to my dad, certain she was spending the rest of her life with her soul mate.

I don't believe in regrets, but I wonder if my mom does.

"I know it's not the year you expected," I say gently, "but I'm glad you're here."

When she smiles, she looks like she's fighting past something. "Me too."

We wander down the street without destination, Mom handing me the beignets she held while I was signing autographs. The liveliness of the city luminesces from every storefront and corner. Under the stately railings, the endless rows of signs scream out their names in vibrant light. Clubs, live stages, restaurants. Music is practically physical here, part of each crossbeam and doorway.

While I've spent plenty of nights in New Orleans, my mother's words seem to make the scenery new. In fact, neither of us could have imagined visiting the city like this.

Honestly, I'm not sure how to speak my feelings about my parents' divorce. For one, I haven't figured out how exactly I feel. Of course I cried when I hung up the phone after my dad gave me the news. I felt like I was holding the hand of something dead.

I wondered if their split was my fault, or something similar. If my fame, the way the edges of the spotlight reached even my once-normal family, had somehow contributed strain or scrutiny their marriage could not withstand. It wound up being one more worry, one more open file on the rare nights when fame frightens me, one more item on the list of places I can never again visit inconspicuously and former friends who've pressed me with manipulative agendas.

Even so, I respect my parents' individuality, their maturity, their freedom. I know they would not have made the decision unless in some way it was what they needed. I have my own life, my own home, my own relationships. They have theirs.

The whole pop-star paradigm makes knowing how to feel even harder. One misconception about me is that I didn't grow up pretty much just like everyone else. I lived in the same Midwestern suburban home where my parents do now, or did. I struggled with math in school. I loved soccer.

Instead, people unconsciously pretend my life started with my first charted single or my *Billboard* cover. Reporters and documentarians grab hold of the fragments of musicality in my childhood, the piano recitals, the high school performances—the start of the *story* of Riley Wynn—and forget the rest.

I kind of forget it myself sometimes. It scares and saddens me. I don't like the feeling of falling for the illusion, of following fans and critics into pretending I never existed outside the stage. It makes me want to hold on to the hurt of my family's wounded remains.

No matter how hard I cling, I still haven't wanted to get into it with either parent, or known how. When my mom helped me move, we only ever reached *her* feelings on the end of my parents' marriage, although in fairness she was the shoulder for *plenty* of my crying over my own failed marriage.

Another misconception about me is how narcissistic people say I am—they assume my musical preoccupation with my own feelings, my own relationships, means I'm uninterested in anyone else's. It does not require world-class sociology to understand why people assume it of me, a very famous, very wealthy young woman.

Nevertheless, it's flat-out fucking wrong. I've known my mom was having real difficulty with the divorce. Getting into my own more complicated feelings in the meantime has felt . . . I don't know. Unfair. Upside-down.

I will eventually. I know I will.

Just not yet. I have enough heartache of my own for now.

"You know, I moved around a lot as a kid," Mom says into my silence. "My dad was always relocating us for his work. I hated it. I decided, when I grew up, I wanted to put down strong roots in one city for the rest of my life."

The overture surprises me. My grandfather was in the Navy. While I never met him, I've heard stories of everywhere my mom lived, far-flung corners of the country captured in the changing locales of her old family photos. I did not know it was what inspired her to settle down so decisively at twenty-six, when she married my dad.

She bites into her beignet, the lights of New Orleans reflecting off her eyes. "But then my only daughter became a pop star and I got divorced," she continues. "It's funny. Not *ha-ha* funny, just . . . I guess I'm realizing just how easily my roots can be pulled up again."

I nod solemnly. My imagination can't quite grasp what she's

describing. Living in one place with the family she raised was everything for my mom. It was *her* dream.

What I'm doing now, this tour, is all I've wanted my whole life. If I lost it overnight . . . It's impossible to comprehend.

"You can put down new roots, Mom. You don't need Dad for that," I say. It feels simplistic even to suggest. Shallow. The idea of imparting wisdom to my *mom*—to either of my parents—seems outlandish. Still, I want to help.

"I know," she replies. "But . . . I'm not sure. Maybe I'm ready to want something new."

Something new. I find myself thinking of Max. Music was never his dream, not enough to sustain him. Now he's trying it on for new reasons, with new perspective, with more life in the rearview mirror. Maybe what you want in life *can* change. Maybe now he'll finally fall in love with music.

With—everything.

Like she's reading my mind, my mom eyes me inquisitively. "Why were you and Max so stiff tonight?" she asks.

I feel my shoulders slouch. The New Orleans clamor seems to press inward, chaotic now instead of cheerful. "Tell me it wasn't that bad," I plead.

"I'm sure only your mother noticed," she reassures me.

"He kissed me." Like all my favorite lyrics, the simple statement isn't really one sentence. It's hidden verse upon verse, questions I'm unable to face, inchoate feelings crashing into each other in the depths of me.

Nevertheless, it doesn't seem to surprise my mom. "*Mm-hmm*," she hums, fixing her gaze on the street corner we're approaching, where the peeling paint does nothing to diminish the facade's finery.

"Nothing to say?" I press. I doubt the humor in my voice hides how desperately I want her opinion. I need help with the Max question.

"Oh, I don't know," Mom replies.

I purse my lips impatiently. "Mom, just say what's on your mind. You think it was a mistake? Max and I did this once already. You think I should focus on myself after my divorce? Or Max is too unsure of what he wants to start something real? What?"

The look my mom gives me is searing.

"No," she says evenly. "That's what *you're* thinking. *I'm* thinking . . ."

I wait, hungry for clarity. The questions in my head grate like dissonant chords waiting for resolution.

"You wrote a whole album about heartbreak," my mom says.

"Yes?"

"Well." She pauses. "I'd like to hear a love song at some point."

SEVENTEEN

Max

SOFT STRUMMING IS the first sound I hear when the jostling of the bus wakes me up. I've slept fitfully on the long drive to Miami, roused by every deceleration on Florida's turnpike.

The gentle progression Riley is playing on her guitar drifts inconspicuously in past my closed curtain. I consider just lying here, letting the sound lullaby me to sleep.

What stops me is the conviction I won't be going back to sleep. I wish I could curse the highways for my restlessness, I really do. Instead, the truth is I haven't slept well since my kiss with Riley. Fever dreams of her mouth on mine, forming love songs without lyrics, have woken me countless times in the past couple nights. Now is no different.

I have the same dreams in my waking hours. Whenever we play "Until You," in rehearsal or onstage, I remember how my lips against hers silenced our song. It's left me hopelessly distracted. The first night in New Orleans, I almost missed my intro. The second, I almost skipped the bridge in the song. Every time we reach *you say you'll see me soon*, my heart pounds, the miserable metronome I wish I could ignore. I'm going to mess up one of these nights.

Riley won't. Watching her, there's no escaping the fact that she's entirely unaffected. While she isn't singing "Until You" with the same emotion she gives the rest of her set, I'm pretty sure it's not because of the kiss. Instead, it's like she can't muster the feeling she used to.

I reposition in my bunk, wretchedly hoping the emptiness in the window will help me convince myself I'm elsewhere.

Until I hear Riley's voice join in with her guitar, soft and scratchy. She sounds curious, like she's discovering the song herself.

I stop tossing and turning. I listen.

Her voice comes through the darkness, wrapping around me like my sheets. *"I walk Heartbreak Road, feel your hand in mine on Heartbreak Road. Traveling for ten years."* Every word is pained, reaching out for ungraspable hopes. I've never heard the lyrics before. She's writing something new.

In the hush of the night, pervaded only by Riley's music, my body isn't my own. I find myself getting out of my bunk, the music compelling me, the song rendering me sleepless. My reverse lullaby. Her siren's whisper pulls me into the living space like a sailor dragged to the depths of the sea.

Riley sits in the dark, guitar on her knees. She's hunched over the instrument, writing something down on a pad of paper. "Heartbreak Road," reads the underlined title over what I recognize instantly to be handwritten lyrics. I have visions of dorm rooms, of hasty penmanship on napkins. It's startling to find out Riley writing songs looks *exactly* like I remember. No matter how large the stages get, the music starts here.

Before she starts strumming again, she tucks her pencil behind her ear. Her voice is fragile when she sings, even wary. "*I walk Heartbreak Road, feel your hand in mine on Heartbreak Road. Traveling for ten years on Heartbreak Road. Kissing you is fine on Heartbreak Road, leading us to nowhere.*"

In the entryway, I feel ripped in half. Pieces of her lyrics snag in my head. I'm under the point of her pencil, I realize. Part of me is uncomfortable finding she's already using me for songwriting material—again.

However, it's her story as much as it is mine. I chose to kiss her. I can't ask her not to lyricize her own life, especially not when I knew she likely would. If I end up her malcontent muse, it's my own fault.

"Another breakup song?" I ask.

Riley looks up, noticing me for the first time. The inspiration in her eyes shifts into the flicker of a challenge.

"Should it be something else?" she replies.

The question is precarious. I don't know how to answer, so I don't.

Riley watches me in the dark, waiting. When she realizes I'm not going to reply, she sighs, her stare drifting into open space. "Honestly," she says, "I think I'm only good for breakup songs."

"That's not true." I reply without hesitating. In fact, words have not often found me quicker. The need in me for Riley to understand this is fierce. I walk farther into the room, the moonlight cutting a line between us.

Riley drops her gaze. She starts strumming again, like it's the only response she's capable of giving. While we fly quietly forward on the highway, I'm stuck, suspended, struggling with what to say. I want to apologize for kissing her, for making her hurt enough to write *another* breakup song about me. I wouldn't undo our kiss even if I could. Not the fever dreams, not the fraught performances. None of it.

Not when, as I'm starting to realize, it meant something to her just like it did to me. *She kissed me back.* Now she's writing every hope, every fear, every question it left her into song. Despite how cool she's played it over the past couple days, from her disaffected performances to her casual friendliness in rehearsals . . . I'm not the only one up past midnight remembering the kiss.

It wasn't nothing.

Not to her, not to me.

I just don't know what it could be yet. While possibilities drift past my grasp, I can't help forming chords with my fingers on the countertop in time with Riley's strumming.

She notices. "Thoughts? On the music, that is. Although I would welcome any other insights you feel like sharing," she says, continuing in her gentle completion of each chord.

I drop my hands to my sides, thinking. Eagerly, I grasp on to the first part of her question. While kissing Riley might be the defining mystery of my life, music theory I can manage. "Try inverting the D minor," I suggest. "It'll make the 'kissing you is fine' sound uncertain."

If Riley finds secret meaning nestled in my recommendation, she doesn't react. She nods, completely immersed in the creative process. "*Kissing you is fine on Heartbreak Road,*" she repeats with the new chord progression. The spark in her eyes shows me she likes the change. It's quietly thrilling.

In what feels like invitation, she shifts the progression. Her vocal melody changes into what must be the verse. "*Holding out hope or knowing what we know,*" she sings softly. "*Retracing our steps or never letting go—*"

She stops. With the quickness of inspiration, she picks up her pencil, one nimble hand still on her guitar's neck. Efficiently she erases *or never* on her pad, then scratches in new lyrics.

"*Retracing our steps until we're letting go,*" she continues.

I watch her, feeling reverent. Riley's poetry is my favorite part of her songwriting, her not-so-secret weapon. Sharp, emotional, clever. Listening to her draft "Heartbreak Road" feels like watching collisions of elements form a star. While some of it is unfinished, much of it is there. Riley plays through until, unceremoniously, she strums the final chord.

Slowly she looks up, her eyes finding mine. She wants my opinion.

Instead, what comes out of me is the question never far from my mind when I'm listening to her. "How do you do it?" I ask. "How do you put your deepest, most personal feelings into a song?"

In the low light, Riley's face is hard to read. I expect it would be the same in full sun. "I have to. Where else would I put them? Writing can feel like cutting out my own heart, but sometimes cutting out my heart is the only way to stop the hurt," she says calmly, like she's repeating some secret prayer or wisdom.

Without waiting for my reply, she restarts the song. This time, her voice is steadier, her expression more settled. Her chords come together like friends instead of strangers meeting for the first time.

Watching her, I realize I'm envisioning Riley elsewhere. Instead of the road rushing under us in the darkened tour bus, in this vision I have, she's in empty rooms of her house, wrestling with pain she doesn't know how to exorcise. Memories of . . . me. She picks up her notepad. In my imagination, she moves to the piano, searching for solace.

I hear the question in my head. *What if writing "Until You" looked like this? What if I wasn't forgotten feelings handily converted into radio gold?*

What if she wrote our song to get over us?

The idea hurts. Some deep, sad part of Riley, staring into the impenetrable dark of the past, wondering what went wrong. Needing to put the feelings into song even so many years later.

Maybe the hurt I feel isn't just sympathy. No, because I'm not just imagining what Riley's going through.

I know *exactly* how she feels.

Every day. Even now.

Watching "Heartbreak Road" emerge with confessional honesty has unlocked in me some piece of myself I forgot I was holding on to. Some part of me, some days small, some days heavy enough to drag me down like concrete, has missed Riley since the day our relationship ended.

It screams in me now, demanding to be felt.

I watch her play, hands moving over her guitar. The serenity on her face looks hard-won, her hair framing her cheeks the color of mercury in the moonlight. Futility is part of the pain in my chest—I know I can't kiss her again. No matter how much I want to.

Not when she's in front of me, writing a song about walking the same road to heartbreak. I won't force her down it now.

"*Kissing you is fine on Heartbreak Road, leading us to nowhere,*" she continues.

She pauses, reaching the unfinished part of the song. The

faraway look in her eyes is the picture of imagination, until something hits her. She plays the next chord and finishes the line like she's pulling something out of herself.

"*Lights go green and even with you,*" she sings, "*same old road leading nowhere new.*"

"What about—"

Riley's head lifts in surprise hearing my voice, hunger in her eyes. I know it's not only for creative collaboration.

"Lights go green, and maybe with you," I say softly, slightly revising the line's ending, "same old road can lead somewhere new."

Riley's hands don't move. Her guitar sits in her lap, silenced. The pause is charged. Speaking my heart in lyrics feels like nothing I've ever experienced. Like flying on wings of hope.

There's no way Riley could misunderstand the meaning of my changes. While my sixteen-syllable letter to her is no declaration of love, it says *maybe*. I'm not even sure if the maybe I'm proposing is possible. I just know I want it to be.

She doesn't reach for her pencil. Something indecipherable flits over her features.

"I have to write the truth, Max," she says.

"Feelings are the truth," I reply, the pounding of my heart putting force into my words. Right now, a couple lines of lyrics have become the center of my world. I continue, mustering courage. "It's . . . how I feel, anyway," I say.

She studies me for a long moment.

When she returns her hands to the song's opening chord on her guitar, she's smiling faintly. She starts the song.

She follows its now-familiar pathways, leaving me waiting, no longer feeling like I'm flying. I'm suspended in midair, wondering whether I'll plummet or soar. In the dark confines of the room, Riley plays the chorus. Then starts the next verse. Then finally—

"*Lights go green, and maybe with you,*" she sings, "*same old road can lead somewhere new.*"

EIGHTEEN

Riley

IT FINALLY HAPPENS when we're leaving Miami.

Something is shifting between Max and me while we're on-stage. It started with our midnight writing session for "Heart-break Road," which hasn't left my head once in the days since. While we only spoke about our kiss in a song, I've felt the wall we've built up over ten years starting to crumble.

I notice it in small differences. Moments our eyes lock on-stage. The real, furtive flash of a smile he gives me heading into the first chorus of "Until You" with the southern humidity sur-rounding us. Over the past couple shows, we've started playing *to* each other instead of *with* each other. The crowd loses it every time.

Until finally, it happens. After our show in Miami, I'm doing my cursory scroll of social media mentions when the frame of one video catches my eye. It's not from the concert—or, not from this concert.

It's me and Max from college. One of our first open-mic nights. We're playing "Can't Help Falling in Love." While café patrons watch politely, I look like I feel like the luckiest girl in the world. Which I did.

The speculation spirals. Max is identified, then our college history unearthed. It isn't long until the entire internet knows we were involved romantically. We consume the social media sphere. Every gossip site, every celebrity news TikTok is captivated. *Riley Wynn reuniting onstage with her college boyfriend.*

The link to "Until You" is easy. In just hours everyone figures out the song is about Max. The next morning, Max, with hair mussed, holds up his phone, showing me headlines with his name in them while he says reporters have started reaching out to Harcourt Homes to ask if we're back together.

We work out our media strategy over cereal in the kitchenette. Larissa and the publicists are on speaker on my iPhone, in full planning mode. What we'll say, what we won't. *Riley Wynn and Max Harcourt dated in the past. They're delighted to reunite for the Breakup Tour.*

The press isn't entirely positive. Internet searches of my name promptly yield new rankings of my exes, which I can't help finding unpleasant despite the lists playing into the album's concept exactly. I don't click on them.

I hope Max doesn't, either. Chatter on social lets me know plenty of people still love Wesley—of fucking course, it's what he does—and consider Max "in the way." I don't. It's the opposite, if anything. I desperately hope he understands I hold nothing in my heart for the man who so deliberately poisoned it.

Like I've found over the past few months of *The Breakup Record*'s success, I can only engage with the publicity so much. My story spirals into others', interacting with their own stories, their own feelings, warping out of my control into something I know is no longer only mine anymore. I couldn't control it even if I wanted to.

While I reserve no frustration for most of the public spectators, whose discussion of me and my personal life is exactly what I've signed up for, I grow more irritated every day with how uncooperative my label is with foregrounding Max and "Until You." The mentions and suggestions of promos with Wesley don't stop.

I figure it out on one long drive of publicity emails—*of course* they want to deflect focus from my unfamous ex to the internet-loved, dangerously provocative star who holds plenty of headlines and millions of followers on his own.

They'll get no help from me, I decide. What I *can* do is keep singing *my* story. Keep living the story *I* want. If my label doesn't like it, they're going to have to cancel my tour.

I know the entire process is hard on Max. His discomfort with instant fame, his hesitation in discussing his romantic history with label executives on speakerphone is easy to read. In his round, wire-framed glasses, his eyes have the look of prey in unfamiliar wilderness. He fusses with his sleeves once every five seconds, sometimes more. But despite his unease, he's mentioned how much the media hype is drawing publicity to Harcourt Homes.

Still, with a couple long drives ahead of us, I know the constant clamor of notifications on his phone is going to overwhelm him like, frankly, it overwhelms me.

Max *isn't* me. He's a private guy, one for long phone calls instead of social media posts, for nights in with favorite records instead of music-festival weekends. I want to show him social media and fame won't eclipse the rest of his life. He decides his story, not the other way around.

One lesson I've learned this year is how much the public eye *doesn't* perceive. How many private fights or fears. How many moments of giddy fun, of surprises, of hidden joys. They've helped me remember I'm not *just* the Riley Wynn of the headlines.

Max needs to feel hidden joys of his own.

With the long drive from Atlanta to Houston coming up, I get an idea for how I'll help him over the many miles. Deep down, I know maybe it's not only for him, either. I need a reminder of how I'm not just a paper doll. I'm not just their Riley to spin into whatever story they want.

I gather everyone onto our bus—the whole band, my mom, and Eileen. We cram in, window to window. The booth is full. People perch on the counters or sit on the floor when there isn't room elsewhere. It feels like the close quarters of the studio where I recorded my very first demo, except with even less space.

While highway signs pass us outside, I pull Max into the bunk corridor.

"I want to play a game today," I say nonchalantly. "I need your help, though."

He eyes me warily. He looks, I've noticed, less sleep-deprived these days. "What do I have to do?" The patience in his voice is playful.

"How do you feel about a fashion show?" I ask.

Confusion flits over his features like it's having fun. "Riley, I'm sure you could walk, like, an actual runway instead of the aisle of a moving bus."

I shake my head, very much enjoying myself. "Not me," I say. "You."

His eyebrows rise. He leans forward, drawing millimeters off the space separating us. "You're joking." He states his question. "You want me to show off my rotation of seven button-downs? I'm pretty sure the band has seen them already."

"I have something else in mind. It'll be fun, I promise," I reply. I meet his eyes, smiling hopefully. It's not the smile I give execs when I want them to pay for more studio time, or the one I give Eileen when I'm going to pester her for one more rehearsal. It feels sweeter, shyer. Less often used, yet somehow more myself.

The skepticism fades in Max's expression, the way the wind carries fog from cloudy streets. "Okay," he says easily, like he can't resist or he doesn't want to. Like we both want to put our heartbreak away just for a little while.

"Great." I grab his hand to pull him into the living space. The second skin meets skin, I remember how he doesn't want the band to think we're together. "Sorry," I say, releasing him hastily. "I didn't mean—"

"It's okay," he interjects, something melodic in his quiet reassurance. "I don't mind."

I don't mind. I know my heart is hungry when it hears whole love songs in simple words like Max's.

"Right," I reply.

We stand in the hallway, suddenly awkward, until Vanessa calls out. "I was promised entertainment!" our drummer reminds us.

Max holds his arm out, gesturing for me to lead the way. I do, then nearly stumble when the bus changes lanes. Reminding myself I'm a literal rock star who walks stages in heels every night, I recover my stride. I can't get weak in the knees now.

When we reach the living space, every pair of eyes finds us. It is *hot* in here, the result of the population density, with no help from the Southern sun coming through the windows over the open highway. The air conditioning is no match.

"Thank you for coming to Tour Bus A today," I say to the group. "We have a very important task ahead of us! Our own Max Harcourt is recently famous."

I pause while people whistle and applaud him. Max looks bashful, but not entirely uncomfortable.

"On our drive to Houston," I go on dramatically, "we will be updating his stage wardrobe accordingly. We need to find his very own rock god look."

Max laughs in surprise. "No offense, but you're likelier to win fifty Grammys than pull this off."

"I *will* win fifty Grammys," I inform him. With a flourish, I usher him through the hallway and into the back bedroom. "In," I order him while the bus cheers.

Following him, I find everything exactly the way I planned. Shopping bags sit full on the bed. I provided the page with detailed instructions of everything to procure before our departure time this morning. Unable to help myself, I study his reaction intently. He doesn't look daunted, only intrigued.

"Wow. You really planned everything out. Okay," he says, "where do I start?" He takes off his glasses, ready to get into it.

Before I can turn my back to him, he's pulling his shirt over his head.

I halt, stunned into staring. I don't regret the way my eyes linger. While I've spent nights with leading men who devote hours daily in the gym perfecting their physiques, Max's chest is . . . lyrical. It's *him*, understated yet impossible to ignore. His stomach muscles look somehow like guitar frets, the outline of his ribs like piano keys. I want to put my fingers on them to find out what melody comes forth.

He catches me looking. His quiet pride changes quickly into concern. "Shirtless isn't one of my wardrobe options, right?" he asks, holding his shirt in one hand protectively.

I find myself flushing. "Don't be ridiculous," I say, fighting to formulate the single sentence. Needing to remove myself from the rush of feelings I'm caught in, I toss him the bag labeled *Emo*, then leave the room.

Out in the hallway, heat prickles the back of my neck. It has nothing to do with the warm stretches of Georgia flying past us outside.

I head into the living space to join the band, ignoring the knowing glance my mom gives me. Instead, I focus on making myself inconspicuous among the small but cramped audience. I manage to find open space on the floor in front of the coffee maker next to Kev, who's reorganizing his Spotify playlists on his phone. I notice heart emojis in the title of the one he's working on.

He runs calloused fingers contemplatively over his goatee. He glances up, my presence distracting him momentarily. "Favorite love song," he says out of nowhere. He speaks slowly, something calm in his low voice.

I don't follow. "What?"

"*Your* favorite love song," he clarifies. "I have one of those collaborative playlists going with my wife. Home in Carlsbad. Listening to each other's choices helps us feel, you know, connected." I nod. "I need your favorite love song," he continues. "Pronto."

I say what comes instantly to mind, not knowing if I'm just remembering the video fans found of me and Max from college, or if it would be my choice if I weren't.

"'Can't Help Falling in Love,'" I say softly.

In silent endorsement, Kev adds the song while I retreat into my heart. *Max's and my old songs on my lips. Our kiss in New Orleans. "Unchained Melody." Midnight writing sessions. Me blushing when I see him shirtless, for fuck's sake.*

If I'm not careful, I'll find myself halfway down Heartbreak Road with no direction home.

I'm shaken out of my introspection when everyone hoots. Max is coming down the "catwalk" dressed in the look I designed. Everything is obsidian black, obviously. His T-shirt, his cut-off shorts, his high-top vans, his metal-studded belt. I was going for My Chemical Romance reunion meets Nine Inch Nails. It's perfect.

It's very not Max, of course. Still, he has fun with it, gazing over us with jaded eyes and sweeping his hair conspicuously from his forehead with one hand. I laugh, delighted. It's deeply gratifying watching him get into the game. This whole experience is meant to help him try something different—so why not fashion?

I hop up from where I'm seated. "Okay," I call out over the noise of the crowd. "Who votes yes?"

Everyone votes no, and Max looks relieved. When he retreats

into the bedroom to change into his next look, I fight how my daydreams want to pull me in there with him.

He returns in the indie-pop style I chose, pastel corduroy paired with a patterned button-down. The garb of college-radio hipsters who dabble in elegant synthesizers. The outfit garners some yeses. We proceed to grunge revival—ripped jeans with the heaviest leather jacket the page could find—then classic rock stardom's combo of a vest and leather pants.

The voting is evenly split for each, everyone wanting to see what Max will strut out in next.

He finally comes out in the '50s Rat Pack–esque look I contrived. It's over-the-top, whimsically formal, but it complements him immediately. It's like how every great song feels meant for the singer's voice. While Max's outfit isn't the obvious choice, it works because it reflects him. Harcourt Homes onstage.

I feel the flush in my neck spread. He doesn't just look like himself. He looks *good*. The lapels, the ebony-on-ivory colors, the way the cut of the suit makes him seem to smirk without moving his lips. It's profoundly handsome.

It isn't *exactly* right, though. While the group laughs as he grandly tips his cap to my mom, I stand up again. Stepping closer, I hear the chorus of my pulse in my ears, refusing to let up.

In front of Max, I reach for his bow tie. "May I?"

He nods, maybe a little breathless.

I take his hat. When I remove his jacket, we're pulled even closer. His chest rising and falling is its own tempo, coming in and out of synchrony with mine. With unsteady fingers, I loosen his bow tie, leaving it draped around his neck, then undo his collar button.

Under my ministrations, Max is silent.

"One more thing," I say over my own uneven breathing.

I slide past him down the hallway into the bedroom, where I grab his glasses from the vanity. Returning to the living space, I put them on him, positioning them just right on the features I know devastatingly well. His expression looks poised, like he refuses to move under the careful presence of my hands.

When I finish, I can barely face him.

I spin him quickly to face the group. How is standing with Max now shaking my composure like performing on late-night shows couldn't? With one more precisely placed glance from him, my feet would go right out from under me. I plaster pride onto my face in hopes of hiding everything colliding in my heart.

Hamid is the first to react. "Hot damn," he declares.

Everyone joins in enthusiastically. The whole rhythm section joins the slow clap Savannah starts. Eileen looks impressed. Vanessa whistles.

"Oh my," my mother remarks.

"Sign me up for Harcourt Homes!" Vanessa calls out. The shy smile stealing over Max's face pulls hidden strings in me. I step around him, discreetly finding my seat again next to Kev.

Our audience is right. Max is . . . sexy. Sinatra, the morning after. Old-school swagger exudes from his new look, changing him from shy pianist into rakishly weary musical raconteur.

It's charming how readily he embraces the character. Of course, everyone votes yes for his new look. Soon, he's posing for pictures with the band and examining his reflection in the windows.

The entire time, I work the hardest I've ever worked in my life *not* to be noticed.

I don't want to meet the green opal of Max's gaze. I don't want to feel the hooks in me of standing close to him. I don't want to hear the complicated melodies of questions his presence murmurs to me.

For the first time outside of singing a song about the love we used to share, I find I have to look away from Max. I can't risk doing otherwise. If he catches my eye—if he smiles—I'm afraid for my heart.

NINETEEN

Max

WHEN WE ARRIVE in Houston, there's already a crowd of fans waiting for Riley outside. The moment she exits the bus, she steps easily into fame, signing autographs for fans with genuine smiles despite the long drive and the fact that we're heading to sound check soon. She's had no time to herself. Right now, she looks like she doesn't need it.

I linger near the bus, wanting to stretch my legs on solid ground. The evening is welcomingly warm, not as sticky as Florida. Looking over the spacious landscape of skyscrapers rising from the dirt, I find myself starting to dread entering the stadium. I expect its mazelike corridors will feel claustrophobic like the others have.

I'm distracted when I hear someone in the crowd call my name.

Instinctively I want to avoid the summons, figuring it's one of Riley's fans hoping to extract information from me, her rumored love interest. The idea exhausts me the way the prospect of darkened stage wings does.

Then I hear my name again. *Maxwell*, not *Max*.

I face the line of fans and find one woman's eyes fixed on me. She's about my age, maybe a little younger. While we've never met, I recognize her. Hers is the face I've seen in photographs on an overstuffed dresser.

"Delia?" I say.

The woman grins widely. Despite my weariness, I can't help returning the smile. Linda's granddaughter looks just like her, right down to the gap in her front teeth. When I walk up, she leans over the metal railing, excitement lighting up her sharp features.

"I'm so glad I caught you," she says. "My grandma got me tickets for my birthday and insisted I get a photo with you."

I want to do what Riley does. Draw on some hidden reserve of perfect poise. Snap the perfect selfie. Instead, I don't move, my heart clenching hard in my chest.

It's startling how fast homesickness hits me. I don't even know Delia outside Linda's stories. She's the smallest, flimsiest fragment of home. Still, with the mere mention of my favorite Harcourt Homes resident, the fragment pierces me through.

"Of course, let's take that photo," I say earnestly. While I have to force the cheer in my voice, I'm genuinely glad to oblige. "How is Linda?" I ask once Delia's gotten the photo.

"She's good. She told me not to talk about her to you, though, because you have way more exciting things going on," Delia replies. I notice more of Linda in the wry mischief in her granddaughter's smile. "She also asked me to pry for personal information, which I'm not going to do since I don't know you that well."

I laugh, my shoulders loosening slightly. "Thanks for that. Say hi for me, if it won't get you in trouble."

"I will even if it does," she says. "Hey, um, if it's not too much to ask . . ." Her eyes wander from me over to Riley, who is facing the wall of cameras like they're old friends.

I smile graciously. "I'll get Riley. Hold on."

I walk the length of the metal barricade over to her, not used to the way onlookers' eyes follow me. When I reach her, she glances up, Sharpie in hand with the inky point positioned over the concert poster she's signing.

The pre-show promise of the night is glowing right under her skin. She looks like I've caught her in the middle of doing her favorite thing in the world.

"Hey!" she says. "You ready for your wardrobe reveal tonight?"

"Are *you*?" I ask. "Hey, maybe I'll move up to second or third place in the official rankings of your exes."

While Riley rolls her eyes playfully, I catch discomfort in her frown, which I didn't intend. Honestly, I don't love the unflattering listicles. Still, I know they're not her fault.

"Don't read those stories," she counsels me seriously. "And come on," she adds. "You know you're number one. Easy."

My heart races in the way only she can provoke.

"If you don't mind," I reply, probably not hiding how I feel like I'm flying, "one of my residents' granddaughters is over there in the yellow dress wanting to meet you."

Riley searches the line until her electric eyes find Delia. She waves. "On it," she says to me while she collects more CDs and vinyl records from people who want them signed.

I step back, not wanting to deprive them of the precious few seconds they have to tell her how much her music means to them. Sweat is starting to stick my hair to my forehead in the heat. Withdrawing from the crowd, I retreat to the side of the bus, where I find Frank on the steps, finishing a sandwich.

Wanting the moment to myself, I return my eyes to Houston. Low freeways pass over endless streets. The setting sun reflects ruthlessly from the skyscrapers' mirrored sides. I'm struck by the overwhelming scale of the emotionless landscape. I won't *know* this place. It'll just be one more hurried swipe on the slideshow life I'm living.

Deep down, it exhausts me. The cities we visit feel like the fans we meet—whole personalities we'll never know, full of life we'll never really understand when they're whisked past us by the rigors of the tour timing. Houston is no different. Another night, another unfamiliar city.

Quietly, I start to indulge in memory, guiltily immersing myself somewhere else. The mere mention of Linda has me conjuring up Harcourt Homes' dining room, the familiar smell of cooking. The chatter of residents I love like they're family, the carpet under my feet. The way the keys of my favorite piano move under my fingers.

I don't need Riley's lyrical gifts to describe this feeling. I miss my home desperately. I'm deadlocked in the middle of the tour. I haven't felt the comforts of home for seven weeks. I won't return to them for eight more.

I'm not leaving early, though. Home will be there, in one form or other. Whereas Riley will move on to new music, new people, new cities. In songwriting terms, I feel sometimes like I'm one note played endlessly. Riley is whole set lists end to end, never ceasing, ever evolving.

"That's a unique one there."

Frank's raspy voice startles me. I look down, finding him studying me, having clearly seen me staring at Riley.

"Of course she is," I reply. It feels strangely like the easiest thing in the world to say. "It's why she's Riley Wynn."

Frank crumples his sandwich wrapper, shaking his head. "Nah, I don't mean like that, although she is. I mean she's unique because she's one of the few musicians I've ever met who doesn't get homesick."

I furrow my brow, Frank's perceptiveness surprising me.

He smiles, leaving me with the impression I'm not the first musician with whom he's started this conversation. "I can read homesickness on someone like I can hear whether they're using Zildjian or Sabian on the cymbals."

His words hold no judgment or doubt. I nod, the only response I can find.

"Some of the biggest rock stars in the world feel homesick," he remarks. "While they're living their dream, they're worried about what they're missing at home. Then they're frustrated because they're worrying instead of living their dream, especially since they know how fast those dreams can dry up."

The wind passes over me while I weigh his words. I'm . . . relieved. It's comforting to know homesickness doesn't mean I'm not cut out for this life. Because I *want* to want it. I want to want it for Riley.

I learned one lesson with certainty from our past—she could never want someone who can't reflect her dream back to her, who's unable to chase the lightning she craves. When I didn't join her on the tour we planned together, she left no possibility of us staying together. No discussion. We were just over.

It's left me certain Riley will only want me if I join her on this endless journey, this road where the only destination is her wildest hopes. If what Frank is saying is true, I still can. If dreams like these might fit me despite my longing for home, then kissing Riley doesn't need to lead to nowhere.

I feel a rush of gratitude for Frank's impeccably placed kind words. As I'm about to thank him, Carrie comes up to us. "You still want to see the show tonight, right?" she says to Frank.

Every hint of our conversation flees from Frank's features. He stands quickly, straightening his shirt. "I'm ready when you are."

"Let me just change, and we can catch sound check," Carrie says. When she heads up the steps, she and Frank do the halting dance of figuring out which side he's going to step to let her pass.

Frank waits, watching her continue inside. When she's out of earshot, his eyes return to me. "Quick question. Carrie and Riley's dad . . ." He trails off.

I can't help grinning. "Divorced," I say, hoping that with the information I'm returning the favor of his encouragement.

He nods a few times, pumping himself up. I clap him heartily on the shoulder.

In the past few minutes, Riley has left the line of fans. With new lightness dispelling the dread in my chest, I head for the stadium. From where we've parked, I find my way to the performers' entrance, the geometry of places like this intuitive to me now. Each stadium is like the set list we play every night—different, yet the same. Inside, the usual corridors of overhead electric lighting greet me.

I go through the familiar motions. Checking my mics, heading to the stage to play the piano before sound check, showering in the bathrooms. Despite the shower's dimensions, the steam is nice. I don't mind my routine, not tonight. I feel . . . competent. Experienced. More like the fleet-footed musicians I first met in New York, less like Harcourt Homes' dining-room regular.

When I get out of the shower, I change into the clothes unanimously decided upon during this morning's surprisingly fun drive. My favorite part of the ensemble isn't the rakish bow tie or the whole lounge-pianist vibe. It's the memory of Riley, inches from me, placing my glasses on my face with her nimble fingers.

I head to the greenroom, pleased with how it came together.

The cocky smile on my lips dies the moment I see Riley.

She's . . . entirely changed. Sitting at the edge of a seat with her headphones on, she stares straight forward, her eyes fixed on the wall.

I've rarely ever seen her this way. Stressed, withdrawn, wrecked instead of energized before the show. She usually looks like lightning. Right now, she looks like the scorch mark where lightning once struck.

I head toward Vanessa, who's standing near the table where the items on Riley's rider sit untouched. She's watching Riley, worried.

"What happened?" I ask under my breath.

"There were flowers waiting for her," Vanessa replies, fury flashing in the depths of her eyes. "From . . . that actor. I guess he heard the speculation that 'Until You' isn't about him." I'm grateful she doesn't pry into or imply who obviously *is* the subject of the song.

My eyes return to Riley, my stomach winding into knots.

I don't know what to do. Of course I want to help. Of course I have no idea how. I've never even met the Riley in front of me, the nervous, shattered statue. How do flowers from Wesley Jameson have her this shaken?

The reason hits me hard. *She's not over him.*

Instantly I feel ridiculous for assuming she was. She just got out of a relationship—a *marriage*—with him. If her love for me left her with the pain she put into every syllable of "Until You" a decade later, of course her recently ended marriage hasn't yet vanished from her heart.

I feel childish for forgetting it, not to mention for the jealousy pounding in me. It's weird in some of the same ways playing in Madison Square Garden was. I mean, I know who Jameson is from entertainment news headlines when he does something charming, from the auto-play scroll on Netflix—from Jess liking his fucking Instagram posts.

It's surreal. While I hold Riley in my heart, the man closest to hers is . . . the internet's boyfriend.

With minutes until sound check, with Riley sitting vacant on the leather couch in front of me, I embrace the harsh reminder. I needed it.

I may have inspired Riley's greatest song, but I'm not her greatest love.

TWENTY

Riley

WILL YOU LIVE forever with me, Riley?

I have only minutes until I need to leave the dressing room. I spend them with headphones on, listening to "Homemade Rollercoaster," desperately hoping I can use my own words to drown out the roar in my head. It works for my fans, I know it does. I've seen the TikToks saying I help them escape their self-doubting whispers or their parents fighting or the ugly words of their exes.

Why can't I work on myself the same way?

Will you live forever with me, Riley?

While they came with no note, Wesley's flowers have left plenty of his words ringing in my ears. I hate him for them. I want to forget him as much as I regret him.

In the dressing room, I wonder if I ever will. In the midst of everything, the tour, the recognition for *The Breakup Record*, the photoshoots—*Max*—I've pretended I couldn't feel him. His memory. The shadow of my greatest mistake has caught up with me now.

It's easy to say I was young. I didn't know what I was doing. I was wild. I was impetuous. I didn't know fast love was different from real love. Or I was chasing fame, glitter-eyed, in love with the idea of the imposing movie star loving me.

I've heard every version. Cheap commentary cover songs explaining my doomed love story on the endless jukebox of public opinion.

None of it is right. I fell for my ex-husband for one reason I won't ever disavow, despite hating the consequences.

He is like me. In desirable, destructive ways, I saw myself in him. I saw it when we first met, some magazine party the January before last with iPads in the gift bags. He was famous, with enough movies to his name for his dark magic to demand recognition. I was newly famous, notable singles making me "one to watch," "on the rise," "on the verge," or whatever phrase each publication or podcast wanted to drop. The lights of the rooftop party glittered in our eyes. When my publicist introduced us, he kissed my hand.

The gesture was like him, I would come to learn. Overdramatic, except not. He has uncanny finesse for flourishes other men's execution would make outlandishly overdone. Yet for him, they . . . work. The effect intrigued me in ways the formalistic flattery of the kiss did not. I understood, in the moment, how his cool star could continue to rise.

We exchanged numbers. Over the next months, I discovered his disarming other side. In texting, he wasn't just informal or conversational. He was . . . chatty, effusive, even goofy. He sent me *memes*. We didn't get together much due to his demanding international shooting schedule for *Reckoning*, yet I felt like we knew each other deeply when we met up in Paris for Fashion Week in March.

Instead of scheduled events, we returned to his hotel room. We had hours of sex. His penthouse opened onto the hotel rooftop, where I joined him, overlooking—what else?—the Eiffel fucking Tower. Once more, it was ridiculous, eye-rolling in its romanticism. It was *him*.

I was swept up. He was thirty-eight, I was twenty-nine. I could hardly comprehend my life carrying me here.

In the Paris night, he strode to the railing with imperial possession. When he started speaking, he couldn't stop. He shared everything with me, how he felt like reaching long-held dreams only made him want more. He wanted *everything*. He wanted me.

I watched him, enraptured. The love in my chest felt like my own dreams did. Dangerous enough to demand I give them everything. He said he no longer just wanted fame or prestige. He wanted his work to live forever.

His monologue unceasing, he faced me. He swept over, the hurricane of a man he is. With my hands in his, he said he wanted me in his life for real. No more DM flirting. He wanted to date me. He wanted to love me. I'll never forget his exact words. They repeat in my head now, the horrible refrain the flowers in front of me wrench up.

Will you live forever with me, Riley?

I said I would. In the lyrical workings of my mind, I found myself marveling, loving his phrasing, understanding exactly how he'd managed to convert overdone poeticism into undeniable charm. Part of it is swagger. Part of it is intelligence. He's read hundreds of scripts. He's reinvented Shakespeare on London stages. He intended the question within the question. *Live forever*. Immortalize ourselves. *Live forever with me*. Entwine your life with mine.

Will you live forever with me, Riley?

He'd finished important scenes for the *Reckoning* pilot. It was HBO's new darling, which I knew made him happy. Fuck, it made *me* happy. Not just for him, either. I was starting to understand the stratospheric feeling of creative promise. I remember the loneliness of my new heights, however joyful. I remember feeling how fucking cool it was I found someone who could sing in the same chords of perilous promise and limitless hope. In him I felt I'd found the mirror of myself.

I didn't notice how he never wanted to hear my same effusiveness when label meetings went well, or I booked my first stadium, or the cover story pitches started coming in, until I did. Then I noticed every day. I hid the glimpses from myself, pretended with my damn optimism not to care if this magnetic man didn't want to know my career was soaring. I spent our fraught months waiting for him to feel lucky the way I did, waking up every day delighted to have found the mirror image of my own relentless joy.

Except he didn't want a mirror image. He wanted a *mirror*. He didn't want me to match his stardom, his stature, his legend. He wanted me to *reflect* it, so his showed larger.

Will you live forever with me, Riley?

Eventually his lack of praise changed into discouragement. Opportunities dismissed, recognitions downplayed. His dismissals hurt like the dull roar of online criticism never could, subtle knives instead of psychological steamrollers. Of course we were over in months.

I refuse to regret what I learned from our relationship. Seeking out someone exactly like you isn't love. It's narcissism. Someone can live like you, speak like you, strive like you, without *loving* you. Without caring for you. Our marriage was like playing the notes right next to each other on the piano. They don't harmonize. They conflict. Their complements wait elsewhere. Not close, yet compatible.

It's why he's interrupting me now, why he's grabbing onto "Until You." I know he has nothing to offer me in the way of the companionship I've yearned for deep down.

Wesley, however, knows I *could* give him what he wants. He knows how dazzlingly I could shine my spotlight on him. The fact that I'm not makes him furious. He's determined to steal from me like he's convinced I've stolen from him.

It makes him want to exploit my song. It makes him want to upset me in every way he can.

Including the flowers. Their mocking faces peer into mine from next to the mirror. They're white, with long, lip-like petals. I don't know what kind.

It doesn't fucking matter. They're not the point.

It's the *echo*. He sent me flowers the day I returned home from Paris.

Sending them now wasn't out of kindness or a desire to win me back. It was a reminder. He knows how to speak in metaphors and images the same way I do, and he's weaponizing the elegant language with unmistakable intent. I may have moved on from him, he's saying, yet I'll never really *move on*. I'll always be at either the end or the beginning of the next relationship. My cycle of breakups is in the flowers.

He knows Max's emergence in my life, in my headlines, is the perfect moment to carve his masterpiece message into me. It's what reminding me of him when I'm moving on to someone new really means. Over and over, whether it's Wesley or a guy from a bar, or Max, it'll always end with me writing my hurt into a song.

It's Max right now. The other rider on the next spin of my doomed carousel. I feel myself falling for him, or maybe dusting off feelings I never pulled down from the shelf. It's not even our history worrying me, although yes, I'm scared he'll walk out of my life once more. The real fear runs deeper.

I don't think love can last for me.

Having put so much of myself into writing about heartbreak, I've written myself into a self-fulfilling pop prophecy. I'm the living embodiment of my lovelorn songs, the direction of my relationship to my music reversed, my romantic life reduced to main-character misery. Instead of writing my choruses, I find them writing me.

I wish it weren't this way. It isn't my choice, not entirely. The Riley my fans want is the one who offers them her endless romantic woes. I'm their favorite lovestruck Icarus, soaring for the sun right until I plunge from the sky, only to rise once more on new handmade wings. Everyone loves a doomed lover.

If I need to continue this way, ever reliving my own lyrics— the heartbreaks keeping me singing, the songs keeping me heartbroken—I will.

If love is the price I need to pay for my dreams, fine.

I've perfected using the pain in service of my shows instead of fighting its efforts to spite them. I remember fucking *great* performances I've given on the heels of sorrow. The Spotify Live session I did the week my parents told me they were getting divorced, the Nashville show I played promoting my first album on the night Jacob Prince—*fucking Jacob Prince, with his horrible fans*—dumped me. I sang stripped and shattered and honest, and it was great.

Tonight is not one of those nights. Leaving the dressing room with my hands shaking, the sweat slick on my face, I feel stuck, caught in the cage of regret the past year of my life has constructed for me.

Every night of the Breakup Tour starts with me stepping up to the microphone in my wedding dress while Vanessa hammers out the intentionally clock-evocative opening drum line of "One Minute." When I join with my white Fender's first chords, I spit out one of my favorite lyrics I've ever written.

Unfortunately, it's long, multisyllabic, requiring me to preempt the verse's first measure.

I walk into the wings with Wesley's vicious reminder lingering with me like the rancid-honey smell of the flowers. Over the opening rhythm, I step onto the stage, adorned in the dress I walked down the aisle to him in, my head in pieces. The spotlights shock my eyes, the enormity of the crowd overwhelming.

Sweating into my silk, I fuck up the line.

"You want—"

The syllables don't fit.

Instead of compensating, shifting the wording years of stage intuition should've helped me do, I just—stop. I feel my throat close off with tears, startling me so much I don't even have the confidence to keep going. To pretend I meant it.

Even in the moment, I know why. I feel overwhelmingly embarrassed. Of how high I dream, of how deeply I let myself love the man who ended up inflicting on me the cruelties I relive in my lyrics every night.

Because while the song is Wesley's, I start it describing myself.

You want a story of a lamb who led herself to slaughter
A romance of a wayward son who met a favorite daughter

Of course, while my mistake was amateurish, my musicians are not. With seamless flourish, they restart the verse.

It's awkward. Everyone, probably every single person in the massive audience, knows I messed up. Riley Wynn, under whose neon lights they came to worship, fucked up within seconds of setting foot onstage.

Instantly, I scold myself into focus. On the repeated verse, I hit the line perfectly. I quietly commit to playing everything with precision. For the rest of the show, I'm in my head, focusing on my own lyrics and not letting myself feel the emotions of my own songs, fearing they might swallow me.

It's not the performance I want to give, not the show my fans hoped for. I don't want to be this human jukebox, offering my audience only the living reification of music videos. Nothing else goes *wrong*, exactly. I'm just not *me*. I feel guilty staring out at the thousands of people who came here for this show, who won't get the chance to see me next weekend when I'm over this. Which I will be.

So I compensate. I add songs into the set list, stuff from my earlier albums. I play them just me and my guitar. Wanting to make up for the distracted performances of the main set list, I hope the extras come off intimate, even if in my heart, they feel desperate. Under the lights, I'm drowning up here for three hours.

When I step offstage at the end of the night, exhausted in every way, I feel like I gave everything I could. Still, I'm furious with myself. It overwhelms me quickly, the switch suddenly flipped without the music to distract me.

I shouldn't have pushed myself. I shouldn't have gone on-stage when I knew I wasn't ready. I should have delayed, should have given myself the mental space I needed. It's common for concerts to start fifteen minutes late, or forty-five. Nobody would have noticed, and I would have given my fans the show they deserved.

Instead, I went on distracted.

Unable to fight the compulsion, I check my phone, in emotional damage-control mode. I have no doubt reviewers were in the audience, not to mention the fans who often double as my harshest critics. While I'm pretty sure one shitty show won't hurt the entire tour's reputation, I need to know exactly what magnitude of compensation I'm facing.

What I find on my first search is . . . worse. Yes, a few music press headlines and pop websites have chided me for the "embarrassing" opening moment. For the most part, however, the internet is chattering over a different story. The one of how, per a "source close to the couple," Wesley sent me pre-show flowers. *Reconciliation?* the stories wonder. They praise my ex-husband for the elegant, high-road gesture of support.

Close source?

I fume. Close source, my ass. It's undoubtedly Wesley's agent. I clench my phone in my hand, ready to smash the device on the concrete floor.

No. I restrain the urge. I know what I need to do instead.

Charging into the corridors of the stadium like I'm half

chasing, half fleeing, I find Eileen. No doubt reading my expression, she meets me with calm.

"Don't worry about it," she says. "The show was fantastic."

I shake my head vehemently, not wanting reassurance. What I want is to cut the hurt out. To make it productive. In my career, I've learned to be grateful for every wound. Everyone has survival instincts they cherish like secret admirers, and this is mine. Emotions like these mean I get to press my pain into platinum records.

"Can you get me studio hours in Houston?" I ask, resisting my impatience.

Eileen's eyes widen. "We leave tomorrow—"

"I know. I mean now," I say. "Tonight. Only for a few hours." The staccato of my voice grates on me. I exhale in the claustrophobic corridor, feeling ready to climb out of my skin under the uncompromising lighting.

Concern shadows over Eileen's features. "We had a long drive," she replies. "You just did a show. Maybe you should rest?"

"I can't. I—" Tears reach up my throat once more. "I need to—" *I need to use this while I have it.*

The long look Eileen gives me lands on sympathy. She nods. "Of course," she says with reassuring resolve, then repeats herself. "Of course. I'll see what I can do. I imagine *somewhere* in the city of Houston would want Riley Wynn to record there no matter the hour." She endeavors to smile.

I manage to return the ghost of one. The way she's used my name, invoking my recorded self, feels right. I want to use this hurt in service of *Riley Wynn* instead of feeling stuck with the sadness of just Riley, the me who signed divorce papers with not-yet-thirty-year-old hands.

I thank her. When I go to my dressing room, I shed my stage look as quickly as I can. I wipe my makeup off in front of the mirror, where my silent reflection stares back.

Holding her gaze, I'm grateful silence isn't the only thing I'll be left with tonight.

TWENTY-ONE

Max

I COULDN'T SPEND one more sleepless night agonizing over Riley.

In my hotel room, the show hung over me. From the moment Riley set foot onstage, I knew she hadn't shaken off everything she was feeling in her dressing room. When the lights went down on her last song, she still hadn't. With the Houston night skyline drawing slanted shapes on my floor, questions persisted—had Wesley come to the show? Was she with him now, or out with someone she hoped would help her forget?

It made me wish we'd discussed our kiss when we had the chance.

Finally, instead of retreating into the crisp white sheets where I would find no rest, I decided to face the problem head-on. Not letting myself lose my nerve, I texted Riley. Nothing elaborate— I asked if she was okay and if she wanted to talk.

She replied with an address.

Which is where I am now. I step out of my Uber, grateful for the city's warm nights. The low white complex is unassuming, the neighborhood residential, with chain-link fences surrounding grass.

While I wait outside the fence, it dawns on me where Riley has led me. It's a recording studio. Even after two in the morning, there are lights on inside.

Eventually one of Riley's handlers—the guys she brings out for heavy crowds—emerges from the front door, looking for me. He nods when I raise my hand in greeting. The studio's gate rattles open.

He leads me inside, into hallways where framed photos of musicians jamming line every wall, until we reach a door where he stops. The recording light is not illuminated.

I open the door, recognizing well the gravity pulling me.

In the small, hushed room, Riley is alone. No producer or engineer is with her. She's sitting on the floor, headphones over her ears, lost in listening to something I can't hear. It's funny to realize I've seen the same look on her face on plenty of occasions when she hasn't had her headphones. Maybe Riley often hears music in the world the rest of us don't.

When I walk in, her eyes fly open, landing on me. Her distraction from onstage is gone, replaced with her usual electric intensity.

Relief isn't exactly what I feel. On one hand, I'm glad she's looking like herself. On the other, her being here in the middle of the night, after the day she's had—everything isn't okay.

"You came." She gets up, removing her headphones.

I'm unable to keep the wariness out of my voice. "What are you doing here, Riley?"

She ignores my question. Instead, she steps over to me and

puts the headphones over my ears, letting her hands linger a little longer than needed.

"Listen to this," she says.

When she presses play on the computer, the loud, immersive sound of the music startles me. It takes seconds for me to recognize what I'm hearing. *Retracing our steps until we're letting go.* She's sped the song up, given it a tempo that makes it feel like it's racing toward something, or maybe on the verge of spinning out.

It's not just exhilarating. It feels dangerous.

I lift my eyes to Riley's, speaking over the music. "You're recording 'Heartbreak Road'? In the middle of your tour?"

At the reminder of her tour, some of the luster in her eyes fades. She takes the headphones back, holding them defensively, or like they're defending her. I notice the shadows under the shimmer in her expression. She's hiding exhaustion with relentless, reckless excitement.

"I have to do *something*. I have to turn this—tonight, everything—into something good. I'll get my label on board and . . ." She stares past me, her gaze sharpening like she's searching for the imagined solution to what she's feeling. "Release it as a surprise single. Or—I don't know."

She sits down in front of the studio computer. With frantic movements, she reaches for the keyboard to make adjustments.

It hurts, watching her press pain into the service of music. I want to help.

I sit down on the couch near the door. "The concert was great, you know," I say.

Riley stops, but she doesn't face me. The room is perilously still.

I seize the silence. She deserves my every effort to get this right. "It's like you told me—sometimes mistakes just make a live show better. They're proof it's live. If your fans wanted perfection, they'd listen to the recorded album."

Framed in the widescreen monitor, Riley's silhouette is motionless. Until finally, she lets out her breath.

"Thank you for saying that," she replies. With reluctance, she removes her hands from the keys, returning them to her lap. She spins the chair to face me fully. Something slowly wakes up in her eyes, like she's realizing how hungry she is for someone to listen. "It's not just the concert. . . ." she says.

"Wesley," I confirm. *Of course.* He's who put her here, fraught with sad inspiration. However many miles we get from LA, he's never far from her heart.

"Jealous?" she asks, no doubt hearing the dark current in my voice. She doesn't sound snide or challenging or even flirtatious. She's genuinely curious.

I look away, even though the emotion is painted all over my face, exposed to the "Breakup Queen," as Spin referred to her. My gaze lands on the upright piano. I can't lie to Riley, not here, where she's singing straight from her heart. I can't desecrate the altar of her music.

"Of course I'm jealous." I say it quickly, hoping the speed lessens the sting.

When I dare to meet her face, I find her eyes wide. She nods, cataloguing my feeling. Probably coming up with a fucking song lyric about it. Even despite what Riley's dealing with, I can't ignore the spark of resentment the idea strikes in me.

I snuff the rogue indignation. I'm here for Riley. I focus on her.

"Don't be jealous," she reassures me. Her wry half smile, like she finds it ridiculous, is comforting. "I don't have feelings for Wesley. I just . . ." She reaches for her guitar and starts strumming, like she needs the music to unlock her innermost private corners. "I sometimes feel like it's my gift—ruining things."

Her gaze goes vacant. It's like she's looking over landscapes of rubble, skylines she feels she's leveled herself without knowing how or why.

"My show. My parents' marriage. My *own* marriage," she goes on hollowly, obviously not her first repetition of the list of casualties. "Everything I touch crumbles, because to do what I do—to reach everyone with my music—I have to pay for it. Become my own muse."

I watch her closely. It sets in how deeply she feels this—how constantly. No matter how many miles we cover from city to shining city, stadium show to show, Riley navigates private maps in her heart. Ones with heartbreak roads spiderwebbing in every direction, connecting the desolation of places where she can never return.

"I don't believe that. Not for a second," I say.

Riley looks up at me, her eyes searing. Hope fights with frustration in her face. Like she can't decide whether she wants my reassurance to convince her or she scorns my naivete.

"You left me, Max," she says accusingly. "What we had was good, and you broke it and didn't even look back."

"I looked back," I insist, not in control of the emotion in my voice. I feel my heart starting to pound, the drum in my chest coming in right on cue. "Believe me, I looked back. But you had already moved on."

Riley laughs with vindication. "So it *is* my fault." She grips the guitar's neck, reveling in the guilt. "I guess I should've waited, right? For the day you would want to come with me? It only would've taken ten years."

What she's said catches the sharp edges of spite I've hidden even from myself. "Well, if I'd waited for you to stay, I'd be waiting forever."

In the empty echo of our words, I remember the small studio room is soundproof. It feels like it. The long-unsaid things we've finally spoken have forced everything else out of the space. Never has the woman in front of me reminded me more of the Riley I used to know. She's not the pop star ruling the charts. I'm not her rumored romantic interest. We're just two people who fell in love only to rip each other open.

It makes my chest physically hurt, enough that I have to sigh. "Look, we can't change the past," I say. "But I'm here now."

When Riley speaks, her whisper comes out desperate. "For what?"

Her chest rises and falls. No night onstage—not Madison Square Garden, not New Orleans in the wake of our kiss, nothing— matches the perilous, perilous wonder in me now.

"What do you want?" I ask.

She stares at the floor, then collects something inside herself. "Play the piano on 'Heartbreak Road,'" she says calmly. "Let me record you. If . . . this falls apart like everything else, I want to have that."

I hesitate. Not just over the implications of recording a song with superstar Riley Wynn, either. I hear everything she's not saying, every implication. *If this falls apart.* Imagining the end of something means first imagining the start. It means Riley is daring to suggest some fragile new us.

It means maybe we'll walk down Heartbreak Road together again, counting every step, hoping—just hoping—we might escape the destination.

My mind made up, I move to the piano. "What do you want it to sound like?"

"Like . . ." Riley chews the inside of her cheek, familiar starlight emerging in her expression. "Like sunrise after sleepless nights," she finishes.

I consider the description. Placing my hands on the keys, I recall the sunrises I've seen in the past month over freeways from the window of the bus and from hotel rooms when I couldn't shake the memory of spotlights shining on a wedding dress.

I start to play.

Hours pass while we record take after take. The song forms gradually, our collage of sound. We explore different flourishes for the piano melody, different styles of playing, chasing the feel Riley wants. She adds her vocals, and we adjust, mixing the instruments, finding places to stretch or to rush.

The sun is nearly rising when we finally listen through the finished cut.

I've never felt more awake. While Riley plays the recording, she smiles, nodding. Watching her make music, her music, *our music*, is like nothing I've ever experienced. I would spend every night sleepless if they looked like this.

The final chord fades, leaving us in the quiet studio. Riley lets out her breath like a great weight has left her shoulders. I wait for the outpouring of emotion, or for the exhaustion to hit her. Instead, she giggles.

"It's fucking *good*," she declares.

Where we're sitting on the floor, Riley collapses backward,

playfully overdramatic. Lying flat on the rug, she stares up into the room.

I don't reply. I can't. I'm overcome by how perfect she looks, undone by her own music. Propping myself up on my elbow, I lie next to her.

One lock of hair rests on her cheek, one reckless tributary from the golden delta splayed over her shoulders. I can't resist reaching out to trace its course. "How could you think you ruin anything?" I murmur. "Your touch is magic, Riley."

Riley only gazes over, her eyes holding unmistakable intent. Then she kisses me.

The kiss is long, profound, full of quiet sureness. It does not feel like recklessness, like the collateral collision of passions we can't control. It feels like *certainty*. The contrast with our kiss on the piano bench in New Orleans could not feel more pronounced. This kiss is less like want, more like need.

Instantly I feel myself giving in, deepening the kiss, mind-shatteringly lost in the intoxicating heaven of my lips on hers. God, she's perfect. Her scent is everywhere. Her body is poised, every curving contour in reach. She's the woman of my every desperate dream, impossibly real. She's Riley—

My Riley.

I hardly recognize the me kissing her, the depth of emotion leaving me close to crying. I want her so much it hurts. No longings I've dared let cross my heart have hit me like this. I haven't let them. Now I do, hearing our chorus in my head.

I didn't know what love is . . .

Until you . . .

Reaching forward, I cradle the soft sculpture of her neck

while I kiss her. It *doesn't* feel like reliving the past, picking up where we left off.

It couldn't, because when I first loved Riley, I hadn't yet known the deprivation of every day without her. I couldn't feel what I feel now—every wound of losing her closing, every scar erased under the ecstatic salve of her mouth on mine, the echo of the song we made together ringing in my ears.

When we part—Riley staring into my eyes, shocked seriousness on her face—I know instantly she feels the same.

She sits up. Somehow I know she's not going to leave.

She pulls her shirt up over her head. *Who ever made music of a mild day?* Mary Oliver's words greet me under Riley's left breast, inked on the skin I see where memory meets fantasy.

She unclasps her bra.

I feel my sigh shudder out of me. Seeing her exposed chest, physical desperation rips me down the middle.

"Touch me, Max." It's the wildly sexy echo of how she directed my piano performance. *Don't pause into the verse. Sustain there.*

Harder. Faster.

I need no more encouragement. I crush her to me, kissing her, her neck, the tops of her breasts while she reaches her hands up, winding them into my hair.

It's like something snaps, some filament of restraint or reverence. Suddenly we're fervent, furious, seized in the passionate grip of a decade spent without each other. The grip of hunger is instant, and it is fierce.

I want her. I want her so fucking much.

I press her into the recording studio floor, high on the joy of consummation, soaring straight into passion—knocking the piano bench out of the way, giving ourselves room. Our breathing is shallow, hearts hammering in untraceable rhythm. Our hands grasping, everywhere, *wanting, needing*, hungering for every inch of each other. There's nothing careful in our ecstasy. It's hectic. It's years of deprivation crashing into one heat-lightning explosion of *us*.

Riley closes her eyes, her breath whimpering out of her. I feel her pulse pounding, her frame curving forward to meet me.

Fingers find my belt. We push clothing aside, hands shaking, unable to wait long enough to remove it properly—I drag Riley's underwear halfway down her perfect legs—until I can touch her under her skirt. She closes her eyes. I don't close mine. I don't need more than this, only to feel her *here*, watching her cheeks pinken while she gasps with every move I make.

Woke up with my heart under your fingers.

I don't care how long Riley makes me wait for her. I would wait forever. Of course I would wait forever.

Her lips purse, and she stops me, groping to reach her bag by the chair.

When I see the condom she retrieves, momentary surprise flits over me, and Riley shrugs. "I know exactly what I want when I want it," she exhales.

I nod. Honestly, any explanation would suffice. *Yes*, everything in me shouts. *Yes. Now. Yes.*

Her smolder ignites. The desire stalking us across miles and years and songs consumes her whole.

I sit up, pulling my shirt over my head, then tug her into my lap. Her legs wrap around my waist, shattering my mind. I don't know how we got here or where it'll lead, but I'll give myself to her. I'll have her. Here, in this studio, our sanctum, like our duet never ended. Like we're playing it on each other now. Music is the soul of our love—now it's going to be the stage for it.

She shoves me until I'm lying down, waiting for her while she trails kisses down my chest, leading lower and lower. Only with restraint do I manage not to climax into her hand, feeling the fingers she uses to coax magic from her guitar gently running the length of me.

When I can take no more, she rolls the condom on. My stomach flexes as she slides up my body, returning to capture my mouth in hers. I meet her with harried, urging kisses, running my hands down to stroke the back of her thighs.

Slowly—reverently—she sinks onto me while I hold her close for the first time in ten long, long years.

With consumed, desperate rhythm, Riley fucks me. I grip her waist, grinding her into me with hungry intensity. With every thrust, I pull her to me, my lips everywhere, her collarbone, her neck, her breast in my mouth. I worship every inch of her like I could live my life in devotion to the goddess with the voice of honeyed thunder.

I'm torn in two, wanting to see every part of her while wanting to press her heart close to mine, burying my face in her hair. Riley isn't torn, however. She knows what she wants, just like always. She puts her hands on my chest. Her whole body shakes. One unbridled note rips from her lips when we finish together.

It feels like the return I've longed for. Like I've spent the last decade wandering in solitude, only to finally come home.

Her whole frame heaving with exhaustion, Riley eases herself off of me. On the floor, she stretches out. Resting her head on my chest, she smiles a lazy, satisfied smile.

I can't resist kissing her head, smelling the sweetness of her sweat, savoring her. In the afterglow of our ecstasy, the silence is wondrous.

Finally, Riley speaks. "Are we going down Heartbreak Road again, Maxwell Harcourt?" Her voice is soft.

I pull back to look at her. I feel like I'm dreaming.

I feel like I'm wide awake.

I feel like I love her so much it hurts.

"Maybe. I don't know," I say. I don't want this to end in heartbreak. I don't know if I can survive it. Still—I don't want to disappear into silence, either, instead of facing the music of us. Not yet.

She kisses my chest, her eyes meeting mine. "Even if we are," she says, her voice full of fire, "we'll have this. This night. This song. Would it be so bad?"

The answer is obvious. This feeling will last forever, no matter where it leads. If it's preserved in Riley's next hit single, if I think of holding her close on the floor of a music studio every time those opening notes come on the radio, will I be sorry?

My voice doesn't shake. "No, it wouldn't. Not at all."

TWENTY-TWO

Riley

ON THE RECORDING studio floor, we decide how we'll handle the new us. In the end, caution wins out. I don't want to share us, I don't want to rush us—I don't want to subject us to the punishing force of the spotlight when part of me is scared we'll shatter like everything else. I have enough of my breakups on public display right now.

We decide what we have is real. It wasn't one night, or something we can discontinue and resume whenever we feel like it. It's worth holding on to, which means it's worth protecting—from my management, and definitely from the unforgiving public.

So we tell no one. We let no one see us.

It isn't easy. Not when we're on a music tour, every day of the next week composed of hectic hours constantly surrounded with close collaborators. Not when every moment, I wish I could pull Max onto the floor for more earthshaking sex.

The lexicon of every love song I've ever heard is not enough for me to put into words how it felt being with him. Finally returning to him. I didn't know how much I needed it until I was there, under his touch, living out heart-pounding pleasure lyrics could never capture.

The echo of how I felt with him doesn't leave me once over the week. It joins with the rhythm in my heart, possible to ignore only for its regular presence in the background of every breath I take. If I stop for one second to feel it, it's suddenly the center of myself.

Fortunately, the tour provides us with plenty of obstacles. When we leave Texas, the schedule intensifies, demanding my entire focus. I return to New York on the label's plane for a magazine cover shoot, after which I fly directly into Palm Springs. I'm headlining Coachella, the centerpiece of my tour.

In the sweltering valley of Indio, California, my car drops me off in front of my rental house. The band, Max included, flew in yesterday while Frank and the other drivers are spending the next couple days driving the buses to Chicago for the second leg of our tour. My mom is taking the week for herself, having chaperoned me to Coachella when I was fifteen and declared she would never return. I'm alone.

I head into the house, my rented space for the week. The place is stunning, vintage Palm Springs, full of midcentury modern flourishes. Exhausted from the flight, I know I'm not fully taking in the elegant comforts of the desert design.

Nevertheless, I walk from doorway to doorway, noting the details—the low geometric furniture, the extravagant light fixtures. Out the wide windows running the length of the sitting room, it's only rocky hills the color of coffee with cream covered with the crooked fingers of yucca plants. I collapse onto the gray couch, enjoying the stability of solid ground if not the solitude.

I won't need to occupy myself for long. I have dinner with my label tonight. In the meantime, I know just how I want to spend the few hours before I need to get ready. I text Max, telling him I've arrived.

Finding my luggage waiting for me, I change into my swimsuit—a white one-piece I haven't worn since I moved out of the Malibu house. I used to love swimming as a kid. When I moved to Los Angeles, I thought I would spend every day at the beach, plunging into the ocean in between songwriting sprints. That was before I realized how massive LA was, though, and that an hour in traffic both directions didn't accommodate my shifts at the ice cream shop.

I open the massive sliding glass doors leading to the back patio and step into the 90-degree heat. Over me, the sky is uninterrupted turquoise with no whisper of clouds. The infinity pool reaches from the patio out to the hillside. In the Palm Springs swelter, the sheet-crystal surface of the water is inescapably inviting.

Easing myself in, I sigh involuntarily in relief.

While I love every second of what I do, touring is punishing physically. Strain lingers in my shins, my knees. Stinging blisters cover my feet. Saying nothing of the costs of poor sleep, I effectively work out for three hours onstage for every performance. The comfort of cool water on my exhausted body is indescribable.

I'm in no less need of respite from the emotional exhaustion of the past few days. The fucking Jacob Prince people have gotten worse, with my onetime fling himself deciding he would play into their fun with some choice reposts of memes featuring me. Inconspicuous shit he can pretend is good fun while knowing full well—and enjoying—what and who he's encouraging.

I hate how much it upsets me. They're ugly, cruel people who deserve none of my emotional energy. Yet—I can't help it, I guess. Could anyone? I'm desperately happy in my new relationship, which is dangerous. Has Max noticed the horrible names they call me? The accusations?

Has my mom? Has my dad?

Under the Palm Springs sun, I'm determined to ignore them. Closing my eyes, I unwind until I hear the sliding doors open.

When I turn to look over my shoulder, I find Max smiling.

Just seeing him makes the relief of the pool feel meager. He's perfectly himself, vintage-desert version. His linen short-sleeve button-down goes nicely with the gold-rimmed sunglasses for which he's exchanged his usual scholarly round frames.

It scares me how my mind, my heart, say *my Max* when I see him. It feels hasty. Unearned.

Shaking off the worry, I return his smile. *Self-doubt isn't how I got from the St. Louis suburbs to the Superdome,* I remind myself sternly. *Self-doubt isn't how I wrote the number one single of the year.* Self-doubt will not stop Riley fucking Wynn from loving Max Harcourt.

"This is sort of different than the last time we did Coachella," he says.

I laugh, hearing the humor in his understatement. He doesn't seem like he cares about the recent online chatter, which makes me happy.

I swim to the edge of the pool near him, where I look up, wanting to inscribe into my memory every detail of Max surrounded by the sky. The sleek house behind him accents his words.

"When we shared a hotel room with way too many people, pretty much got heatstroke camping out early for spots close to the main stage, and narrowly avoided getting puked on?" I ask, remembering. "Yeah, this is different."

I'm not giving our relationship's only Coachella enough credit—or rather, our *first* Coachella. We're here, together, now. On our last visit to Indio, California, we pushed the speakers in my Volkswagen to their limit, blasting the playlist I made of the headliners. I danced in his arms for every set. On the way back, I started a song I never finished about the promise of desert nights. *You make days feel like nights of stars*, went the first line, echoing in my ears now.

It's not the only love song I've abandoned. Honestly, their fragility frightens me. Breakup songs focus on the past, on what *has* happened. There's no changing the past, so their feelings stay real. With each rendition, they're no less present. Endings never end.

Love songs, though, exist in the present. Possibility is their premise. Which means they're perilously easy for life to invalidate. Then what? How do you stand onstage singing sermons of hopes you no longer hold? How do you write them knowing heartbreak will likely rob the feeling from every line?

I've never embraced the idea. It doesn't feel like courage. It feels like naivete.

Or, felt.

The way Max looks now makes me want to finish it. He kicks off his shoes and sits, dangling his feet in the water. "I had fun, though."

"Me too."

It's quiet out here, in the Palm Springs hills. I find the stillness comforting. The only sound in the spacious landscape is the lapping of the water when I push myself forward, up to Max.

I stand between his legs, resting my hands on his knees. With one wet finger, I trace cool water up his arm. When I kiss him, I wish it would never end.

Desert nights, I decide, have nothing on desert days.

"I missed you," I say. "It's been a long, long time."

Max smiles, recognizing the song title. He knows I don't just mean the week since we were last alone together, in the recording studio. This place rings with long-forgotten echoes, reminders of the years we spent without each other.

In reply, Max hugs me close. While the imprint of me soaks the front of his shirt, he doesn't seem to mind. He hums the song's melody in my ear.

I'm wonderfully, surpassingly happy, which makes me sad. How could it not? I feel like I'm looking out from the highest pinnacle we'll ever reach, the best thing I'll ever have. I know the descent is coming. I need to prepare myself to enjoy the downhill momentum instead of fearing the crash.

"I have to tell you something," Max says softly.

I stiffen, not ready for the unraveling to have come quite this fast.

Max pulls back, undoubtedly noticing the change in my posture. He reads the fear in my eyes immediately. "No, Riley, nothing like that," he reassures me. "Jess has to fly to New York this week, and Harcourt Homes is short on staff. With the new interest in the home, I can afford to hire someone, but I have to interview them and train them while Jess is away."

I feel cold in the sweaty heat. "You want to go home."

"I don't, actually." He smiles when he says it, like he's surprised by himself. With delicate fingers, he sweeps my hair from my forehead. "I want to stay with you. But we don't have rehearsals between the two Coachella weekends. I could train someone new and be back in time for our second show. I would invite you home with me, but . . ."

I shake my head reluctantly. I have press to do and an ad campaign to shoot. They're obligations I usually don't mind. Often I enjoy them—the outfits, the photos, the chance to share or explain my music.

However, now they only feel like the forces that will pull us apart. Inevitable. Painful, yet without cruelty.

"I can't. Not this week," I say. Hearing the resignation in my voice, I force myself to fight. "It won't always be like this, though. Tour is unique." I'm half reassuring, half pleading for the universe to prove me right.

"I know." Max's reply is light, floating on the wind where my words fell like stones. "It's just five days. Then I'll be back. We still have more tour left together."

He cups my face in his hand. His skin is soft against mine, his fingers placed with loving precision. Everything he does with his hands is deliberate.

"We do," I tell him.

You make days feel like nights of stars, repeats my discarded opening line in my head. It joins with other lyrics unraveling unbidden from my memory, coming to me only now. *You make days feel like nights of stars, when the pressure ends, when the sky is warm.*

It feels significant, finding myself suddenly writing the song I was working on when we were last here. Like musical memory reminding me not to lose faith. I wonder if we could be like the lyrics I started on the drive home a decade ago.

Not lost. Unfinished.

TWENTY-THREE

Max

I WAKE UP in her bed.

Riley is stunning when she sleeps. She looks like she even dreams devotedly. It leaves gorgeous serenity on her sunlit features, her cheeks desert pink, her lips—the lips I felt everywhere last night—parted in the imitation of invitation.

Her nocturnal shifting has splayed her hair on her pillow in shimmering gold. She runs hot—of course she does—so in the night she sloughs off the sheets, exposing the crests of her curves and the soft skin of her shoulders, her neck, *her*.

I love her.

The recognition feels inevitable—like it's emerging from where it's waited within me for the past ten years—yet revelatory. I don't know how or whether I even deserve loving her. I just know I want more mornings like this one, more nights like yesterday, more of her in every single way.

I don't have long for my feelings. With the morning sun filtering into Riley's stylish bedroom, I watch her eyes flit open with ready excitement like it waits there even while she sleeps.

I've spent every moment of the past week knowing full well we might not work out, remembering our conversation in the recording studio. Even if circumstances or existential directions sever us from each other once more, the passion will have been worth the pain. Every precarious day, I feel like I'm walking the harrowing edge of us.

The thing is, it's one of those edges where the view is *stunning*. Riley is my Empire State Building. She's my Mississippi River. She's my Grand Canyon.

Still, the love I feel when I'm with her makes me unable to eradicate certain fragile hopes. Questions I can only whisper to myself in the dark.

Is this really possible?

Will I finally get to love Riley the way I'm desperate to?

Despite the tranquil comfort of her bedroom, we can't linger. When stylists arrive to ready Riley for the day, I don't leave, instead staying nearby in the sunlit house. I know my presence here will start to spread rumors, but I don't care. I'm going home tomorrow. I want to spend as much of today with Riley as possible.

When she emerges, she's wearing a flowing white skirt with a macramé crop top. It's eye-catching. The stylists did their job perfectly—Riley looks like herself.

On our way out the door, she sneaks her hand into mine for several furtive seconds. One short drive later, we step out onto Coachella's dusty grounds.

We wander the festival together, checking out sets, stopping to meet her fans. With Riley's headlining set closing out the night, we have the day to enjoy ourselves. It's not at all like the last time we did Coachella together, and yet in some ways I feel exactly the same.

Listening to live music with Riley is almost as good as playing music with her. While we're in the VIP section now instead of sweating it out just to secure spots in the front of the crowd, I still feel the way her heart picks up with the start of every song, still see how she can't resist dancing to every beat. They're reminders of how everything Riley's earned, every headline made or record set or stadium filled, started here—with her love for music.

When her handlers tell us we need to return to Riley's trailer to get ready for her set, we leave the stages early. She looks like she's absorbing all the energy around us, the joy of the crowd, the enchantment of the music, the sear of the midday sky captured within her. When I touch her, I feel it, lighting me up from within.

It makes me wonder if I belong here. For the first time, I start to imagine setting up Harcourt Homes to run without me and helping out whenever needed. Maybe everyone was right. Maybe my place is here, on the road, onstage, in the studio. Maybe I've found what my heart is meant for.

When we're nearing Riley's trailer, she squeezes my hand. Unlike this morning, she doesn't let go, her fingers resting entwined with mine. It pulls me into the moment, out of the future I'm contemplating.

"You really don't have to come in if you don't want to," Riley says.

I look at her, finding concern etched on her features. She thinks I'm quiet because I'm dreading something, I realize. Not because of the unforeseen possibilities unfurling in my head. "Why would I not want to?" I ask.

"You have no reservations about meeting one of my exes?" Riley doesn't hide her skepticism.

I laugh. It's been on the schedule since before I signed on to the tour for Hawk Henderson to be the surprise guest at Riley's Coachella performance. She'll bring out her ex to sing together the two acerbic songs they've written about each other. "Riley, I've been watching you sing eleven songs about other men every weekend for months. I think I can handle meeting Hawk."

The relief I catch in her eyes is quick. Nevertheless, its fleeting presence suggests situations like this probably went very differently with Wesley. The portrait Riley's offered renders her ex-husband full of petty jealousy, the kind to smile with his hand on her waist, then sulk in silence in the limo home.

Her reaction is gone swiftly, veneered under playfulness. Riley raises an eyebrow. "If you're sure," she says.

We walk into her trailer. In contrast to the day's heat, the hyper-cooled box is welcome comfort. It's generically stylish, with a patterned rug on the floor, wireless speakers on the end table, and organic snacks near the mirror. It's much like the greenrooms in the stadiums we've played. The only feature out of place is seated on the small couch.

Hawk Henderson looks exactly like every photograph of him. He's lanky, with long, wavy brown hair framing surprisingly blue eyes. The way his tattoos peek out from his white tee looks precisely rugged, designed for the impression of working-man swagger.

When he sees Riley, he smiles with unmistakable warmth.

"Nightmare Girl!" he greets her.

Riley meets his grin with one of her own. "Mr. Maybe," she

replies with scolding flair. Hawk's song on *The Breakup Record* happens to be one of my favorites. It's one of the funniest, full of perfect lines, detailing how often in their relationship he would say "maybe," only ever meaning no.

Hawk gets up from the couch gracefully. He and Riley hug like old friends.

I watch from the doorway, lightly surprised. I expected Hawk Henderson to exude *asshole* the way he presents himself in his music. Instead, the guy in front of me looks ... sort of nice. Easygoing.

Stepping back, Riley turns to me. "This is Max 'Until You' Harcourt. Max, this is Hawk."

Hawk extends his hand readily. When we shake, his smile doesn't change. "I feel like we're brothers separated at birth. Comrades of *The Breakup Record*." He leans a little closer to me. "And we got the good songs, too."

"Excuse me," Riley interjects, hand on her hip. "I remember seven of them making the Billboard Top 10 in the first week."

Hawk scoffs grandly. "I don't mean like that. The whole album fucking rocks. I mean we have the songs that don't make their subjects look like absolute shitheads."

Riley's eyebrows steeple pityingly. "Did you listen to 'Mr. Maybe'?" There's no venom in her voice.

"Hell yeah, I did." He shrugs. "I come off inconstant, self-involved—everything you knew I was before we started dating. I'll take that over being, you know, the nice guy who slowly destroyed you. Which, speaking of ..."

I laugh. I can't help somewhat liking Hawk Henderson.

"Wesley is coming tonight," he finishes.

I watch the color wash from Riley's face. "Jesus," she manages with weak humor. "Do you guys have some sort of group chat or something? How do you even know that?"

Remembering her reaction to the flowers he sent her, I find myself in worry's clutches. One simple bouquet in her dressing room had her looking like smashed ceramic, forgetting her lyrics onstage in Houston—which *wasn't* the centerpiece set of the tour. Wesley in person here is . . . not good. The way she's keeping her composure now is the perversely perfect testament to how well she's capable of covering her emotions when she wants to.

Hawk grimaces with good humor. "We were at a CAA event. He mentioned it to me. That guy sucks, by the way. Of all of us to marry, you chose *him?* What's wrong with me, or Max here?"

I have to look away, reminded of when I first saw Riley on-stage in a wedding dress, the replica of my fantasies.

With his namesake's keenness, Hawk notices. He gives me a knowing look.

Riley doesn't take the bait, clearly used to his games. She stares past us, expression fixed, eyes charged, like instead of the wall of the trailer, she sees waiting crowds. "If Wesley wants to come to my set, let's give him a show."

Hawk grins. "Hell yeah."

"I have to change," Riley continues. "You need anything?"

He shakes his head. "I'll chill with Max."

When Riley leaves, I settle into the seat by the couch. "There isn't really a group chat, right?" I ask.

"God no." He laughs. "I hate most of those dudes. No offense."

"None taken. I'm not a fan, either."

We fall silent for a few seconds. On the couch, Hawk crosses one shoe over the ripped knee of his jeans. While his gaze on me is evaluative, there's no judgment in it. Or, I'm pretty sure there's not.

"So you're the first to go in for two rounds," he finally says. "I got to hand it to you. It's brave. Or stupid. I never know which is which." His self-effacing smirk feels practiced.

I know there's no point denying it. Once you've been in love with Riley, it's probably easy to recognize the symptoms in others. I meet the rock star's calm stare. "You're saying you wouldn't try again if she gave you the chance?" I return.

Hawk points one lazy finger at me in concession. "Nice one. Okay, let me think about it." He pauses, considering. For the first time since I walked in, seriousness falls over his expression, even vulnerability. It surprises me. "I'd consider it for sure," he says. "She's a creative genius, and it's invigorating to be around. But"— his eyes lift—"the girl loves drama. She feeds on it."

I'm starting to object, knowing how many critics have mistaken Riley's epic-scale, emotionally honest songwriting for "drama," when Hawk smiles wide.

"The problem is, I love drama, too," he concedes. "We delighted in pushing each other, and I think it really did bring out the nightmare versions of ourselves. So no," he concludes cheerfully. "I'm good. You clearly don't mind it, though. I mean, you know what you're getting into."

I clench my teeth, not caring if his sharp eyes notice. I don't like the way he's characterized Riley. Like she's something to be tolerated. Sure, she draws inspiration from her life. She feels huge, unafraid feelings. Yes, sometimes she'll even chase a reckless idea for the thrill of it. But she doesn't pick fights or push people just so she can spin songs out of screaming matches.

The fact that Hawk thinks she does tells me why Riley really ended things.

Hawk shifts on the couch. "Did I touch a nerve?"

"No. It's fine," I reply. "You're right. I know what I'm getting into." I wish I could gloat that I know her best. I wish I could claim some secret supremacy because I knew struggling-songwriter Riley, the girl none of the celebrity men in her life knew. *I knew the real Riley*, I want to say.

Except it isn't true. The famous Riley *is* the real Riley. I know it. I think Hawk knows it. I have nothing except hope that I've managed to figure out Riley's soul in ways no one else has.

The grin Mr. Maybe gives me now is not magnanimous. "You have it bad," he comments. "I get it. I really do. I look forward to hearing the next song Riley writes about you. Hey, it might not even be a breakup song this time."

I smile politely despite wishing I'd taken Riley up on her offer of my own trailer. It's not that I care about Hawk's opinion. I don't. What he said isn't far off from what Riley and I decided in the recording studio. If all we get out of our new relationship is "Heartbreak Road"—four verses and one chorus of consolation prize—we would be okay.

No, what's silenced me is how his words have made me imagine how I'll really feel if everything ends with Riley for the second time. If I'm left with nothing except the souvenir song we recorded when we were us. In this trailer, the truth comes over me like the rising shrill of guitar feedback.

I *won't* be okay.

While I don't want to be just her next breakup song, I'm worried Riley's mindset is different. Because if she's okay with just a song, then she won't fight for us. Not for real. We're facing daunt-ing pressures—her music and my work at Harcourt Homes, the impossible-to-ignore presence of the press, the nasty shadow of the exes who remain intertwined with Riley's legacy. In the midst of everything, we're going to *have* to fight for us.

It's the only way we can last where twelve relationships before now—twelve great, gutting songs—didn't.

TWENTY-FOUR

Riley

THE SET WAS fucking perfect.

The Coachella stage was everything I dreamed of when I was fifteen, nineteen, twenty-three—imagining myself in the middle of its illuminated glory, my throne of lights in the center of the festival. The crowd stretched out to where the grounds' iconic Ferris wheel endlessly revolved. The crystal-clear night sky beneath the ceiling of desert stars opened up like it was expecting every song, waiting for them.

I hit every cue, climbed every high note, drove every chord into the stage with perfect precision. When I invited Hawk out, the crowd lost it. I could hear screaming for literal minutes. We dove into "Nightmare Girl," then "Mr. Maybe," our voices perfect opposites, the interpersonal theater of our joint performance captivating even me. No matter my ex's faults, the man is talented.

Of course, he wasn't the ex who demanded most of my focus. Nor was Max, whose outpouring of heart into "Until You" I wasn't expecting.

It was Wesley I kept imagining, somewhere in the VIP section. I wasn't shaken, though, or insecure, or heartsick. I was *loving it*. Envisioning him possessing not one ounce of musical talent, wishing he could join me while I fucking ruled this stage—wishing he could siphon my spotlight, leechlike—

It was incandescent.

I didn't finish my set until one in the morning. Even then, the night wasn't over. I'd decided to host my own after-party, requesting my team invite a very select list.

They've already arrived when the label's car pulls into my driveway. Night in the Palm Springs suburbs is smothering in its darkness. The stylish contours of my rental house stand out lit up on the quiet street.

On my own doorstep, I find myself waiting, hesitating. I recognize intimately what I'm feeling, the whispers in my head of how fleeting this could be, how I might never have this again.

I smash them resolutely under the heel of the dark boots I performed in. *This is my moment.* I've worked so hard to get here, sacrificed so much. Right now, it isn't ethereal lightning fleeing my fingertips. It's a goddamn victory lap, one I'm going to enjoy.

I walk inside, and everyone applauds me. I bow in thanks, then wave my hands in deference. "Please," I say over the noise. "You've spent enough time watching me tonight. Have fun!"

Instantly, I notice Max sipping a drink by the bar. My oasis in the desert. He raises his glass in toast to me.

I smile before I'm pulled in multiple directions. People from my label want to congratulate me, or, likelier, discuss every imaginable relevance of Wesley's appearance at my set—I avoid them. The only journalist I invited, the young woman from *Sound-*

bite whose career I want to help, is hovering politely. Other musicians I've looked up to my whole life want to meet me.

Part of my heart pulls me to Max, whose side I'm ever drawn to. Even so ... I don't want to miss one minute of *this*. While Jodi Hitchcock, the legendary keyboardist for the Years, compliments me on my set, I can't help glancing at the bar.

When I next look for Max, I find him outside, seeking solitude by the pool.

While I don't resent him for it, it dims my excitement in complicated ways. I know this isn't his scene. A house crowded with celebrities is pretty much the opposite of his scene. I appreciate him being here despite it.

This *is*, however, my scene. It unnerves me, feeling out the edges of this fundamental difference between us. I'll never give up nights like this, though. Not even for him.

I don't have long to dwell on the problem.

There's a shift in the party. *He* walks in, charging the air with dangerous potential. Whispers and glances race around the room.

I stand straighter. This is part of my moment, too.

His path is slow. Wesley Jameson never hurries when he feels eyes on him. He moves with possessive charm, shooting his movie-trailer smile at every A-lister in striking distance. I recognize his movement, his mannerisms, his magnetism. I recognize the man who charmed me in Hollywood, who captivated me in Paris, who crushed me in a million moments afterward, in the quiet outside the spotlight.

I don't approach him. I won't have to. I know why he's here.

While I'm getting a selfie with the lead of my favorite supernatural romance show, he makes his move. Crossing the rest of the room in effortless strides, he's suddenly right next to me.

"Riley," my ex-husband says. "Wonderful as usual."

I'd imagined this moment would feel like pressing magnets together, full of resistant repulsion. It doesn't. It's rather like staring into shadowed corners. No matter how dark they seem, one only needs light to render them harmless.

The actress I'm posing with reads the room immediately. She excuses herself to scurry to the bathroom.

I look at him, delighted with how calm I feel. "I heard you came to my set. I would have gotten you passes," I say.

He smiles. His fake smile, the one he started giving me only at the end of our marriage. Its reemergence ignites the first rogue flash of anger in me. I don't care how genuine the conversation I'm having with him now is. I just can't control my residual reaction to the memory of how fucking *small* his cheerless smile could make me feel. I'm indignant on behalf of my former self.

Unfortunately, his hollow expression doesn't change the fact that he looks good. Wesley is handsome, but not obviously so. He just carries himself like he is, which makes him something more valuable—intriguing. It turns heads in every room he's in.

It used to turn mine. It doesn't now, like I've defied whatever gravity the dark-haired disaster in front of me once held.

"Don't be ridiculous," he drawls. His magnanimity is like the scent of his cologne, his favorite. Sickly synthetic. "I'll always want to support your career."

"Funny you waited until our divorce to start," I reply.

Even during our relationship, I was never surprised when he could perform contrition or woeful offense like he was just running lines. I'm not surprised now. "Riley," he pouts. "We had our differences, but you can't really think I didn't support your career."

Will you live forever with me, Riley?

For once I don't want to make myself into a spectacle. What I want is an apology—anything to prove the love we once shared came from something real, something worth the months I gave him and the hurt he left me with. I fight to keep my voice pleasant, or pleasant enough not to push the guests' intrigue over into scrutiny. "You hated it whenever I performed," I say.

"I did not," he replies genially.

The outright lie pushes me over the edge. I won't be his goddamn scene partner for one second longer. "I was offered the chance to play the Hollywood Bowl, and you said it was inconvenient," I remind him.

He looks sideways, chuckling like I've made a joke. "It was the one weekend I was home that month. Is it a crime I wanted to spend Saturday night with my wife after a month of shooting in Croatia?"

"Did you ever think you could spend time with me by, oh, I don't know, coming to my show?" I fire back.

When his face darkens, I'm delighted. Getting Wesley to break the character he's performing, to reveal his real self, is rare. I doubt even his costars can do it.

This is better than an apology, I decide. I don't need to know my pain was worth it. I just need him to feel as small as I did. I want to embarrass him. The way I was embarrassed when I called Eileen to decline the gig of a lifetime.

The pause on the line carried the disapproval she was too kind to voice, and I rushed to fill the silence, offering empty excuses to spare Wesley. *I don't feel up to it. It's just not the right time. Not yet.* He made a liar out of me.

"I told you there would be other chances to play the Bowl," Wesley says, quieter, a warning note in his voice. "And I was right. Call them tomorrow and you could have your pick of dates."

I step toward him, not yet finished. I won't let him smooth this over—smooth *me* over. He never faced my rough edges. He'll have to now. "That's not the point, Wesley," I reply, my voice sharp like snapped guitar strings. "I turned down a dream of mine for you. And it's not just that. You were constantly pulling me away when I was trying to write—"

"To spend time with you!" he interrupts me. "I didn't realize husbands weren't supposed to want to spend time with their wives."

"You don't want a wife. You never did." I'm picking up momentum now, racing toward the truth I hid in the corners of verses I couldn't sing. "You wanted someone to adore you every waking minute of their day. You wanted a live-in, permanent *fan.*"

His face reddens. He's suddenly far from handsome. He's indignant and weak, and I should have seen it sooner. He's *not* worth what I gave him. I can't write him into some epic tragic ending when he was nothing more than a farce.

"Well, all you wanted is this, right?" he asks, gesturing to the room, the night, the tour. "At least one of us got what they wanted. For now. I personally think your breakup-songs bit was old before you did a whole album of them. But eventually everyone in this room will get bored of it, just like those exes you wrote about got bored of you. I wonder what you'll sing about then. Something that matters, maybe?" He shrugs, like he's already tired of it. Of me.

It hurts. Everything he's said is something the internet has repeated endlessly, of course. Hearing the dismissal from him hurts immeasurably worse. Not surprising, in the end. Sometimes one voice, if it's the right voice, cuts without mercy where others strike dully.

When I read smug victory in his eyes, I decide I won't give him the satisfaction of walking away from me. Holding in my tears, not wanting him to see how he's reached my deepest insecurities, I spin on my heel, muttering "Excuse me" to the people nearby.

I steal into the hallway, heading for the bedroom where I woke up. The sound of the party is close yet strangely far, past the gossamer curtain of the sadness I'm stuck in. I just need a moment.

Stepping into the room, I close the door quietly.

I should have known. I should have fucking known I wouldn't get an apology from him. Still, I didn't expect *this.* He loved me once, I know he did. Why can I hear no echo of it in the way he speaks to me now? Instead, it's twisted into something ugly and mean, warped into the howl of distorted feedback.

Because I deserve it, I can't help feeling.

There's something wrong with me that drives everyone in my life away, leaving me with songs as my only consolation prizes.

The door opens. The click-creak is painfully loud. I turn my face, not wanting some agent or producer to see me looking like the caricature they've decided my songs render. "Crying in the Coachella Valley." Whoever it is could probably write the single for me.

"Riley, are you okay?"

When I hear Max's voice, I sob.

Instantly, he's there, wrapping me in his embrace, comforting me, stroking my hair. I cry into his shoulder, having never known someone else's presence could mean this much. If the right voice can cut, maybe the right shoulder can heal like nothing else.

"He's an asshole," Max reassures me. "Whatever he said to you, don't listen."

I pull back to look at him. Right in the eyes. "Did you ever hate me, Max?" I ask.

He blinks. "What?"

"When you didn't come that summer, when you realized I'd moved on, did you hate me for it?" It's the easiest question to reach for—the one lingering in the periphery of every conversation I've had with Max over the past months—yet the hardest to speak out loud.

"No," Max replies easily, like it's obvious. Only when he notices the fear scrawled everywhere on my face does he repeat himself forcefully. "*No.* Do you hear me? I never hated you."

I focus on him, trying to listen. Pushing myself to ignore the little chorus of whispers I never manage to escape. *Not yet*, they say. *You don't hate me yet.* I stand up, wanting to shake them off. "I'm fine," I insist, hating my lack of conviction. If I were listening to myself recording, I would throw out the take, scorning my inauthenticity. "It's nothing. Just more inspiration, right?" I laugh darkly, my heart not in it. Not yet.

"Don't do that." The soft sternness of Max's voice surprises me. "Don't turn someone's cruelty into some kind of gift."

I know he wants to help, but I resent the reprimand. I've lived my own life, with my own wounds, for ten years without him. It's gone pretty okay. "Why not?" I snap. "Why shouldn't I take something for myself?"

"Are you?" he replies. "Or are you just hurting worse?"

I don't answer, not knowing what the truth is anymore. It used to be so clear to me. It's hard now to even remember which petty prizes I imagined myself holding on to, not when they're slipping through my fingers like sand.

Max sighs. "Why did he even come? Why crash your ex-wife's party?" he asks.

"He didn't crash," I say. "I invited him."

I'd known I would need to the day I got his flowers in Houston. It was the only hope I had of exorcising him from my life, no matter if I shredded my soul in the effort. Of giving my label the confrontation they've desperately demanded, but on my *own fucking terms*. I had to face him.

Max frowns. For once, he actually looks mad. The shift in him is startling. "Why?" he demands.

"I thought he might apologize. I guess I was wrong," I muster weakly, feeling foolish. The downside of dreams is how unprepared I'm left when fate fucks me over. "I figured even if he didn't, maybe just knowing he saw this, me in this moment, would . . ."

Max stands up. "What? Give you a new song? Make you feel better? Which is it?"

Hating the rising doubt his questions have left me with, I seek higher ground. "I'm going to write about my life, Max. We've been over this." I notice ruefully how easily this defensiveness comes to me, like riffs I could play in my sleep.

"That doesn't mean you have to put yourself in positions that will hurt you," he replies. While he's close enough to touch me, I suddenly feel like ten years or thousands of cross-country miles don't compare to the distance separating us now.

I wonder if maybe it's one we'll never close.

Hot anger leaps in me. "Falling in love *always* leads to hurt.

Why do you think I've sold so many records? Everybody relates. It's naive to think there are no risks to this."

I've cut him to the quick. Like he can predict my improvisations when we play together, I know Max feels the change in the conversation's register now. I don't only mean love. I mean us.

"I know there's a risk. I'm ready for it," Max says. His voice is low, retaliatory. "I've been here before. I've loved you only to lose you. But I can't give my heart to someone who isn't afraid to break it for the *inspiration*."

I feel time slow down, the moment's tempo collapsing into nothing. No longer rhythm. Just pounding. My heartbeat races erratically in my chest. Wesley was right. *He was fucking right.* While I've long styled myself as the unflinching fortune teller, he got one prophecy over on Riley Wynn.

Everyone grows tired of me.

I want to fight it. I want to tell Max I won't break his heart. But I can't. There's no use resisting. I know there isn't. Every one of my songs knows there isn't.

The center of my music is not its moving melodies. My songs resonate for their undeniable conclusion. Like I've repeated on stages from Houston to Hollywood, my relationships *always* end with someone hurting. Heartbreak Road isn't the journey—it's the destination. The song of my life is written. I suspect fate will leave me singing it long after the stage lights have gone down.

So I don't say anything. I can write this familiar song in silence.

I watch as realization washes over Max's face. I know I'll remember every detail of this. The flash photograph of his expression imprinted on my soul.

It's better he leaves now, before we're in so deep he walks

away hating me like Wesley does. Because I couldn't handle Max hating me. There is no consolation prize that would ease the pain. No song. Nothing.

Max walks to the door, and I know we've reached the same horrible conclusion.

When he speaks, his voice is quiet, but I hear every word. "I'll head home early. I guess you got two songs out of tonight. I hope they make you happy."

He walks out.

I want to curl in on myself. Like stars out in space, I want to implode, devoured by my own gravity into nothing. I want to give in to the heartbreak I pretend I've mastered.

I can't, though. Tonight is my night.

In the bathroom, I fix my makeup. Staring into the mirror, I see the Riley they're expecting.

I put on a smile, then head back into the party like I'm walking onto a stage.

TWENTY-FIVE

Max

MY OLD LIFE welcomes me easily.

I return to Harcourt Homes from Palm Springs, right into the comfortable routines I could repeat with my eyes closed. I drive Sunset Boulevard. Riley's billboard is down now, replaced with CBS's latest drama. I hire and train new help. I review the home's financials, seeing how the new residents who learned about us from the media spotlight on me have provided enough income to stay open.

Every evening, I drive home to my apartment. I keep the radio firmly on the oldies station. I sleep soundly. I've hung up drapes.

The reversion is so smooth it makes my cross-country months of music and Riley feel almost like a dream. The same sense of improbability surrounds them, their details sharp yet disjointed from the sturdy familiarity of the world into which I've reimmersed myself.

Only one part of my new-old life is different. I don't play the piano in the Harcourt Homes dining room.

Playing music is too connected to Riley—Riley, who I remember coming to the very same dining room with an encore on her lips—and I'm afraid to look directly at the wound my departure left in my chest.

I know how reality will hit me when I do. There will be no hiding from myself. The victim of self-inflicted heartbreak for the second time.

I hate how ugly things got between us. I hate that I left her. Again. Often when I close my eyes, her tear-stained face in our last conversation is the first thing I see. It's the only part of the past months I can't compare to dreams. It's my worst nightmare.

Some of it is the helplessness I feel. I don't know how to convince her she deserves love, not heartbreak. I don't think it's something anyone can convince her of except herself. Unless she does, our love will feel like this. Like instruments with no one to play them.

So I avoid the piano. I cut off that part of myself. I put away the questions and fears for just a few days before I have to return to the desert. To Riley.

On Thursday, I have dinner with my parents. It's nice. We eat in the dining room after the residents. It's empty, most of the staff having gone home. I answer their many questions about the tour, about Riley, about the improvements I can afford for the home. Patiently, I explain how different the financial picture is now. When they ask me to play for them, I tell them another night.

My mom stops in the doorway as I walk them out. "You look . . . different," she says.

"Tour is tiring. I just need a few days to recover," I defer, not entirely honestly. I might spend my life recovering from Riley.

I'm surprised when my mom shakes her head. "No. Not tired. You look—I don't know. Settled, maybe. I'm proud of you for trying out music," she says.

I catch the glance she exchanges with my dad. It has the feel of their characteristic silent coordination.

"With the home doing well now," she continues, "we leave the choice to you. We won't sell it if you don't want."

I nod. My parents pause like they are waiting for me to make the decision now. Instead, I see them out with polite cheer, stuck in my head the whole time. I'm not sure how to process what she said.

All I wanted months ago was to ensure Harcourt Homes survived. And I did it. My onstage reunion with Riley gave me everything I wanted.

Or—not everything.

What do *I want?* It comes to me instantly, with visceral clarity, like the glare of the spotlights, the scream of the crowd, the soul-stripping resonance of the perfect duet. *I want to return to Riley's side.*

To do whatever she needs me to do to convince her we can make it. I'd give up everything for that.

But should I? The old countermelody plays over my sudden longing. I return down the hallway into the dining room, wrapped up in thought. Its emptiness reminds me of pre-show stages or midnight recording studios. Places I've stood, wondering if they felt like home. If they ever could.

If Riley weren't part of the question, would my answer change?

I walk to the piano, where I sit down.

Play the way you want to kiss me.

Out of my memory, Riley's voice comes to me. In the shabby

practice space where we would sometimes rehearse, with heavy repainted layers on the walls and nicks out of the concrete floor, I glanced up from the piano. I found Riley sitting on her amp, watching me with the sort of gaze I could never resist.

When I went to stand, she shook her head.

Play the way you want to kiss me, she said.

I did. Feeling her stare on me, I gave the piano everything. Everything. I only stopped when I felt Riley sit next to me. With gentle fingers she pulled my chin, pointing my lips to hers. She kissed me with the same undeniable everything.

Her request lingers with me now. I start considering whether it's what I've done since the start. *Play the way you want to kiss me.*

Has every chord I've chased, every song I've rehearsed, found me following Riley? Reaching out for her? Playing with her in mind? Maybe it has, I wonder now. Every open mic, every stadium show, even every night in Harcourt Homes.

Maybe I kept music close so I could stay near Riley.

Her smoldering voice isn't here now. I sit in front of the piano, solitary. The room is dark. No one is listening. I haven't played for just myself in months.

With a deep breath, I put my hands on the keys. When I play the first chord, I feel like I'm listening to my own heart.

I start with "Heartbreak Road," the stinging wound not yet closed. I follow it with "Until You." Next, I transition into the standards I perform for Harcourt Homes. I play them all. I finish with the music of my childhood, the Mozart and Beethoven I learned at this very piano.

I play my thoughts, my feelings, my regrets, my hopes. No one hears them but me. I'm sweating, breathing hard, but I'm comfortable. I'm like my mom said—settled.

In the piano's voice, I hear the harmony I was looking for. I know what I want. Not who. *What.*

I want this. Filling the lives of those who pass through Harcourt Homes with music. Keeping this place running. The comparisons I felt here to stages and studios fade into nothing. It's something greater—home.

I *could* give this feeling up for Riley, the woman I love. But it wouldn't be fair to either of us. Riley deserves someone who dreams the same dreams she does, who won't leave her the way I've done twice, fleeing home to dreams of my own. I deserve someone who believes in our love, who wants to fight for us. Who won't end things out of fear, leaving me with nothing except the life I only chose for her.

The song urges me forth, the music reading my mind. I follow, hearing the melody's message.

My place is here. I've given music the greatest chance I could, played on the grandest stages imaginable, and now I know without a doubt I was only living out the hopes of others. Playing in this room isn't just enough. It's everything.

I know what I have to do now. It won't be easy, but I've survived it once.

I finish playing and remove my hands from the keys. Gently, I fold down their lid. In the empty room, I hear the echo of Riley's encore months ago.

When I turn to look, though, she isn't there.

TWENTY-SIX

Riley

I SIT ON the edge of the pool, feet in the water, guitar in my lap while the sun rises. The desert is painted in soft purples and oranges. I woke up early, hoping the view would inspire me.

It should. It's the kind of perfect moment I chase.

Instead, I strum emptily. I wait for lyrics to rise from the desert, for the light wind to whisper verses in my ear. I'm met with only the morning light, yielding up nothing. I'm stuck. Like I have been all week since Max left.

Every spare moment, I've worked to fill his absence with writing. Nothing has come. It's infuriating. Even ironic, I guess. The songstress of doomed love so heartsick she can't write. I mean, come on.

I'm trapped wondering what he's doing, how he's feeling, where we stand. I haven't called him, though, simply because he's the one who left me. If he wanted to talk, he would call. While my iPhone hasn't lain vacant of notifications, none of them were from him.

I'm not fucking surprised. I'm not going to chase him. Max is a quitter. He always has been.

I set my guitar down. The instrument's hollow body clunkily protests the concrete. Sighing, I climb out of the pool. In the heat, my legs dry quickly.

The problem is incredibly frustrating. I can't write a breakup song when I don't know if we're really broken up. I don't even know if he's still coming to our second Coachella weekend set tonight or not.

I've told myself I don't care. It's one of those lies I want to be true. I shouldn't be headlining Coachella worried about whether my boyfriend will come.

Repeating this sustains me through my joyless day of festival stuff. I drop in to parties. I wander from set to set seeing some bands I don't know, some I do. I ignore the familiar ripples of cell phone cameras held up wherever I go. Closer to the time of my set, I retreat to my trailer, where I let my team prep me for the performance.

The hour comes. My handlers escort me to the stage itself.

It's then that I see him.

Max stands in the main stage's expansive wings, hands in his pockets. His eyes find mine. They look . . . neither longing nor resentful. No different from the way my other touring musicians would meet me. He's just showing up for work.

It's quick resolution to the question of his silence this week. He wasn't yearning, waiting for me to reach out.

Instantly, I find I'm *pissed*.

He stormed out, then didn't feel he owed me even one text? He's only here for the show, I realize, not for me. If not for the concert, he never would have come back.

I suppose it's *some* growth from him. The last time he bailed on me, he didn't come to any of the shows we had planned.

I walk past him, not wanting to talk. I'm ready to sing some fucking breakup songs.

Max doesn't want to explain himself or figure this out? Fine.

I strut onstage to the familiar opening drums of "One Minute." My march. My herald. I hit the opening notes full of spite. It's sort of great, in fact, one of the rare moments when I give myself chills. If I get nothing out of Max's return except for the fervor of my performance, I'll scorch the sky with this silver lining.

The crowd is feeling it. I draw in their energy, converting it into my own. Over the chorus of screams, I shift into the second song, judgmental. *The Breakup Record* is about twelve people, but tonight every song is about Max.

It's cathartic, knowing he's my captive audience. While he has to watch backstage, I fill every note with every feeling I want to say to him, imagining them wrapping his heart in constricting chords.

When I reach "Until You," I feel lighter, like I've gotten some of the wounded weight off my heart. It's like I'm returning to the Riley who played stages like this—well, not *exactly* like this— for years without this fresh pain. Under the lights, I can start forgetting the feeling of losing Max Harcourt for the second time.

Sipping water down my stinging throat, I walk to the front of the stage. "I'm pretty excited to play this next one," I confess to the crowd. They roar their reply. "I think tonight I really need to hear it. Do you?" I pause playfully. "Do you need to hear it?"

Out of the corner of my eye, I see Max walk onstage. It's noticeable how different he looks from his stumbling entrance to our first show. I'm struck by how much life we've fit into these couple months.

"I'd like to bring Max Harcourt up to play with me," I say.

With one modest nod to the fans, Max walks to the piano bench. I wait for him to sit. I prepare myself for him to play the song the way he did when I told him to unleash his feelings. When he played it like he hated it. Full of sound and fury, signifying everything.

Instead, when he starts, he plays the song like I intended it to sound. Broken.

His chords drop like birds with bent wings to the stage. His flourishes reach for heights they will never grasp. It's horrible. It's perfect. When I meet his eyes, I find only hurt in them.

I hold his gaze, and the whole audience disappears. I sing my lyrics to him alone. Into the night, I make their message ring loud. Like I'm reminding him he can abandon me again, but this song and the feelings he knows we shared will follow him forever.

"*Long days, fast years,*" I sing. "*Old hopes, new fears. Future, present, past run in reverse. Feeling best when I expect the worst.*"

I'm furious. I'm heartbroken. I'm pathetically hopeful. He doesn't flinch from my feelings. He faces everything, feeling them with me. It is the purest duet, where the harmony reaches past the notes into songs unsung.

I don't need to see the crowd to know our performance is magnetic. When the song ends, applause roars over us. I hear the fervor distantly, like I'm holding my hands over my ears.

With my stare lingering on Max, I find my face is wet. I don't wipe away the tears. It wouldn't matter even if I did. I imagine I'll feel the imprint of their pathways forever. Facing the crowd, I bow while Max does the same, then leaves the stage.

High on the painful drug of heartache, I play the show of my life. I forget myself entirely, the music holding me under. I don't even know how long passes. I only know when I've finally run out of set list, feeling like I've shed my last skin. I walk offstage, numbly overwhelmed. I don't speak to anyone.

Max is waiting in the wings. Our eyes lock for a flash, and we don't need to say anything to know what will happen next. We said it onstage.

Ignoring everyone who wants to congratulate me, their voices joining into one indistinct chorus, I head to my trailer. Max follows. While the night nips my skin, I hardly feel the cold. I step into my trailer, leaving the door open. I don't turn, not even when I hear him shut the door. Not even when his hands come around my waist, or when his lips find my neck, or when I feel his heart beating against my back.

I press into him, reveling in his warmth. The week I've spent without him feels somehow like eternity stranded in the fog. In every caress, his lips, his hands, write one line onto my skin, repeated endlessly.

This is a bad idea.

I know it, and I know he knows it. The conversation we're going to have afterward waits in the other room. I ignore it a little longer, lapsing instead into one inescapable fact of me. *I love bad ideas.*

I spin in his arms, capturing his lips with mine. I'm crying, or he is. It's the same, in the end. In this moment of collision, we're one. He pulls my dress over my head—I reach for his belt. Major, minor. Music, lyrics.

We pick up speed like we're in freefall. *One last time.*

Max pushes me against the wall while my instincts override

every filament of coherence in my head. I'm pulling off his pants, his shirt. When our chests meet, the contact is electric. It shatters me. Fully no longer in control, I lift my chin, looking up, where the ceiling of my trailer provides our temporary substitute for heaven.

Unable to wait, I reach down. Max pauses in involuntary response, surprised momentarily into stopping the kisses he was devoting to every exposed part of me.

I'm operating on pure instinct, the way I do when I'm in the middle of my set, singing songs I have hundreds of times. The muscle memory of it does not make them less *me*—it makes them more so. Nothing is in my own way. Not even myself.

Riding this unstoppable wavelength, I feel myself collect the condom from my stuff on the couch next to us. I feel Max—the length of him. His hands shift from caressing me to clutching me to clenching, grasping my naked curves like he never wants to let go.

Except he will, I know.

One.

He presses me to the wall in one forceful push. I gasp from the ecstatic surprise, my breath still frayed from my set. Lifting my knee, perching one foot on the end of the couch, I position him where I want him.

He doesn't hesitate. Slowly, he joins us. I press my lips to his shoulder, exhaling with my whole body. I focus for every heart-splitting second on how it feels. Him inside me. Within me. It's the same. It's the culmination.

Last.

We find our rhythm. Every thrust pushes me into the wall of the trailer, pressing the surface to the small of my back. It's like everything happening now, rolling smashes of pleasure coming right up to the edge of discomfort. The reminder that there's something waiting for us on the other side of this one glorious fuck.

Something unyielding. Something final.

Time.

I lower my hands, holding his hips, feeling every movement of his muscles with each stroke he makes into me. The friction sends electricity running through my whole body, smothering every thought silent under the wonderful static.

With feeling rising higher in me, I'm suddenly struck with the sense I'm . . . finishing out the song Max and I have spent the past ten years writing, in one form or other. In literal songs, melding our music. In the soft refrains of pillow talk or wandering conversations. In crushing choruses like this one.

It's the perfect expression of us. This, right now. No harmony has ever felt this way.

Like he's experiencing the same thing, Max suddenly moves deep into me, where he stays. He presses his forehead to the side of my face, his lips dragging over the corner of mine. "*Riley,*" he sighs.

For once, I can't speak. I kiss him, hoping it says everything. *I missed you. I need you. I'll remember you, Max.*

I grip him hard. I grind into him harder. When I explode, everything in me lighting up like the spotlights I love, he does the same.

Until, while we hold each other, the spotlights go dark. I feel like each of us has given up something we will never have again. The room is quiet. The chill of the night dries our sweat commingled on each other.

No matter the peace, the moment is stained with the sense of the ending—the echo of us.

TWENTY-SEVEN

Max

RILEY PULLS ON the sweats and hoodie draped carelessly over the couch. I put my clothes back on. We're silent. We've played our encore. All that's left now is to go home.

Riley pours herself a glass of water. "Did you have a good trip?" she asks.

It's small talk. Stiff, impersonal. It's how I know this is really, really over. In the past decade, we've swung from the soul-exalting heights of passion to silence so huge it swallows years. It's almost impossible to remember that her lips were just pressed to my chest, that I was touching every part of her, writing love songs like frantic scribbles on the map of my heart.

"I did," I say. Gathering my resolve, I press on into the quiet. "I'm sorry for how I left."

She drops into the chair near the door, farthest from me. The way she moves is unfamiliar to me, her limbs slack with exhaustion. I want to pretend it's only from the epic concert she just played. Deep down, I know it isn't.

"I shouldn't have been surprised," she says hollowly. "I honestly didn't expect you to return to finish the tour."

I wish I didn't deserve the stinging shot. "Well . . . ," I begin, shifting on my feet, facing down the message I decided in Harcourt Homes' dark dining room I needed to deliver. "I think it would be best if I dropped out."

Riley puts her glass down. "There it is," she says. Her sarcasm is humorless.

"Riley." I hear the plaintive strain in my voice.

"What? You're bailing on me just like you did ten years ago." She's angry, but I can hear how beneath her anger, she's hurt and trying to cover it. The last thing I want is to hurt her. It doubly breaks my heart.

"Can you honestly ask me to stay when you've practically said we can never be more than another breakup song?"

She stares straight forward, her dull glare fixed on nothing. Her silence says everything, the one answer she's able to give. I feared it no less for knowing it was coming.

It makes me reach down into myself, ripping up something rooted deep. "I love you," I say. Words I haven't spoken to Riley in so long. I can't decide if they sound like dissonance or utter clarity.

She looks at me. "Don't," she warns. "Don't say you love me in the middle of breaking up with me. It's not fair."

I flinch, feeling racked with urgency. "You think I want to do this?" I reply. My words pick up speed, the unique momentum of downward spirals. "I don't. *Of course* I don't. I've spent every waking moment of this week trying to talk myself out of this, to believe if I just . . . gave myself to you, if I let you break my heart,

I would still be happy to have however many days, weeks, years with you."

Her eyes have gone wide. I know I'm not one to share my every feeling. Right now, though, I can't manage to stop.

"But I don't know if that's true," I continue, staring into the center of my words. "I think I have to live my life on my terms. Until you believe what we have is strong enough to last, it's nothing."

"It's not nothing," Riley replies instantly. Her voice crackles with dark charge, like while I was speaking, she carefully seared the exhaustion out of every corner of her. "You. Us. It's everything to me. Can't you see that? Can't you see the fact that I would risk even more pain just to be with you is proof of how much I love you?"

The declaration she's snuck into her question cuts the conversation clean open. Everything stops until she goes on. Her voice is different. Where she was protesting, now she's pleading.

"I *love* you, Max," she says. "I never stopped. Every song. Every fucking note I sing is inspired by you."

They're the words I've yearned for. It makes them deadly now, dreams sharpened into daggers.

I don't know how to explain to Riley why they don't fix what's wrong with us. In the end, the question isn't whether you love someone—it's how you love them.

"Then I'm giving you what you want, right?" I ask. "Just write the breakup song now."

Riley wilts, wounded. "I didn't— That's not what I meant. You're more than a song to me."

I shake my head, hating how everything in the room is imprinting itself on my mind. In some ways, I feel I'll never leave this trailer. Heaven changed into purgatory.

"It's not me you don't believe in," I reply. "It's yourself. You don't think you deserve a love that lasts. I feel like you've told yourself the same story too many times not to believe it. You're the Breakup Queen."

Riley's rearing up to cut me off when I continue.

"But I wish you knew you write incredible breakup songs because you're you," I say, "not the other way around."

Her expression closes up. The light in her looks fragile. I understand why, I do. Hearing yourself mischaracterized hurts—of course it does. Hearing yourself described exactly right, down to the flaws whose painful costs you can't escape, hurts worse.

It's why I keep my voice gentle. "You could write anything, Riley. You could *be* anything. I really hope you see that one day. I'll be listening until you do."

I fall silent, having reached the end. Not just of my speech. Of . . . everything. I wait, not knowing why.

Riley watches me, steeliness resolving in her eyes. The unrestrained conviction that makes her *her*. She's not going to give. She's not going to promise something she can't uphold.

I love her for it. I really do.

At the end of the conversation, I start to notice sounds outside, like I'm returning to the world. The pounding of the music from festival parties still going in the late-night tents. The security staff outside. The cars on the city streets not far from the grounds.

The surrealism of it, the improbability, is overwhelming. I'm having the most important, most painful conversation of my life in the middle of Coachella, in the headliner's trailer.

She stands up, holding her hand out to me. Impossibly, her

lips curl in a small smile. "Thank you for playing with me, Max Harcourt."

I take her hand, knowing it might be the last time I touch her. It splits my heart into pieces. But I'll hear her voice on the radio, or on my record player whenever I want. It's something. A torture I'll relish forever.

The idea of her releasing my hand, severing the connection, is unbearable. I don't let her, not yet. Instead, I pull her into one final hug, crushing the sob in my chest into her frame.

She strokes my back. "You're going to have the happiest life," she says. The quiet whisper is nearly unrecognizable from the woman whose voice could fill the world. "You deserve it. You'll find someone who's everything I'm not, everything you need her to be. You'll be okay."

My body shudders. They're words I know she's spoken to herself in the depth of other nights, ones she's lyricized like no one else could. She isn't just saying goodbye. She's singing me the purest song she knows.

Her voice is choked when she continues. "It's an honor to have my heart broken by you."

I laugh wetly. It's strange, this feeling of searching for the last things I want to say to her. I find one. "You taught me what love is, too, you know. It's why I couldn't listen to 'Until You.' I didn't want to remember that," I confess. "I won't forget it now."

Riley smiles sadly. "Would you rather I'd written you something unmemorable?"

Whether knowingly or not, she's hit on the question I've struggled with since the day I found out I was the song's inspiration. Would I rather she not have spun our fleeting love into the pop charts' greatest heartbreak hit?

"No," I say with the deepest honesty. "It's perfect."

In the smallest shift of her body, I feel it—her relief.

I pull back. "Take care, Riley." Every word, every second, is effort. When I walk toward the door, I feel like I'm ripping myself from her. If I didn't, I would never leave. She's my siren, even when she's not singing.

I have to concentrate on every movement my legs make as I move to the door. With only the night waiting for me, I walk out of Riley's life for the last time.

TWENTY-EIGHT

Riley

I'M LIVING MY lyrics once more.

The next weeks pass in the forgettable haze of what's become my life. I fly from Coachella to Chicago to continue my tour without Max. In every seat in Soldier Field, rings of light surrounding me from the floor to the sky, I see someone who might feel like I do, or might have, once. I put all my heartache into my performances, not letting myself forget the opportunity I have in the open wound from which I can let music spill.

I sell out stadiums. I play "Until You" on my guitar.

Whenever I catch myself wondering if I just saw Max's face in the audience, or in the stadium corridors, or in the green room, I chase off the guilty hope. Whenever my mom asks, I say I'm *fine* with him leaving.

I'm not, of course.

Speculation has gone wild. Online and in magazines, everyone declares I've gone through yet another breakup. Instead of working to ignore it like usual, I indulge in the nasty commentary. When I read about strangers wondering if it's *some sort of performance art*, I wonder with them.

I go on a late-night show, and the first question is whether I'm single. I smile. I say I'm never not in love. I perform my music under the studio's lights, singing pain like it's second nature. I return to my hotel, where I keep performing it in other ways. In some sense, I start to feel like I'm performing it every minute of every day.

I lie awake on the bus, fighting not to imagine Max sleeping just feet from me. When I fail, I seek solace in the living space, where song after song comes to me. It keeps happening. I've never slept so little in my life, nor have I felt myself so frighteningly in the grip of inspiration. I scribble lyrics everywhere. Coffee cups, receipts, napkins, even my hand.

I think about Max so much while I'm writing that the memory of us loses its sting. I still miss him in an ache that never fades, but I have no more tears to shed over him.

I continue from city to city. In St. Louis, I make excuses for not visiting home, knowing deep down I'm not ready to combine losing Max with what I know I'll find, cardboard boxes of my mom's possessions waiting for relocation when she moves somewhere new.

Whatever my feelings on the new shape of my family, the middle of my tour, with hours until my show, is not the moment to rattle myself with them. Instead, I hole up in the hotel, where I get nothing done.

My mom, I expect, does the same. We haven't spoken more on the changes she's considering in her life. Regardless, I'm guessing she's using the tour to get some space from the collapse of her marriage, not to fit in some quick packing in the suburbs fifteen minutes from here.

My dad joins me for lunch in my room. It's really, really nice, even if he sees right past my upbeat, prepared veneer to the wounds I'm hiding. Of course he's read every headline. He knows how, just months since my divorce was finalized, my *next* relationship has now failed. Yet here I am, playing for fans like I'm the same old Riley.

He says it worries him. I laugh it off.

I give my St. Louis show everything, like the city has given everything to me. The next morning, I'm gone.

Indianapolis's Lucas Oil Stadium is unexpectedly one of my favorite stops. Inside the stadium's stately walls, I guess I just feel for the first time recently like everyone is *glad* to see me instead of curious. After the first show, I don't return to my hotel. I've found writing in the hotel is harder. The rooms are designed to feel like blank slates.

I don't need blank slates. I need texture. I need the place where Max shaped piano chords with his hands on the table in the middle of the night, where he made us laugh and stunned us in the costumes I chose for him. I need the home I've known for the past few months, the hardest and happiest of my life.

It's pleasant outside in the middle of the night. The bus waits in the hotel's rear lot where we parked. I hum the melodic line I have stuck in my head while I walk up, the urgency of exciting ideas speeding my steps.

When I reach the doors, though, I find . . . duct tape on the window.

I stop, confused, remembering the conversation I had with

Max about how we should indicate we'd brought someone back to the bus. Max is gone, though. Only my mom—

I feel the color drain from my face. It's safe to say the melody I was humming has disappeared from my head. Slowly, delicately, I retreat like the parking lot is littered with land mines.

It's too late. The door flies open, revealing Frank.

I'm lost for a moment. How did Frank even learn the system? Did I misremember the duct tape discussion? Was he there? Did *he* bring someone back to the bus?

While I'm sorting out what I'm seeing, my mom emerges in the doorway next to him. Her face is the color of pink carnations.

There's no fighting the way my mouth flies open.

"We were just, uh, finishing—I mean, leaving. We were leaving," Frank fumbles to say. With effort he forces something like nonchalance. "What are you doing here, Riley?"

Honestly, he's sort of adorably flustered for a hulking, tattooed long-haul driver. He shifts in the doorway, shoulder pressed to the metal frame.

I put a hand on my hip playfully. My mortification is subsiding under the strength of his.

Yes, it's a little weird knowing anything about my mother's sex life, and even weirder that it no longer involves my dad. Still, I'm glad my mom is moving on. I know better than anyone how important it is. The recovery is its own ritual, with its own joys, its own opportunities. Sunrise has wonders sunshine doesn't.

"How long has this been going on?" I ask, genuinely curious. From the way my mom naturally leans closer to Frank, I get the sense this isn't the first time. I'm impressed how discreet they've remained.

My mom winces. "Since you left for Coachella," she confesses.

With the pieces fitting into place, I smirk. "And you said you didn't want to come because it was, quote, *too hot, too loud, not enough bathrooms*," I chide, enjoying reprising the excuses I heard plenty in the weeks leading up to the festival. "You could have just said you wanted to spend time with Frank."

"Riley, I'm sorry. I'm sure this is uncomfortable," Frank says. He rubs his head, looking distinctly uneasy. "I've probably crossed a line here."

"Oh, shut up," I reply unhesitatingly. "I love you, Frank. If anyone was going to hook up with my mom, I'd want it to be you."

Frank nods, still stiff, but he manages a smile. "Okay. Good. I have a lot of respect for, um, both of you. Obviously."

In the funniest way, I'm reminded of how tours like this don't just come with the self-evident, headliner joys. They're full of secret gifts, unexpected flourishes of the universe. Perfect beignets, impromptu jam sessions, people I never would have encountered otherwise. Frank is one. Without nights on the road, I never would have met one of the most unfailingly loyal, profoundly kind men I know. Nor would my mom. "It's okay if you leave now," I encourage him gently.

"Thank god," he says emphatically.

I laugh, exchanging a look with my mom, who's fighting not to smile. Sweeping my arm aside, I usher Frank out of the bus. When he passes me, he stops and faces my mom.

"I'll call you later," he promises. It's nice to hear his unflappable Frank-ness return.

My mom loses the fight with her smile. She doesn't need to reply. The way she's lit up says she would very much like it if he did.

She retreats from the doorway. I follow her inside, where she collapses into the booth. It's dark in the little living space, the familiar stage for many moments I'll never forget. This is definitely one of them.

"Now I know how you felt when we caught—what was his name? Nick something?—sneaking out of your room when you were in high school," my mom says weakly.

"Nick Lynn," I supply. "And I didn't give you half as hard a time as you and Dad did me."

She nods, knowing I'm right. I was grounded for weeks, including missing the Yeah Yeah Yeahs show I was looking forward to. Nick's nighttime visit was honestly not worth it.

My mom meets my eyes, her expression more serious. "Sincerely, you're okay with this?" she asks.

I don't hesitate. "Yes. I know Dad is dating. You should do the same. It's weird, but weird isn't bad. Just . . . something to get used to."

My mom studies me, determining whether I'm being honest. Her conclusion reached, she nods. "You were right to bring me on tour," she says. "I'm glad I came."

I notice the pull of unfamiliar rhythms in her words. Interrupting my mom's hookups is new, definitely. A discussion like this is revelatory in other, deeper ways. Here, I'm not *the daughter*, high school ground-ee or precocious popstar, or her *the mom*, weary with wisdom. We're closer to equals, sharing life.

"I'm glad, too," I say.

She straightens up, looking around like she's realized something. "What are you even doing here?" she asks. "Why aren't you in your hotel room?"

I gaze past her. My guitar in its case is leaning against the counter. I sift through everything I could say. *I can't sleep. I can't stop writing. I can't stop.* "I write better in here," I settle for saying.

Mom frowns. She can read volumes in verses no matter what I say. Knowing where this is going, I get up and grab the guitar. I'm hoping to signal I don't want to have this conversation.

"Riley." Her voice is patiently firm.

"I'm fine. Really," I preempt her. "I've been dumped before. I'll get through it like always."

"You don't have to put on a brave face, though. Not with me," Mom replies. "I know what Max meant to you."

I unlock the guitar case. The instrument inside is one of my oldest friends in the world. I pull out the Taylor, fixating on its shiny body, the strings silver in the moonlight. "I pour my heart out in song every night," I remind her. "I'm not exactly putting on a brave face."

She shakes her head. "I don't mean then. I mean now, when it's just us. No music."

Only with my fingers on the strings can I fight off the frustration her words leave me with. She doesn't understand. I resent myself for resenting it.

I let out my breath. "I can't," I explain patiently. "I can't let a moment of sadness spoil this. I've worked toward this tour for practically my entire life. If I let *breaking up with my boyfriend* ruin this, I'm exactly what every one of my haters says I am. Overdramatic. Shallow. Besides . . ."

My next words don't come readily. It's because I need my mom to understand, so she'll let go. Sinking into the booth opposite her, I focus like I do in the middle of the night when I feel the perfect chorus just past my fingertips' reach.

"I don't really think I have a right to be upset. I mean, this, my career, is because of my breakups. I should be grateful," I say, repeating words I've routinized into daily recitations. "I *am* grateful. Who's to say I would even have all this if Max and I had lived happily ever after ten years ago."

The truth is, I have details deep in me I've never dared write into song. I've rendered the hurts, the joys, the hopes, the fears. I've never written the could-have-been. Its images have become seared into my eyelids from how often I've imagined them. *We go on tour together. We graduate together. We move in together, somewhere near Harcourt Homes. While Max helps his family, I never stop chasing my dream. We do it together.*

It's the only thing I'm scared of writing.

"That's—" Mom starts to say. She stops herself, staring out the window into the dark of the parking lot, reconsidering. "I understand."

My eyes widen. It's certainly not the response I was expecting to my guiltiest personal quandary. I don't know whether I'm more surprised or relieved.

"When your life is good, when you've achieved your goals, when you have reasons to look forward to tomorrow," she goes on carefully, like she's fitting puzzle pieces into place, "it's easy to justify everything else. Everything that isn't good. They feel like necessary sacrifices, or payments. What life wants you to put on the other side of the scale."

I watch her, my nervous hands going still on my guitar. While I'm realizing where some of my poeticism comes from, this revelation isn't what silences me.

"I . . . ," she goes on. "Well, I never said it out loud, but I wasn't happy in my marriage for a long time. I told myself the unhappiness didn't matter. It was small on the scale of everything else my marriage had brought me—everything else I wanted. You, family, our home. I knew something was missing in the way your dad and I interacted. I just convinced myself it didn't matter."

I've never witnessed the sadness in my mom's eyes right now. Years' worth, like she's never cracked the door where the feeling hides. I watch her close it now, smiling softly.

"It took your dad making that decision for me, and I'm so glad he did," she says. The humor in her voice is self-conscious. She knows *glad* is not exactly how her daughter would describe the distraught conversations we shared on the floor of my new house, or how she knew I noticed when we would go weeks of phone calls without her laugh.

Writing has given me instincts for feeling each word's every meaning, though. Sometimes *glad* means warmth without meaning light.

While I listen, she goes on. "I shouldn't have suffered through anything just because of what it once gave me," she says. "You shouldn't, either. You don't need to live with heartache, Riley. You don't have to pretend it's a good thing," she says. "Because once you let go of the thing that hurts you, you could find so much more."

She takes my hand. It's funny noticing the different calluses we have. Mine from guitar strings, hers from gardening. With her hand in mine, they feel very much the same.

"I never would have come on this tour. I never would have met Frank. I never would have considered living somewhere new." Her voice is choked up, the way it was in our newly divorced conversations, except with the exact opposite emotion. The same sound, yet subject to the universe's incandescent revisions. "I'm so glad I have this chance, because I really believe great things are ahead for me."

I squeeze her hand. "They are."

She smiles. "They are for you, too."

I let myself really hear her. My breath catches a little, almost a sob, almost a sigh of relief. I don't know what to say. I know only how much I need my mom. Even now, with my name written on reverse in the windows I'm gazing out of, the sound of the stadium I filled still ringing in my ears. Especially now, maybe.

"I'll leave you to your music," she says, standing up. "But maybe not too late tonight, okay?"

"Okay, fine." I laugh, nostalgic for school nights in my childhood bedroom, for songs I was only just learning to write, for dreams whose costs hadn't revealed themselves to me yet.

Satisfied, my mom grins. She leaves the bus, heading for the hotel.

With only my guitar for company, I sit in the stillness of the night. I pull the instrument into my lap, thumbing the callouses on the fingers of my left hand. I've put so much pain into this. I've turned heartbreak into art, into success, into fame and wild fantasy. I've made it the cornerstone of monuments I've sent soaring into the sky, unable to be ignored. I've reveled in the splendor of my kingdom of sorrow.

But it's fucking hurt.

I start to believe my mom is right. What if I have held myself back from something even greater? I've tried to believe my sacrifices were worth it.

Now, without Max, I'm not so sure.

On unsteady legs, I return to where the guitar case leans on the kitchenette counter. Fighting myself, I unlock the latches, exposing the velvet interior. I place my guitar inside, then close the lid.

In the moonlight, I let myself cry.

TWENTY-NINE

Max

PIANO MUSIC FILLS the room. It occupies the space like the sunlight filtering in the curtained windows, everywhere and nowhere. It's "Für Elise," gentle, enigmatic. It isn't perfect—while nearly every note is in place, they're played haltingly. I find myself remembering what Riley told me. Music doesn't need to be perfect. Sometimes it's more human if it's not.

On the keyboard her granddaughter got her for her eighty-ninth birthday, Linda plays the piece. I tap a leading tempo with my foot, relaxed. We're in her room in Harcourt Homes, where I've picked back up the lessons I was giving her before I went on tour.

I'd be lying if I said I've been happy since I left the Breakup Tour. I've been heartbroken, even if being here has felt right. I know without a doubt it's where I'm meant to be.

Still, I wish I could have worked things out with Riley. I wish she believed our romance didn't have to end one way.

I miss her. Or, I miss *being* with her, because in other ways she's inescapable. Her voice, her face, headlines featuring her name. She's everywhere, like she has been for years. My old labyrinth where the walls just keep getting higher.

When Linda finishes the song, I applaud. I'm a second too late.

She whirls on me, her eyes accusatory. "Am I boring you?" she asks.

I straighten, embarrassed. "No," I reply earnestly. "That was lovely. This week, let's work on tempo and not emphasizing every beat. Think of every measure like a sentence. Only some words get emphasis."

Linda waves off my instruction. I knew she would. Once provoked, her imperiousness is not easily stifled. "If you're going to be lost in thought during the lessons I pay you for," she replies loftily, "you're going to share those thoughts."

I exhale a laugh. "I was just thinking it's nice to be home," I say honestly.

Linda narrows her eyes.

"I really am happy to be home," I insist, not entirely sure why I feel compelled to convince her. "I tried music out. I just prefer it . . . like this." I nod to Linda's keyboard. "Harcourt Homes is my place."

"Well, of course," Linda replies impatiently. "But it wasn't really *music* you were giving another shot, was it?"

I stand. This I won't discuss, not even with my favorite resident. "It doesn't really matter," I say.

While some decisions measure their rightness in the comfort they provide, others weigh it in their hardship. I know the choice to let Riley go was right *because* I haven't wavered despite how deeply it hurts. The pain is the proof.

Under Linda's inquisitive disappointment, I change the subject. "You're coming to Jess's going-away party tonight, right?"

This week is my sister's last at Harcourt Homes before her move to New York. I've been planning this surprise party with the staff for weeks. It's helped distract me from the reality of Jess's departure. First everything with Riley, then my sister departing for New York—I'm set on life changes for the foreseeable future. Of course, I haven't overlooked the irony. Me firmly staying while Jess is firmly leaving.

"I certainly am." Linda looks indignant I dared imagine otherwise.

I smile. As I start to head toward the door, she reaches into her pocket.

When the opening of "Heartbreak Road" fills the room behind me, I wonder if perhaps I'm dreaming. I once found Riley's unexpected presence in the dining room downstairs mirage-like. I feel the same now, hearing our creation, our love's legacy. One of life's echoes, resonating into now.

It's coming from the speakers on Linda's phone. The sound is small, even frail.

Riley put the song out a couple weeks ago. She called and asked me for permission first. I granted it, only requesting I receive credit under a pseudonym. Privately, I found it fitting. Hearing the recording, I felt like the person who played the piano in the studio in Houston was someone else. Not me.

It's another hit, dueling with "Until You" in the charts. Of course it is. The song is fantastic, no matter what now-disappeared versions of us played its chords.

I don't want to hear it right now, even if the money from my writing credit has let me look into buying the empty lot behind Harcourt Homes to expand. I like the feel of this new dream. It's what I want—not what I *could* want, one day.

In this way, I've remained grateful for "Heartbreak Road" without listening to the song itself. I can't. It would make me miss Riley unbearably. Not even just because I would be hearing her voice. With this song, I know from exactly what corners of her heart she pulled its parts. I would remember every detail of the night we wrote it, one of the greatest of my life.

"Beautiful song," Linda remarks. "I especially like the piano part. Whoever recorded it really thought of every measure like a sentence." Her eyes practically twinkle in the fading afternoon light.

I laugh. "So you *were* listening. Glad to know you're getting at least some of your money's worth out of our lessons."

She waves me out good-naturedly. "I'll work on it this week."

I reach for the door, feeling somehow better. Maybe there's something in this—sharing your music with people. Maybe it helps you bear the emotions inside the notes. The realization only makes me feel closer to Riley.

"Max." Linda's voice halts me in the doorway. "I really think she loves you."

I don't face her. "Yeah." I nod. "I think so, too."

I close her door behind me, stepping out into the hallway. It's quiet but not silent on Saturday afternoons. Some residents have their doors open. From them I catch fragments of conversation from visiting families. It's one of my favorite parts of this place, honestly. How many independent stories, lives in their infinite complexity, it contains in neat rows. I could compare them to the rooms of hospitals or hotels. In fact, it's some of each.

Yet the comparison my mind makes is to the sound booths of recording studios, for no reason except Riley.

Needing a moment to myself, I head to my office. On the way,

I pass parts of the home I note need fixing. The wobble in the banister, the water damage from a leak we patched in the sunroom's ceiling years ago.

They don't weigh on me now. I like improving them. I'm grateful to Riley that I'm able to.

It's nice, except in the one way it isn't. In every repair, I find new remembrances of Riley, new pinpricks of longing. I wish I didn't have to feel the loss comingled with the joy in the changing pieces of this place. I don't know when every reminder of her will no longer hurt. Will there be a day I don't think of her unless I pass her billboards on my drive or hear her voice on the radio?

I can't imagine it now. The missing is constant.

I close my office door and sit down in my chair. While I've sat here on countless days, in every circumstance, the memory this place rings clearest with is the day she was here, when she asked me if I'd listened to her album. It's like I can still see her, like her scent still clings in the room. It's the impossible way Riley is, leaving me always either hoping or haunted.

Giving up performing music wasn't hard because it wasn't my dream. Riley was my dream.

I would do anything to not have to give her up.

In the depth of moments like this, I know there's no use fighting the pain. I might as well indulge it. I want to hear her voice. I *need* to hear her voice. I can't possibly feel worse.

I find "Heartbreak Road" on Spotify—when I hit play, the intro I heard in Linda's room fills the office with suffocating force. Its rhythm whisks me onto highways paved with passion, lined with rest stops I rarely visit now. The dark of the tour bus, where we made music together. The sound of her breathing when I would wake up in the night. The kiss we shared at the piano.

The smaller moments, not the ones onstage. They feel fleeting now. They feel stolen.

I'm so lost in the music I don't hear anyone approach until my door flies open. I reach hastily to shut the computer, but I'm too late.

Jess stands in the doorway. "Oh my god, Max," she chides playfully. "I feel like I'm in high school again, walking in on you listening to one of the songs you would duet with Riley and moping."

"You're not supposed to be here. You're no longer an employee of Harcourt Homes," I muster, knowing she's right. Comparing me to myself in college is, frankly, charitable. My present love-sickness is way worse.

"I didn't want to be late to my surprise party," she says, rolling her eyes.

I don't bother reprimanding her for knowing about the surprise—Jess has always had a knack for getting privileged information out of our parents. She's known the contents of every birthday and Christmas present since we were kids.

She sits in the chair that used to be hers, in front of the desk she cleaned out days ago. "For real, bro. You okay?" she asks, concern in her eyes.

I know Jess feels like she's abandoning me in my heartbreak by moving. But I also know I can't lie to her. She'd see through me. Like she saw through my parents' ruse to drop by the home tonight before dinner with her to pick up a sweater my mom "forgot."

"How do I get over someone like her?" I can't hide the searching strain in the question. It's sort of nice saying it out loud instead of just repeating it endlessly in my head. "I mean, how could anyone get over her? The whole country loves her. She's everywhere except here with me."

Even while I'm saying it, I hear how vain it sounds, my pleading with the universe. I'm not entitled to hold on to my daydream just because I held her once.

"I just miss her," I go on weakly.

Jess nods sympathetically. Then her eyes light up. "Yeah, you're right," she says, like she's working something out. "She's everywhere. If you miss her"—she shrugs like the conclusion is obvious—"go see her."

I slouch. "We've said everything we have to say to each other."

"No, I don't mean talk to her," Jess replies intently. "I mean, *go see her*. The same way the entire rest of the city of Los Angeles is looking forward to seeing her."

I glance up, my heart leaping.

Of course. I've watched worshippers flock to the shrine of the music of Riley Wynn for months. I can be near her the same way. I can be there for her without being *with* her. I don't have to close myself off from her completely. I broke my promise to play on her tour, but I can still be there for the final show.

Reading my face, Jess smiles.

In a rush of new urgency, I open my computer again. It's surreal, feeling the longing start to lessen. With my heart lighter, I do what I should have done the first time I saw Riley was going on tour.

I buy tickets to her concert.

THIRTY

Riley

I'M GLAD TO be home.

Being back in LA is welcome in ways I didn't expect. While I love the road, returning here carries the soul satisfaction of finishing something. Despite its personal upheavals, I'm proud of the tour. While it wasn't necessarily everything *I* wanted, it was everything I wanted to give fans.

This earned, even weary, fulfillment is what finds me in the dressing room on the night of the Breakup Tour's final US show. I'm playing the Rose Bowl, the city's famous stadium. It's one more dream improbably within my reach. I haven't gotten used to the magic of far-flung hopes realized. I hope I never do.

In a few months, I'll start the international leg of the tour. In the meantime, I'm looking forward to spending some settled days here. I'm ready to return to my empty house, to make it *mine*. To write new music there. To find out what my next chapter will be.

First, however, I'm going to say goodbye to *The Breakup Record* for a little while. And I'm going to do it with my whole heart.

I put on my wedding dress, which no longer feels like Wesley's. It feels like sixteen cities across the United States—enclaves of memory, stages where I split the kaleidoscope of myself open on other nights like this one. It feels like my fans, like the love I share with them. Where the dress once stood for romance, it now represents a different kind of relationship, the one I'm grateful to have with the people who have been touched by my music.

In the pre-show hour, I head into the greenroom. Everyone is feeling the way I do. I pick up on the pride combined with sentimentality immediately. It's like walking in electric haze. The band isn't joining me on the international segments of the tour, so the sense of finality is even greater. I shake everyone's hands with sincere thanks for each. Kev, solemnly focused. Hamid, jumpy with excitement or caffeine. Savannah, headphones on until I come over. Vanessa, her fingers pattering endless rhythms on every surface in reach.

Finally, it's showtime.

I walk to the stage, hearing the pre-show countdown and music. I let it speed my pulse, like the opening drums drive my heart itself. When the lights hit me, I beam at the stadium—at the people who've been there for me, who made everything possible.

The Rose Bowl is radiant. The view is distinctly Los Angeles, the mountains dusky pink past the high white rim of the stadium. On the edges of the floor standing room, the green of grass hides.

Endless flashing lights greet me. I allow only one single pang in my heart knowing Max isn't one of them.

I kick off the show, determined to enjoy every second. Which I do. I race up the steep sides of "One Minute," revel in the sweet swing of "Sacramento," lose myself in the quiet of "Novembers."

When I reach "Until You," which has been hard for me to play since Max's departure, I remind myself the song is no longer only ours. It's found its way into other hearts, entwining itself with losses I'll never know, feeding flickers of hope in private corners of other lives.

I strum the opening chords, still unwilling to play the song on piano. With Max gone, my own skill on the keys is not up to the performance I want to give, which left me with the prospect of having someone else play the piano part.

I haven't wanted to, of course. I can't imagine playing the song with anyone except Max. While "Until You" has found homes in endless other hearts, the way I hear it in mine is inextricable from him.

I picture him at Harcourt Homes, playing something old on his piano. Maybe he's thinking of me. Is it pride or narcissism to imagine he might? It feels more like peace, the idea that his song will play on elsewhere, even if it's one I will no longer hear.

I hope he's happy.

While my chords fill the stadium, I decide happy isn't all. I hope he knows I'll always love him, in the way of loving my first favorite song. It stays in my heart even while my musical lexicon widens, the love changing form, with nostalgia, grace, and gratitude shaping it into something past pure passion. I want him to know he's part of me now.

Instead of continuing into the intro of "Until You," I strum open chords as I walk to the front of the stage, where I address the audience. While the cheering is unceasing, I feel the collective pause, something indiscernible shifting in the night. It's like the whole stadium feels the edge I'm stepping up to.

"You know, I used to think all my heartbreaks were worth it

as long as I got a new song to sing," I say. "I love my art. I love writing breakup songs. I think we need breakup songs—I know I certainly do."

I pause, smiling to my fans, letting them inside the joke. It's the magic I work on every stage, the marvel of making intimacy out of places like this. I love it. I want everyone here, packed in with strangers surrounding them, to feel like they have a private pass into the hallways of my heart.

This morning I woke up wanting to make this show something special. With one performance, I can end one era of my career and open the door to another.

I shift the chords under my fingers.

"Until You" does not rise from my guitar. Instead, what forms is decisive, firmly sweet. With repetition, melody starts to sound like structure, like sentences into poetry. It's no longer strumming. It's a song.

Feeling the change, the crowd starts to shriek. "I'll never stop writing breakup songs," I say. "But I think I need to admit that I'm sort of tired of having my heart broken."

I hear someone shout loudly enough to be heard. "You'll be okay, Riley!"

Smiling, I play on. "I think next time I fall in love, I'll write more songs like this one. Love songs," I say. "This is 'Unsung.'"

It's the song I started in the desert a decade ago. I finished it yesterday, in the music room of my house in the Hills, in my own private emotional exorcism. I was feeling off whenever I set foot in my former favorite room because one of the only memories I have of it is when Max played "Until You" for me. I felt like he was still there, or should have been.

So yesterday, I let him in. Finishing the song he inspired with sunlight shining in on the piano, it was like I could feel him there.

I sing the opening lines. *"You make days feel like nights of stars, when the pressure ends, when the sky is warm."* My voice floats over the crowd, who have lost it hearing me play something new. *"You wrote with me in the dead of dark. Held me in your words, made me feel the spark."*

It's hard. No, it's *fucking* hard playing this untested piece. I have none of the usual struts I use for self-confidence. No one has heard the song. Not Eileen, not my mom. It has a newborn fragility—and it's painful. It hurts to think of the feelings of love that haven't faded from my heart, to remember writing some of this when we were together.

It hurts like I knew love songs could. I'm living out the very reason for my fear of writing them. Breakups remain forever. Love can vanish. I'm standing on one of the grandest stages of my life, singing what's supposed to be the happiest song, full of sadness instead.

No, I correct myself.

Sadness is not the only feeling I find in this song, because it isn't only about Max. It's about myself, the Riley who dared to write it. Who dared to love. For the next few minutes, I'm her. Even though it hurts, it's not a punishment. It's just a complicated gift.

It feels right. It feels like hope.

Hope that one day, with someone, it'll last. Because I'm worth it.

THIRTY-ONE

Max

HUNDREDS OF FEET from Riley, I watch her sing a love song on a giant screen.

The audience around me is hushed, held silent in joined rapture. In the dark of the night over the Rose Bowl, the stage where Riley strums her guitar is a stunning center of light, like the moon descended into our midst. While Riley unravels the first verse, everyone is listening carefully.

None as carefully as I am. *"Past the studio door, shaken to the floor. You gave me everything, then you gave me more,"* she sings in the song's rolling rhythm. *"I reach into songs I never knew I could finish only in the name of you."*

With strumming like punctuation, she hits the chorus. *"You make me sing songs I would've left unsung."*

I recognize the lyrics. They're . . . about me.

And it's a love song.

Riley wrote me a love song.

The studio door. Shaken to the floor. With "Until You," Riley rendered unforgettably one of the hardest days of my life. With

"Unsung," she's memorializing my most wonderful night. *Our* night.

I watch her, riveted. The screens show everything in grippingly familiar detail. The way her lips move, the way she sways with the song's rhythm, the way her chest rises and falls with her singing.

Only the song's power pulls me from how gorgeous she looks. It's . . . stunning. There's still sadness in it, the melancholy Riley writes so well, but it's loving, and sincere, and hopeful.

The way Riley sings, the way she puts herself into her music while connecting with the crowd, it's like she's singing *all* of us a love song. I grip my armrest until my knuckles turn white. The love of my life is singing a love song to me and she doesn't even know it.

I want to stand up, to wave my arms, to shout and tell her *I'm here. I'm here. I'm listening.*

I love you, too.

It isn't just about the song. It's that she even wrote it. That she heard me when I said I need her to try to believe in us. To believe she's worth writing a love song.

Now that she does, I don't want to spend another second without her. It hits me with painful irony that I could be onstage with her right now. She could be singing this song to me and only me. I'm jealous. I want to be the only one in this stadium. I want to be at her side. I want to go home with her. To wake up with her tomorrow. To hear this song sung at the kitchen table, in the shower together, when her voice isn't warmed up yet and the notes crack.

Instead, I'm stuck hundreds of feet away, watching, with nobody but myself to blame.

I feel Jess nudge my elbow with hers. When I pull my eyes

from Riley's onscreen, I see my sister looking at me with tears in her eyes. She smiles, telling me she's with me. She understands.

Grateful for her presence, I lean into her arm while Riley finishes her declaration of love to an audience of eighty thousand people she doesn't know I'm part of. I want desperately to believe I haven't ruined us. That I haven't destroyed our last chance of happiness together. It makes Riley's performance equally wondrous and wrenching.

When she finishes the song, I applaud with everyone else. Just another nameless face in the audience of people who love Riley Wynn.

On the screen she smiles at me—at everyone—beautifully bashful. Her eyes sweep the stadium. *Is she looking for me?* my battered heart wonders. More likely, she's just taking in the moment. She hands her guitar off, then picks the mic up out of the stand.

She's breathless when she speaks. "Thank you for humoring me. I'll never forget playing that one, here, in my own town." She waits while all of Los Angeles cheers. "Now," she continues, her voice stronger, her winking smile returning, "back to breakup songs."

I hang on to her words, lost under her spell. She looks freer. The whole show, she's put everything into every song, having fun. She's captivating, like always—I've just never had the chance to feel her radiance from the audience. Watching her has been a gift, better even than performing with her. It's let me sit in awe of her.

"I want to do something different with this next one, though," she goes on. "It's no secret that I was accompanied for most of this tour by an incredible pianist. Without him, I've played 'Until You' on guitar. I'm not the strongest piano player, and I . . ." She looks down, swallowing hard, like tears are climbing up her throat.

The pounding in my chest could fill the stadium. It could fill the world. I don't know if I'm ready to hear "Until You" played to me without me. It won't just ring with the memories we've spent months on tour sharing. It will resound with the ones I've spent so much of my life writing.

"I haven't wanted to play with anyone but Max," she admits.

Hearing my name over the Rose Bowl's speakers—it's heart-break in one syllable.

Riley fidgets with the mic in her hand. "But on the final night of this tour, I want to do this song the way it's meant to be played," she says. "Please be kind about my piano playing?"

The crowd replies with roars as she walks, shakily for the first time onstage, up to the piano that should be mine. I don't know whether the moment seems stolen or whether it's in exactly the hands it was meant to find.

Riley sits, adjusts the mic, and places her fingers on the keys.

The music she draws forth is hesitant, like it isn't sure it welcomes its new master. She plays some chords in the key of the song, warming up, then hits a wrong note. In front of the stadium's imposing rings, their rows glittering with camera lights, she winces dramatically. It's unselfconscious, one more little way she lets the rest of us feel part of the world she's conjuring onstage.

Recovering her composure, she starts anew with a simplified intro. The elegant skeleton of "Until You," rendered in its neat structure.

It leaves me hungry for every note. While Riley isn't as confident on piano, she's an incredible musician. The choices she makes to strip the song down to her capabilities are smart—despite her physical limitations with it, she understands the piano. No dexterity could match the intuition in her playing, the way she guides the song's emotional strokes with offhand finesse. It's the charcoal sketch of the melody.

And it's . . . hurting her.

In a flash I see what the rest of the crowd can't. The struggle in her eyes on the massive screens. She knows she's not giving the song everything it deserves, and she doesn't like it.

Her skill on the piano is not the only hardship, either. Knowing her well enough to read every inflection on her face, I realize she's wrestling with the change from song to song. She was just putting her heart into the love song, *our* love song. Now she's singing our breakup. Wedding vows to our eulogy. It's weighing on her in ways "Until You" hasn't on other nights, in other cities.

In an instant, I know what I have to do.

I don't care if it's impossible. Riley makes the impossible look possible to me every day. Impossible like hearing someone else write the songs in your heart. Impossible like changing into twelve versions of herself under the spotlights. With Riley, I can find in myself someone who doesn't recognize fear or reservation. Only need.

I need to play this song with her.

I turn to Jess, opening my mouth to explain. She cuts me off. "Get up there," she says.

Standing from my seat, I move on pure impulse. I slide down the row. Reaching the aisle, I pull my phone from my pocket. Every moment feels like improvisation, like putting fingers to keys, waiting for my instincts to find the melody. I know what I *want*, know where I'm going. How it happens is forming second to second in front of me.

I keep improvising. Heading down the stairs of my section of the stadium, I call Eileen.

While the phone rings—and rings, and rings—I hit more stairs. When I'm sent to voicemail, I start to sweat as I look at just how far the stage still is. Despair's dark spiral drags me closer.

When I've reached the foot of the steps, the standing-room floor section opens up in front of me. Close, yet out of reach. If I started running, I could make it onto the floor. But if I did, I would get grabbed before reaching the stage.

No, I reprimand myself. I'm not giving up.

This is everything. Music, love.

Resolve reinforced, I press forward. I weave past people, and when no one is looking—I make the jump to the floor. The impact shakes into my knees.

My flight's soundtrack is ripped from my dreams. Onstage, Riley hits the chorus. The chords fall like heavy rain under her fingers' urging. Her voice strains with emotion. I remember finding her in the dead of night writing "Heartbreak Road," how vulnerable her singing sounded then. That was nothing compared to the naked pain in her every word now.

I understand why. She wrote "Heartbreak Road" to deal with the present, with what she was feeling then. She wrote "Until You" to reckon with the past.

Now, the past of "Until You" has become present, rebounding in her life in devastating reprises. She isn't struggling with *reliving* its lyrics. She's struggling with *living* them. Once more because of me.

I want desperately to unwrite its new resonances. I want, in Riley's figure of speech, to render its saddest parts *unsung*. I don't want the only thing I have of Riley to be memories of her—

Writing on the bus.

Out of improvisation comes inspiration. Everyone on the tour got the numbers of their drivers for emergencies. Frantic, I call Frank.

When he answers, relief rushes over me. "Frank," I say, my voice breathless.

"Son, what are you calling me for?" Frank sounds like he's only pretending he's impatient with me. "You're not on my bus anymore," he reminds me.

"I'm at the show," I explain. I'm hurrying every word, feeling the magnitude of my life narrowing into the span of one song. "I need to get onstage and play with Riley."

With the noise surrounding me and in the phone line, it's hard to hear, yet Frank's voice is unmistakably clear when he replies. "Fucking finally." Over the line, I hear more indistinct talking and—is that Riley's voice? She sounds louder. "I'm watching the show with Carrie. Here," Frank says.

I hear Riley's mom's voice next. Frank has handed her the phone. It's interesting she's with him, part of me notices idly. Is it just them? "Max, you hurry up there," she orders me. "I'm getting Eileen to tell security to let you onstage. Can you make it to the front?"

Hearing her plainspoken practicality, I'm gripped with gratitude I've hardly ever felt in my life. If this works, I'll owe the two of them everything. "I will," I tell her.

The pause on the other end is only just perceptible. "I hope this means what I think it means," Carrie comments with world-class nonchalance.

I shove past people, earning dirty looks. I don't care. The racing rhythm of my heartbeat is consuming me whole. "I hope it does, too," I say.

"Good," Carrie replies. "Go."

I hang up. The front of the section is coming closer. I'm walking into the mirage. Riley is on the second verse now, and she's fully crying onstage. It's making her miss notes on the piano and swallowing her voice. She presses on, pushing herself forward. Only her musicianship keeps it sounding like a song despite what it really is—a march over shattered glass.

I'm desperate to pull her into my arms, but no one is letting me to the front. I can't push forward without risking knocking someone down, which of course I won't do. I'm stuck feet away, my musical hourglass emptying. All I can do is watch Riley break onstage.

"Holy shit," someone suddenly says nearby, interrupting the grip Riley's singing has on the crowd. "Is that Max Harcourt?"

Other voices reply. *"Oh my god." "It is." "Max!" "He's who this song is about."*

The crowd shifts, faces full of curiosity scrutinizing me. It feels like the last thing I need . . . until I realize it might be *exactly* what I need.

I speak directly to my new onlookers, holding in none of my desperation. "I need to get onstage."

A girl in front of me swats her friend's arm. "I *knew* it. You still love her. Oh my god."

I wait, unsure how to handle this kind of attention, while counting every measure of "Until You" passing onstage.

I don't need to wait long. The girl, my new champion, straightens up. "Clear a route!" she says to the people around her. Her urgency is inspiring. Whispers start to spread. Some fans watch me with wide eyes, others with swooning hands over their hearts.

It works, though. I watch a path to the stage open in front of me, the crowd parting like magic or magnetism is pulling them. With the stage finally within reach, I don't let myself feel hopeful. Not yet. I've had hopes crumble in my hands even when I felt like they were certain.

I find my way to the front, where a security guard is eyeing the disruption in the crowd. I approach hesitantly. If Eileen didn't get the word out, my hope ends here.

"You Max?" the guard asks like he knows I am.

I nod. I can't speak. My nerves have constricted my vocal cords. Riley's voice fills my ears.

Without warning, the security guard ushers me over the fence. He escorts me, practically pulling, up to the stairs leading to the stage. Dragging me headlong right into my lovesick dreams. My heart is pounding. I was so focused on *reaching* the stage, I didn't think about what I would do when I got there. Am I really going to ask Riley to take me back in front of an entire stadium?

Absolutely I am.

The decision sharpens everything. I don't stumble this time. While I've joined Riley onstage on other occasions, it's never felt this way. Not only in how my entire romantic fate waits for me, either. On every other night, part of my soul knew I wasn't really living my deepest dream. In this moment, I'm present with my whole heart.

Riley doesn't notice me. She hits a wrong chord in the bridge, and it throws her off. I know she's lost. Her heart is too heavy for her to find her way.

Watching her, I'm in my dorm room, with sheet music

everywhere. My keyboard on my desk. Riley, lost in focus, patiently finding the chords of "Songbird." The Rose Bowl fades like the world unraveling. It's only us, lost in music together.

I'm not miked. My voice won't carry past the stage. Knowing this, I speak out to Riley only. "D minor, then C. You've got this. Just walk it down." The chords of "Until You" are written on my heart.

She looks up when she hears my voice, hope catching in her eyes. She hits the chords like she's reaching out for handholds to slow her descent into the dark.

It works. Her voice sounds surer as she sings the bridge. *"Will I ever hear the songs we would play,"* she repeats the endlessly familiar lines, *"without wondering why we ended this way? Will I be okay with losing everything now? Will I ever feel free without remembering how—"*

Her gaze locks with mine.

"—I'll spend my life pretending," she sings. *"You're a verse without an ending."*

Giving myself over to the song, I do something I haven't since our earliest dorm-room duets, when we had no idea what roads they would lead us down.

I sing with her, finishing the line. I'm no singer like Riley is no pianist—but when our voices join, it's the greatest sound I've ever heard.

Her eyes crinkling with joy, she laughs through the lyrics. It's spellbinding. Riley seems to shimmer with delight, which makes the song into something otherworldly.

When the line ends, Riley watches me, stunned and stunning. "What are you doing here?" she asks me into the mic, her voice ringing out into the stadium.

I could fill records with the confessions of love waiting in my heart. I settle for the simplest answer instead. "I came to play with you, if you'll have me," I say.

Riley nods, and I walk up to the piano to sit down next to her. In my head, I remember the endless reaches of fans watching us, memorizing every moment. In the rest of me, though, it's only us.

While she's playing, Riley lifts her left hand, surrendering the bass clef to me. I fill in quickly, watching her fingers on the keys. For the next measure we share the piano like we're holding hands over the span of ebony and ivory.

When Riley withdraws her right hand, our fingers brush in the quickest kiss before I complete the chords. She leans against me, and we continue "Until You" this way.

Despite the song's despondence, every note is luminous. It's "Until You" like I've never heard it, like *no one* has ever heard it. It's the culmination of each perfect moment I've shared with Riley, experiencing what I feel now in one ecstatic shock of recognition. Every song is a love song if you play it with the right person.

In the final verse—the hopeful one—Riley sings to me. The mic is right in front of me, and Riley doesn't pick it up, instead leaning into me while she delves into the lyrics and putting our faces close. Her voice, exhausted from crying, is sweet with new hope.

I hold her eyes the whole time, putting all the love I have for her into the melody in my fingers. Unhurried, she climbs into the chorus, confession and plea and promise in one.

"*I won't know what love is,*" she sings, her whole heart in the refrain, "*until you . . . come back to me.*"

The song is over too soon. Staring into Riley's eyes, I hesitate, wrestling with the enormity of the wish I carried with me when I stepped onstage. I'm hoping the end of the music might be the start of something new. It's left me overwhelmed with excited nerves, part of me wishing I could live in the sweet refuge of the lyrics with Riley forever.

Instead, while the crowd roars, she gently covers the mic with her hand, looking like her heart is unimaginably full.

"You came to my show," she says.

I smile. Everything has led to here. The long road has finally, maybe, carried us home.

"I came for this," I say.

I put my thumb on her chin and pull her face to mine. In front of the whole world, I kiss her.

When she kisses me back fiercely, it feels like flying—high over the Rose Bowl, over the city, over every city I've shared with Riley, over life itself. We ignore the thousands of people cheering us on. The lights surrounding us wrap our kiss in endless radiance. I reach my other hand to her waist.

I was wrong when I compared holding her to catching lightning. Holding Riley Wynn is like holding a love song.

When she finally withdraws, she's beaming. She gets up, taking the mic from the stand. "Thank you, Los Angeles," she says, her voice wavering with emotion. "This has been a show I'll never forget. I love you. Good night!"

In the lowering lights, she returns to me, grabbing my hand. She leads me offstage into the dark of the wings. She draws me into the shadows, where immediately she kisses me. The kiss is deep, desperate, joyous, like the greatest love songs. It's everything. I revel in her, the feeling of her mouth on mine, leaving me close to crying.

Riley. I don't know if I whisper the exhalation into her lips or if it's restless in my chest. *Oh, Riley.*

I hold her tight. She does the same, pressing herself close to me like she can't stand for even inches to separate us. "It's good to see you," she whispers, her lips near mine. While I can't completely see her face with how we're enmeshed with each other, I feel her smile in the contours of her cheeks, hear it in the shape of her voice.

My heart feels full of light. "I liked the love song," I say.

"Me too," she replies.

"Take me back, Riley. Please take me back," I implore her. The words fly out of me, impossible to restrain. I don't know whether I've waited ten years, ten months, or ten minutes to say them. It couldn't possibly matter. I need to say them now. "I promise I'll never leave you again. I'll give you all of me."

The audience is still cheering—waiting for the encore. Crew members hurry in every direction around us. None of it reaches me. My whole world is the woman in front of me right now.

"I'll love you forever," I say. "I already have."

Riley doesn't rush. She presses her forehead to mine. Then she takes my hands in hers, entwining our fingers. Everything slows down. Everything is quiet.

"You're going to put me out of the breakup-song business for good," she says softly, her chiding humor not hiding the fragile joy in her voice, the hesitant hope of dreams emerging into life. "But I think we'll get more than a song out of this."

Hope fills my smile. "A whole record, maybe?" I venture.

Riley shakes her head.

"No," she says. "We could get everything."

When she kisses me, I know we already have.

EPILOGUE

Riley

I WAKE UP in the middle of the night, finding the music from my dreams is still playing.

In the moonlight, I smile, then climb out of bed. The floor is cold, so I hurry into the hallway. I'm unpacked now, my house finally home, full of the signs of life lived not only on the road. Photos from tour, the incredibly old record player on the credenza, the cookbooks we pick something out of to cook every weekend.

The last one still makes me laugh. I own *cookbooks* now. It makes my mom laugh, too.

When I reach the stairs, the melody gets stronger. It's not one I've heard before. Dreamy, wistful, romantic. It's played deftly with sweeping runs along the piano keys.

I don't know when the nocturnal music will end. I just know I don't want it to. I pick up my pace down the stairs, shivering in the cold night—or, cold for the Hollywood Hills. With only the faint natural light illuminating my way, I navigate my home's now-familiar hallways.

In the doorway of the music room, I stop.

There he sits, his glasses askew, his hair ruffled, in the soft T-shirt he wore to bed.

Watching him, I feel the reprise of the night I first laid eyes on him. It's like our chorus, life repeating this refrain to embed it in our hearts. When I woke up in our college common room to find Max Harcourt playing piano, I couldn't possibly know I would one night wake up in the house we share to find him downstairs, playing piano.

Except, maybe I did.

Then, though, I couldn't hear the melody he was playing. Tonight, I can. I hear everything with Max now.

As he plays the song, lost in his own music, I stay silent, enjoying it. Lyrics start to come to me. Something to span the memories, connecting the choruses. Something to remind us where we started whenever we remember where we've ended up now.

I want to play your favorite piano, the one in your family's home, I hear in my head.

I don't sing them, not wanting to interrupt him. Listening to him is one of my favorite parts of our new life together. He's been doing this for the past few weeks, writing when he returns from Harcourt Homes. Sometimes he plays his compositions for his residents, sometimes just for me. Even though running the home is his passion, he hasn't given up music.

He gives up so little, I've realized. When Max loves something, he loves it always.

He hits the final chord, and his shoulders relax, like now he will finally be able to sleep. I smile. I know the feeling well. While he and I love music in our own ways, the depth of our devotion is the same. It's our hidden harmony, our reminder of what hasn't changed in years when everything else has.

Softly, from the doorway, I applaud him. He spins, startled until he sees it's me. "Encore," I say, my voice raspy with sleep. It's another of our lives' repeated choruses.

He grins, holding his arms out to me. It's second nature to cross the room, sit in his lap, and press a kiss to his lips while he tilts his head up to me.

"I'm sorry I woke you," he says.

"Don't be," I whisper with my whole heart. "Play it again."

I start to stand, eager to hear the song once more, but Max holds me in his lap. I'm now facing the keys.

"Stay," he says with something like urgency as he kisses my neck.

Resting his head on my shoulder, he reaches past me to the keys.

Refusing to let him play just yet, I touch the ring on his left hand. The one I put there just hours ago, in a private ceremony. *Our wedding.* The very idea feels improbable, even magical. Only our parents, Frank, Eileen, and Jess and April were there. We stood in the yard right outside this window while the sun set over the hills.

I'd been the one to propose to him one week ago. He'd been the one to set the date—we'd waited ten years, and he didn't want to wait even a day longer than we needed to.

I wouldn't have even worn a wedding dress, honestly, not caring what I was wearing as long as I was marrying Max. Except when I mentioned it to him, he smiled and went silent. I realized—*of course.* He'd watched me perform in a wedding dress for months, one I'd worn for another man.

I couldn't let it be the only wedding dress he ever saw me in. I needed a Max dress.

It surprised him when I came out of our bathroom wearing it minutes before our guests got here. It was nothing like the dress I wore onstage. My Max dress was—is—all lace, soft, romantic. He teared up, and I wiped his eyes before we welcomed our family and friends.

My mother fluttered with pre-wedding jitters she failed to hide. She lives in New Orleans now when she's not on the road with Frank. My dad flew in from St. Louis, his hair freshly cut. They greeted each other warmly.

I don't pretend they're happy to see each other—I know all too well the painful distance of exes—but for today they were more than exes. They were the parents of the bride. When my dad saw Frank, they shook hands, having met on my first tour.

It made the day feel old and new. Different except in the ways it *wasn't* different.

I cried. My mom cried. My dad cried. He walked me from one end of our yard to the other, where Max stood under the orange tree. Our wedding party consisted solely of Jess, who hugged me eight times, and Eileen. While our guests sipped champagne, I read the vows I'd written as poetry, lyrics for the rest of our lives.

In my young life, I've sold out stadiums, slept with movie stars, and pressed platinum records. Getting married for the second time surrounded by everyone I love in my backyard, I've never felt luckier.

The day was ours—only ours. No social media. No statements. No notification even to my label, who Eileen swore not to tell. They'll hate that I intend to be happily married forever, but

I'll send them new, better songs. The rest of the world won't know the Breakup Queen is married, not for now, unless they hear it in the music I'm writing.

The night . . .

The night was ours in other, inexpressibly wonderful ways. Our own bed, instead of our lonesome bunks. The glorious haze of the happiest moments of our lives not yet gone from our cheeks. Kisses like dreams. Love like promises. Nothing separating us, losing ourselves in the sense of sweet forever.

Not every day will feel like this one, of course. In a few weeks, I leave on the European leg of the tour. I'm overwhelmingly happy we had our wedding before I go. Max will remain here, managing Harcourt Homes, for most of the months I'm in Europe. However, we've decided to make a week in Italy into our honeymoon. He's even going to join me onstage in Rome.

We're fitting our separate lives into one, finding how they resonate. Melody and countermelody. Not the same, yet harmonious.

We approach every day as just one day. If Max wants to stay in LA while I'm on tour—fine. If he wants to join me—also fine. If he wants to play with me or not, or write with me or not, everything is an open conversation. We can play our love song as infinite variations on the same theme.

Max's fingers move over the keys, his ring shining in the moonlight. He plays slower with me in his lap. It's enchanting.

"What's it called?" I ask, meaning the song.

"It's for you to decide," he replies. I turn in his lap, looking for his answer in the peaceful lines of his face. "It's my wedding gift to you," he explains. "You can write lyrics to it. If you want to, that is."

My face flushes with happiness. I find my voice easily, singing the words softly over the refrain he's playing. "*I want to play your favorite piano, the one in your family's home. I want to sing our endless love songs, in melodies our own.*"

Behind me, I hear Max's smile in the sound of his voice. "People will know you're not single when they hear this one."

I shrug. "I don't mind. I want to be just us for a little longer," I say. "We have forever, after all."

Max plays on. His agreement, offered in his favorite language.

I listen, knowing I'll hear it this way only once. Like every love, every rendition of a melody is unique, each the harmonious reflection of the people making the music. Without us to cherish their complexities, to infuse them with life, to make them our own, they vanish into silence.

So when you find a song you feel filling every corner of your soul, you stand onstage, and you sing your heart out.

While Max kisses my neck, I stare out over the yard, where the sky is finally starting to lighten.

Sunrise, after so long.

"Until You"

Riley Eleanora Wynn, songwriter (Riley Wynn)

Stereosonic Records, 2024

> *Late nights, new homes*
> *Your hands on the piano*
> *Woke up with my heart under your fingers*
> *Played me slowly so the notes would linger*
>
> *Little lights, close hearts*
> *I felt the end in the start*
> *Words I didn't know you didn't mean*
> *"I" and "love" and "you" would make me see*
>
> *I didn't know what love is*
> *I don't know what love is*
> *I won't know what love is*
> *until you*
> *opened the door*
>
> *The day of, I want you*
> *High roads, see us through*
> *You look like you're hoping I'll be fine*
> *I know I'm helpless even when I try*
>
> *We know it isn't true*
> *when you say you'll see me soon*
> *Cut me cleanly with your gemstone eyes*
> *which is when I realize*

I didn't know what love is
I don't know what love is
I won't know what love is
until you
say it's this.

Will I ever hear the songs we would play
without wondering why we ended this way?
Will I be okay with losing everything now?
Will I ever feel free without remembering how
I'll spend my life pretending
You're a verse without an ending

Long days, fast years
Old hopes, new fears
Future, present, past run in reverse
Feeling best when I expect the worst

I'll change, you'll stay
Love won't obey
I'll wait, wish, wander, wonder until I
learn to think of you and not to cry

I didn't know what love is
I don't know what love is
I won't know what love is
until you
come back to me.

"Heartbreak Road"

Riley Eleanora Wynn and Joseph Nash
(pseudonym for Maxwell Joseph Harcourt),
songwriters (Riley Wynn)
Stereosonic Records, 2024

Once upon a highway, you were with me
picking up distance with hair flying free
Fast lane running with nothing in the mirror
The skyline closer and never getting clearer and

I wish I couldn't guess where this pavement ends
With heart-shattered passengers who started out friends
Holding out hope or knowing what we know
Retracing our steps until we're letting go

I walk Heartbreak Road
Feel your hand in mine on
Heartbreak Road
Traveling for ten years on
Heartbreak Road
Kissing you is fine on
Heartbreak Road
Leading us to nowhere

Map unopened 'cause I've been here before
Pain in my chest with the pedal to the floor
With lanes wide open, nothing slowing us down,
we're driving,

driving,
driving

Hands on the wheel like I'm holding on to you and I
Foot on the gas 'cause it helps me not to wonder why
Lights go green and maybe with you
Same old road can lead somewhere new

I walk Heartbreak Road
Feel your hand in mine on
Heartbreak Road
Traveling for ten years on
Heartbreak Road
Kissing you is fine on
Heartbreak Road
Leading us to somewhere

I pass stop signs screaming and
lonely hearts leaving and
parking lots full of lovers dreaming
with you

Where does the road go?
I hope one day I'll know

I walk Heartbreak Road
Feel your hand in mine on
Heartbreak Road
Traveling for ten years on

Heartbreak Road
Kissing you is fine on
Heartbreak Road
Leading us, leading us, leading us

"Unsung"

Riley Eleanora Wynn, songwriter (Riley Wynn)
Stereosonic Records, 2025

You make days
feel like nights of stars,
when the pressure ends
when the sky is warm

You wrote with me
in the dead of dark
Held me in your words
made me feel the spark

Past the studio door,
shaken to the floor
You gave me everything,
then you gave me more

I reach into
songs I never knew
I could finish only
in the name of you

You make me sing songs I would've left unsung
You make me feel like I'm the only one
You make me sing songs I won't leave unsung
You fill my voice, my forever only one

On the road,
cities come and gone,
Played with love hard-won
Like a secret song

You left me lonely
You found me home, we
heard notes our own, we
Refused so long

We were never meant
To have stayed content
With the days unspent
Fine and not okay

Now I wait for you
Like a song offstage
Hope in every phrase
Like a nameless grace

You make me sing songs I would've left unsung
You make me feel like I'm the only one
You make me sing songs I won't leave unsung
You fill my voice, my forever only one

I wish I hadn't
wasted years
when everything I
need is right here, reaching out with chords of endless love—
Right here with you

You hold me close
When the chorus stops

Cause in the end
Every song I write
Every line I live
Every reckless night
Every lullaby
Every faded rhyme
Is the sound of you,
like an echo only my heart can hear,
when the darkness closes everywhere,
I hold on to the light you remain inside my life
You free the songs I would once have left
Unsung

ACKNOWLEDGMENTS

Like many great songs, *The Breakup Tour* is the product of collaboration, inspiration, and support from others whose contributions we're endlessly grateful for. Thank you for singing our harmonies.

Katie Shea Boutillier, nine books in, we couldn't be more honored by your continued championship of our work or happier to call you one of our truest, long-standing friends in publishing. You know all too well what you mean to us. For never steering us wrong, for fighting for us, for keeping us dreaming big, we love you. You're a superstar in every sense.

Kristine Swartz, we continue to be humbled and grateful for your insightful, graceful, incredible editorial guidance . . . even under the tightest of timelines. Our deepest thanks for encouraging us to chase this story. We remember when we were discussing possible ideas for this book and you told us you wanted to read "the Taylor Swift romance." Look what you made us do. We couldn't be gladder you did!

Vi-An Nguyen, every version of this cover was lovelier than

the last and left us speechless and immeasurably grateful for your remarkable powers of envisioning exactly the right image for this story, in vivid color. Three Berkley books in, we don't know how you keep outdoing yourself, but we're very, very glad you do. Design like this never goes out of style. Thank you to Andressa Meissner for the stunning illustration.

Working with the Berkley team has been something out of our wildest dreams. This book owes its gorgeousness to Katy Riegel, who brought the story (and lyrics) to life. Thank you to Caitlin Lonning, Kayley Hoffman, and Claire Sullivan for the invaluable polish you provided in every line (and for helping us learn a few new style rules, which we found fascinating!), and to Megha Jain, Christine Legon, and Mary Baker for harmonizing everything like the notes of a chord. Jessica Plummer and Hillary Tacuri, our profound thanks for your wonderful work spreading this story's reach. Kristin Cipolla and Tina Joell, our returning publicists, we remain enchanted to have you helping readers meet Riley and Max!

Our dear friends Bridget Morrissey, Maura Milan, Gabrielle Gold, Gretchen Schreiber, Rebekah Faubion, Derek Milman, Brian Murray Williams, Farrah Penn, Lindsay Grossman, Kalie Holford . . . this love is good. For coffee chats and group chats, commiseration and celebration, you fill our publishing journey and our lives with light. The romance community remains a welcoming and inspiring home for our work, and we're ever grateful for the readers and authors alike who have offered kind words and encouragement we cherish. Jodi Picoult, you've more than earned the famous keyboardist we lent your name to with incomparable blurbs and incomparable friendship.

Finally, thank you to our family, without whom none of this is possible.

The
Breakup
Tour

EMILY WIBBERLEY

AUSTIN SIEGEMUND-BROKA

READERS GUIDE

DISCUSSION QUESTIONS

1. Do you prefer breakup songs or love songs? Why?

2. While Riley is living out her dreams, she faces stress, insecurity, and loneliness. Do you sympathize with her struggles and the price of stardom?

3. Max closely associates memories with songs. Do you experience this as well? Why does music endure over our lifetime?

4. Until the end of the novel, Riley believes her best art comes from her pain. Do you think this is true of other artists? Do we as a society look upon art about suffering as somehow deeper or more meaningful than art about joy?

5. Max chooses family over trying out a dream he doesn't know if he wants. Was it the right choice?

6. Which musicians do you think served as inspiration for the character of Riley Wynn? Do you think they feel similar expectations and pressures as Riley in the book?

7. Do couples need to have a common dream—not necessarily professional, but something beyond love and attraction—that puts them on the same path in life?

8. Riley is criticized for writing about her ex-boyfriends. While Max is uncomfortable with it at times, he always recognizes that it is her prerogative to write about her own life. Do you agree?

9. How do you think the journey of self-discovery of Riley's mom, Carrie, on the tour affects Riley's growth? Did you like their mother-daughter relationship?

10. Riley believes in taking inspiration from her heartache because in some ways it gives purpose to her pain, like turning lemons into lemonade. Do you agree this is something we should always try to do?

Keep reading for a preview of

Emily Wibberley and Austin Siegemund-Broka's

THE BOOK BOYFRIEND,

coming soon!

In ELYTHEUM, NO one ever has a hard time finding parking.

I've rounded the quiet streets surrounding the College of Hollisboro four times on my hunt, desperation growing with each circumnavigation—feeling probably much like Val when he knew Kethryn was captured within Nightfell's walls with the hourglass running out on her life. Except, of course, for the smell of the "Cherry Evening" air freshener pervading the interior of my sister's Prius.

When I *finally* find parking outside of one of the neighborhood's overwhelmingly common frozen yogurt places, I'm frustrated. I *hate* being late. As a person, in fact, I define myself by my punctuality. If you're late, you're late. If you're early . . . you've just given yourself extra time to read the book you have brought with you.

I have no book with me now. I'm late. *Well,* I remind myself, *isn't acting out of character the entire point?*

Very out of character, honestly, except for where I'm going. The planner in me could hardly imagine how, fresh after dumping my now ex, Scott, ending the worst fight of our relationship in front of the elevator while my mean neighbor Rudy glared, I *didn't* nestle myself into my pillows with my favorite *Elytheum Courts* chapters. Instead, I called Sarah, took NJ Transit to her condo, picked up her floral-scented Prius and drove eight hours into the wooded heart of North Carolina.

Why?

The Elytheum Experience.

I've wanted to go since the Experience was announced. I pretty much worship everything Heather Winters has ever written, essentially. For the past decade, while *Elytheum Courts* has grown into one of publishing's most popular enduring successes, I've hung on to every word of the unfolding epic of warring Fae and mortals in the dark, magical, Regency-meets-medieval-derived realm of Elytheum—especially the forbidden love story of mortal Queen Kethryn and her Fey paramour, Lord Valance.

I'm not alone. Far, far from it. While Elytheum flourished, I found other fans online, at events and festivals, and eventually in my professional life, from my very first publishing assistant job coordinating calendars and helping project-manage to my present position in the publicity department of one of Parthenon's commercial fiction imprints. I wake up every morning with videos of fan theories and funny reenactments of events from the series, and I procrastinate with Instagram feeds of fan art and character memes.

Which is why the Elytheum Experience is literally a dream made real. About a year ago, a few fans decided they wanted to organize an Elytheum "immersive experience," complete with costumes, character actors, and scene-inspired events, held on

Hollisboro's campus because of how perfectly the Gothic architecture reflects Elytheum's darkly dramatic setting. For intellectual property reasons, the founders reached out for Heather Winters's endorsement.

Not only did Winters endorse, she offered to fully fund the Experience, even working in close collaboration with the founders in developing original lore for the expansive immersion.

Original. Lore. The very words make me feel like I've just downed espresso with nine sugars.

Which, for the record, I would never do. Cinnamon dolce lattes only, please.

It was the ultimate gift of gratitude and honor for her fans. The Elytheum Experience was official—and my friend Amelia Gupta was part of everything. She works with Heather Winters's IP and was involved intimately with every step of the planning. While she couldn't divulge details, when the first Experience was scheduled, she *could* offer her dear friend a free invitation, which she did months ago.

I pleaded with Scott to go together. He said no, of course, which made my hope feel foolish. Despite everything I loved about Scott—his conscientiousness, his patience, his impeccable memory for the details of my day and my life, not to mention his gray-eyed, sharp-blond-haircut nerdy hotness—his persistent resentment of my love for Elytheum was one of our relationship's only real problems, one I forced myself to forgive in light of everything good.

It was part of why, after our relationship-ending fight in front of fucking Rudy, I had an epiphany. I refused to cry. I called Amelia, and with a waver in my voice I knew my friend could hear, asked if her invitation stood even on the day the Experience was set to start. She said yes, and here I find myself, about to enter Elytheum-via-North Carolina with a new resolution.

I don't need another Scott. I don't need another relationship. Why do I keep dashing myself against the rocks of online dating when I have the love in my favorite series, where it's never disappointing? Did a date *ever* measure up to a night of reading about the passion and connection of Lord Valance and Queen Kethryn in Elytheum? Where men are noble warriors and devoted lovers?

Okay, not exactly men—*males*, with wings and horns. Still—when they say *I love you* it means something.

I grab my cloak from the Prius's passenger seat, resenting a fresh reminder of Scott when my fingers catch the Elytheum emblem I embossed into the fabric. When I made the garment for Halloween, he said I looked hot, referring to what I wore underneath, the leather video-game-character costume I felt reasonably approximated Kethryn's Assassins' Convent armor.

The compliment, flattering in its un-Scott-like forwardness, helped me ignore the thought that he knew the cloak was inspired by Elytheum and purposefully refused to ask me about it. Honestly, I liked how I looked—how my dark brown hair fell over the strips of leather crossing my skin. For the night, I wasn't average-height, average-everything Jennifer Worth. I was my favorite heroine.

Right now, I have only the cloak and shirt and jeans I dumped Scott in—no strappy leather costume, having left it at his place. It's fine. Amelia says the Experience will include opportunities to buy or craft other Elytheum-appropriate costuming.

Hollisboro is wonderfully warm in the summer night, cooling off enough for me to fling the cloak over my shoulders without overheating. I hustle down the quaint streets with

Google Maps's guidance in the direction of the campus, ignoring how my driving-wracked stomach yearns for Starbucks—the Experience started an hour ago, and I won't miss one second more.

Passing grad students and college-touring families, I feel a little ridiculous. *A grown woman, walking around in her costume.* I hate the automatic reaction, knowing I wouldn't feel the same if it were a sports jersey. Once, flush with the confidence of feeling like our relationship was working, I'd asked Scott to read the first *Elytheum* novel. *Just one!* I urged him playfully.

He hemmed and hawed. He pretended he had overwhelming workweeks. He said *he would see.* He was polite—of course he was polite. Gentle. The man I loved, gently desperate to avoid what he knew meant the world to me.

Whatever. None of my exes are here. No one is here who will make me feel uncool for loving Elytheum. I don't have to hide my cloak *or* myself.

I step onto campus emboldened—and impressed. The Experience's location is perfectly chosen, with sculpted archways of gray stone under intricate Gothic spires. Ironically, the grounds look fit for the courtly intrigues, clandestine cunning, and dark magic rituals of Elytheum, not for Economics 101.

Reaching the dining hall, I pause, remembering the doors of the elevator closing on Scott's face, on the hope of the future I'd started stupidly imagining with him.

I fight the feeling. *No.* I'm not heartbroken. I'm in Elytheum.

Pushing open the door, I walk into another world.

None of the vivid dreams I've had prepare me for what I find inside. The Elytheum Experience is ... enchanting. Intricate production design has converted the College's dining hall into the

"Great Hall," the imposing room where Fae declarations of war are delivered and queens mourned. Only candlelight illuminates the hall, into which romantic violin music plays quietly from musicians near the fireplace. Everyone is dressed much more elaborately than me.

At the front of the room, a stunning woman in armor sits on an actual throne.

Chills spread down my arms. *Kethryn*. Which means . . .

Heart pounding with excitement, I gaze eagerly around the room until I find him.

With prosthetic horns peering out from his sweep of ebony hair, he's unmistakable. The man in ornamented dark garb watching Kethryn from one corner of the room was the central preoccupation of a good number of my aforementioned dreams—or his character was. Lord Valance is exactly how I imagined him.

I find I'm grinning my first grin of the day. Elytheum really is magic, one way or another.

"Okay, I'm amazed you got here in time."

Only Amelia's voice pulls me from my unabashed scrutiny of Val. I haven't seen her in months, and just hearing her has me immediately emotional. Amelia is my former work wife, once my favorite Parthenon publicity coworker. The "divorce" was amicable. Amelia, like me, loves Elytheum. It forged our friendship fast, in memes DM'd during meetings and weekend readathons with cheesecake. She's the Hazelheart to my Spindleshear, which is how we introduce ourselves at Elytheum events. It's hilarious if you're a fan.

Nine months ago, Amelia got the worst and happiest news. She interviewed for a developmental role with Heather Winters's

IP—and she got the job. We knew it was the right move for her professionally, but we cried her entire last day at Parthenon.

I spin, crushing the clipboard she's holding with the hug I sweep her into.

"You did *not* exaggerate," I say when we part, referring to the room.

Amelia shrugs, smug. She's shorter than I am, and even the heels she's wearing as part of her impeccable courtly look don't bring her to my eyeline. Her hair is braided into an elaborate black crown, her thick mascara accentuating her dark eyes. "I really didn't," she says. "Here, I snuck your key from check-in so you can go up after this."

While the key card she offers me is plastic and obviously nonmagical, reasonably required for use of the dorms for the summer week, it's painted to resemble a playing card, one whose design I recognize from fan art. *Of course.* Demoniaca is the recreational card game of Elytheum, a cross between poker and Pokémon, in which deals are struck or secrets exchanged. *Spindleshear*, mine reads, with the demon's portrait. I hold it up.

Amelia smiles. "Cool, right?"

"God, I've missed you," I say.

"You too, hon." Her expression shifts into hesitant sympathy. "Are you—is everything . . . ?"

While I know she means well, I don't welcome the distraction of the hurt welling up in me. "We're not supposed to talk about the outside world here, right?" I reply. It was on the email confirmation's list of rules, emphasized to prevent "bleed" from the real world.

Amelia's mouth flattens with my evasion. "Convenient for

you," she remarks. "Well, we're going off campus for coffee and you're telling me what happened," she orders me.

It's how Amelia is, always on the fine line separating domineering from encouraging and defending me like no one else in my life ever does. "It's really not worth talking about," I say weakly.

"Yes," Amelia replies. "It is." Excusing my further resistance, her eyes catch on a girl waving her over nervously. "Heather's assistant needs me," Amelia says with forced patience, her gaze returning to mine. "We'll catch up later," she promises me meaningfully.

I nod, my stomach knotting. Honestly, I don't want to discuss my pathetic love life—not when Elytheum is here to experience.

While I walk over to sit at one of the long tables, another epiphany descends over me in the rose-scented room. For the next week, I'm *not* Jennifer Worth. I don't have to be the woman who spent the past year loving a man—a damnably cute, unfailingly loyal, otherwise perfect man, unfortunately—who would prefer watching paint dry instead of embracing my favorite fandom.

No, I'm . . . *whoever I want to be*. Warrior. Princess. Fae. Demon.

I don't know yet. I just know the question is exhilarating.

Sipping from the stew one of the many footmen has delivered to me, I listen, scouring the snatches of conversation surrounding me for inspiration. The man and woman next to me make illicit plans, their offers to "exchange sensitive espionage information" sounding like pretense to exchange something else.

I stay silent, still figuring out what I want my story to be.

Darting glances at Val in the corner, the women across from me swap fictional war stories from the Western Court Campaign. It's wonderful realizing I'm following every reference, expecting every detail. Who knew a fantasy world could feel like home? I'm about to insert myself into their conversation when I hear a familiar laugh.

No. It can't be.

I look over my shoulder while the room seems to move in slow motion, as if under the Forgotten King's hourglass magic. The man who laughed is chatting animatedly with an older woman in elf ears, his grin upturned roguishly. In full leather armor, he looks like he's in the Queen's Guard.

Or it's how I know he looks to everyone else here.

To me, he just looks like Scott Daniels.

My ex.

Mike Yoon Photo

Emily Wibberley and **Austin Siegemund-Broka** met and fell in love in high school. Austin went on to graduate from Harvard, while Emily graduated from Princeton. Together, they are the authors of several novels about romance for teens and adults. Now married, they live in Los Angeles, where they continue to take daily inspiration from their own love story.

VISIT EMILY AND AUSTIN ONLINE

EmilyandAustinWrite.com